GHOSTV

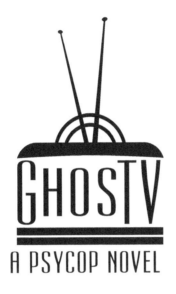

GHOSTV

A PSYCOP NOVEL

Jordan Castillo Price

JCP BOOKS

First published in print in the United States
in 2011 by JCP Books LLC.
www.jcpbooks.com

First Edition

ISBN: 978-1-935540-22-9

The PsyCop Series

PSYCOP EBOOKS:

Among the Living - PsyCop 1

Criss Cross - PsyCop 2

Body & Soul - PsyCop 3

Secrets - PsyCop 4

Camp Hell - PsyCop 5

GhosTV - PsyCop 6

Many Happy Returns - PsyCop Short

Mind Reader - PsyCop Short

Striking Sparks - PsyCop Short

Thaw - PsyCop Short

PSYCOP PAPERBACKS:

PsyCop Partners
(contains Among the Living and Criss Cross)

PsyCop: Property
(contains Body & Soul and Secrets)

Camp Hell

GhosTV

www.PsyCop.com

Chapter 1

Sunshine, fresh air and junk food. I told myself I could enjoy those things—or that's the line I was feeding myself, anyway. This was the reality: my underwear was soaking wet and my head was ringing; I'd taken one too many Auracel and spun around a few too many times. If I was careful, really careful, the best I could hope for was keeping the chimichanga and the fried Snickers bar from making a reappearance.

I wasn't obligated to talk to any dead people. I supposed that was something to be thankful for.

I did, however, feel somewhat obligated to talk to Jacob's sister, Barbara. But only somewhat.

"...scored two goals during the first half of the game. You'd think the coach would have been proud, right? Instead, he said Clayton wasn't a team player. That he didn't pass the ball."

"Must run in the family."

Normal sounds, like screaming children, screaming adults, and the general wall of screaming humanity, continued on. But the conversation Barbara and I were diligently attempting to have fell down dead between us.

It belatedly occurred to me that I'd spoken aloud.

"I mean, uh, that's what I like about Jacob. If he's good at something, he doesn't stand around waiting for someone else to take a turn at it. That's fine for little-league soccer, maybe, but when it's life or death, you want the best guy on your team to step up to the plate." Okay, I was mixing baseball metaphors with my soccer, but I really didn't know shit about soccer.

I risked a glance around the side of my cheap plastic sunglasses toward Barbara. She was watching me, which made me want to squirm—despite my damp underwear. Over at the Gut Scrambler, or whatever they were calling the latest ride that neither Barbara nor I were willing to be strapped into,

Jacob and Clayton disembarked. They were quite the pair, all flushed cheeks and smiles. They stopped to peer at a bank of monitors that snapped shots of all the scream-laughing riders getting scrambled like a bunch of eggs.

"Aw, jees, he's gonna talk Jacob into…" Barbara stood and cupped her hands around her mouth. "Clayton. You do not need a ten-dollar picture of yourself on that ride. I took plenty of pictures today with the phone."

Clayton set his jaw, and holy shit, I hadn't really seen it when I'd met him last November—but now that he was half a year older, I totally did. That was Jacob's stubborn-look. In spades.

Genetics can be kinda creepy.

"Tell 'im he'll wreck it on the log flume," I muttered.

"You'll get it wet on the log ride, and then what? You want to be stuck carrying that thing around all day?"

A tinge of bewilderment touched Clayton's mulish expression. Jacob said something, maybe a promise to stand in line another half hour, ride again and get a photo on the way out. He probably didn't want to be stuck carrying the thing around all day either—but he also had only one nephew, and as far as he was concerned, kids were made for spoiling.

Jacob and Clayton approached without the photo. One small success. Although I wouldn't have minded being the photo carrier; it would've excused me from riding rides.

"I wanna go on King Chaos," Clayton whined. He had exactly two modes of speech: whining, and bragging.

Our small group milled for position, and before I could drop to the rear, Jacob looped an arm through mine and pulled me against his side. "What do you say, Vic? You choose the next one after that."

"I'll, uh, keep my eyes open." The list of rides I could actually stomach was pathetically small. Fast spinning and Auracel didn't mix well. The act of getting strapped into anything and my own demons didn't mix well, either. Even thoroughly potted on Auracel, I had no desire to ride through long, dark tunnels where God-knows-what might pop out. And my legs were too long for those teacup things. That left log rides. I tried to tell myself they were fun, but it seemed like every time my underwear finally dried off, I ended up sitting on one of those wet seats again—plus, as the tallest guy there, I was always the one to get nailed in the face with the funky, chemical-laced water. But at least it didn't look like I was too wussy to ride anything.

The contraption Clayton was angling for was some mad scientist experiment that took a row of people and whipped them upside down like they were riding around inside a big bicycle pedal—though in addition to the "you must be this tall" sign, there was also a maximum height.

Yes.

"Gee, sorry," I said. I was a good two inches taller than the sign, and even Jacob would need to seriously slouch to fake his way through it.

Clayton turned plaintive eyes toward his mother, who said, "Not in your wildest dreams."

A train pulled up beside us with lots of fake steam and recorded clanging, and Jacob looked at it, and then at me, and raised his eyebrow.

Clayton whined, "I don't wanna go on that stupid—"

Barbara said, "Give Uncle Jacob and Vic a break for ten minutes, okay? We'll get some popcorn."

"I dunno why *they* wanna go on that stupid…."

I climbed onto the emptiest train car, with only one other rider in it who was staring out at the amusement park and keeping to himself. "Thanks, Barb," Jacob said. He gave his sister and nephew a little wave. Clayton gave me the evil eye in return. I hoped psychic ability didn't run in Jacob's family like stubbornness did.

Without much thinking about it, I sucked white light and put up a barrier between myself and Clayton's scowling face. I didn't really feel the power—not like I would have if I weren't on antipsyactives—but psychically shielding myself was second nature to me by now, like blowing on my coffee to lessen the scald factor or positioning myself upwind of a rotting corpse.

Jacob eased an arm around me and said, "I'm really glad you came."

I didn't see why, but I did my best not to sigh or roll my eyes. I'd figured it wouldn't kill me to sit there for a day and zone out on meds if this family time meant that much to him. "Long as you don't mind me being a spectator." I hadn't realized the buckles and straps would trigger a restraint-reaction from me. I told myself it was just a seatbelt, but my subconscious didn't buy it, and I ended up bowing out before the spiral flingy upside-down coaster got going.

It was easiest to say the Auracel wasn't sitting right. In theory, sharing your burdens should make them lighter. But in practice, I hate watching it register on Jacob's face when he catches me in a Camp Hell flashback.

The train chugged through some Mardi Gras section that looked like a cartoonist's vision of pre-Katrina New Orleans, and then a stand of palm-looking trees that had absolutely no business growing in the suburbs of Chicago. Jacob pulled me closer and nuzzled my hair. "Next time we both get a day off at the same time, you pick. Anything you want to do."

I leaned into him. It felt risky, like someone might pop out of the fake woodwork screaming for his autograph, the famous Jacob Marks, darling of the local media—and there he'd be, rubbing up against some guy. But people you see on TV look different in person. Over the airwaves, they're taller, tanner, younger, and more coiffed. And people were accustomed to seeing Jacob in a suit instead of a sloppy, faded T-shirt and cargo shorts. He'd grown his hair out maybe an inch, and while it had started its day immaculately combed, the whirling and scrambling and whipping around and splashing had left it no better off than mine—and given the relative failure of my most recent haircut, that was saying a lot. For today, at least, Jacob was just a regular guy.

A hot as hell regular guy who was breathing in my ear, but a regular guy, nonetheless.

"You can be my slave for the day," I suggested.

"Really?" he purred, directly into my ear. I'd been kidding—but maybe it wasn't such a bad idea. "What'll that entail? Feeding you?" His breath was warm on my cheek. "Bathing you? With my tongue?"

"I don't know yet. Gotta keep you on your toes." No doubt about it—between Jacob and me, he's got all the testosterone. And yet, maybe he really would get off on the idea of waiting on me hand and foot—and tongue—like that. Problem was, experimenting in bed was kind of like riding amusement park rides. Sure, they were fun, but sometimes you rued the day you ever got in that line.

A big-kid ride roared past us and the wall of scream trailed along in the wake of the metal cage full of freshly flung people. Jacob and I watched. Horror and delight, all mingled together.

I wondered if I would've liked rides—if my life hadn't been…my life.

"So how're you hanging in there—really?"

"It's uh…I dunno. It's fine."

"You had a look."

I shook my head. Sometimes I got really sick of myself. "I've always got a look. Never mind. I'm having fun."

We chugged through a really artificial-looking garden, with flowers in colors you never see in nature planted in rows with military precision.

Popcorn bags and paper cups drifted against the planter and mounded around the bases of the garbage cans that were set in every few feet, with yellowjackets swarming their swinging lids.

"It's too bad about the Auracel. Remember those swings?" Jacob nodded at an older strip of rides with much shorter lines than the new, popular attractions. The swing riders were achieving liftoff as they spun in a big circle. "They had those back when we were kids."

"Did they?"

"Sure. Those, and slides, and bumper cars, and wooden coasters."

"And funhouses." I couldn't be sure if I actually remembered being in a funhouse or if I'd just seen one on TV. My patchwork brain likes to keep me guessing.

"Now it's all how fast and how far you can fall." Jacob pulled me against him tighter. "Don't let me say that in front of Clayton. I probably sound as old as my dad."

I gave his knee a squeeze. King Chaos loomed up ahead of us. Cripes. I was glad I was too tall to ride. It looked like a stiff neck with Valium written all over it, even from the ground. The train tooted and chugged and pulled up to the spot we'd first climbed on. Jacob turned to give me a hand down, and then didn't bother letting go of my hand. This was unusual for him. He's not really into public displays of affection. But he was having a sentimental kind of day.

Barbara and Clayton both stood and walked over. Clayton said, as if we were all talking about whether the clouds would turn to rain, or if we'd prefer pizza to burgers, "This kid Tyler at school says that faggots are perverts and they should all be put in jail."

Barbara went white. I let go of Jacob's hand not because I gave a rat's ass what an eleven-year-old snotnosed punk thought of me touching his uncle, but because I wanted to attempt to catch his mother if she fainted.

"Clayton Joseph," Barbara barked. She sounded like Jacob telling a crackhead to drop his weapon. "You apologize this very second."

"But that's what he said." Clayton's whine cut through my head like a dentist's drill. "I'm not making it up."

Barbara put her face directly in her kid's. "You are old enough to know when you're repeating something that will hurt somebody's feelings."

"Barb." Jacob sounded...I couldn't quite place it. Maybe he sounded like I did when things went south—not like I'd been expecting anything better, but maybe I'd held out a glimmer of hope that it didn't necessarily need to be all that bad. He sounded weary. "Clayton's going to hear things. I'd rather he heard them from me."

He put his arm around Clayton, and what a relief, the kid didn't flinch. I suspected he might not be at the point where he really got what sex was even about, not deep down in his balls.

I might've noticed other boys "that way" when I was his age, but come on. Back then Teen Beat was full of boy cheesecake, and I was assailed by images of smooth chests, long, feathered hair and limpid, dreamy-eyed smiles at the checkout line every time I grabbed a pack of gum. And maybe I was just ahead of the curve in that department—or maybe you'd have to be dead not to notice.

Jacob walked Clayton toward the snow cone stand while I jammed my hands in my pockets and wandered in a holding pattern, and Barbara dug around in her purse as if she might unearth the answer to all our problems there, if only she looked hard enough. Instead she found some clear lip gloss, the kind with the sponge tip applicator, which she applied with a vengeance.

"It's not like it's news to him that Jacob is gay," she said. "We've always been upfront about it."

My wet underwear clung to me like a trick who'd worn out his welcome. "Uh-huh."

"I don't know who this 'Tyler at school' person is."

"Does it matter? I mean, if it's not him, it'll be someone else. Right?"

Barbara spotted a bench covered in cartoon characters and sat down hard. I hovered behind her. Ten yards away, Jacob handed Clayton a green snow cone. The kid took it and gave it a lick, all the while looking daggers at us. At me. The snow cone vendor handed Jacob another one. Red. Jacob caught my eye and pointed at his blindingly red snow cone as if to ask me if I wanted one. I shook my head.

"It's nice of you to sit out all the rides so that Clayton can be with Jacob. He idolizes my brother, you know. It probably doesn't seem like it, what with that outburst."

"No, I um…" I perched on the back of the bench and my wet underwear rode up my ass. "He's probably, uh, y'know." Damn it. Words were so useless sometimes. I did my best to figure out a way to say he was just being especially bratty because some fag was monopolizing his uncle—without coming out and using those exact words. "He probably feels…things…more intensely. Because they're so close."

She gave me a sideways look, one of those zingers where I totally saw Jacob around the eyes, the type of look he'd give me when he knew I wasn't being polygraph-level truthful with him. Then she sighed and re-settled her purse in her lap. "Yeah. Probably."

"I'm not so big on rides anyway."

Another Jacob-ish look, a notch or two more analytical. "Is there some medical reason…?"

"No, uh…not exactly." Was Post Traumatic Stress Disorder medical? No doubt. But I'd been diagnosed by my backstabbing ex, and not a real doctor—although Stephan *was* technically a health care professional nowadays. The whole thing made me want to break out in a cold sweat. "Maybe."

"Huh." She found a pair of sunglasses in her purse, blew the lint off the lenses, and put them on. "I always pictured Jacob with someone a little more athletic."

What was that supposed to mean?

Jacob and Clayton had taken the long way around the food court, and they approached the bench, Clayton with green-tinged lips, Jacob with a wicked red mouth. Jacob stopped a couple of steps back and Clayton shuffled forward. I'd figured he was going to ask his mother for something, but then I realized he was aimed, more or less, at me. Neither one of us cared to initiate eye contact.

"I'm sorry I said something rude about gay people," he said. There was no inflection in the sentence, as if he'd read it, poorly, from a teleprompter.

"Yeah, uh…" what was I supposed to say? Apology accepted? You're forgiven? How queer. "That's okay."

The tension was thick enough to cut with a spork, but then, as if nothing had just happened, Clayton suddenly brightened, turned to Jacob and said, "If we can't go on King Chaos, can we ride the Scrambler again?"

Chapter 2

"Always remember—your most effective tool is your mind. Safety and liability can go hand in hand, but it's critical that you assess the situation and determine the correct amount of force."

I did my best not to roll my eyes at the trainer, a brick wall of a guy named Sando. I don't know if the name was Greek, Hispanic, or what—or even if it was supposed to be his first or his last name. Or neither, or both. Like Cher.

Well, probably not much like Cher.

Evidently some meth head was suing the neighboring Sixteenth Precinct because he'd broken one of the small bones in his wrist by flailing around while he was cuffed—the fact that he'd been caught in the act of robbing a Stop 'n' Go convenience store armed with a baseball bat wrapped in a rusty bike chain notwithstanding—and so now we all needed to learn how to use nylon restraints.

My neck was sore from too many log flumes the day before, but I resisted the urge to rub it. I've always found that staying very, very still tends to keep trainers' focus off me.

"When you size up a situation, first thing, determine your tactical advantage. For instance…" Sando scanned the room.

I held my breath, but unfortunately, he spotted me. I glanced at my partner, Bob Zigler, who gave me a subtle shrug. Damn. I should've stood in front of a darker wall. Or maybe the unfortunate sunburn I'd scored at the amusement park was to blame. Nothing like a big pink target.

"Detective?" Sando motioned me to the center of the room. I tried to pretend I didn't see that smug jackass Raleigh from down the hall smirking at my discomfort.

I sighed and stepped forward. "Now, in your case, you take advantage of your reach." Did he know I almost never arrested anyone? That I was there to wander through crime scenes after the fact? Really, I had more in common with the forensics techs than the beat cops. He took me by the wrist—I hate being touched—and furled my arm up toward my chest. "Defensive stance. Now. Say I take a swing at you." He did a slow-mo swing. "Put your hand on my shoulder and push. I don't connect. See?"

Right. Are we through yet?

"Grab the arm, twist, and pop the elbow."

I fumbled with Sando's arm. He was pretty muscular. Not like Jacob, but still. A beefy guy.

"Plant your foot next to the perp's—make a fulcrum—throw him off-balance. Now twist the arm, pivot, and slide the loop."

I went through all the motions. The chance of me ever getting my foot in the right place at the right time in real life was slim to none, but the sooner I got the nylon cuffs on Sando, the sooner I could get back to standing against the wall and trying to be invisible. I pulled the tab, then tried to wrangle his other hand into the second nylon loop. This time, he actually resisted me—which was a lot more like real life. And I was so not up for real life at that particular moment.

"Use your reach. Pop and twist."

I tried to figure out where to "pop" the elbow. His bulging biceps was distracting.

"Tactics. Think smart. Training wins out over size, so even if you're at a disadvantage with upper-body strength—moving fast, knowing where to hit, that'll be the difference that makes the apprehension."

Nice of him to point out my upper-body strength…or lack thereof. Maybe he'd always pictured the Fifth Precinct with someone more *athletic*. I wrangled the second loop onto his other hand and pulled the tab, and turned back toward the place where I'd been standing, minding my own business.

Sando's hand closed over my wrist. "Again."

Oh, fuck me.

◊ ◊ ◊

The only good thing about the nylon handcuff training was that we'd started at six and wrapped up at ten, so it was almost like having another day off.

I went back home and changed out of my suit, then turned on the TV. It showed about two and a half commercials, and then the screen turned to snow when the cable went out—which it seemed to do every two days, and which left me with nothing to do but ruminate over the faggot remark. And the *athletic* remark. And the lack of upper-body strength remark.

Sticks and Stones opened at eleven. I found myself on the landing in front of the store at five 'til. I knocked.

There was movement behind the door, shuffling and footsteps, and then the door opened a couple of inches before a security chain stopped it. One of Crash's eyes appeared in the space, and his single-eyed gaze raked me up and down. "Where's your polyester suit?"

"I'm done for the day."

He closed the door, undid the chain, and opened it again. "Good. I need a hand with this display. And you brought lunch. The day's looking better and better. Set it on the counter for a sec."

When I stepped into the store, the incense smell was mellow, like Crash hadn't burned any copal since the night before. The store's vibe, its island of calm in the static of life, sank in right away—and when I thought about it in that safe haven, the trip to the theme park felt more like some kind of life lesson than a reason to hate all children forever more.

I set the McDonald's bag on the counter and had a look around, but I didn't see Miss Mattie. I even lingered briefly, but she wasn't there. She could've been invisible, I suppose, but I had the feeling that she wasn't exactly the type to stand around eavesdropping—and if she was, doing that with Crash around would probably result in a hell of an earful. What she did while she wasn't there, I'd never been able to figure out. Did she have places to go, people to see? Could she appear anywhere she wanted, anytime? Did she have a job? No idea.

I hurried back to the front of the store since I didn't want to seem too obvious. Crash gets annoyed when I'm more excited to see his dead neighbor than him.

I joined him beside the front door. We were both in jeans—his were rattier. Both in T-shirts—his cooler, with a mostly washed-off Black Flag logo and the sleeves cut off to showcase his ink. To top it off, he had on a pyramid-studded belt with a skull and crossbones belt buckle. He could pull it off. I couldn't. Not anymore.

He looked me up and down again. He was chewing gum, and somehow he managed to do it critically. "Don't tell me you tried a tanning bed."

"No. I went outside."

"Uh huh. You've got that milky white, blue-eyed Irish thing going on. There is such a thing as sunscreen, you know."

Did I have Irish blood in me? I'd never given it any thought. "I was wearing sunscreen." I snuck a quick glance at the counter to see if Miss Mattie was there yet. She wasn't.

"How long did you stay out of your cave?"

"I dunno. All day."

Crash blew a small bubble, then cracked it loudly. "Right. Live and learn. Here, hold this chair so I can reach the ceiling."

The chair in question was so rickety it would have made a better tripod. "Don't you have a stepladder?"

"Yeah, I have a whole stepladder collection, I just dig standing on chairs 'cos I like to live dangerously. What do you think?"

He probably didn't want to know what I thought. I decided to cut my losses on that particular portion of the conversation and hold his damn chair for him. He climbed up and started sticking pushpins into the ceiling. I kept my eyes on his hands, because it was safer than letting on that I noticed his belt buckle in my face. Dollar bills—or drawings of dollar bills in his weird, cramped hand—were tethered to the pushpins on clear fishing line. A few well-placed pushpins, and suddenly it was raining money inside Sticks and Stones. Pretty cool.

"What's the, uh…concept?"

"The fucking economy. People who're trapped in a bad mortgage, who lost a job they thought was secure to outsourcing, all of 'em are desperate to patch up their wallets."

"With occult supplies?"

"Sure." Crash hopped down, put his hands on his hips and looked up at his handiwork. "My top three sellers, in order, used to be love spells, money charms, and revenge hexes. Now the love and money are flip-flopped."

I glanced down at a few boxes of merchandise Crash had pulled. Soaps, incenses and even aerosol sprays with names like Fast Luck Money Drawing, Horn of Plenty and Luck in a Hurry. I knew that if Crash sold it, it must have been legit in some sense of the word—and if I could exorcise ghosts with salt from the Stop 'n' Go where they sold lottery tickets and Freezee drinks, someone could increase their cash flow with Nine Lucky Mixture bath and floor wash. I wasn't sure who. But someone.

"What should I call it? I was thinking it might be amusing to make a poster that says Golden Shower of Wealth and see if anyone notices."

"Serious?"

"Eh, maybe not. Most of my customers are either too old, too religious or too foreign to fully appreciate my sense of humor."

I wasn't sure a pee joke was the best moneymaking idea, but Crash seemed to enjoy it. "It's your store. Why be your own boss if you can't please yourself?"

"Pleasing myself—is that a double entendre?"

"No."

He stuck an arm through the slats on the back of the chair and slung it over his shoulder, then batted his eyelashes at me, turned, and sashayed back toward the counter. "You sure? Maybe you know who I was thinking about the last time I jerked off."

I sighed, and said, "Miss Mattie? Is that you?"

"Nice try, but she's not here. Your aura would've spiked if you were really talking to her." He dropped the chair in front of the counter and opened the McDonald's bag. "What'd you get?"

"Two combo meals."

"What about me?"

"One is for you."

"I'm a vegetarian, you knucklehead."

"What?"

"You're seriously that oblivious—how long have we known each other?"

"Uh, I dunno. You can have my fries."

"Good. I'm starving." He flicked his gum into the trash and stuffed a good dozen fries into his mouth. "These used to taste better when I was a kid, but I think they were fried in lard back then."

"So how long have you been a, uh…."

"Five years. It's a religious thing."

Crap. I'd always figured Crash had some sort of nonspecific New Age belief system. I didn't know he considered himself a member of an actual religion. Maybe he was Hindu or something—he seemed to know an awful lot about chakras and meditation. Did Hindus eat meat? And if they didn't, how come the Indian restaurant down the street had such amazing Chicken Tikka Masala? Once upon a time, back when my training had been less about snap-and-pop and more about esoteric concepts, I probably could've told you what religions made which demands, especially the more arcane ones. But I'd probably killed the brain cells that held that knowledge with one too many hits of nitrous.

"It's okay," he said. "You can eat meat in front of me. I'll deal."

I hunkered down over the counter and chowed down half a burger. Maybe I'd been hungry too. Aside from the hunger, the other thing that had been gnawing at me—underneath the litany of criticism I'd been subjected to lately—was the idea that the amusement park hadn't been riddled with ghosts. Because even through the Auracel, I can usually sense their presence. The drugs just allow me to tune it out.

"D'you think ghosts take up space?" I asked.

Crash took a long, thoughtful pull on the massive soda. "Don't know. You can see 'em. What do you think?"

"They don't stand inside other people. Living people. They don't stand inside each other. But they walk through walls and furniture and stuff like it's not even there."

He nodded as he finished the rest of one super sized fry and continued on to the next. "Subtle bodies."

Was he serious, or was that another Crash-joke along the lines of golden showers? "What's that?"

"Astral. Etheric."

Those, I knew about—enough that maybe I could figure out his religion without having to resort to actually asking. "What discipline talks about that?"

"Oh, you name it. Subtle bodies pop up in everything from Tantric to Crowley. Spiritualists, too—the Victorian table-rappers who said ghosts shot ectoplasm, the ones who staged fake photos of garden fairies."

Super.

"So it's bullshit."

"You're pretty quick to get defensive, for someone who's seen it all in action." Crash crumpled up the greasy cardboard sleeve, threw it back in the bag, then took the top bun off my second burger and stole the tomato slice. I ignored his tongue stud as he licked off the mayo. "I think a few of the table rappers were probably real mediums. Plenty of shysters along with 'em, but you figure one or two had to be legit."

"Hard to say." At least without tracking down their graves, seeing if any were still lingering around, and then trying to figure out if they'd be willing to level with me or not.

"I thought you could see people going astral. Why the second-guessing?"

"No. I can't, usually. I need to be on psyactives." Or drunk. "I was just trying to figure out why crowded places don't tend to be haunted, but isolated places do."

"Or what if it's the other way around?" Crash sucked grease and salt off his fingers like he was giving his own hand a blowjob. I didn't notice. Not at all. "What if places get deserted because on some sub-sensory level, the mundanes of the world know there's something spooky about an area and they start avoiding it? It's like the chicken and the egg. Maybe you'll never know."

I picked the second burger off the bun, ate the meat and cheese in few bites, wadded the soggy bun into a ball and shoved it back in the bag. Miss Mattie was still nowhere to be seen. It wasn't fair. I was playing nice with her little Curtis and everything—hadn't I even brought him fries? Regardless, she remained indifferent to my thirst for arcane knowledge. I took a long swallow of Coke instead.

Crash folded a piece of gum into his mouth. "So…I can't help but ask… what's with your hair?"

"I got it cut."

"Where? At the Moe Howard school of cosmetology?"

I could tell Jacob wasn't too keen on my hair lately either, but it had grown way over the dress code length, and I kept missing my appointment at the real salon because I'd been scouring the scene of a domestic stabbing all week to see if the spirit might know where her loverboy took off to. Unfortunately, it seemed she'd moved on before I had a chance to chat. "Just one of those places where you don't need an appointment."

I ducked when Crash grabbed for my head, but he was just as fast as me. I felt his fingers slide through my hair, watched him peer down his nose at whatever he was seeing. "This angle's all wrong. Sit."

I'd been kind-of kneeling in the tripod chair so I could hover over the counter while I ate. It creaked when I turned and tucked my leg beneath me. Crash pulled a comb out from under the cash register, rounded the counter and started pulling up hanks of hair from random parts of my head, measuring them between his fingers, and scowling. "I can save this cut. Lemme get my shears."

I'd be stuck with it a while. Then it would start all over again, the awkward haircut that grew out some and had a few decent weeks, then was suddenly too long for the dress code. A never-ending cycle. "Yeah, sure."

"You not too proud to let him help you. Almost—it still be hard for you. But you got trust built up between the two of you now."

I whipped around. Crash was gone, and there was Miss Mattie, big and glossy-skinned mahogany, fanning herself with her paper St. Anthony fan.

"I'm so glad to see you. Listen, don't go. I need to ask you—"

"I done told you, I'm not here for you. You got to find your own path."

In one of the cramped rooms behind the store, drawers and doors squalled open and banged shut.

I sighed. "Fine. Do you have something you want to say to Curtis? I'll tell him. I'll even write it down so I get it right."

"He do want the best for you. He need to be needed—we all need to be needed. He be a good friend to you if you let him."

I knew that.

Suddenly, that seemed pretty profound. I'd known that for a long time—and it wasn't one of those things I took for granted. The people I considered to be my friends were few and far between. Really far between. "Okay. Yeah."

Miss Mattie scowled down at a handmade sign propped on the counter. It was cobbled together from the glossy Sunday Tribune ads, where a hastily cut out male underwear model with a really prominent package had been pasted over the world's cleanest stovetop. A comic book style dialog balloon that read, *Did you sign up for the Sticks and Stones newsletter?* hovered beside him.

She couldn't seem to make heads or tails of the sign. Neither could I, really, but maybe that was the point. To make you look, even if you didn't quite get it. "It don't make you no less of a man to ask for help." She pronounced it *axe*. "You got to ask yourself what's more important—to try to do everything your own way and lose it all, or to ask for help so you can get what you need, when you need it. Always remember, you not here in this world alone. You got friends."

"It's just a haircut—but him and me, we're cool. I know it might not always sound like it, but that's just the way we ta—"

"Sometimes the only place you find help is the last place you look. Remember that."

Then she was gone, without even bothering to exit through the closet door.

Chapter 3

I stared at the last place I'd seen Miss Mattie, then dropped my gaze to the underwear model. The hodgepodge sign was vaguely disturbing. That was probably intentional, too.

"I gotta unlock the door." Crash swept back into the store and set a pair of scissors, a bottle of Windex—or probably what used to be Windex and was now water, judging by the fact that it was clear and not bright blue—and a jar of some trendy hair paste on the counter. "Don't worry. It's usually pretty dead before noon."

Just because he'd said that, people were milling around on the landing waiting for the store to open. One of them was a short, round Hispanic woman who went right for the Santeria supplies. The other one was a white guy with long, greasy hair and a patchy beard. From where I sat, he looked smelly.

Crash said, "Just a sec," to me, dug around for his keyring and unlocked his register. Within seconds, the Hispanic woman was at the counter with an armload of prayer candles. Crash wrapped each one in newspaper before he bagged it, gave the customer her total in Spanish, and made quick change for her twenty. She took her bags and left without a word. "One of my regulars," Crash said. "She doesn't have a lot to say. I think she feels guilty for shopping at a gringo store." The grubby guy was still browsing.

"Sit," Crash insisted, and shoved at my shoulder. I hadn't even realized I'd stood up. A cop-thing, most likely. When I thought about it, how rote a majority of my responses were, it felt pretty bleak. Or maybe that was the point. Maybe that's what training was really all about.

I sat.

He spritzed my head with Windex water. It didn't smell like ammonia. Probably just plain water. Then he combed through and parted my hair in a bunch of places. "You want me to go conservative, then?"

"I uh…" I didn't. Not deep inside. But I could hardly ask for a mohawk. "Whatever you think is best."

"I always knew you could sweet-talk me like crazy. Don't worry, baby. You're in good hands." He tilted my head down and snipped at my hairline in back, tiny nips. "I wish the butcher who got to you before had left me some length to work with."

Points of wet hair sprinkled the floor beside the chair. Very small, a quarter of an inch, even less. Crash kept working my hair, fingers and comb, comb and fingers, measuring and finessing while the tiniest bits of hair rained down.

"You cut hair?"

Crash let go of my head and I looked up. The grubby guy was standing closer to us than I would've liked, especially with me sitting down.

"How much?" he asked.

"You can't afford me. Is that all, or do you need some charcoal?"

"Uh, no. I'm good."

Crash rang up the sale, then came back around to the front of the counter and picked up wherever he'd left off. "Another regular?" I asked.

"I dunno. He's shopped here a few times, but there's something in his vibe that rubs me wrong. He's always buying bouncebacks, curse deflection stuff. Which raises the question—look down, there you go—is he really surrounded by people who continually fling hexes and whammies his way, and if so, what did he do to deserve it? Or is he just paranoid? Either way, I'm not exactly itching to add him on Facebook."

Crash grabbed my chin and tilted my face up. I held my breath while he leaned over me and put his face right in mine to check the sides of my hair for length. He gave his gum an annoyed crack and took another quarter inch off one side.

Had he felt my aura spike when Miss Mattie showed up, or had the creepy guy's vibes thrown enough interference from out on the landing to cover it? Hard to say—but my guess was, Crash would've had a comment or two if he'd known I was just chatting with his long-lost neighbor. Why had she bothered to talk to me just to tell me it wasn't wussy to ask for help? I was well aware of how much help my hair needed—and I'd already resigned myself to the Crash treatment. Overprotective, I guess.

Crash traded the scissors and comb for the little jar of hair stuff and rubbed some paste between his palms. "I know you can't be bothered to style it—"

"Not necessarily."

"—but humor me just for today."

He worked the paste through my hair and tweaked it. I used to put my 'hawk up with Elmer's glue and egg whites. I could manage a dab of paste.

"Yeah, not bad. I wanna give you a trim in a couple of weeks when the front has a chance to recover from the chop shop."

"Uh, how much do I owe you?"

Crash waved it off. "Never mind. It's enough to know you won't be scaring my customers away. So what else was on your agenda today? Did you need any actual supplies?"

Bob Zigler had downsized my stealth exorcism kit to a repurposed pocket-sized breath spray and an emptied out Chap Stick tube. I was at the point where I could zap a repeater with a quarter teaspoon of Florida Water and a pinch of herbs, and I had enough sandalwood powder to last me through Christmas. Still, if Crash wasn't going to accept money for the haircut, I figured I should probably buy something. "I dunno. I'll look around."

What would he stand to make the most off if I bought it? The statuettes, probably. They were the biggest ticket items in the whole store. If I bought one, though, he'd probably look for it the next time he came to visit—and if there's one thing I can't stand, it's clutter. Throws too many shadows.

Also, he'd probably ask me why I wanted to buy Ganesh in the first place, given that I'm agnostic. It'd be a lot easier to simply drop a few twenties on his floor when he wasn't looking, but in all likelihood they'd end up in the pocket of the bearded guy, or someone just like him.

I turned and scratched my head, wondered when the last time was I'd washed my hair. Then I remembered the paste, and *then* I laid my eyes on a row of books. Books had a decent markup, right? And I might actually find some use for them. "What do you have that's recent?"

"Lucky you've got a hot little ass in those jeans or I'd have to smack you for asking such useless questions. Recent what? Ephemerides? Meditation guides? Hymnals?"

I felt my cheeks warm up, so I cranked my internal faucet and pulled down a white balloon between the two of us before he could get off empathically on my embarrassment. "Psych stuff, I guess. General facts. Post-eighties."

"Ah. Now, that's a challenge." He brushed shoulders with me as he came to stand beside me at the bookshelf. "That's when the books got bland. Before that, psychic research was actually interesting—but the second they found something real, poof. The writing tanked."

"How come?"

He lowered his voice. "Who was the one who set up a cloak-and-dagger meeting with me in a public toilet to find out more about F-Pimp? You know better than anyone that Big Brother is real."

The Federal Psychic Monitoring Program—could I go one single day without being reminded that the FPMP was keeping tabs on me? Was that too much to ask? I sidled away from him. He managed to brush up on me some more without even seeming to move. "Maybe Jacob would like…this one." I scanned the shelf frantically for a title that didn't look asinine while I pumped white light into the shield between us like I was putting out a flaming house with the energy. *Psychic Self-Defense.* How appropriate. I pulled the book and showed him the cover. "Any good?"

"Adequate. I wouldn't stock it if it wasn't at least moderately informative, not unless it had a tacky cover that fairly screamed *For Entertainment Purposes Only.*"

"Okay. I'll get it for him."

The second mention of my lover—Crash's ex—finally got him to back out of my personal space. "So how is Mister Tall, Dark and Infuriating these days?"

"The same, I guess."

"Doubtful. We're all evolving."

I grabbed a couple more titles—*Elemental Magick,* and *You Too Can be Clairvoyant.* The Clairvoyance one was thirty-five bucks. Good. I wouldn't feel so bad about the free haircut if I bought it.

Crash rang up my books and swiped my Visa, then did a double take at my hair. "Come here a second." He motioned me forward and I leaned over the counter, figuring that I had something out of place. I felt his fingers against my scalp and a tingle shot down my spine. I turned up my internal faucet another few rotations. "You've got a wicked sunburn right up your part." Crash snapped a triangular chunk off an aloe plant that was hidden behind a big incense burner and a Seven African Powers prayer candle, then pushed my head down and squeezed the cool juice onto it. I figured that the aloe might add character to the paste—or at least it wouldn't be terribly noticeable.

I looked up, and Crash's fingertips hovered at my eyebrow like he might stroke my cheek. I stepped back and strengthened the white balloon yet again. It had to be as thick as a steel-belted radial by now.

He was a lot easier to resist when he was acting like an asshole. Time to get out while I still could. I gave him a stilted wave, and I could hardly move my arm through the thick membrane of protection I'd been pouring light into for the past quarter of an hour. He smirked and gave me an ironic finger-wave in return. "Ciao, baby."

I stumbled out onto the street and let my balloon drop. Crash was great, don't get me wrong, but keeping him from feeding off my emotions felt like drinking three refills of Coke at a restaurant, finding the bathroom out of order, and having to hold it all the way home down a road full of potholes.

On my way back to the car I glanced at the fortune teller's window—not that you can ever see anything, between the neon and the thick black drape—and got a load of myself reflected back in the glass. Holy crap. My hair looked friggin' awesome.

Crash had given me rock star hair. Subtle rock star hair, like a pseudo-intellectual kid on an indie label might have, hair that looked like he didn't give a shit about it, that he just happened to tousle it the right way and it fell, by chance, in the most flattering way it might have landed. Hair that might not have been washed lately, but it didn't matter because it only added to the just-rolled-out-of-bed charm.

It was the hair I'd been born to have—if I were a pseudo-intellectual in an indie rock band, and not a cop.

Would I have to get an even shorter nerd cut to cover it up? I didn't want to. Besides, it probably wouldn't look quite as good without the hair paste. It might even look cop-like, if I didn't tousle it.

Though I didn't know how I'd resist. It was the best hair I'd ever had.

My phone rang while I was waiting for the light on Damen and Lincoln that I've never once made. Crash. "Hello?"

"So what do you think?"

"The hair? It's uh…yeah. It's good."

"Oh, go on. Really. Go on."

"It's really…good…hair."

"That's it? Good? Just good? You look about five years younger and smokin' hot."

"What about…athletic?"

There was crackling on the line. I realized it was Crash torturing his gum for a good second or two. "What're you talking about?"

"You know, more uh…athletic."

"I think I have the wrong number. I could swear Victor Bayne just asked me if I thought he looked athletic."

"Never mind, I gotta g—"

"My grandma is more athletic than you."

"Thanks a lot."

"You break a sweat lifting a coffee cup."

"Okay, okay, I get it."

"Athletic? I must've told you a dozen times today how you well and truly rock my world, and you go fishing around for the one compliment you'd never get in a million years." I heard a slurp of Coke in a straw, and the muttering of the word, "Athletic…."

The light turned and the car behind me beeped. I gave him a "yeah, whatever" all-purpose wave and rolled forward. "So what do you think it would take? I mean, for me to, I dunno, maybe bulk up a little."

"Protein and weight training. But I just watched you scarf down half a pound of beef, so I'm guessing your protein is adequate."

We had protein drinks in the fridge. They tasted like the can. But maybe if I held my nose…. "You mean like, uh, barbells and…stuff?"

"Most guys your age—how old are you, forty?"

"Thirty-nine."

"They'd kill to have your bod—not an ounce of fat on you and a full head of hair with hardly any grays."

What? I had gray hair? Since when?

"I'm all for physical fitness, but I think you're pretty much stuck with your basic body type. What the heck's gotten into you, anyway, that now you suddenly need to be athletic?"

"I just thought that Jacob might like—"

"Jacob's ga-ga over you as it is."

"Well, I don't know about—"

"I do," Crash said. "He's smitten. Lust-addled. Head over heels." I replied with a long, gusty sigh at the thought of going through all the trouble of diet and exercise only to end up as beanpole-like as ever, and Crash said, "Besides, I can't believe you're being this shallow. The body's only a shell."

I considered that logic. "Then why should it matter if I have a good haircut or not?"

"Go fuck yourself, then…and think of me while you're doing it." He made a wet kissy-noise and hung up.

Chapter 4

Psychic Self Defense by Muriel S. Sullivan ended up being a lot more interesting than I would've imagined. I suspected the author was visual, like me, so I could relate to the way she talked about things. My visual representation of protective skins might have looked more like condoms and body bags than hers, but even though she wrote about rings of mystic fire and halos of purifying white light, I could still scrape together some sort of internal reference.

The book had been written in the sixties, so it was definitely weird. Muriel's instructions would be making perfect sense, but then she'd tell you to grab an iron spike, invoke Thor, force the negative energy into the spike and drive it into the ground. Granted, as Marvel Comics superheroes go, Thor is pretty cool. But I've never seen an iron spike just lying around waiting to be planted.

Despite the weirdness, the book must've really been holding my attention, because I didn't hear Jacob come in until he spoke.

"Did you do something different with your hair?"

I jumped, and the book fluttered out of my hands like a living thing, pages fanned open, hovering in mid-air while I grabbed at it, and then tumbling to the floor, shut.

I touched my hair. It felt funny. Hair paste. "Yeah, uh, Crash gave me a trim."

Jacob turned on the overhead light. I hadn't even noticed the room getting dim. He hooked a finger through the knot of his tie and loosened it as he approached, all the while nailing me to my seat with his most intense dark-eyed stare. Silk hissed on cotton as he whisked off his tie, and then he leaned over me, eyes level with mine. "Take off your clothes."

He said it, and then he didn't even give me a chance to do it myself. He yanked my T-shirt over my head and threw it on top of the book, then went at the fly of my jeans like he'd rip it right out if it didn't cooperate. I undid the buttons on his tailored dress shirt, then Jacob pulled it off and threw it on the floor beside mine. His undershirt followed. Then it was just him, and me, and everything we were wearing from the waist down—which didn't stay in place for long.

All the while we stripped, Jacob didn't say a word. He just stared. He dug the hair…maybe.

Or maybe he was wishing I was more *athletic.*

"Let's try something," I suggested, before I'd even fully formed an idea.

He nodded, all ears.

"Something more, uh, active."

He gave me a dirty smile. "What did you have in mind?"

Something that would make me seem like I wasn't out of shape—though nothing I could picture seemed to fit that bill. "Well, we could…." I trailed off and hoped that, in his enthusiasm, Jacob would come up with something.

He pulled me against him chest to chest, moved to stroke my hair back and then changed his mind at the last second, as if he was afraid he'd wreck it by touching it. "You want to fuck me?"

Um. Oh.

He looked pretty jazzed, so I made myself nod as if that was exactly what I'd been getting at. It's not that I didn't think Jacob's ass was a damn fine ass, but with our bodies—him massive, me gangly—I felt like a greyhound attempting to mount a mastiff whenever we changed things up.

"Let's do it in the bathroom," he said. "In the mirror."

Oh God. Not only did I have to do the deed, I had to see myself in action. I'd be lucky if I could even get it up.

At least we kept the primo lube in there—the silicone that lets you hump for hours, even underwater. Hopefully he wouldn't notice if I kept my eyes shut.

I followed him in and he turned on me suddenly, and nuzzled my jaw. "Tell me what to do."

I tried to think athletic, but absolutely nothing came to mind, so I said, "Kiss my neck." I'm notoriously weak-willed when it comes to my neck. Maybe I'd get into the spirit of things more quickly if he was working on my…yeah.

Jacob's mouth was a thing of beauty. I slipped my arms around his shoulders and pressed myself against his body—big and warm, solid, hairy where I liked it, smooth along his back, inside his thighs. I slipped a hand alongside his balls to remind myself how silky smooth he felt down there in the crease of his thigh, and hot and moist, the heat of the day. He moaned against my neck, and I felt a most definite stirring.

I could do it. No problem. I could be very…athletic. All I needed was the proper motivation.

"Touch my nipples. Not hard, not yet. But make me feel it."

Jacob mumbled against my neck and slid his hands up my ribs. He took both nipples at the same time, one in each hand, and rolled them between thumb and forefinger. My cock twitched, and he made another pleased sound along the spit-wet skin beside my Adam's apple.

"No hickeys, mister. You're in deep shit if you mark me up."

A rumbly laugh. A gentle bite. My cock rose and made a right angle to the rest of my body. I let the head glide over his hip, and he made another satisfied sound against my throat.

Bossing Jacob around, I could get used to it. For the evening, anyway. "Enough of that. Kneel. Hands behind your back."

He pulled away and paused to look at me for a moment, then smiled to himself as he complied. Or maybe it was my hair he'd been admiring. Same difference. Maybe.

He knelt on the tiny rubber-backed square of machine-washable carpet. It wasn't exactly the most padded thing in the house, but it would do.

I grabbed him by the head and let my fingertips rake along the sides of his scalp. I liked his hair a touch longer, the way it was now. It gave me something to hold onto while I said, "Kiss my cock."

Jacob leaned in, keeping his hands obediently clasped behind his back. His arms were thick and strong, with defined parts that I didn't even know the names of, since my knowledge of anatomy stops after biceps and triceps—and a golden tan from mowing our ragged strip of lawn in nothing but a pair of gym shorts, a determined scowl, and a sultry sheen of sweat.

His beard tickled my shaft. Small kisses. Brushes of lips teased my cock, fluttering along the underside, the base. My knees felt a bit weak. I leaned against the sink. "Lick it."

Hot and wet, like he'd been dying to taste me. I closed my eyes and felt his head advance and retreat while his tongue slid up and down to wet my dick.

I could come like that. If he started to suck me, and I looked down and saw him kneeling there, submissive and naked, I would totally shoot my load.

Not very *athletic*.

So what was it he said to me that got me off when he was being the bossy one? Oh yeah. I grabbed his hair harder and stilled his head so he knew to stop and listen. "Get up. Show me that hole."

When he stood up again, his cock was thick and hard. He was wearing his "I wanna pound you through the mattress" expression, but it was taut now with his effort to keep it all in check and do only what I told him. His thighs flexed and released as if he was spring-loaded, and the tiniest slip would send him flying into action. But for now, he could wait.

He knocked yesterday's newspaper, folded to the Lifestyle section, to the floor, then eased his chest onto the counter beside the sink. He walked his legs out. More muscles I couldn't name, or maybe tendons—and the sweet, rounded rise of his ass, which was mostly muscle, too—all of it spread out before me. All of it mine to do whatever I pleased with it.

I ran my hands over him, down his back, over his ass, to the backs of his thighs. His skin flicked in response. Everywhere, he was rock hard.

"I need it," he mumbled into his forearms. "Do it."

The fact that he could hardly bring himself to tell me to fuck him sent a thrill zinging down to my groin. I licked my finger and trailed it down his hot, moist crack. He exhaled carefully against the countertop.

I figured I should probably say something about that being "my" hole and how I was gonna "own" it, but it sounded too fake, even in my thoughts. I bent over him instead, and laid a slow, wet kiss along the spot where his tailbone ended, and the curve of his spine turned into ass crack. He moaned.

I tongued him, farther down, and farther down still, rich and salty and end-of-the-day musky, and my cock started to throb in anticipation of going there too and knowing what that hot, wet hole would feel like clenching all around it.

"Sweet ass." I let the words play over my spit, and Jacob shivered all over. I licked him, right on the pucker, hard, and pressed a wet fingertip in.

"Oh God."

I closed my mouth over his hole and pressed my tongue in where my finger had been. I was high on the scent of maleness, and sex.

Jacob was really moaning now, a string of encouraging sounds, and tilting his ass as if maybe angling it just right would encourage me to cram in something bigger and stiffer than my tongue. Seeing him beg like that with his body, his mega-ripped, rock hard body, was a total rush.

The lube was cold, but warmed to my touch fast. Super slick. I gave my cock a few quick, slippery pumps then swiped my fingertips over Jacob's ass. He moaned again.

I didn't waste any time in pushing in. Tight, so tight. I hadn't barebacked with anyone since I was a teenager, and it always shocked me, the molten hot wetness of Jacob's body squeezing at my cock. I started slow, because neither of us were particularly accustomed to me serving it up to him, but his hole was so deliciously slick I ended up buried in just a few thrusts.

The musculature of his back shifted as his ribcage heaved, and he drank in great, loud breaths, still moaning, still encouraging me with his sighs and the needy arching of his spine.

"Fuck me. Jack me off." The words were half-buried in moans and groans and breathing. Jacob usually has no problem at all doing the dirtiest dirty-talk, but not now, not with my dick up his ass.

Everything would've been perfect, if it weren't for the mirror. I could try to focus on Jacob with his arousal-flushed face, and the chiseled perfection of his bod from every angle, but there I was right in back of him. Good hair or not, I couldn't stand to look. Most people in long-term relationships occasionally fantasize that they're *with* someone else when they fuck. I wished I *was* someone else.

I reached around to stroke him, but even then, there I was—looking right back at us from the mirror.

I could turn off the light, but that would be too obviously weird, leaving us panting and puffing in the windowless, pitch-black room. The shower—I could turn that on and steam up the mirror so all I saw were shapes. But I couldn't reach the tap. And we'd never gotten around to upgrading our hot water heater.

"Harder," Jacob mumbled into his arm. "I'm ready."

Oh—he thought I'd been taking it slow for his benefit, and not figuring out a way to stop seeing myself. I shut my eyes and focused on the tightness, the feel of myself gliding in and out, in and out, the way he arched under me to meet each thrust. So hot. So slick. So tight.

Then I opened one eye, and there I was. Damn it.

I pulled out, flipped the toilet seat down, and sat. "C'mon, get on top of me. I want to look at you face-to-face while I'm in you." I wanted to look at anything but the mirror—but I thought it was a pretty good excuse.

Jacob straddled me, and his quads bulged as he found his position with the deliberation he'd use mounting a machine at the gym. I strongly suspected he was working his abs as he did it.

He braced himself on the towel bar behind my head and lowered himself gingerly, until the fine hairs that dusted his ass and my thighs tickled together. "How's that?" he said.

"Tight."

He grunted, and began to move. It was awfully intense, watching him watching me—watching him trying to get me off—but it was a hell of a lot better than the sight in the mirror. I lubed my hand again and started to work his cock like I meant it. He caught his lower lip between his teeth and shuddered all over.

His eyes closed and he focused hard on just moving, riding my cock. He found his rhythm and worked it, and I jacked him with one hand and held him by the hip with the other so I could feel his body rise and fall. His face—what cheekbones. What a mouth. Great eyebrows, too. Expressive. A hitch formed between them, and he said, "Is it good for you?"

"Yeah."

"You're so quiet."

"I am?"

"Yeah. I mean, usually…."

"Oh, uh…it's different. A different feeling. But just as good. Totally."

He shifted his angle, as if he didn't believe me—like he thought he couldn't please me, not that way, without some serious determination and focus.

Crap. The last thing I needed was for both of us to have an inferiority complex. I tried to think of something to say that didn't sound fake. "You know how tight you are? So tight I can hardly breathe, let alone talk to you."

His expression softened, but he kept on riding me like this thing we were doing was a puzzle, and he needed to crack the code.

He clenched himself harder—and now I was positive he was working his abs, because I could feel contractions rolling through him, coaxing me to come.

My breath caught, and my hand flew over his cock. "Come with me inside you," I gasped. "I wanna see that. Come for me."

Jacob raked his jaw over his biceps to wipe away the sweat that was starting to bead his face from all the quad work. "Touch my balls."

I let go of his waist and slipped my other hand between us. It felt weird, no two ways about it—his taut ass slapping down on my hipbones. He'd probably have a bruise in the shape of my pelvis to show for our experiment. Stroking his nuts seemed to turn up the heat. He threw his head back, and the way his body clenched me started to feel less deliberate. I dug it, the trembling contractions, erratic, desperate.

"I'm gonna come…" I whispered. "You're making me come…"

"Fuck, yeah." He grit his teeth and squeezed his eyes shut, squeezed his ass around me too, and damn, there it was, a surge, and another surge, and fuck, it was so hot and so wet, my juice inside him—and it was worth it, totally worth it, even if I'd looked like a big dumbass in the mirror. He spattered my belly while I came, and that made my hips twitch up even after I thought I was spent, and my dick gave another grudging throb in his hole.

Jacob pressed his forehead to mine, sticky with sweat, and we both breathed hard. "That was really intense," I said. "You feel incredible."

"Yeah?"

"Yeah." I tilted my face up for a kiss. His mouth tasted salty.

He eased his death grip off the towel bar and ran his fingers through my way cool hair. "I love you so much."

"I love you too." It seems like there should be a better answer than that, but sometimes it doesn't pay to try and talk fancy.

I kissed him some more, slow, satisfied kisses, drowsy kisses. It seemed like I could have stayed there forever, kissing him. But then I felt his thigh tremble. "Are you not sitting down on me?"

"Well I…." He looked surprised.

"Do you think you can't sit on my lap?"

"No. Of course not. It's just…we're at a weird angle. That's all."

I sighed. I didn't need to be a Human Polygraph to know that people who said "of course not" were unlikely to be giving you much of a truth.

He stood up fast and offered me a hand-up. I couldn't not take it without shoving him into the shower and cracking his head on the not-quite-retro tiles. I was feeling mildly ticked, not sociopathic, so I accepted.

"I thought maybe the toilet seat was digging into you."

"Forget it."

He turned on the shower, and the sound of water ringing on tile filled the awkward silence nicely. "Don't be mad," Jacob said over the rhythmic stream. "We just had a really great time. There's nothing to be mad about."

"It's fine."

He stuck his hand under the shower, tweaked the temperature, then climbed in and pulled me along with him. He hustled me against the wall and started in again with the kissing, and maybe I was irked enough to tell him enough with it already, we'd shot our loads and what more did he want—other than someone *athletic* enough to bear his weight? But as I planted my foot and tried to pivot, I felt a horrible twinge race up my calf.

Jacob's mouth closed over mine, and now he tasted like the shower. I kissed him back, reluctantly at first, but then he slid a bar of soap between my legs and started making lather, and I decided I could stay put for the moment.

At least until the charley horse subsided.

Chapter 5

Since Jacob now had over an inch of hair, he also owned styling products. Things had changed a lot since the eighties, when I'd primped my hair with office supplies. The cramp in my leg was nagging at me, so I decided to burn a sick day rather than letting the jackasses like Raleigh down the hall see me limping. Jacob was at work, I'd actually slept in for a change, and now I was home alone with my new haircut.

I rifled through the medicine cabinet. There was hairspray, but supposedly for "shine" rather than "hold," in a tiny little spritzer bottle. I also found a small round jar of something with the consistency of pudding. That was it—two things. Undoubtedly, if Jacob had more hair, we'd have more hair stuff. I figured the hair pudding would have to do.

I took a very small dab and worked it through my hair like Crash had, fully expecting to look ridiculous when I was done.

I didn't. It looked great.

I wondered if working out, especially if I followed that workout with some kind of stretching, might help the calf situation. But you didn't do your hair and then jump around and get it all sweated up—everyone knows that. Besides, I didn't actually have any idea what "working out" would entail. So I went and turned on my computer instead. If I put together a plan of action for bulking up, it would be a step in the right direction. And it wouldn't wreck my hair.

Sifting through websites took time. A lot of them pimped home gyms, or weird pieces of plastic that were supposed to help you push, pull or gyrate your way to a spectacular six-pack. Even though I knew they were probably crap, the before and after pictures did give me pause.

But I figured that if any of these things did work, we'd already have one downstairs. In the basement.

Hitting the gym is as much a social thing for Jacob as it is about keeping up his hugeness, but since he was now a homeowner and he had his very own basement, he'd collected a few basic pieces of equipment for those days when his job kept him from his normal routine.

Since I didn't trust the overhead light not to sputter into oblivion the second I was smack-dab in the middle of the basement, I grabbed my pocket flashlight, just in case, and headed downstairs.

Jacob had worked hard to make the space respectable—half of it, anyway. The now-finished portion of the basement had a fresh, white acoustic drop-ceiling and a smooth concrete floor he'd fussed over for hours, only to cover it with interlocking rubber gym tiles once it was absolutely perfect.

I walked around the weight bench to size it up, and from the far end, caught a glimpse of the other half of the basement. A couple of folding screens separated it from Jacob's home gym; he hadn't quite figured out if he should build some walls and divide the space into rooms, or have the big ancient canning equipment hauled to a junkyard and expand the finished area into a giant rec room. So for now, his solution was to not look at the part he didn't know what to do with.

Who was I to criticize?

It was pretty creepy, though. Darkness lurked behind the screens, and hulks of big metal machinery. The unfinished ceiling absorbed all the light, until all that was left were dozens of shifting shadows.

I looked down at the barbell and counted up the metal discs. Over a hundred and fifty pounds on one end alone. I stared at it stupidly as I realized he bench-pressed two of me. On a regular basis.

The dumbbells, then. There they were, colorful and rubberized, stacked on their unassuming metal pyramid. The weights were printed ever so helpfully on the ends. I took the second-smallest weight, a green 12-pounder, and wondered what to do with it. I tried a curl and thought, seriously, is this how guys get buff?

I put it back before I hurt myself.

The clear course of action was to ask Jacob for advice. So naturally I wanted to do that least of all. Did I think he would look down at me, think I was a wimp because I couldn't press and squat and lift what he could? He already knew that. Heck, he thought I couldn't even handle him sitting on my lap.

Maybe I thought he'd push me harder than I was ready to go. That's what trainers did, wasn't it? Though Jacob was so notorious for cutting me slack, I couldn't really fathom him telling me to drop and give him fifty. Not unless we were naked, and role-playing, and he'd only make me do about ten before he spread me open and showed me who was boss.

I visited that pleasant daydream for a few seconds, then turned and headed upstairs. I suspected what I was really scared of was that as disgusted as I was with my scrawniness, I didn't have the motivation to do anything about it. It was bad enough Jacob had to live with the protruding hipbones. He didn't need my personality flaws highlighted, too.

My laptop was still open to the latest miracle piece of plastic, so I decided to see if there might be a legitimate-looking site that would tell me how to use something we already owned. I grabbed a banana and a fresh cup of coffee, and I started poking around for dumbbell workouts. I quickly saw they were now called freeweights. Fine. Freeweights, then. I found a simple routine, went to print it out, and got a message that my printer was out of ink.

Why did everything always need to be so complicated?

Sure, I could go to the store, buy ink, come back, try to install it and find I'd somehow managed to get the wrong cartridge—but was it worth it? Who was to say I wouldn't try the workout once and then give up?

Who was to say Jacob even wanted me any bigger—besides Barbara, of course?

It seemed like a shame to go through all that effort for nothing. If there were only some way I could know for sure if Jacob even wanted me to beef up. Without asking him, of course, because he'd only say I was great just the way I was. That's what boyfriends are supposed to say—that's just the way the world works.

However…I did know someone who could tell me for sure.

Even as I thought it, I felt petty. My ex-partner, Lisa Gutierrez, was teetering on the verge of locking herself in a room and using her *si-no* talent to solve every crime in every precinct known to man, and then probably a few that hadn't even been committed yet. Did I deserve to use her to find out whether or not Jacob wanted a little something more to hold onto?

The thing was, we were friends, Lisa and me. And whether or not she used the *si-no* to come by her answer, I'd bet she'd be able to give me some good advice. I opened my email and typed:

Hey Lis

What's going on with you...how had summer been treating you, I bet its nice in C.A.

I was thinking about weight training...what do you think Jacob would think about it...I can't always tell if hes just saying what I want to hear.

You missed vinyl wrist restraint day with some muscle bound guy named Sando, lucky you...I bet you were meditating at the time.

Keep in touch,

Vic

p.s. call me sometime

There. That didn't sound too desperate. And if her answer didn't sound like a *si-no* to me, I could always figure out a way to get Carolyn to ask Jacob for me.

I grabbed another cup of coffee and set out to find three exercises I could get started with that were so simple I could memorize them without printing them out, when I saw I had new mail.

My heart raced. Lisa must have been sitting at her computer and done it then and there. *Si?* No.

Briefly, very briefly, it occurred to me to not look at her answer—because if it was no, Jacob didn't need me to step up the fitness regime, then I'd be missing out on a perfectly good opportunity to increase my strength and endurance—and I'd also squander the chance at a potential hobby, which would be a shame. I'd finally admitted that I had no idea how to play Sudoku.

And if she said yes, then no doubt I'd feel like crap, and I wouldn't be able to tell Jacob about it either since there'd be nothing he could say that would make me feel better.

I thought both of those things, for maybe half a second. But I'd asked, and if she had an answer for me, then I owed it to her to see it.

I pulled up my email and saw the message I'd just sent, with this in the header:

550 user lmgutierrez23, quota exceeded

550 <lmgutierrez23@Q-mail.com>... Can't create output: Error 0

My first thought was that I'd typed it wrong, but no, she was in my address book and the emails always went through before. Besides, when I looked at the message, it didn't say it was an invalid address. It said the quota was exceeded.

On a Q-mail account? Those things hold like a million messages.

I memory-dialed Jacob, who picked up after two rings. "Hey, it's me," I said. "You busy?"

"Not for you. What's up?"

"An email bounced back from Lisa. Don't you think that's weird?"

"I don't know." He considered. "Maybe her account was full of spam so she created a new one."

"The account was still there, but it was full. A Q-mail account."

"Huh. But remember when my mother got the digital camera and she sent me a hundred megs of photos because she didn't know how to work the settings? It might be something like that."

"When was the last time you actually heard from her?" I scrolled down. "Lisa, I mean. Not your mother. Because now I'm looking, and I see she didn't answer my last two emails. So it's been a week. No, two."

He gave a short sigh. "Okay. I'll check tonight when I get home."

I was in the basement attempting a lateral raise when the sound of the front door slamming nearly sent me through the ceiling. My gun was in the bedroom. I glanced down at the fifteen-pound freeweight in my hand. It would have to do. I crept up the basement stairs soundlessly and poked my head out, only to hear Jacob's familiar footfalls on the stairs to the loft. "Vic? You home?"

A sick surge coursed through me as I realized I wasn't experiencing a home invasion. Only my adrenaline level needed to catch up. "Here."

Jacob turned on the stairs with his tie half-off, looking like a male stripper who'd gotten the address to the bachelorette party wrong. Then he scowled, which diminished the stripper-like quality. Slightly. "What were you doing in the basement?"

I could hardly drop the weight behind me and hope it bounced quietly down the stairs, especially since it would probably take out half a dozen of them. "I, uh…." I shrugged.

"Were you working out?"

Busted. "I was bored."

Jacob backtracked, got over the shock of seeing me with a dumbbell in my hand, slipped his tie the rest of the way off and dropped it over the back of the couch. "I took half a day. I couldn't stop thinking about Lisa."

◊◊◊

It had been two and a half weeks since she'd emailed Jacob.

"You can level with me," I told him. "If she gave you her phone number and not me, I won't be mad."

"Me? What makes you think she'd trust me over you? I was the one who couldn't stop asking for *si-nos*."

We both looked at each other hard, and then I said, "Carolyn."

While Jacob set to tracking her down, I called Sticks and Stones. "Hey, do you have Lisa's number?"

"Nope. I got an email address, the same one you have."

"The Q-mail? It's bouncing. The message says it's full."

"Must be a glitch. Those things never fill up."

"That's what I said. What if something's wrong?"

"You're the detective. Do something about it."

I wished I was there in person so I could smack Crash upside the head with my phone. "You're sure you don't have a phone number."

"Are you calling me a liar? I already told you. No. I have an email. That's all I have."

"Okay, okay." I cast around for some other idea. "So...do you have any kind of feeling about it?"

"Don't be an ass. I'm not a precog any more than you are."

I hung up with Crash. Jacob had his phone pinned in the crook of his shoulder and was busy going through his wallet. I watched, torn between curiosity and dread, while he pulled out a business card. He looked up as if he'd sensed my eyes on him. "Carolyn doesn't have her number either. I've got one more idea, and it's a long shot."

I stared harder.

He dialed.

He waited. I waited. He fiddled with the card. And finally, when I'd decided his long shot wasn't going to pay off, someone picked up. "Hi, this is Detective Jacob Marks. I'm not sure if you remember me, but last fall you performed an exor—"

A raised voice on the other end of the line cut him off. Talking. A lot.

"That's actually why I—"

More talking. I couldn't make out the words, but I caught the tone, all right. Urgent.

"Hold on," Jacob said. "The Santa Barbara police are—? Uh huh. No, they're not part of the PsyCop program. It doesn't necessarily say anything about their procedures…it could be that a referendum wasn't approved to spend the—right, they're probably not trained to keep psychic evidence uncontaminated."

What? Hell, even I wasn't trained in keeping psychic evidence uncontaminated. I did my best to apply the procedures I learned for mundane crime scene evidence, but ultimately, I winged it.

"What have they done so far? Searched the—uh huh. Did they remove anything?"

Psychic evidence. I wasn't even sure what constituted "psychic evidence." It would depend on the Psych, wouldn't it? For me, it meant ghosts. For Carolyn, statements. For Lisa…well, anything was fair game, with the *si-no*. Which would be a pretty damn threatening realization for a criminal.

My stomach was doing an unpleasant churny thing.

"When was the last time you saw her?"

Lisa missing? A very unpleasant churny thing.

"Hold on." Jacob thumbed the mute button and asked me, "Do you know anyone named Karen Frugali?" I shook my head. He unmuted the phone. "And how long has she been gone?" He listened, then cut his eyes to me. "I'm not positive my partner will be willing to fly out there and take a look…but I'll ask."

They said their goodbyes while I wondered if I might throw up, and once Jacob hit the disconnect button, I said, "If something's going on with Lisa, you bet your sweet ass I want to go take a look."

He gave me a wry look, and said, "I was counting on it."

Chapter 6

While Jacob dealt with the airline, I called Betty at the Fifth Precinct and let her know I needed a few personal days since I was taking a little trip—which undoubtedly seemed shifty, since I'd just called in sick—and then I set about getting my shit together. Since I didn't have any kind of instinct about what to bring with me, I watched Jacob pack for California and brought one of whatever he brought. I'd always figured if I visited the West Coast I'd bring shorts and sunglasses—not a suit and a sidearm.

"Leave your Florida Water here," Jacob told me. "It won't make it through security. It looks too much like mace."

I stared down at the Blast o' Mint container that Zigler had painstakingly refilled. "So…I can bring a Glock on board, but I can't bring some scented water."

"Airport security is what it is. They understand what guns are; if we go through the right channels, we can carry. But explaining an exorcism…let's just say I can't imagine that'd go down very well. Besides, I'm sure they have Florida Water at PsyTrain."

I stared at my tiny exorcism kit. I had no idea I'd become attached to it. "What about salt? I can bring salt on board, can't I?"

Jacob glanced up from the undershirts he was folding and gave me a look.

"What," I said, "I can't?"

"Any substance that looks iffy stands the chance of getting us grounded."

"You've got to be kidding me! It's…it's salt!"

Jacob smoothed the clothes into his garment bag, then turned toward me and planted his hands on his hips. He was practically as wide as the king-sized bed between us. "How many times have you been through airport security?"

I paused as if I needed to count, and then after a moment, said, "Never."

"Then take it from me—keep your Auracel in your checked luggage, don't put mysterious granules, powders or liquids in your pockets, and make sure you don't have any holes in your socks so you don't feel dumb when your shoes are going through the X-ray machine."

I went through my pockets. A vinyl tie from the previous day's training was coiled in one of them. I left it where it was. I might need it in California, and if they had a problem with it, they could keep it. It was disposable.

At least I'd be able to bring my pills, though I wasn't exactly sure which ones I should carry in my luggage, and which ones would be better off in my stomach. I went through my nightstand and pulled out some bottles. Valium? No-brainer. I swallowed one dry. Auracel? That was a tough call. Being trapped on a plane for four hours with a ghost, and me with no exorcism gear, would suck.

Getting off the plane and not being able to see something scary creeping up on us would suck worse. I threw the bottle into my bag.

"Don't take all of them with you. In case your pills get confiscated."

"Cripes, we're law enforcement. Doesn't that cut us any slack?"

"Roger Burke was law enforcement, too."

I sighed heavily, retrieved the Auracel, and dumped half the pills out on my nightstand. Then I did the same with my Valium.

The only item of interest left in my drawer was a bottle of lube. I held it up. "I don't suppose…?"

Jacob's mouth turned up at one corner. "Security'll have a field day with that."

I put the lube away.

It was when Jacob pulled into long-term parking that I started to get nervous. Because long-term parking implied that he and I might be out in California for a while—that maybe something really was wrong. That I wasn't just the scrawny kid on the back of the bus freaking out over the car accident no one else could see.

People traveling for business as opposed to pleasure are easy to spot. They walk with purpose from point A to point B. They don't stop to consult every flight schedule sign, then look around as if they woke up in the airport with no idea of how they'd gotten there. They don't have a half-dozen screaming kids to corral.

Jacob seemed to know where point B was, or in this case, Terminal 2, from our choices of 1, 2, 3 and 5, so I followed his lead. We each had one of those slick rolling suitcases—obviously he'd had an extra that I could borrow—and he was able to maneuver his case with our garment bag rolled on top like it was weightless.

I managed to keep from getting mine stuck on the moving walkway.

Everything at O'Hare International Airport is reflective. Glass. Mirror. Chrome. I kept catching glimpses of the two of us in our suits and sunglasses, half a head taller than everyone around us, striding along like we had an appointment at the Pentagon to rid the world of an alien threat—and I had to admit, it was pretty damn cool.

Security at the gate seemed to be geared for much longer lines than it was processing. A guy behind a podium checked I.D.s, then the passengers shuffled, boarding passes in hand, through a snaking maze of stanchions linked by nylon belting. Jacob handed his badge and boarding pass to the podium guard who said something into a two-way radio—indiscernible even from our end—and another security guard came out of an official-looking door and nodded to us both.

"Detectives," she said pleasantly, and she led us to the special express-lane I'd seen pilots using.

I got to go through the pilot door. Cool. I did my best to look grim, since cool guys take special treatment like that as a given.

The guards at the pilot door had a different demeanor to them than the regular guards. Most of the airport security seemed robotic and terse, like they were having a bad day, and that bad day had begun in 2002. But the express-lane guards were relaxed. They made eye contact. They smiled.

I figured they had seniority.

Jacob and I showed our service weapons and they didn't even flinch. We were on the list. It was expected.

Our luggage went through an X-ray machine, though we weren't asked to take off our shoes, not like the woman in the sun hat with the beach-ball figure who was struggling to get back into her sandals ten yards away from us. "Looks like rain," one of the guards said to Jacob, who glanced out the window and said, "Could be." And of course neither of them gave a shit—it was more like a macho-guy way of saying, "I'm okay, you're okay."

In the regular-people line, more passengers scrambled in their stocking feet to capture their luggage from the stream that poured out of the X-ray machines, and to make sure no one else dipped into their basket of car keys and change.

A female guard handed Jacob his carry-on with a smile. Jacob stacked the garment bag on top, and my carry-on emerged. The guard handed it to me—same smile she'd given Jacob. Like she thought I was cool.

I'd caught a glimpse of us walking together in the chrome, the glass, and the mirrors. I was having a good hair day, finally. And we did look cool. Both of us.

We strode together toward the door that led to the terminal, and I felt like maybe together, Jacob and me, we could get ourselves to PsyTrain, kick some ass and take some names. Or at least figure out where Lisa was.

But then a noise rose above the crowd murmur, radio crackle and conveyor belt hum—a whine—and I turned to see a couple of airport security guards who'd been talking to each other without a care in the world, now startled, with a German shepherd between them scrabbling at the linoleum. The dog let out another high-pitched whine.

It was looking right at me, ears pricked, tail wagging.

The whole group of guards on the VIP line who'd been smiling, chatting, acting like human beings—every one of them froze.

"I left the Florida Water at home," I told Jacob. "I swear."

The biggest VIP guard caught up to us in long strides while we'd paused to see what the noise was about. "Detectives, if you could step over here."

"I'll bet he smells the gunpowder," Jacob said, low in my ear, as we turned to face the guards. "Their sense of smell is incredibly accurate—a thousand times better than a human's."

We walked back to the guard station, pulling our carry-ons behind us. I didn't feel nearly as cool anymore. The German shepherd's tongue lolled out, and he pranced in place beside the handler, who was holding the leash short. The dog's toenails skittered against the floor.

"Sorry for the delay," said the woman who'd smiled at us. "We'll just need to check your carry-ons."

Jacob said, "It's probably our service weapons."

"Detective? Please, place your luggage on the counter."

Jacob draped our garment bag over the counter, and he and I both hoisted up our carry-ons. The dog whined again. Its big brown eyes were trained directly on my face.

"I should probably take off my sidearm," I said, figuring that obviously Lassie would be more interested in the gun than me if I separated the two of us.

The female guard picked up a clipboard and started scribbling into a form. "Do you have any substances to declare?"

"Substances."

"Medications, pills, inhalers?"

"I'm getting out my wallet," Jacob told the now-alert guards as he pulled out his badge. He reached behind the shield and pulled out his tiny paper PsyCop license and handed it to the big guy. "We can't miss our flight."

I patted down my pockets to see if maybe a stray half-tab of Auracel had stuck to the lining. "I have prescriptions…but not on me. I checked them in."

The big guard cleared his throat and the other guards looked to him. He cut his eyes meaningfully to Jacob's PsyCop card. I wondered if it would help if I added that I had one of those, too.

The female guard looked from the tiny white card to her clipboard, and back to the card again. The guards, all four of them, were so still, I don't even think they were breathing. I know I wasn't.

"Sorry for the delay," the woman said, once she'd weighed the pros and cons of detaining us. "Please make your way to the ter—"

The dog woofed. Its tail was going like a windshield wiper cranked to the highest setting, and it stared at me as if I had a giant T-bone steak for a head.

"Drop it," the handler said, quietly, even though there was nothing to drop. The dog touched its ass down to the flooring, then stood right back up again, gave a piercing whine, and started digging like it was trying to put a hole right through the linoleum.

The handler looked to the woman with the clipboard for guidance. She blanched, pulled out her two-way, and said, "Code sierra bravo at Terminal 2." Those weren't police codes. I would've recognized those.

Indiscernible words crackled back. She glanced at us, then looked away fast. "Clearance nine. Yes. Over."

The tension between the guards was thicker than day-old coffee. They must have all understood the static—and they seemed to be communicating solely with their eyes. The big guy positioned himself between Jacob and the door to the terminal and said, "Sorry for the inconvenience. We'll need you to step in back. The sooner we start, the sooner we'll get you on board."

Jacob pitched his voice low and casual. And he didn't fool any of us. "Start what?"

"It's procedure," said the big guard. "Not you," he glanced at Jacob's badge, "Detective Marks. But him." He nodded at me.

"This way," the guard with the clipboard told me. When I moved to follow her—because what else could I do?—the dog strained toward me and started doing a tapdance. The click of its claws on the floor sounded like a high-powered nail gun sealing my coffin.

"Listen," I whispered to her, "I must've picked up some kind of smell in the evidence room."

She glanced at me, but didn't offer any words of encouragement.

"I'm a PsyCop too," I went on. "I've got a card. If I show you my card, can I go catch my flight?"

"Before you do anything," Jacob was saying, "let me call my sergeant and see if we can straighten this out."

I heard the big guy tell him, "It's procedure…" as the woman led me through a thick metal door into a windowless office with more doors on three sides. The walls were blue. My scalp began to prickle with sweat.

Here I'd been worrying about ghosts at the airport. Who knew I'd be revisiting Camp Hell at the security station?

"Place your weapon and your cell phone in this locker," the guard told me. I didn't want to, but what else was I gonna do, shoot her and then call an ambulance? "A security specialist will meet with you in room three. Step in, remove your clothing, and place it in the marked tray."

"You're not serious."

"It's procedure."

"You can't strip-search me," I said. But a sick feeling in my gut told me they damn well could—because of the Patriot Act, and Terror Level Orange. Because of that fucking dancing dog.

If I'd thought it would help me to fall to my knees and implore the guard, in the name of everything that's right and good—mom, baseball and apple pie—to take a few steps back and let me out of that damn room…I would've done it. In half a second. But that look in her eye, flat, closed-down—I'd seen that look too many times to count on the faces of the nameless, rotating orderlies at Heliotrope Station. *Nothing personal, man. Just doing my job.*

The panic attack had Heliotrope Station all over it, no doubt, but the thought of being strip-searched threw the panic right off the charts. The notion that had my uvula quivering and my gut clenched up like it'd just taken a sucker punch was this: I can't deal with you strangers seeing me naked.

"Non-compliance is a federal offense," the guard told me.

"I need to call my lawyer." I didn't have a lawyer, but the Fifth Precinct had one, didn't they? I'd call Sergeant Warwick, that's what I'd do. And he'd figure it out.

"Look," she said in a hushed voice. "We're being videotaped. If you have something to declare, do it now. It'll all go faster if you start cooperating—and maybe we can even get you on the next flight."

"But I'm not not-cooperating. I don't have anything on me."

"Put your sidearm and your phone in the locker. Please."

I flipped open the phone and hoped my panicky brain hadn't scrambled the location of my memory-dials.

"Detective," the guard said, "if you do that, then procedure dictates we physically restrain you. Save us—and yourself—the embarrassment. The quicker we search you, the quicker you're out of here."

Physically restrain? I'd thought I was panicked before, but now I actually couldn't have told you Warwick's memory dial—or my own phone number, for that matter.

My hand was shaking when I placed my phone in the locker. Great. I'm sure that made me look totally innocent. While I wasn't so crazy about putting my Glock away, I knew the chances of me getting shot by security (and their "procedure") had to be less if I was unarmed.

The guard showed me to a room. My brain was in overdrive trying to find Camp Hell connections—blue wall…blue wall…blue wall—but the room smelled different, felt different, which kept me from totally losing it. I heard Stefan's voice in my head, counting me down, calm and relaxed, deep and melodic, reassuring me that I was in the present, and Krimski couldn't hurt me. And I knew it was bad if I was dredging up memories of goddamn Stefan for comfort.

"A federal agent has been summoned," the guard told me, "and there won't be any female guards present."

And that was supposed to make me feel better?

Fuck.

Chapter 7

There was a built-in bench along one wall of the windowless room, and that was it. Not even a hook to hang my clothes. Even though my shirt was stuck to my back with sweat, I left my jacket on, sat down on the bench and jammed my face between my knees. The little black motes dancing at the corners of my vision didn't subside, but they did stop swarming toward the center.

A big part of me wanted to just go along with the airport guards, because I'd survived this long by going with the flow, letting my body be incarcerated, sleep-starved and drugged, but not my mind, never my mind. What're they gonna see? A skinny naked guy. So fucking what?

That's how I tried to talk myself into complying with them. Only I wasn't twenty-three anymore. And I just couldn't do it.

Time expanded for me. I could've been sitting there for hours with my head between my knees. Days. Weeks. Only some small part of my brain, some bundle of neurons that still had a sketchy sense of temporal reality, told me it was more like minutes.

There was a tap on the door. I looked at it, baffled. Someone was knocking? Worse—it was a "shave and a haircut" knock. I stared at the sturdy metal doorknob—sure that it was just some kind of fucked-up coincidence, that my battered brain had heard it wrong—and I waited for it.

Two bits.

The doorknob turned.

A man in sunglasses and a sweatshirt with the hood pulled up let himself in. At first I figured they'd dragged some pothead out of line and accidentally stuffed him in the same room with me. Then he slid his mirrored shades down his nose, and I recognized his eyes. Con Dreyfuss, the FPMP's head honcho of the Midwest.

"I wondered if you'd actually strip or not." He plunked down on the bench beside me, dug a small bottle of water out of his pocket and offered it to me.

I stared at it like he was handing me a live snake. "Who're you supposed to be? The Unabomber?"

"Whoa. It takes a guy with major cajones to say the word 'bomb' at an airport. But both you and I know you're a lot pluckier than you let on."

"How'd you get here so fast?"

"I'd tell you…but then I'd have to kill you." He said it with a big, cheesy smile…which didn't really reassure me. "Listen, Bayne, you've had a few months to read up on exorcisms. Tell me—how's it going?"

"It's going."

"Uh-huh. I thought as much." Dreyfuss peeled off his wraparound shades and dangled them between his bent knees. "The HVAC system is still on the fritz in my office. Cold spots. I'm thinking that maybe now that you've brushed up on your medium skills, you could convince the causes of said cold spots to vamoose."

"You can't talk to them. They're repeaters."

Behind Dreyfuss' easy smile, his eyes grew hungry. I recognized that look from Jacob, who got very still the minute I started talking ghost, in hopes of not spooking me out of finishing my thought. When Dreyfuss saw I had nothing more to say, he waved the water bottle at me, as if maybe I'd somehow managed to not see it. I ignored it. He shrugged, cracked the seal, and downed it in a few pulls. Then he said, "You're pretty calm, cool and collected for a guy who's about to have some stranger rooting around for drugs in his rectum."

"Haven't you heard? I'm a faggot. I get off on that kind of thing."

"I can dig it—when life hands you lemons, make lemonade."

I stared at a spot on the wall.

"You know your plane's boarding right now," he said, "right?"

I've never ground my molars, but I was tempted to start. I planted my elbows on my knees and pressed the heels of my hands into my eyes. Ahh. "What is it you want, anyway?"

"Just making sure you've got a good overview of the situation. That right now, you're stuck here in the bowels of Terminal 2—while who-knows-what is happening to your friend out in California."

I stopped pressing on my eyes and glanced sideways at Dreyfuss. When the sparklies dissipated, there he was, looking at me. Dead serious now. I said, "What do you know about Lisa?"

"Not much. The western edge of my territory is the Nebraska border, remember? But Lisa was a Chicago girl…if only for a couple of weeks."

"Look up your FPMP buddies in the company's California directory. I'm sure they'll be happy to score some points by filling you in."

"They've got their hands full with the universities out there trying to ban telepaths from qualifying for scholarships. What do they care about a single precog who isn't even a California resident?" He leaned toward me and lowered his voice. "Especially if none of her paperwork happens to mention the fact that she's practically omniscient?"

On one hand, I suspected he was just trying to scare me by acknowledging how powerful Lisa's little *si-no* actually was. On the other, it was working. "So why're you here?"

He set the empty water bottle on the seat between us, then propped his elbows on his knees, mirroring me, and laced his fingers together. His nails looked just as chewed as they had in February. "When someone goes missing, the chance of finding them grows exponentially more improbable each and every day that passes. Lisa's three days gone. Her roommate's been AWOL for a week."

The thing with missing adults is that unless there's some obvious clue, like a bloody candlestick in the conservatory, law enforcement needs to go with the theory that they've up and left on their own accord. Cold feet before the wedding, a secret rendezvous with an online fling, the sudden urge to see the Grand Canyon. People do all kinds of crazy shit. Some adults are considered lower risk for ditching their lives than others. People with children. People with steady jobs. People in loving relationships.

I had no idea what the roommate's deal was, but Lisa was single and childless, and her job status was vague.

Even worse, she'd been struggling hard with the meaning of life. That might sound existential, but for a Psych, it ranks in importance with all the other big pieces of the identity puzzle: job, friends, home, kids, and whatever else keeps people from jumping off bridges.

Here's where most people whose loved ones are gone say, "But I know them. They wouldn't have left without telling anyone. It's just not like them."

We cops hear it all the time. And after the first few missing people are found on the wrong end of a drinking binge, you can't help but feel skeptical about how well anyone really knows anyone else.

The thing was, I did know Lisa. And I knew that she was probably the most grounded person I'd ever met, and she was a cop. A good one. She had enough backbone to tell people to leave her alone if she needed space to think, something I'd experienced personally, so there was no reason for her to slip off in the middle of the night.

Unless she got sucked into something trying to bail her roommate out of trouble.

And what about her email account?

It might not be a bloody candlestick, but it was reason enough for me to be worried.

"I was hoping you might work with me on this," Dreyfuss said, "but you've always had a chip on your shoulder when it comes to the FPMP that I've never been able to figure."

"Chip on my shoulder? Try a chip in my cell phone. I never signed up for a party line."

"We're tapping everyone's phone. That's like being pissed-off 'cos we're breathing your air. Don't take it so personally."

Color me paranoid, but I took my phone tap very personally. And besides, how was it that I happened to end up in the strip-search room to begin with? I didn't have anything on me other than the gun, which I'd been cleared to carry. Normally I would have figured a bribe passed hands. But how do you bribe a dog? Unless….

"Animal communicator." I said it without unclenching my teeth, but it was perfectly understandable.

"Bravo. You think it's all about the level-five talent, but you really don't give yourself enough credit for your deductive reasoning. Which is why you should throw your lot in with me and really exploit your full potential. The Army's not the only government agency where you can 'be all that you can be.' I'm great with Psychs."

The very last thing I wanted to be was exploited. "Screw you."

"Firm stance. I admire your negotiating skills, really, I do. But right now, do you honestly think you have enough time to go back and forth with me on this?"

The clock was ticking, and we both knew it. "You can only keep me here so long."

"Now you're making me out to be the bad guy. Look, as soon as we're done with our chitchat, you're free to go." He pushed up the sleeve of his sweatshirt and glanced at his watch. "Your problem isn't me—it's the appalling lack of airline service at the Santa Barbara airport. At this point, you'll be wandering around all night at some terminal waiting for your connecting flight. I thought you might be interested in a route that was a little more direct."

I said, "You can't fly direct from Chicago to Santa Barbara."

"Not commercially. No."

"You're saying you can make that happen."

"That's what I'm saying."

Did I want to tell him to go shove his chartered flight up his ass? Sure. But my gut was telling me I needed to find Lisa before her trail got any colder, and my need for speed trumped my loathing and distrust of Dreyfuss. "How do I know my flight doesn't get diverted to Area 51, where all the good Psychs go home to die?"

"You're mixing your life up with the X-Files. Don't worry. I want you back so you can help me clean up my office, remember?"

"And that's all I'd owe you in return. An exorcism."

"Yes. Fine. If you need to be so formal about it—that's our agreement. I fly you to Santa Barbara right now, and in return you owe me an exorcism. Does that sound kosher to you?"

I hated it when Constantine Dreyfuss made sense. I glared at him. It seemed to me as if I should have been able to stack up my options and choose the best one, but my brain was looping around in "holy hell, I'm locked in a room" mode and nothing was particularly obvious to me except the desire to get out.

"I can tell you're right on the fence," he said, "so I'll sweeten the pot. I can't tell you what the bonus would be, but I guarantee you, it'll be worth your while."

So now he was resorting to breakfast cereal tactics with a "secret prize" at the bottom of the box. I don't know if he'd actually needed to go that far, since there's only so long I can deal with a locked room, but it was good to know my hard-won suspicion was finally paying off. "I guess," I said as grudgingly as possible.

He stuck out his hand. "Deal?"

Great. Now I had to touch him. At least I wasn't naked. I shook his hand, and said, "Deal." His palm wasn't moist or anything, but I still felt like wiping my hand on my pant leg afterward.

When we emerged from the dreaded back room, the terminal security had a new group of travelers in it chasing after their baskets of watches, wallets and spare change, and then struggling into their shoes. The woman who returned my gun and my phone wouldn't meet my eye, and the guards around the VIP door all stood ramrod straight, and their faces were professionally blank. A dozen yards away, Jacob was on his cell phone, pacing like he was just about ready to snap. A bunch of emotions played over his face when he saw me come through the door behind Dreyfuss: relief, surprise... worry.

The guards exchanged glances as he stormed past them and up to Dreyfuss and me. Maybe they were wondering if they were supposed to stop him. Probably they all hoped it was out of their jurisdiction.

"Detective Marks," Dreyfuss called out cheerfully. "Con Dreyfuss. Pleasure to finally make your acquaintance."

He held out his hand for a shake. Jacob planted his hands on his hips and ignored it. And his jacket rode open and flashed the front edge of his holster. "You wouldn't happen to know why a drug dog just went apeshit over my partner, would you?"

"What're you suggesting? That I had an invisible agent run over and plant something on Detective Bayne? Ha ha! That'd be a good trick, wouldn't it?" He winked at me. How sleazy. "I've known a motley group of Psychs in my day, unfortunately I've never met anyone who could turn themselves invisible—and the amount of energy it would take a telekinetic to pull that trick from across the room would probably send his brains leaking out his ears."

I thought one of the airport security guards heard us. And I thought he was doing his best to pretend he was anywhere else but there.

Dreyfuss checked his watch and said, "Detective Bayne just agreed to fly the FPMP skies to Santa Barbara, since that'll put him in California by sundown. Care to ride along?"

Jacob cut his gaze to me. I wasn't quite sure how to convey, *I know we hate him, but based on the circumstances, it was the most logical thing to do,* with a nonverbal signal. I widened my eyes a little.

Jacob blinked, just a smidgeon more pointedly than he normally would have. I took that to be shorthand for a drawn out, long-suffering sigh. And maybe an eye roll. "Let's go."

Constantine Dreyfuss had his everyman persona down pat. His brown hair was long and curly, and I imagine that when he first started growing it out, it probably went through an afro state until it got heavy enough to weigh itself down. Currently, a black and gray striped scrunchie was holding it in a frizzy ponytail. He was a big federal so-and-so, but I'd never seen him in a suit. Probably because he was a big federal so-and-so. He wore T-shirts and sweats, and as far as I could tell, he didn't even carry a gun. If you ran into him at the grocery store, you'd probably figure him for something low-rent and benign, like a minimart attendant or a library assistant. Unless you got a look at his running shoes and happened to know they would cost a month's salary to either of those professions.

We walked in a chevron formation, Dreyfuss on point, Jacob to his left. Since Jacob was right-handed, it would be easier for him to flatten Dreyfuss from that angle if the situation suddenly went south. I was right-handed too, but I was fine keeping Dreyfuss on my left. I trusted that if things got physical, it would be better to have Jacob in position than me. Given that I really wasn't very athletic.

For just a second, I was glad we'd checked our roller bags, because dealing with the carry-ons was bad enough. Then I realized my pills were in my checked luggage. And everything else I'd thought I would need for the trip. What would happen to our stuff? I had enough to worry about trying to keep up with Dreyfuss and Jacob without worrying about my bag.

Dreyfuss moved fast and he didn't get winded. I seemed to remember he was a runner. Jacob's got incredible stamina, so he kept up without a problem. My long legs helped, some, but I needed to make a conscious effort to conceal the fact that I was out of breath after the first fifteen minutes of power-walking. By the time Dreyfuss finally let up the pace, I was just about ready to plant my hands on my knees and suck air. I breathed through my nose carefully and hoped my cheeks weren't flushed.

Dreyfuss got in line for a pretzel.

"What are you doing?" Jacob said. He wasn't winded either.

"Don't worry. The plane won't take off without us."

"You think this is some kind of joke?"

"On the contrary, Detective. I think it's dead serious."

A really big guy peeled away from the register with a pretzel the size of his head, a huge knot of dough covered in frosting, coconut flakes and chocolate chips. I like junk food as much as the next guy…but, yuck. The line moved up, and a suburban-looking mom with a couple of kids ordered three regular with salt, and the boy, maybe Clayton's age, said he wanted what that other guy had. And his mom said there was no way she was paying ten dollars for a pretzel. I resisted the urge to press against my eyes with my thumbs. After all, the detour gave me a chance to catch my breath, didn't it?

The family argued for a few more volleys, the kid got a plain pretzel with the implication that it was that or nothing at all, and then Con Dreyfuss ponied up to the counter. He ordered a cinnamon sugar pretzel with frosting on the side and paid for it with a fifty.

Once that was settled, the power-walking started again. I figured we were on our way to Terminal 3, but Dreyfuss passed by that security stop and kept on going. A map on the wall showed Terminal 5 as being the next point of interest—an International Terminal so far away from the main hub of the airport that it could only be reached by a shuttle bus. Then he turned down the hall that led to the bathrooms.

I imagined bacteria settling all over his pretzel and I quelled a smile, just in case Jacob looked back at me. Because I didn't want it to look like I thought it was some kind of joke, either. I knew in my gut that what we were doing—whatever it might be—was, indeed, dead serious.

Family bathroom—what the heck? Ladies' room. Drinking fountain filled with old gum. Men's room. "Staff Only" door. Unmarked door. Dreyfuss stopped at that one—why was I not surprised?—and handed his pretzel to Jacob. "Hold this."

Jacob frowned at the pretzel while Dreyfuss dug a keycard out of one of his pockets and slid it through an unobtrusive reader in the wall. He propped the door open with his hip and took his pretzel back. "Don't tell me you never wondered about Terminal 4."

I glanced at Jacob, who scowled harder—which meant he probably had. Jacob notices things. I ignore things. I guess we complement each other.

The unmarked door opened to a set of industrial metal stairs that led down to a huge, high-ceilinged space so vast I could hardly call it a building. There were airplanes, helicopters, buses, vans, even Humvees. And even though nothing was currently running, the metallic hollowness of the hangar was so stark that the very silence inside it reverberated enough to make my eardrums throb.

"The official story," Con said, "is that Terminal 4 was lost to renovation. I personally thought it would've been less conspicuous to keep 1, 2 and 3 the way they were and just rename Terminal 5 'International,' but that all happened before my time. Sometimes I wonder if the powers that be did it just to see if anyone would give a rat's ass—or if 99% of the public is happy to look the other way and never question what happened to the fourth terminal. Like the way they accept that the floors in skyscrapers go right from twelve to fourteen."

Everything in Terminal 4 was metal and concrete, and when Dreyfuss spoke, it sounded like his voice was coming from everywhere. I was surprised everyone else at O'Hare didn't hear the hangar humming like a giant tuning fork. I was fairly certain I could hear my own heart beating.

We walked past rows and rows of huge, testosterone-driven machines, some gleaming silver, some dull black, none with any sort of insignia to mark them, until a familiar smell tickled my nostrils over the smells of oil, jet fuel and metal.

Frankincense.

Chapter 8

We rounded a commercial-sized jet to find a small gray plane surrounded by people. Most of them had Airport Security getups, only they were nothing like the guards back at Terminal 2 who'd seemed relatively human, at least until the drug dog went berserk. These guys were all male, all young, and all over six feet tall. And they all looked pretty damn athletic.

They were carbon-copy guards we could take in with a single glance. The interesting individuals were the two FPMP employees kneeling in their midst, heads bowed, hands clasped in prayer—my old Camp Hell pal Einstein and his sidekick, the janitor.

Einstein—who went by Richie nowadays—glanced up from his prayers and broke into a huge smile. He made the sign of the cross and leaped up to greet me, and I saw he and his compadre were kneeling on some kind of elaborate padded panel—that, in fact, they had a heck of a lot of specialized gear with them. "Hardcore Vic!" he said.

I reminded myself not to sigh. I liked Richie, I did. He was a good guy. Even if he was sleeping with the enemy. "Hey, Richie. Good to see you."

"You get to fly in the Learjet? Heh-heh. Lucky duck."

So that's what a Learjet looked like. Small. Very, very small, small enough to fit in our loft. Granted, our house used to be a factory. But I still had a hard time feeling secure about boarding something that I could stash in the living room if I moved the couch out of the way. "You know what they say. Some guys have all the luck."

The janitor—heck, he probably wasn't a janitor, was he? Assistant medium? Co-medium? Incense specialist? He went about snuffing the candles in a particular order, same as I'd seen him do back at the FPMP's Chicago headquarters. And just the same as then, he didn't say a word to anyone as he did it.

Candles weren't my thing, but even so, seeing their tricked-out kit and realizing mine was back in my bedroom made me feel like I was chasing down an armed suspect with an empty holster. If I had known my gear wouldn't be confiscated after all, I would've brought it along.

"Hey, Richie," I said. "You have any Florida Water with you?"

He looked bewildered for a moment, then said, "Like Hoodoo?" Then he grabbed me by the sleeve, hauled me out of range, and whispered, "Just 'cos Carl's black doesn't mean he goes for all those hokey superstitions. He's a good Catholic. Just like us."

"Oh, uh, right," I said. "Sorry." I had no idea what ever made Richie think I was Catholic—or any other religion, for that matter—but I could see Dreyfuss getting a report from one of the big, athletic guards while Jacob scanned the area, undoubtedly noticing all sorts of things, and I decided it wasn't the time or place to tell Richie that I believed in the power of Florida Water a heck of a lot more than I thought eating fish on Fridays would secure me a place in heaven. Or that heaven existed at all.

I slid another look at the gear Catholic Carl was now stowing away in a wooden box covered with crosses. Candles and incense. Tools used in so many diverse religions and ceremonies you'd think they'd be intrinsic to any kind of Psych work. So, of course, they were the ones I'd eliminated with no ill effects whatsoever. Just because I didn't need any fancy trappings, though, didn't stop me from feeling an unwelcome pang of envy from watching Richie wallow in all the gear his simple little heart could possibly desire. Richie, the functionally retarded level-two medium, had an assistant to light his candles for him and a special padded panel to kneel on, while all I got were a handful of vinyl ties and a morning in hell with a trainer named Sando. Then I told myself to stop being a jerk and cut him a break. It wasn't as if I'd personally touch his job with a ten-foot pole, not for all the fancy gear in the world. Not considering who his boss was.

When we rejoined the crowd beside the Little Jet that Could, Dreyfuss held up the pretzel with a flourish. "Hey, Richard, look what I found." Richie's face lit up and he danced in place like he had to pee. Words failed him.

"Go on," Dreyfuss said. "Take it."

Richie reached for the pretzel like it was a spiritual experience and took a big, blissful bite. Dreyfuss dug into his pocket and pulled out a small plastic container. "And there's frosting."

Richie warbled something happy around his mouthful of dough and snatched the tub of frosting from his boss. I wondered if they sold Florida Water in California. And I did my best to stop thinking about what kind of "big pretzel" was in store for me. Because watching Dreyfuss take care of his own—that gave me more creeps than a visitation from your garden-variety spook ever could.

"As you can see," Dreyfuss told me, "I did my best to ensure the plane was clean, but feel free to poke around and make sure there aren't any stowaways."

I took a step toward the jet and snapped back when Jacob grabbed me by the shoulder. "I'll check it out." One of the interchangeable agents opened the door for him, and didn't even flinch when Jacob pulled his sidearm. Maybe the agent's eyes followed the gun, but since they were hidden by those mirrored shades, I was none the wiser.

It hadn't even occurred to me that there might be someone waiting in the cabin for me with a syringe full of knockout juice. My initial impulse to be annoyed with Jacob for elbowing in gave way to a profound sense of relief that I had him on my team. That, and fear. Because the FPMP was way bigger than both of us. They had a Learjet.

And a tranquilizer jab could take him down just as easily as it could me.

"Say, Richard," Dreyfuss wondered aloud in a breezy, casual tone that I didn't buy for even a second. "D'you suppose it's even possible for an airplane to be haunted?"

Richie said, "Sure," through a wad of chewed pretzel, but then he scowled as if he was second-guessing himself. Or maybe choking on cinnamon dough.

Dreyfuss looked at me and raised his eyebrows expectantly.

I stared back blankly and gave him the look that always pisses off everyone who're so damn sure I'm hiding something. I wasn't. How would I know if spirits stick to aircraft? It wasn't as if I'd ever flown before.

Except, in the pit of my gut, I kind of suspected it was possible. Ghosts with personalities, the kind of spirits you could hold a conversation with… they might have a home base, but they could also start following you around if they thought you'd be able to help them grab that brass ring and get off the merry-go-round for good. Repeaters, though—hard to say. I'd seen repeaters going through the motions long after the building they died in had been razed to the ground.

Richie swallowed hard and said, "If a ghost doesn't leak through the floor of a building, why would it fall through the hull of a plane?"

Brilliant. No, seriously, I meant it—brilliant. Why didn't ghosts fall through the floor, and keep on falling until they hit either the center of the earth, or maybe China?

Dreyfuss' gaze flicked over toward me. I did my best to look as blank as humanly possible so I didn't let on that Richie had actually said something so simple it was profound. While I was doing that, Jacob leaned out of the Learjet. His broad shoulders barely cleared the door. "You want to have a look before we take off?" he asked me.

"Yeah, why not?" Mostly, it was a relief to be able to stop doing my mannequin impression. Jacob lingered until I was practically fighting him for the tiny oval door, then brushed against me as I tried to figure out how to get through it without doing the limbo. He gave me a small nod.

I cleared the door and blinked in surprise. The entire Learjet cabin was a creamy, plush white, from the carpet to the leather seats to the built-in cappuccino machine.

I couldn't have decorated it better myself.

No ghosts, that was obvious. I would have spotted them among all the cushy white seats. But I walked in a crouch to the back of the cabin where a long, inviting-looking bench spanned the plane, and wondered when the wisecrack about Jacob and me joining the mile high club was going to surface.

"What do you think," Dreyfuss asked me when I stuck my head out the door. "Are we good to go?"

I looked at the goons in suits and mirrored shades. Were they capable of flying a plane? Some of them were ex-military, maybe. But they didn't really fit my idea of what a pilot would look like—although I suspected that my mental image of a pilot was probably shaped by a series of dubious movies from the late seventies.

"Don't worry," Dreyfuss said. "I'm leaving them here. Too heavy. They'd only add to the payload and shave time off our flight."

I glanced back into the cabin to see if maybe the jet was some ultramodern self-piloting deal. The military had unmanned aircraft, right? Why not the FPMP? The cockpit had a couple of plush swivel chairs in front of its bank of dials, readouts and buttons. And no robot. "We're not taking off without the pilots," I said, "right?"

Dreyfuss laughed. "That'd be some kind of trick, now, wouldn't it? Especially when your average telekinetic gets a nosebleed from moving a golf ball." He made an "after you" flourish to Jacob, who gave him a thorough once-over, then angled himself into the swanky white cabin beside me. I blundered against the cappuccino bar and squeezed awkwardly into a seat that faced the opposite wall. The cabin felt spacious enough, once I was sitting. Like a nice, big van, or maybe a limo. Jacob took the seat with the best tactical access to the door and the cockpit, and sat there with his coat pushed back behind his holster and his sidearm in plain view.

After Jacob, Dreyfuss slipped through the door nimble as you please, and the thugs sealed it shut. I glanced at the pilot seat again, as if maybe the Invisible Man would show himself. Instead, Dreyfuss plunked down in the driver's seat and pulled on a headset.

"Don't tell me..." I said.

"Hey, you're not the only one who'd like to go through life without ever knowing the intimate touch of a bullet. What better insurance policy than making sure I'm the most indispensable guy on board?"

"What about the co-pilot?" Jacob said.

"Here's some aviation background for you: the term 'co-pilot' went out of vogue with the word 'stewardess.' Anyone who's licensed to fly a plane is a pilot. And the chicks and gay guys who show you where the emergency exits are located are now flight attendants. And they're phasing out peanuts in favor of pretzels because too many people are allergic these days—though with gluten intolerance on the rise, who's to say if airline snacks'll soon go the way of the smoking section."

Great. He was the only one who could fly the plane, and I still wanted to kill him.

"Don't worry," Dreyfuss said, "I can do a four-hour flight myself, no problem. The narcolepsy thing is totally under control." He fiddled with the control panel, then caught my eye and grinned.

"Has anyone ever told you you're the opposite of funny?"

"All three ex-wives...but the alimony sure gives 'em something to smile about." He looked at some readouts, tapped some buttons, and the roar of the engine blotted out everything else. His lips moved as he murmured into his microphone, but I would've needed to be telepathic to understand him. Then he tilted the mike away from his mouth and said, "Help yourself to the cappuccino. It's not half-bad. Just be warned there's no bathroom, so if you've gotta go, you'll have to aim into an empty soda bottle or hold it 'til we get to California."

Chapter 9

Takeoff was the worst part of flying. I actually slipped my hand into Jacob's and squeezed as we hurtled down the runway, my stomach stayed in place while the plane angled up and started rising, and the tremble of the tarmac against the wheels gave way to the sickening smooth glide of flight.

Thank God I wasn't on Auracel. I would've tossed my cookies for sure.

Jacob leaned across the aisle, pulled my hand onto his knee and worked it until my knuckles throbbed. "You okay?"

I nodded, but kept my lips pressed shut tight in case I wasn't. I squeezed his hand harder, encouraging him to grind my fingerbones together in that obscenely strong grasp of his so that I could focus on something other than that icky floating feeling. Instead, he shifted his grip and began stroking my palm with his thumb, which I supposed was a better idea if I ever hoped to hold a gun again. I closed my eyes and tried to pretend I was just high, but my body didn't buy it. So I centered my attention on the feel of Jacob's thumb gliding over my life line, undoubtedly hitting all kinds of acupressure points, and I thought about nothing until my roiling gut stilled.

Con Dreyfuss' voice startled me out of my brief moment of Zen, coming from behind me. A speaker. "Sorry for the rough ride—you feel everything more intensely in a small craft. We're climbing to our cruising altitude of 42,000 feet, and then you'll be free to move about the cabin."

I looked at Jacob and said, "Is he serious?" I had to talk loud to be heard over the jet engine noise, and if there actually were microphones planted somewhere in the cushy white seats in hopes of listening in on our conversation, I couldn't imagine how they'd extract our words from the ambient noise without a heck of a lot of cleanup.

Jacob gave me an "I dunno" shrug and peered out the window. A few minutes later, Dreyfuss' chipper voice said, "Okay, kids, we're on our way.

No fighting, now. Don't make me pull over."

Jacob motioned toward the back seat with his head and the two of us crouch-walked as far away from Dreyfuss as we could get without tearing open the door and taking a literal flying leap.

"I'd blow someone for a Valium," I said in Jacob's ear.

"Maybe he's got one…but try offering a hand-job first so you retain some leverage."

Over the deafening engine noise, I almost didn't catch the inflection that would have told me Jacob was trying to come off calm, cool and collected by kidding around…and failing miserably. I don't think he knew about the telltale line between his eyebrows that was as good as a blinking neon sign flashing the words, "Something's Wrong."

I patted him on the knee awkwardly. "It'll be okay." As I said it, I realized it sounded just as hollow as his lame joke. "We'll get there faster than we would have if we'd flown commercial, and that's what matters. Right?"

He gave me a curt nod, smoothed his goatee a few times, and glared out the window. I worked my jaw and yawned to try to pop my eardrums. And we rode like that, uncomfortable in some way or another, all the way to the West Coast. Because, yeah, it was true that we were actually getting there a hell of a lot more quickly than we could've managed by our own devices.

But that didn't mean we were crazy about the reason we were making such good time.

◊ ◊ ◊

I'd expected California to be hotter than Chicago. It wasn't. I expected it to be filled with tan guys carrying surfboards who said "dude" a lot. It wasn't. I expected it to be overrun with hippies and communes and the types of people who'd shop at Sticks and Stones, if Crash's store wasn't tucked away in Wicker Park where they'd probably never stumble across it.

I was wrong, though. Wrong on every count. Not only were there no surfers lounging around in front of PsyTrain, there were no hippies, either. In fact, there was no one at all.

A town car with a driver so silent he could've been a mute dropped us off at the front door, and there we were: me, Jacob, and Constantine Dreyfuss. I'd imagined PsyTrain in the middle of a big, vacant lot, surrounded by a tasteful fence that just happened to be electrified. But it didn't exist in a vacuum, as it had in my imagination. There were townhomes on either side of it, and a Mexican restaurant across the street. There were cars and seagulls and a bicyclist with a mirror on his helmet.

The building was three stories, just under one city-block wide, with an off-white stucco façade, terra cotta roof, and fancy black bars over the windows.

I probably should have offered that hand-job, after all. Even if the first thing I did was tear open my suitcase and dig for my Valium, I doubted anyone would stand around on the sidewalk waiting with me for the meds to kick in. Plus…my suitcase was back at O'Hare.

Dreyfuss slipped on his wraparound shades, took in the building with a sweeping look, smiled, and said, "Don't mind me, kids. Pretend I'm not even here."

Right.

Jacob took the lead, across the walkway, up the steps. Other than the enticing smell of carnitas, the whole street had an empty feeling of abandonment, like we'd stepped onto a movie set, and the buildings were just a bunch of painted plywood fronts, and no one really lived in any of them. Inside, a couple of beefy rent-a-cops converged on us from either side of the doorway. I slid my badge out and Jacob did the same. "Jacob Marks," he said, "and Victor Bayne. We're here to see Dr. Chekotah."

Doctor, as in "an apple a day"? Or one of those guys who's got an honorary title for staying in college too long?

The security guys didn't seem to notice, or maybe didn't care, that Jacob hadn't bothered to introduce Dreyfuss. Jacob wasn't going to let our terrifying brush with security at O'Hare shake his confidence. He got right back on that horse and used his "I'm a manly man—respect me" voice. And they did. One of them pulled out a two-way radio, buzzed, and said, "Your guests are here."

Guests. That felt slightly festive.

"Dr. Chekotah will be right out," the guard with the walkie-talkie said.

I took stock of the lobby while I waited. It was beige, very beige, and very empty—except for a single, large crate, big enough to pack a couple of buff strippers inside, that stood in the center of the room.

The emptiness of the room wasn't creepy in itself. It was the vestiges of use that stood out. Well-thumbed New Age magazines sat abandoned beside empty waiting room chairs. A tall, thirsty-looking potted shrub drooped in the corner. The computers at the front desk were off, and dust clung to the dark monitors. A wall calendar with a picture of a dog in a wig and sunglasses was open to May, even though June was practically over.

I scanned the room and settled on the crate again. From the corner of my eye, I saw Con Dreyfuss watching me take in the room, and I looked up at the ceiling, so as not to appear too interested. Spanish style wrought iron hanging fixture. Cobwebs. The fine tendrils started to sway as an interior door opened and closed, and the air pressure in the room shifted ever so slightly.

A good-looking brown-skinned guy in sandals and a rumpled linen suit rounded the corner. He was maybe my age, maybe a few years younger, with high cheekbones and long black eyelashes—but his eyes beneath those eyelashes were squinty, like he hadn't slept for a week. He cheered up when he saw us, though. "Jacob!"

"Bert."

They strode around the huge crate and embraced like long-lost pals who'd run into each other at a block party. "You made good time," Chekotah said. I might have been tempted to roll my eyes in Dreyfuss' direction and say, "Yeah, we had help," as sarcastically as I could, but Jacob's more adult about things like that than I am, and he only nodded. "Let's get you filled in on what's going on."

We passed through a waiting room with a private secretary. The interior was stucco and tile, more Spanish style influence, though the furniture looked antiquey, with scrolls and flourishes, and some of the vases and hangings could've been Chinese. Not that I'd know a Ming vase from Ming's Lucky Dish takeout.

The secretary didn't bother to greet us, since he was currently occupied having a showdown with his phone. It was a multi-line unit, and though it wasn't ringing, the buttons were all lit up and blinking like Christmas had just come early. Chekotah paused beside his desk. "Lyle?"

The chubby secretary held up his index finger. "I keep pressing the voicemail activation button and they keep coming through."

No wonder my calls never found their way to Lisa. Chekotah sighed. "So let them ring. I need three rooms in the instructor wing."

Lyle rolled his eyes and made a huffy noise. He was way gay—queer enough to telegraph his sexual preference with a flick of his head. I waited for a snap-and-twist and a singsong *what-ev-er,* but he restrained himself.

"Actually," Jacob said, "my partner and I could double up on a room. You remember I told you about Vic."

Chekotah cocked his head and regarded me through a haze of fatigue, and suddenly his eyebrows shot up. "The medium." He then looked between Jacob and me as if he was trying to picture us out of our cop-suits, maybe doing something a bit more blatantly homosexual. "Sure, sure...." He then squinted at Dreyfuss as if trying to figure out where he fit into our relationship.

"Agent Dreyfuss should have his own room," Jacob said.

"Agent?" Chekotah repeated with some concern.

Lyle stopped acting snippy and started acting interested, and I noticed a shift in Jacob's expression, a minuscule tightening of the mouth that told me he was annoyed with himself for letting anything interesting slip. While I was never taught the technique in so many words, I've noticed the best way to get people to show their true colors in a police interview is to act as blandly neutral as possible. Pointing out that the Feds were crashing the party was decidedly splashy.

The notion that Jacob really wasn't "Mr. Perfect" was comforting.

Chekotah wasn't keen on making any more of a spectacle out of our arrival than he needed to. He hustled us into his office and closed the door firmly behind us.

Chapter 10

Chekotah's office was a mess. Lots of half-open, half-packed boxes. It stunk of burnt sage.

"Sorry for the, uh…you can just put that on the floor, there."

Jacob, Dreyfuss and I all stared while Chekotah cleared some chairs. Nervous, yes. Probably at the thought of having a federal agent eyeballing him.

The boxes made heavy thumps on the floor. Mostly books, though one had some pottery in it—Native American and not Chinese, I knew that much, at least.

"Redecorating?" I suggested, when it seemed obvious he wasn't going to elaborate on the boxes.

"New office." He moved a stack of files to a precarious spot atop a pyramid of boxes, then made his way around the desk. "It's all a little sudden."

No one filled in the awkward silence for him.

"Director Park resigned yesterday, so…." He fiddled with a polished obsidian paperweight.

"So now you're in charge?" Jacob ventured. Chekotah nodded. Jacob broke into a broad smile, the type of smile that lights up a room, and extended his hand over the desktop. "Congratulations."

They shook. And just like that, the tension drained away.

Sometimes it's not about doing things right the first time around. It's about course-correcting when you screw up.

We sat, Jacob in the middle facing Chekotah, Dreyfuss and me off to either side. "So what's going on?" Jacob asked. His tone wasn't like a cop to a witness, it was one friend to another. He also didn't have his notepad out—and I knew Jacob was an exacting note taker. I was aware of the weight of my pad in my pocket, square against my side, slightly curved from the way I always leaned it into a ridge in Zigler's passenger door, but I figured if Jacob wasn't scribbling, I shouldn't either. Dreyfuss leaned back, crossed his ankles, and folded his hands in his lap, the picture of relaxation.

Chekotah ran his hand through his stark black hair. A few strands of gray showed at his temples, but only a few. "Karen went first. We didn't think anything of it at the time, though, so we didn't know…." He sighed, fidgeted with a pen. "She was unhappy with the program, so we just assumed she'd left. Even if we'd reported her missing, that's what the police would have thought, too. That's what they told us when they were here."

"So you called them, when?"

"After Lisa was gone. She missed her afternoon class, missed dinner. I called her, and her cell was still in her room…and I just had a feeling."

I was maybe a little jealous that Dr. Chekotah had Lisa's current cell phone number and I didn't. But I'd need to tuck that emotion away until later and focus on his statement, especially since I wasn't writing it down.

"It wasn't an actual premonition—you know I'm no precog. But with Karen taking off without a word to anyone, leaving all her things, and then suddenly Lisa misses a class for the first time, then skips dinner. It just didn't seem right."

Chekotah lapsed into silence, and Jacob said, "Is it possible maybe she met someone? Someone outside PsyTrain?"

"Lisa's an adult. She can come and go as she pleases." That sounded a little snippy to me. "When would she even meet a guy? And even if she did, why wouldn't she wait until after her class to see him? She's only going to be here for another month. She's been doing her best to make the most of the training."

Knowing firsthand how a crisis of faith could derail Lisa if it were strong enough, I wasn't sure I necessarily agreed with him. I kept that to myself. The thing about his opinions that interested me the most were what they might reveal about him.

"So Director Park resigning," Jacob said, "is that anything to do with Lisa and the other woman?"

Chekotah threw his arms in the air as if his ancestors might need to help him answer that one. "That. And the non-stop phone calls. And the reporters."

"What do the reporters want?" Dreyfuss asked. His tone was good. It made him sound like the type of guy who'd buy you a beer and commiserate with you after a hard day. He'd probably put radioactive tracers in that beer, and then stick a bug on the hem of your jacket while you weren't looking. But you wouldn't know it from his voice.

"Is Five Faith active in Chicago? No? Bunch of paranoid anti-Psychs. The Bishop's off in L.A. Meeting with the Cardinal to see if the Catholic church can officially deny any ties with them."

"Are you being threatened?" Jacob said.

"So far, no. They're more of a nuisance. Protests and wild accusations. But they're spreading fear, and it won't surprise me at all when one of their rallies goes too far."

"Do you think we could get a look at Lisa's room?" Jacob asked.

"Sure, sure, right this way."

My insides froze up at the thought finding Lisa right there in the middle of it—and me being the only one able to see her. I did my best to keep my face neutral, but I might have squinted as Chekotah herded us out of his new office. The secretary—Lyle?—didn't seem to have made any leeway at all with his phone, and was in fact looking at the back as if he was seriously considering just unplugging the damn thing. Despite his frustrations with the phone, he paused to give us a good ogle as we passed by.

Doors opened an inch or two and people peered out as we walked down a long, narrow hallway to Lisa's room in the dormitory wing of the building. I smelled the room before I really saw it. The odor of burnt sage was just as pungent there as it had been in Chekotah's office. "Did she smudge it right before she left?" I asked. And I wondered just how much sage she'd burned.

"No…that was from this morning."

We all trooped in. Not much to see. Twin bed, desk, laptop. No decorations, except for a photo of a grim-looking Mexican couple in a faded 1970's green-tinged shot. A half-empty bag of Cheetos with the top rolled down and secured with a hair clip. A Netflix disc. Not particularly lived-in, other than a wad of clothes on the floor at the foot of the bed. Then again, she was going to be leaving in a month.

"The smudging," Jacob said. "Is it…policy?"

"Well, no. I was just…." Chekotah sighed. "I was meditating. Trying to see if I could get a handle on the situation. Any kind of insight that might help."

"Wouldn't a precog be better for that?" I said. It just kinda popped out. He'd said himself he wasn't precognitive. PsyTrain was no Camp Hell, but someone there had to be at least a precog three or four.

How the heck could someone possibly disappear in a building full of psychics without one of them knowing what happened?

"No one's turned up anything," he said. "Obviously. Or we'd have Lisa back." Snippy again, though I guess there wasn't any other way to respond to my precog remark.

"And Karen," Dreyfuss said. Maybe a little too brightly. Or maybe I was projecting.

"And Karen."

Karen Frugali's room was connected to Lisa's by the shared bathroom in between. The furniture was the same, but the bed was set at a weird diagonal to the rest of the room. A red Chinese screen partitioned off another corner, and behind that, stacks of books four feet high stretched up from the floor, teetering slightly, as if we'd just caught them slipping into a dust jacket that was a little more comfortable.

"Feng Shui," Dreyfuss said. "Gotta love it."

I knew what Feng Shui was about, vaguely, but it was slippery knowledge that hadn't fared too well among all the other memories I'd repressed. I mean, I got that it was about the flow of...Chi. Shit. I was surprised I even remembered that much. But what I didn't know was what type of Psych would concern herself with it. "What was Karen's talent again?" I said.

"Light worker," Chekotah said. He was staring down at a picture of a baby on Karen's nightstand, so he didn't notice my WTF-expression.

I glanced at Jacob, who shrugged. Good to know I wasn't the only one who'd never heard of it.

"What level?" I asked.

"We don't rank our students according to level," Chekotah snapped, and again I felt like I'd somehow managed to pogo on his very last nerve. "That's for the government to do."

"You know what I'm thinking?" Dreyfuss said, again in his we're-all-pals-here voice. "Directly upstairs, there are a couple of bedrooms just like these, exact same configuration. Right? Makes sense for us to stay in those."

"But the student rooms are nowhere near as spacious as the staff—"

"It'd really expedite this whole thing."

Chekotah closed his eyes and composed himself for a moment. Even with everyone playing nice, it looked like our visit was sucking all the energy right out of him. Maybe he needed to go stand behind the red screen.

While Chekotah went back to his office to break the news to Lyle that he'd need to get two different rooms ready for us, we cooled our heels in the cafeteria and waited for the students we'd displaced to clear out. Again, I kept my eyes open for something that would set off my Camp Hell alarms, and again I discovered I had nothing to worry about. The PsyTrain cafeteria had framed "inspirational" posters on the walls, and potted plants the size of small trees in the corners. Nothing fancy, but not the cafeteria of a government institution, either.

Dreyfuss bought us each a Coke from the machine without bothering to ask Jacob or me if we wanted one. Jacob popped the tab on his while I was considering not drinking mine out of sheer stubbornness, but then I decided I could probably use the calories. Especially since I'd refused the pretzel.

"So, they don't score the talent here," Dreyfuss said. He was so good at striking up a conversation. What a shame that skill was wasted on someone like him. "Then again, even the regular schools around here probably grade report cards with self-esteem-building words of encouragement and animal stickers."

"Speaking of numbers," Jacob said, probably figuring he'd make the most of it if Dreyfuss insisted on chatting. "What's this Five Faith?"

"Been around for a few years now. At first they were moderate, perfectly reasonable—that's how all good cults start out. And then they turned weird."

"They're made up of five faiths?" I asked.

"No, nothing so egalitarian. Buddhists, Jews and Sons of Islam need not apply. Only Christians who're fed up with the way their own church handles the whole Psych issue. Very bible-centric. Heavy on Old Testament smiting. The 'five' refers to five senses—as God intended. So they've determined by poring through the English translation of the Latin translation of the Aramaic bestseller of 500 B.C."

"What're they gonna do?" I said. "Make converts stand outside holding protest signs while they hand out religious tracts?"

"High-level medium in Florida went kaboom two years ago? That was Five Faith."

"Wait," I said, in an attempt to figure out how Dreyfuss was spinning it. "I thought you said they were Christians."

"So was the Spanish Inquisition. And I'm not talking about the John Cleese version."

Jacob had pulled up some articles on his phone and started to scan through them. "They don't seem to have a big presence in the Midwest."

"And if I have my druthers," Dreyfuss said, "I'm keeping it that way. They had their eye on a hunk of property in Skokie—but they were mysteriously outbid. Hopefully they'll decide Chicagoland real estate's too rich for their blood and go away. But given the tenacity of religious fanatics, I somehow doubt it."

Lyle appeared in the cafeteria doorway looking somehow odd, in a way I couldn't quite put my finger on. "Okay. Your rooms are ready. I'll show you, uh, where they are." Fidgety.

We stood and filed out behind him, and piled into a retro-looking elevator all full of mirrors and Spanish-style trim. Once the doors squeaked shut and we were all stuck breathing each other's air, I noticed he was wearing aftershave. Fresh aftershave, like he'd just put it on. I tried not to look too puzzled, since everyone could see everyone else in all those mirrors, and I like to keep my bewilderment to myself when I can help it.

The second floor hall was a carbon copy of the first floor hall, except there was a window at the far end instead of a door. Stucco walls, moderately tacky carpeting, and more black metal lighting fixtures than you could shake a stick at. Lyle strode to the doors of the rooms directly above Lisa's, pivoted, and started talking in a long rush.

"Okay, so, these are your rooms. I had the linens changed but there wasn't enough time to shampoo the carpets like I'd normally do. We have a wired Internet connection beside the desk, wireless network—password is nirvana—and basic satellite on the TVs. Thermostat's beside the door. Fresh towels in the bathroom. Basic soap and shampoo are by the sink—not tested on animals, of course—but if you need anything else, our visiting herbalist will be here in the morning, and she'd be able to help you." He stopped suddenly, as if the speech he'd prepared for us wasn't done but he'd suddenly drawn a blank, and he was unable to go on.

"I don't know about you," Dreyfuss said, "but I'm dying for a little power nap. Flying always wears me out." Flying, pilot. Real cute. He slipped around Lyle and peeked into the first room. "This one's got the extra bed in it. I'll take the solo room, since the ex claims I snore."

He held his hand out. Lyle stared at it for a moment, nonplussed, then fumbled a key out of his pocket. "Wake me up if anything interesting happens," Dreyfuss said, and headed into his room.

"Wait," Lyle said.

Dreyfuss backed up and gave him a raised-eyebrow "what now?" look.
"What about the crate? It's taking up the whole lobby."
"Oh, that's Detective Bayne's. Just have it brought up to his room."

Chapter 11

Our room was small—but small doesn't actually bother me. The bedroom in my old apartment barely held my bed, a single dresser and a nightstand. I'm not too crazy about clutter, though, and too many pieces of furniture were vying for position in this particular room.

The walls and bedspreads were seafoam green, like the countertop of a faded diner. A full-sized bed hugged each wall, which left the dresser that the second bed had displaced in front of the window. I was fine with that. I'd rather have a view of a dresser, even one with a big mirror such as this one, than a set of bars. The smell of vinegar-based cleaner and burnt sage lingered in the air.

I was too keyed up to know if the place felt good or not, in the way that Sticks and Stones felt good—but it definitely didn't feel psychically stained, like Dreyfuss' office. That was vaguely comforting.

Jacob helped one of the security guards from downstairs wedge the gigantic crate into the gap between the beds while I ducked into the bathroom doorway to avoid being flattened. The guard had to crawl over the bed and pull the dolly along behind him. The green bedspread pulled back and revealed a floral print sheet set so brightly colored it made my eyes hurt.

Once the guard left and closed the door behind him, Jacob gave the room a final once-over, then looked at me. "You okay?"

I nodded.

He indicated the crate with a jerk of his chin. "Any idea what that is?"

"Nope."

"Are we alone here?"

I glanced under a lampshade as if a radio transmitter would be conveniently located there for me to demonstrate for him. No such luck. It was just a lampshade. "I doubt it."

"I don't mean it in that way."

Oh. I was still experiencing some residual queasiness, but that was more from my flight in the Learjet—and my proximity to Dreyfuss—than from my current state of medication. The last Auracel I'd taken, back at the amusement park, was long gone from my system. I looked around to see if a hippy ghost in tie-dye might have been lingering on the sheet set, camouflaged by the barrage of color. Nothing there but the pillow. "Other than your standard crosswalk-repeaters at the major intersections, I haven't seen any dead since we got off that plane."

"I was concerned, since this used to be a TB hospital—"

"And they run a Psych training facility here? Cripes. Was the local Indian burial ground unavailable or what?"

"Bert says it's clean."

"Bert the Director—who you happen to be on a first name basis with. Since when?"

Jacob swung himself over the garish bed so he could talk to me face-to-face without leaning around the crate. "Remember I told you a shaman helped me out when Hugo Cooper was sticking to me after his execution?"

"Yeah?"

"That's him. Bert Chekotah."

My drug-deprived brain struggled with the image of the attractive guy in the gray linen suit shaking an eagle feather over Jacob. Shouldn't he have been wearing beads? And pelts? And buckskin chaps? Maybe I was thinking of the Village People. The knowledge that he and Jacob knew each other in a professional context was comforting to me—surprisingly so—since Chekotah was young, and good-looking, and undoubtedly more *athletic* than me. I hadn't realized that the idea of Jacob bartering his way into PsyTrain with sexual favors was even a thought I'd been entertaining.

"Vic?"

"Uh...right. The shaman. Yeah, I remember." Of course the word *shaman* set me to wondering about that other talent Chekotah had mentioned when we'd asked what Karen Frugali was, since I wasn't particularly clear on what either of those talents actually were. I was about to ask Jacob what sort of talent he thought either of those words meant, in terms I could understand, when Dreyfuss' voice rang out from the bathroom.

"Knock knock!"

I flinched, and whispered, "Maybe we can push that crate in front of the bathroom door when we go to sleep."

Jacob leaned over the foot of the bed and opened the door. There Dreyfuss was, framed in the doorway, holding a toothbrush. "If you take it into your head to dip this in the toilet, just remember. You never know when you might be on Candid Camera."

"Just make sure it gets my good side when I'm using the facilities," Jacob said. He said it cop-faced, which I took to mean that he wasn't trying to convey any actual mirth.

Dreyfuss hung his cheerful purple toothbrush from a holder on the wall. "Your bags were already loaded on the commercial flight by the time I got to O'Hare, otherwise I would've had my men on it—but like I said, you need anything, just say the word. I'll put in a call."

I glanced at the crate, but either Dreyfuss didn't notice, or he was taking his sweet time about mentioning it just to piss me off.

Dreyfuss pulled the scrunchie from his hair, tucked it in his pocket, and gave his temples a quick rub. His hair spread over his shoulders in a bunch of corkscrew curls. "I guess if no one needs anything from me, I'll turn in for the night so I can be bright-eyed and bushy-tailed in the morning."

Jacob cleared his throat. I looked at him. He indicated the crate with his eyes.

I supposed if Dreyfuss wasn't going to volunteer what it was all about, it really was my responsibility to ask. I just hated that he was making me do it. I almost prefaced it with a long-suffering sigh, but managed to curb it. "What about this thing?"

"I told you at the airport I'd make it worth your while. What, you didn't believe me? Don't you always come away from our negotiations with a little something extra for your troubles?"

"What is it?" Jacob asked.

"I'd tell you…" he turned toward the door to his room, "…but then it would spoil the surprise. The combination is Detective Bayne's birthday."

"But there's no room to—" I tried to say, but Dreyfuss talked right over me.

"I've got some phone calls to make before I hit the hay. I'll leave you two to plan out your investigation. You're the detectives, after all. I'm just a glorified paper-pusher."

He closed the bathroom door, which left Jacob and me alone with the crate. Would a normal person be excited? Would they start dreaming up what sort of luxury item or major appliance might be lurking inside to bribe them into accepting that the FPMP was not so bad after all…so long as you didn't value your personal privacy. Hard to say. Sometimes I could manage a pretty good approximation of a normal person's reaction—but now wasn't one of those times.

"I don't want it," I said.

Jacob pressed himself against my back, which at first I took for him trying to move me out of the way. Not that there was anywhere for me to go; I was trapped, with a mattress on either side and a monster crate in front of me. Then his hands slid around my stomach and he pulled me back against him, this wall of warm solidity, and I felt myself sag into him before I'd even consciously decided it was okay to relax.

Damn, he felt good.

"Look first, before you decide."

"But that's the thing." My voice sounded tired, even to me. "If I look, I'm gonna want it."

"You don't know that."

"No. I do. I'm sure of it." I felt Jacob's forehead press against the back of my skull. His breath was warm through my hair. I drew the strength to put words to my thoughts from the feel of him breathing me. "You saw the big pretzel. You know how he manipulates people."

It was wide open for Jacob to try to ratchet down my anxiety by saying something like, "You can fit one hell of a pretzel in that thing," but he didn't take the bait. Instead, he thought for a moment, and he said, "You're better off knowing than not knowing. You need to be able to weigh all your choices so you know what you're getting into, so you can go in with your eyes open."

"I don't want to owe him anything."

"He never said you would, did he?"

"So far, just an exorcism—but I'm sure there's wiggle room for him to tack some extras onto my bill somewhere down the line. I wish he'd just be straight with me. There are too many angles to this thing. Too many ways it can turn out bad."

He held me for several long moments, and then he said, "There's got to be some reason he shipped it all the way to California."

"There's a reason he does everything. That's what I'm trying to tell you."

"Look." Jacob turned me around so that we were facing each other, with a displaced dresser to one side and the crate on the other, and a mattress behind each of us. "After Heliotrope Station, the thought of anyone recruiting you for your talent makes you shut down. I get it. But what about the Fifth Precinct? That turned out okay, otherwise you never would've stuck with it this long."

"Maybe I don't want to screw that up."

He worked my forearm through the sleeve of my jacket with his thumb. "Then you need to look. Because hiding your head in the sand isn't helping anything."

I glanced at the crate. The gunmetal gray plastic was pebbled with texture, with a few scrapes showing on one of the sides right around doorknob-height. The corners and edges were chased with metal, and the whole thing had a strap around it that closed with a barrel lock.

I tried to picture myself opening it up, but I'd gotten myself worked up to the point of imagining a one-way ticket back to Camp Hell, or somewhere worse. Somewhere they weren't just trying out random meds to see what would happen to Psychs' brains. Somewhere they damn well knew... and they used them to manipulate us like a bunch of drugged-out puppets. "I can't."

He kissed me. It was gentle, something I felt more in his goatee tickling my upper lip and my chin than on my mouth, and he said softly, "Then I am."

He turned, keeping one hand anchored on my arm, and thumbed the barrels to 0-2-2-3. The lock clicked open.

"So...you actually do know when my birthday is," I said. And there, it was me trying to cut the tension, not him.

"Of course I do. I'd just lost track and the date snuck up on me." He glanced down at the open lock. "Are you doing this with me?"

I couldn't. I shook my head.

"Are you going to stop me?"

Was I? It didn't feel like it. I was paralyzed. I gave my head another curt shake that could be interpreted as a *no*.

Jacob popped a couple of clasps, top and side, and gave the crate a wiggle. It stayed shut. He ran his fingers along the closed seam, found a clasp on the bottom he'd missed the first time around, and snapped it open.

A dark crack appeared. The front of the crate separated. It didn't open on a hinge like a door; it pulled off like the lid of a big shoebox standing on its side. Before I could see anything, Jacob demanded, "What the...?" as if the case could talk back to him.

And given some of the things I'd seen over the last few years, I really hoped it couldn't.

"It's a TV set," he said. "An old one."

I half-heard that last part over a great whooshing in my ears, because the apathy and avoidance I'd so carefully maintained over the mammoth crate came crashing down like a thrill ride at the amusement park, and my heart was pounding so hard I felt like my blood was going to burst through my veins and squirt out my ears. The lid was blocking my view. I took it from Jacob a lot more calmly than I felt, and held it there to one side of me while I looked.

I'd been expecting the GhosTV.

I was wrong.

Chapter 12

The TV set inside the crate was decades older than the GhosTV I knew. It was a seventies model in a more elaborate wooden console, with sparkly brown fabric covering the panel that hid the speakers.

Even though it was definitely not the set from the motel room in Missouri, my heart kept on pounding as if it knew something I hadn't quite admitted yet. Like it remembered that even though the original GhosTV was in an evidence locker in St. Louis, Roger Burke and his cronies had cobbled together more than one GhosTV. And it was pretty sure I was currently looking at one of those "extras."

"Help me unpack it," I said. My voice was so thick with emotion that it startled Jacob.

"Is this…?"

"Not the one from St. Louis." I took a careful breath and let it out. "But I think it might be one of the others."

"You hold the crate. I'll get the set out."

Fleetingly, I toyed with the idea of ruing my lack of athleticism—but everything's got limits, and the desire to wallow in my self esteem issues couldn't hold a candle to the thought that I could very well be in the presence of a genuine GhosTV—without a gun to my head or a shot of sodium amytal wending its way through my veins. Besides, holding the crate turned out to take a good amount of actual effort. I was glad it wasn't me prying the console out of its protective foam packing. It looked heavy.

"Do something with that crate," Jacob said, struggling to maneuver a TV set as big as him with nowhere to put it.

I slung the crate onto my bed, and hoped I hadn't just pulled a groin muscle.

"It was sideways in the box," Jacob said. "Is that how it's supposed to sit?"

"I doubt it. They're supposed to blend in with their surroundings."

"Then grab the top. I don't want to drop it when we're getting it into position."

I did what he said, and then immediately wished I'd placed my feet in a better stance. Lift with your legs, that's what they say, right? That's all fine and good—but how are you supposed to lower something? The set was at a thirty-degree angle. One false move and it'd crush me. "Got it?" Jacob said. He didn't even sound like he was exerting effort.

"I'm at an awkward angle."

He huffed, bearing the weight with one arm so he could reposition his hand. His fingers appeared, wrapped around the edge of one of the console's feet a few inches away from my face. I experienced a surge of gratitude for those big, strong hands. "How's that?"

I planted my feet a bit better. "Can you pull the bottom back so it's got somewhere to swing down?"

He walked the set back carefully. "You sure you got it? We could switch."

Could we? Not unless I was able to walk *through* him. "Yeah, it's good. Let's do this."

Just when I thought I didn't have any left…me and my fucking pride. We should have switched, me steering, him bearing the weight. But no. I chose to be the one easing the behemoth to the floor—and while I had nothing to gauge its weight by, since it wasn't the size, shape or density of a human being, it had to be a few hundred pounds, minimum.

The console was at 4 o'clock, I had nowhere to back up, Jacob was grasping at wood trim, and my hands felt like someone was trying to tear them off with a big pair of pliers.

"Flex your knees," he told me. "Breathe."

I let my breath out in a loud gasp.

"Easy," he said. "Keep telling yourself, a couple more inches. That's it."

"I…can't."

"You got it, just a few more."

My hands burned, really burned—and my back and my knees and my arms and everything else on me was a blinding, red wall of pain. But I couldn't drop it—could *not* drop it—no matter what. I'd dreamt about it every time I faced the one-eyed headache I got from swallowing too much Auracel. The sickening meds I took just covered up the spirits, but the GhosTV did something else. What if it scrambled the signal? What if it actually affected them instead of just making it so that I didn't need to see?

"Almost there," Jacob said. Calm. Velvety smooth.

Yes. I could do it. I'd set that monster TV down without dropping it. A few more inches, for real this time. The floor was near. I could feel it. Almost there, just like Jacob said. Almost.

But then the console smashed my hand into the corner of the dresser... and pain? The pain I'd been in was nothing compared to the agony of my hand being crushed.

The console slipped.

Blind panic. I could practically feel the delicate wiring tearing from its sockets, the tubes shattering—the GhosTV, dead before I'd even turned it on.

It took me a heartbeat to realize that the pressure on my hand had eased. Jacob's shoulder brushed my arm. He'd shifted around the console. He'd caught it. "Easy," he said. "All the way down."

When the cabinet's feet touched down, I barely felt it over the throbbing in my knuckles. Jacob took my hand—so gently, for such a big hulk of a guy—and brought my skinned knuckles to his lips. "That's gonna swell."

I wiggled my fingers, one at a time. They moved. Probably not broken—just pulped. The knuckles looked white and gristly. Blood started to bead up from the scrapes, belatedly, as if it had been too busy pounding through my panic centers to notice something as unexceptional as a friction wound.

Jacob turned to the console once it was apparent that my hand still worked. "How do you know if it's really...what you think it is?"

"There'll be stuff inside, controls that aren't original to the set."

He crouched, and shone his pocket flashlight through the vents in the back of the cabinet. "When I was a kid, Uncle Leon and I took an old set apart to tinker with, so I might be able to spot anything unusual...but from here it's hard to tell what's what."

I leaned over the console as well as I could without putting my weight on it. The back panel was screwed on. I tried tugging on the top of the cabinet. Nothing. Felt around the tube to see if it hinged out like the original GhosTV. Nope. It was in there pretty good. I slipped my hands underneath. Nothing strange there, either.

Jacob straightened up, pocketed his flashlight, and said, "The original—was it plugged in?"

"Uh. It must've been."

Jacob held up the two-pronged power cord and raised his eyebrows at me. I nodded. He plugged it in, looked to see if I was going to turn it on. When I made no move to do it, he flipped the switch.

Snow.

We watched my favorite channel for a minute, and then he said, "Is this how the other one—"

"No, there was a game on. But it was just a recording. It had a DVD player mounted inside the cabinet. And something else, a thing with a digital readout and some knobs."

Jacob changed the channel. They were all snow. "Even if there was reception, we'd need an antenna and a digital converter."

I didn't think reception was the point. At least, not the reception of TV broadcast.

He switched from UHF to VHF and looked at me expectantly. "Anything?"

I didn't think so, but unless there was a ghost in the room, would I even know? The only evidence I'd had that the original GhosTV was doing anything at all was the fade-in, fade-out of the local spirit population. "It might work, it might not. But if this place has been cleaned out—even by mediums who don't think they need to rate their talent with numbers—we're never gonna know, because there's nothing to see."

"We could ask Dreyfuss…" Jacob began.

"I'm not asking him." Not until I had no other choice.

With my flashlight, I searched for telltale wear, excessive smudging, breaks in the patina, or other clues that might hint at a spot that'd been messed with, but other than the areas where Jacob and I had manhandled it out of the crate and searched it ourselves, there wasn't even so much as a fingerprint on it.

Jacob pulled his keys out of his pocket and unfolded a little Phillips-head screwdriver from the keyring. "Should I?"

It'd be stupid to go this far and not go all the way. I nodded. Jacob turned off the set, unplugged it, and got to work on the screws in back.

"Bring your flashlight over here," he said as he tipped the back panel off. I wedged myself as close as I could, and we both shone our lights in.

The first thing I noticed was that the inside of the console was as squeaky clean as the outside. No dust, no cobwebs, no crud. Other than the pristine state of the old wires and electrical parts, there was nothing special about this TV set. I sat down hard on one of the beds as the strain of the day washed over me.

"On the St. Louis TV—how big were the extra parts?" Jacob asked.

"Pretty big." And pretty fucking obvious, too.

In a move worthy of a contortionist, Jacob pressed his ear to the floor so he could look underneath the cabinet. He straightened into a crouch, sighed—and then caught the look on my face, which I'm guessing was the look of a kid who just figured out that Santa's nothing more than a drunk in a red suit. "Don't jump to any conclusions. Someone went through a lot of effort to ship this here."

"Did they? Or did they find it at a local swap meet and put it here to fuck with my head?"

"I'm sure Dreyfuss knows how it—"

"That asshole next door scares the crap out of me. Okay?"

"Babe." He never calls me *babe*. He tried to reach for me, but there was a big honkin' TV console in his way. "I think you're feeling the plane ride, and you're worn out and hungry." And jonesing for a Valium. He didn't say as much, but I'll bet we were both thinking it.

"This thing's got to work." He plugged it in, reached around, and turned it back on. Perplexing static. "And I'll bet there's some way we can use it, right here, right now." He crammed his way between the TV and the dresser until he squeezed through to the pocket of space in front of the bathroom door. "You don't even need to ask him yourself. I'll do it."

"So he can start fucking with your head, too? No way."

"Then what do you want? Do you want to risk messing this thing up by turning the wrong knob? Do you think you'll be able to sleep knowing that it's here, right here, and you haven't got any idea how to use it?" He turned his darkest, most forbidding laser-eyed look on me. "What about Lisa? Isn't she what really matters?"

"Oh, sonofa…." I stood up from the bed with the intention of giving the console a final once-over, when something in my low back that'd been irritated by the heavy lifting sent a spasm from my ass cheek all the way down to the back of my knee. Before I could catch myself I pitched forward. In our loft, I would've ended up sprawled on the floor. But there's a little thing called "elbow room" in our loft. In that puny room crammed with beds and dressers and crates and furniture, I found myself hurtling straight for the old TV.

I tried to course-correct, as much as anyone can do that while they're falling. Maybe I'd end up splitting my head on the crate on the opposite bed, but at least heads can theoretically heal. Everything happened so fast, though, that all I really did was tilt a bit to one side. I put a hand out, hoping to rappel off the side of the TV rather than land on it full-force, and my skinned knuckles rasped over something surprisingly rough. I bounced off the cabinet, smacked the empty crate, and hit the floor with my shoulder. The snow channel cut out as the power cord popped from the wall socket. The crate lid fell on top of me.

"Stay still," Jacob said. He pulled the lid off me—which, since it was lined with that spongy egg-carton foam, hadn't hurt anything but that dumb pride of mine. "Are you all right? What happened?"

I chose to answer the least embarrassing of those two questions. "I'm fine." My hand had landed in something wet. And red. The knuckles looked like hamburger.

"You're bleeding."

"Only my hand." I pushed myself up off the floor and cast around for whatever had just flayed me. A brown fabric panel lay half-under the bed. The sparkly fibers weren't as visible on the back side of the fabric, though tiny pinprick glints showed through enough for me to recognize the speaker cover, and its sandpaper-like synthetic fabric, face down on the floor. Great. Now I probably had microscopic traces of fiberglass coursing through my veins.

Leave it to me to be laid low by a piece of material.

I snagged the corner of the cover and pulled it out from under the bed. Hopefully nothing was broken, and it'd just pop right back on, no harm, no foul. The framework beneath the fabric felt like it was still in one piece. I knee-walked to the console, hoping I hadn't broken off whatever tabs or grooves held the cover in place, when something inside the speaker well caught my eye.

It was shadowy in the recess of the cabinetry, but then I spotted it, something that wasn't original to the set, protruding from the shadows—a thread-fringed corner of duct tape.

Chapter 13

"You're really bleeding. We need to wrap that up."

"Jacob." A juvenile fear of "jinxing" myself stole over me, and I couldn't even bring myself to say, *this is it.* "Give me your flashlight."

Jacob handed it over and I shone the beam into the speaker well. A device was taped to the side—four dials. No LCD readout like the TV in Missouri. No instruction manual, either. But I knew, with a cold certainty, this was the real deal.

Carefully, Jacob climbed over a bed, rounded the TV, and crouched so he could peer over my shoulder. He admired the machinery for a long moment, then said, "How do you work it?"

I didn't know.

Jacob said, "I'm getting Dreyfuss."

That was about as close as he'd come to asking my permission. I didn't like it—but I didn't stop him, either. He ducked into the bathroom and crammed himself back into the room with Dreyfuss two minutes later. "What's on tonight's lineup?" Con said. "I don't suppose this thing gets HBO."

"How do you work it?" I said.

He stepped over the corner of the bed and into the gap between the beds and the GhosTV with me, but thankfully he'd managed not to touch me. "Plug it in, for starters."

Jacob plugged it back into the outlet he'd used before. "Okay."

"Okay," Dreyfuss echoed.

"Now what?" I said.

He looked at me with raised eyebrows. "Are you shitting me? I thought you knew."

"This is not the time to get cute."

He held his hands up beside his head in mock surrender. "Cross my heart, we all figured you'd snuck a peek at Roger Burke manning the helm and you picked up a few pointers."

"Maybe you should've thought it through better than that before you had him killed."

The tube crackling inside the TV console was conspicuously loud over the sudden silence of the three of us holding our breath.

"Sounds like you've got your mind made up, but I promise you this, Detective. You might think you know everything. But you don't."

Funny. I'd expected Dreyfuss to deny the FPMP's part in killing Burke. Did he realize I knew about them offing Dr. Chance, too?

And speaking of Dr. Chance…if Richie hadn't managed to exorcise her from the FPMP offices, then it meant that at least *someone* knew how to work the GhosTV. But what good did that do me at the moment? It wasn't as if we could shoot her a quick email.

"The GhosTV I saw before had a digital readout," I said. Not that I knew what any of the numbers meant…but it was there. "You turned the dials, and…."

"And they affect different waveforms. Our lab determined that much—but what it boiled down to in the end was that whatever this thing does, our tools, for the most part, don't have the ability to measure it."

I stared at the speaker well as if glaring at the equipment would result in a sudden realization of its inner workings.

"It's science," Dreyfuss said. "Physics, actually—ions and alpha particles. But something else, too. Something the old tube amplifies. Maybe something we don't know enough about to actually gauge."

Dreyfuss crouched in front of the panel, and I flattened myself against the opposite bed. "Right now, everything's in the off-position. The first dial is like a volume button. It acts on the other three equally. Dial two, three and four…we're not so sure. The way the guys from the lab explained it to me, they were kind of like an Etch-a-Sketch. Remember how it was always such a challenge to draw a diagonal line with one of those things? One knob went up and down, the other side-to-side, and turning them both just right was like walking a tightrope."

I'd been in foster care with an older boy, Charles, who was always trying to render boobs on the Etch-a-Sketch. And he always shook away everything I tried to draw. That was the extent of my knowledge…though I suppose I understood the analogy well enough. "How about that last dial?"

"Same thing, only this particular toy can draw in three dimensions."

"What kind of sketch are you aiming for?" Jacob said.

"That…we haven't figured out quite yet." Dreyfuss gestured toward me. "As far as we know, Detective Bayne is the only one perceptive enough to see the pictures."

"You have a medium at the FPMP."

Dreyfuss gave a *whaddaya-gonna-do?* shrug. "He feels cold spots."

"So that's why you brought us here?" Jacob said. "To figure out how the GhosTV works?"

"I brought you here to find Detective Gutierrez." He stepped away from the console and straddled the corner of the bed to squeeze by Jacob and head back to his room. "The TV is yours to keep. If you can use it, great, knock yourselves out. If it clashes with your décor, just say the word. I'll ship it back to our lab."

"He's bluffing," I said, once the door shut.

"He's not bluffing," Jacob insisted, with the certainty of someone who'd been working side-by-side with a talking lie detector for the past five years. He listened for the door to Dreyfuss' room, and once the coast was clear, went into the bathroom himself. He came out with a roll of toilet paper still in its wrapper. The paper wrapping was covered in graphics of leaves. Recycled—extra scratchy. "Let's take a few steps back, breathe, and come to a plan of action we both agree on."

He sounded terribly rational, which should have alarmed me, because the more logical Jacob was acting, the more likely I was to be cornered into a situation I wanted no part in. But I hurt all over—particularly the one leg that hurt from my ass to my knee—and I didn't have any good ideas of my own.

I sat on the side of the bed, and Jacob sat at the foot. The corner of the GhosTV console jutted there between my knees and his, segmenting us each into the tiny slots of space we occupied. Jacob unwrapped the recycled TP, then took my bloody hand in his lap. He swabbed off my hand and wrapped it loosely, enough to stop me from bleeding on the mountain of furniture crammed into the puny room without melding with the wound.

"We need to find Lisa," he said, "and nobody here knows what happened. Right?"

"Right."

"As far as we know, this building's clean of spirit activity, but you've got this GhosTV that might help you locate a spirit that's harder to see. You with me so far?"

"I guess."

"While I focus on interviewing the residents, you see if you can find a surprise star witness."

That's the thing about Jacob. He always makes so much damn sense.

At least someone or something did. As plans went, it was the best one either of us could come up with, and so we planted ourselves in front of that TV set, and we played with those dials until my brain went numb. Jacob created a grid of combinations we could try, but even with the "volume" knob at a constant, there were a thousand possible combinations. I let him worry about the numbers, and I sat beside the GhosTV, and I looked.

I didn't see anything.

The frustrating thing is, a lack of ghosts didn't necessarily mean the GhosTV wasn't functioning. It could've just as easily meant there were no ghosts there to be seen.

In an ideal world, I'd find myself a place where there was subtle spirit activity, maybe a disembodied voice, or a cold spot—yeah, sometimes they only feel like cold spots, even to me—and I'd make a quick call and have the GhosTV set up on site. Then the knobs might mean something. Temperature. Transparency. Time.

But testing the GhosTV in a spirit-free room was like learning to swim in your car. If your car wasn't currently at the bottom of Lake Michigan, at any rate.

I was really sick of playing, "See anything?" "No," by the time a tap on the hallway door broke the monotony. Despite all my creaky aches and pains, I was itching to do something, anything, that was different from the profound *nothing* I'd been doing for the past few hours, and so I slipped around Jacob, climbed the bed and opened the door.

It was Lyle. He had a rolling cart with him, suitcases on the bottom, and a couple of cafeteria trays on top. "The airline dropped off your luggage. And I thought you might want..." he pointed toward the trays, then spoke over whatever he'd been trying to say as if he was having trouble finding words. "It's lentil soup. That's all that was left, but...."

"Great." I realized I was ready to keel over from hunger. "That's great." I opened the door wider, then wondered where we'd manage to fit the soup, let alone our suitcases.

Lyle actually staggered back a step when he got a load of our room. "How…why…?" He gestured at the displaced dresser, the big plastic crate, and of course, the GhosTV. "This is ridiculous. I'll get you another room."

"No, it's okay," I said quickly, because I didn't think I could handle being alone with the GhosTV. "It's late. We'll figure something out in the morning."

As I took the tray from him, and then the suitcases one at a time to hand off to Jacob, I couldn't help but wonder: wouldn't it be a hell of a lot easier if that extra bed were in the hallway? True, it would be a challenge to sleep with Jacob on anything smaller than a king-sized mattress, but I was accustomed enough to having his elbows in my ribs. Lyle was obviously gay—either that, or he was in serious denial—so it seemed like I should be able to lay it all out on the table with him.

Except I couldn't. Not yet. Because once something's been said, you can't exactly unsay it.

"You saw the land line," Lyle said, once we'd crammed the final suitcase in. "I couldn't take it any more and I pulled the plug. We've had our new number all of two days, and those freaks found it already and started crank-calling us again. So if you need anything, here's my cell number."

I took his business card and set it on the corner of the dresser with my bloody toilet paper hand. "Actually, we could use some gauze and Band-Aids, and some first-aid cream."

Lyle gasped—he'd just now noticed it?—but he didn't ask what had happened to me. That was good. I wasn't sure whether to blame the crate, the carpet, or the GhosTV. "I'll be right back—two minutes."

I closed the door after him and sagged against the closet door. "Hand me a soup?"

Jacob passed a warm takeout container across the crate lid. I took it from him, peeled off the lid, and drank it without even chewing the lentils.

Better.

Jacob decided to forego the spoon himself, though I do think he chewed. "Needs salt."

Another Lyle-tap on the door, and there he was, pink-cheeked and breathless, holding out a white plastic first-aid kit. "I think this should work. Unless you wanted the homeopathic—"

"It's fine." I wished I'd asked him for a Coke, but it seemed cruel to make him run back downstairs again. He looked like he was waiting for some other exchange of pleasantries, but I was so worn out, I felt anything but pleasant. I took the first-aid kit, handed him the empty containers, said, "Thanks," and shut the door.

In no time flat, I had my bag splayed out atop the carton lid on my bed, and I was rifling through for the pill bottles I'd wrapped in my spare socks. It was eleven thirty—holy shit, one thirty Chicago time—and I was so wiped out I'd probably sleep like a baby even without a Valium. I told myself I was in an unfamiliar place, so I should make sure I could wake up quickly if I needed to…but I wasn't buying it. I touched the orange plastic bottles to reassure myself that they were there, but it wasn't enough.

Half a tab wouldn't hurt, I figured. Though when I dumped them into my palm and looked for a halfsie, I couldn't find one, and ended up taking a whole dose.

While I re-wrapped my hand, Jacob checked that his stuff was all intact, then changed into a T-shirt and sweatpants. "We should call it a night," he said. "We'll be fresher in the morning." He climbed over the foot of his bed and worked his way under the garish blankets. The full-sized mattress was barely big enough to hold him—I knew as much from my old bed, which had also been a full. The second bed held the crate lid, and now, my torn-apart suitcase. We probably didn't want to put anything on top of the console, lightweight or not. But maybe if I pulled my bed away from the wall a couple of inches I could sneak the crate lid over the far side….

"Can you reach the overhead light?" Jacob asked.

I looked at the train wreck on my mattress. "I need to figure out where to—"

"Don't even think about it." He held up his own blanket in invitation. "Cut the light and come to bed."

I wasn't even going to risk draping a suit over the GhosTV. Heck, if we'd been able to re-crate the clumsy piece of furniture without smashing through the window, I would've voted for putting it completely away to ensure nothing happened to it while I slept. I hung my suit over the growing mountain of stuff on the spare bed, put my sidearm on the floor near the nightstand where I wouldn't fall over it and accidentally shoot myself, then I turned off the light and climbed into bed in my underwear.

"You're not worried about getting cold?"

I was facing Jacob with my head pillowed on his biceps. Our legs were woven together. Every exposed inch of me seemed to be pressed up against somewhere warm on him. "I'll be fine," I said into his neck.

His hand roamed my shoulder blades, skin gliding over skin. The back of my leg was still on fire, but the rest of the aches and pains I'd gathered over the course of the day settled into an annoying throb that Valium and exhaustion would erase soon enough.

First the drug dog at the airport, then trusting my life to Dreyfuss as he flew us here, and now the GhosTV that didn't do anything—all the while Lisa's trail grew colder. The day had been an emotional roller coaster—or maybe an emotional scrambler. Even an emotional people-flinger. One of those rides I would have been better off sitting out.

CHAPTER 14

My head bumped against something hard, and it came back to me that I wasn't in my own bed—heck, I wasn't even in my own state—and I was currently mashed into a room that was way too small, and a bed where two "big and tall" guys could hardly squeeze in with a shoehorn.

Jacob would need to move over, simple as that. I gave a push, in hopes of prying him away from some of the mattress real estate, but couldn't get a good sense of what was where, or which way I was even facing. Talk about disorientation. I usually had a sense of my headboard and my nightstand, but here everything seemed topsy-turvy, as if I was attempting to sleep in an entirely new hemisphere.

Whenever I can, I avoid opening my eyes if I wake up in the middle of the night. I feel like it helps me get back to sleep faster. In this case, though, the cop in me wasn't going to rest if I didn't get the lay of the land. I snuck one eye open and saw the wall an inch from my nose.

The wall? That was some fancy sleep choreography on Jacob's part. I'd finally fallen asleep facing the narrow lane between the beds with him curled against my back. I felt behind me for Jacob.

He was gone.

That's how I'd ended up against the wall—I was alone. Huh? Where was Jacob? What was he thinking, going somewhere without letting me know? He wouldn't do that, would he? That was totally not like him. He was probably just taking a leak, and the feel of him getting out of bed was the thing that woke me up. Nothing to worry about. I rolled to face the tiny aisle between the beds and attempted to make room for Jacob when he came back, but couldn't quite figure out where the edge of the bed was. The more I skootched forward, the more space I seemed to have.

What the…?

I looked, really looked, at the opposite wall—what I could see of it in the murky dark, anyway—and tried to figure out where the crate lid and the luggage and all the other crap on the spare bed had gone. Nothing. The room was an expanse of nothing, all the way to the opposite wall.

Oh, hell. I was the one who'd been abducted, not Jacob. I looked around in panic, and got a lentil-churning look at a mirror on the ceiling—me and Jacob, spooned together and swaddled in an ugly print sheet. Mirror? Where had the mirror come from? Wouldn't I have noticed a mirrored ceiling within the first nanosecond of entering the room? Wouldn't Jacob have at least made a passing attempt to get me to do something X-rated beneath it?

Even though I'd taken the classes, heard all the theories, and drank the Kool-Aid, it took me an extra few seconds to actually understand what was happening. I moved, but the mirror image didn't move. I moved some more. I tried to get a feel for the bed I was laying on, except it wasn't a bed. And I wasn't on my back. And then I finally put it all together.

I was having an out-of-body experience.

At this point, most astral projection newbies usually get so freaked out that they snap right back into their physical shells. I, personally, was plenty freaked. But no snap.

At Camp Hell, they'd said on more than one occasion that our astral bodies are connected to our physical bodies with a silver cord that sprouts from the solar plexus. I looked down at my stomach. No cord.

Did that mean I was dead? Crap.

I tried to swim down to myself, but I felt too buoyant. I made it back to the wall to use it to climb down to my physical body, which did work, briefly. But then my hand sank into the wall. That might seem freaky, but strangely enough, my lack of substance didn't bother me nearly as much as my missing silver cord. I could feel the difference between the open air and the wall. It was like having my arm in the sleeve of a snug sweater. I pushed a little bit more, and felt the freedom of the opposite side of the wall, like my fingertips had just emerged from the sleeve.

I threaded my arm back and forth through the wall a few times, and once that seemed okay, I took a chance and shoved my head through.

There it was. The bathroom.

A small plastic nightlight glowed from the outlet near the medicine cabinet, so I could somewhat see. Luckily, you-know-who wasn't taking a late-night dump or anything. I tried to make out a few details so I could verify later that I wasn't simply having some kind of elaborate sleeping fantasy, but it was too dark to get a really good look—incredibly, palpably dark, like I was wearing a pair of dirty sunglasses.

I pushed myself forward, feeling the strange glide of the wall all around my astral body as I passed through it. And then, there I was, fully, on the other side of the wall. Out of visual range of my physical body. I checked to see if that thought panicked me. It didn't.

Strangely enough, it seemed easier to move around if my physical shell wasn't in the room. I scooted around the perimeter of the ceiling, then experimented with controlling my descent. I was able to get down to about six feet.

Maybe if I was farther still from my physical body, I'd have even more leeway.

I could have just gone out into the hallway, I'm sure. But I'd been presented with a chance to peep at Con Dreyfuss, see if he was doing anything incriminating, and I couldn't pass it up.

I pushed my hand through the far wall of the bathroom and it met with some resistance. I was probably ranging too far from my physical body. All I wanted was a tiny peek, though, so I pushed a little harder and felt a flex, and then a give, as my fingers broke through. I followed with my head.

Dreyfuss' room was even darker than the bathroom, but a sliver of streetlight shone in through the side of the curtain. He was in bed, presumably asleep, wrapped tight in his sheets and curled up in a fetal position. A few corkscrews of hair stuck out the top of the blanket roll.

Okay, I told myself. I've had my fun. Time to go back. Except I didn't feel like going back to that cramped room with its small bed and disappointing TV. As long as I stayed in the building, I decided, I wouldn't accidentally float away, so it couldn't hurt to do a little more exploring. With no one to get in my way, a quick peek around might save Jacob and me a whole lot of time in our investigation.

I pulled my head back into the bathroom and floated to the wall that separated the bath from the hallway, which I tested with my hand. That wall was easy. My hand slipped right through. I followed with my head. There it was—the hall. A row of identical doors on each side, an elevator at the end, slightly worn carpet and stucco walls.

I floated to the room across the hall and pushed my head through the door. A sleeping person. Same in the next room, and the next. The rooms held the same basic pieces of furniture, but they had different personal stuff in them, at varying levels of tidiness. I couldn't say for sure what color anything was, though whether the reason was because it was so dark, or because my astral vision was naturally desaturated, I didn't know.

Not only did it quickly get boring to look at sleeping person after sleeping person, but I felt slimy about invading the residents' privacy, too. I told myself it was no worse than any other psychic search, and that I was well within my rights to pry all I wanted. My paper PsyCop license said so. But a look at a guy who'd fallen asleep with his TV on, muted, his dentures on the nightstand beside him, his hand down the front of his boxers, and his toothless mouth snoring wide—that sent me backpedaling into the hall wishing I could take an astral shower.

What did I think I'd find in the residents' rooms, anyway? The chance that any of them were involved was pretty slim. It wasn't as if any of them were effective, practicing Psychs. Or if they were, they wouldn't know as much, since no one had ever really ranked them.

The thought of getting farther away from my body didn't make me quite as anxious anymore, so I figured I could take advantage of my situation to get a look at Lisa's room with my astral eyes and see if I'd missed anything. Good thinking on Dreyfuss' part to score us the room above hers...unless it was all just part of his nefarious master plan. Which it probably was. Still, I couldn't let his motives stop me from finding Lisa, so I floated back to my door to get my bearings, then I imagined myself sinking down, down, down.

The floor felt permeable, but more solid somehow than the walls. Like pushing through one of those ball pits at a kiddie restaurant. Not that I'd ever played in a ball pit as a child. But a few years before, I'd scoured one for body parts in the investigation of a particularly inventive crime.

My feet popped free, then my legs, my ass, my shoulders and head. I opened my eyes. The first floor was much more shadowy than the second, though the layout was the same. I floated myself down to eye-level with the doorway to try to get a look at the room number, just to be sure I'd been traveling in the right direction.

The number on the door wasn't a number. It was...a shape. A glyph. Some weird combination of loops and sticks I had no way to interpret. My astral head hurt just looking at it.

Maybe it had always been that way, and I simply hadn't noticed when Chekotah had shown me the room. No problem. I'd just poke my head in and look for the bag of Cheetos to make sure I was in the right spot. I mashed my forehead into the door and felt significant resistance. It flexed and held, springy, like a mattress. Distance from my physical body seemed to be making my astral body wimpier. But since I'd made my way through some resistance on Dreyfuss' wall, I decided to suck some white light, gather my will, and give that door a big, hard push.

That's when everything went sparkly. And then black.

Chapter 15

"What are you doing?"

I blinked. It was dark, murky-dark, and after a moment of laggy disorientation, I remembered I'd been cruising through an astral projection. I blinked again, knuckled my eyes, but I couldn't seem to see.

"Can you hear me?"

I looked around for the woman who was talking to me, but it was so damn dark. "Hello?" Stupid thing to say, I know. I could suddenly sympathize with every character in a horror flick who'd never come up with a more logical response.

"It's very common for beginners to have trouble opening their eyes," she said.

They were open plenty before, but then I rammed into...whatever that was. It took a few tries, because I'd begun to get confused about opening my astral eyes as opposed to opening my physical eyes, but as I thought back to the way I felt flying around my bathroom, my astral body figured out a way to replicate the sensation and my astral eyes opened. Someone was crouched over me—a woman about my age with spiky hair and glasses (astral glasses?) Her outfit had a shapeless, hand-dyed, third-world seamstress kind of look to it, and it was topped off with a necklace that looked like someone's jute-and-stones collection had tangled together in their drawer and stuck that way. Her skin was luminous. She was slightly translucent.

"You're astral," I said.

"Well, at least you know what's going on."

"Why was it so hard to open my eyes?"

"Anxiety's usually the main reason, although a high-protein Western diet has a tendency to make projecting more difficult. And alcohol. You don't drink, do you?"

"No." I didn't mention the Valium. "What's your name?"

She crossed her arms and looked at me. "You really are a newbie, aren't you? We can't do introductions; my name wouldn't make any sense to you even if I told you. The right hemisphere of your physical brain isn't in the loop."

Good information, but it seemed to me she was awfully know-it-all about it. "Yeah. I am new. It's my first time out."

Astral Lady nodded gravely. "Good, that's good. I'd rather you were a wandering newbie than one of those nosy Feds they brought in."

By "one of those nosy Feds," I presume she meant me. I glanced down at myself to see why that wasn't readily apparent, and saw I was projecting in an old pair of jeans and my favorite black T-shirt, despite the fact that the physical clothes were in a laundry basket somewhere in Chicago. I decided it was against my best interests to announce I was with Dreyfuss, not that it took much arm-twisting. "I'm Lisa's friend. I couldn't reach her—"

"And you were worried, and so you projected. I'll bet you were thinking about her as you fell asleep, and that triggered the release of your astral body." Know-it-alls were pretty easy to lie to. The ones who really liked to hear themselves talk spun out whatever story they wanted to hear, and all you had to do was let 'em ramble. "She was my friend, too."

"Is this Lisa's room? How can you tell? What's with the number on the door?"

"You really are a newbie." She looked at me with pity, and a hint of smugness. "It's your brain, your right hemisphere. You haven't noticed it's impossible to count in the astral?"

That was about the dumbest thing I'd ever heard, so of course I had to try. A few numbers, just to see….

The numbers squirmed away from me like a half-remembered dream. "No. I guess not. So how come you can't tell me your name, but you understand when I say *Lisa*?"

"Have you even had the intro lecture? Do you know anything at all?"

"I know I'm astral," I said. That should count for something.

"Say we've heard of someone—Bono, or Al Gore…or Lisa—then that name lives in our long-term memories. If we're having a fairly lucid trip, we'll be able to understand the names of people we already know, and even talk to each other about them, as long as both of us know them. If not? If I try to tell you my mother's name, for instance? Here's what you'll hear." She said something else, but I didn't quite catch it.

"What?"

"Exactly. Other concepts are slippery, too. Numbers get scrambled. Other memories? You don't usually know until you try to think them, and you can't. It all depends on where the information fires in the brain. And even that's not fully mapped."

If I were in my physical body, I would have had some kind of reaction to the thought of psychic phenomena being mapped to various parts of the brain—because of course I could always place myself in the guinea pig hotseat and imagine those electrodes sprouting from my own head. Not just glued on, either, but wired through holes that'd been drilled through my skull. Astrally, though, I was able to follow that thought with a certain amount of detachment.

"I tried to get into Lisa's room, but it felt like I'd stuck a penny in an electrical socket."

"Of course. That means it's protected. Our shaman is very capable. He sealed the rooms to prevent them from being contaminated."

Contaminated by what? And what was a shaman, anyway? I was sickened by the idea that I'd imprinted on the talent and level system that had been created by a government that wanted to milk my own talent at any cost.

Astral Lady planted her hands on her hips and looked at me funny. "Have we met before?"

"I doubt it."

"Are you sure? Something about the way you're scowling is awfully familiar."

I shook my head.

"Maybe not in the physical…but it's possible we've had this conversation before and we just don't remember it. Plenty of people project, but it takes talent and a lot of training to remember the trip."

"I've had all the training I care to have, thank you very much. And I'm sure we haven't met. I'm not local."

"You were worried about Lisa and you found yourself outside her room. Distance really isn't an issue—which you'd know if you just took a basic course."

"You seem pretty keen on training."

"Well, I would hope so. It's my life's work."

People tended to get pretty prickly if they thought you were impugning their "life's work," but I had to press. Besides, if you're going to fall out of your body, you could run across a lot worse than a Psych trainer. Even one wearing astral Birkenstocks. "If you're the pro, then tell me. Where's my silver cord?" I looked down at her midsection, and now that I was searching for it, there it was. It glowed gently, and it looked less substantial than she did. "You've got one. Where's mine?"

"Don't worry." She pointed at my head. "You just can't see it. Your third eye's connected to a thick rope of power." She floated up closer and squinted at it. "Lots of power. Two strands, all wrapped together. Someone's looking out for you, someone very strong."

I clapped my hand to my forehead, thinking maybe I could feel this astral power cable. I couldn't. "Really? You sure?"

"You don't know? Or you don't remember. These types of things don't just happen for no reason. You must have participated in some sort of ritual, or you're carrying an expensive charm." Astral Lady took a good look at my silver cord, and followed it upward. Her gaze stopped there as if an image of the Virgin Mary had appeared in one of the water stains in the ceiling. "Would you look at that?"

I looked up, too. I still didn't see any cord.

"The whole ceiling's lit up," she said.

It was? It looked awfully dark to me. Maybe the difference in our perception was one of those slippery things she'd mentioned before, something you don't notice is missing until you need it. Or maybe I should have broken that Valium in half.

She grabbed me by the shoulder. Disturbingly, it felt like a physical hand…except, it kind of didn't. "Let's go see what's up there."

"No, it's okay—"

I might have had a supercharged powercord coming out of my forehead, but Astral Lady was obviously a veteran at controlling her subtle bodies. She pulled me along like Jacob does when I'm dawdling too long at the grocery store, and he gets in front of the cart and hauls it like a team of oxen.

We flew up through the ball pit of the ceiling and into my room so fast it was as if we were astrally greased. We emerged in the sea of furniture. I stood partially in the spare bed, with one foot in the tiny open aisle. Astral Lady was directly in front of the GhosTV. "Here—here's what's glowing."

Maybe it was glowing a bit around the tube, like the old-fashioned sets used to when you turned them off in the dark.

"It's beautiful," she said.

Interesting, maybe. But beautiful? No doubt we were each looking through a different astral lens.

"There's some heavy energy here. But whose room is—?" She looked around, blinking at the extra bed and all the crap stacked on top of it, and then, finally, she turned toward the bed and paused.

There we were, Jacob and me. We weren't exactly spooning anymore. It looked more like he'd taken a sudden header and pinned me to the bed, where I decided it was futile to try to squeeze out from under him, so I might as well surrender and get some shut-eye myself.

Now that I knew to look at my forehead, I finally spotted it: my silver cord. It flickered like a hologram—now you see it, now you don't—but when I tilted my head just so, I saw even more. A thread of red wound through it, a vibrant streak that was more solid and opaque than my shimmery cord. That thread originated in Jacob's solar plexus.

I turned to ask Astral Lady about it, but she was staring at the opposite bed, the still-made bed brimming with clutter. Then she looked back at our bodies crammed into one bed. "Who are you? Who is he? Why are you in Bob's room?" Except she didn't say "Bob." I don't know what she said.

"I can't very well introduce myself here, can I?"

"What're you doing?"

"Sleeping?"

She stared for a moment, then said, "Oh, you're gay."

Well, that might explain the large man on top of me.

"That's not a value judgment," she said. "I voted 'no' on Proposition Eight."

That last word was more of a mushy sound, but I assume she'd said Proposition Eight. Unless she thought her stance on wind power mattered to me one way or the other.

"I just thought, the way your silver cords were connected, maybe it was some sort of…ritual." She seemed really embarrassed.

"Don't worry about it."

Still, she was so mortified, she'd gone pale—meaning, more transparent—and I was pretty sure she was about to bail on me...when instead she shot forward to the edge of the bed, flickered there like a jittery spirit, and got her face all up in my physical body.

"Step back," I said, before she could do anything scary like sneak into my flesh suit while I wasn't wearing it, and she flinched away like I'd physically slapped her. I hadn't meant it to come out quite so aggressive. It was just a cop-habit.

She did back off, some, but she was still staring at my physical body as if she'd seen a ghost. "Victor Bayne."

"Do I know you?" I was still using the I'm-gonna-kick-your-door-in tone of voice, but after the sound of all those non-words where names and numbers should have been, hearing my own name totally freaked me out.

She whirled around to face my astral body and said something very urgent to me. It sounded like…heck, I didn't know what it sounded like. It didn't even sound like words. "What?" I snapped.

She repeated herself. Again, nothing. She wailed, "Don't you recognize me?"

"Look, lady. I don't know who you are. If I met you at some Psych thing or I worked a case for you or whatever—I'm sorry. I don't remember."

A jumble of emotions played over her face—excitement, fear, agitation—and then, finally, understanding. "Wait a minute—I know why you can't hear what I'm saying. When you knew me, I went by the name *Faun Windsong.*"

◊ ◊ ◊

There was a sickening lurch. I opened my eyes. My mouth tasted terrible. And my lower back hurt like hell. Maybe I hadn't appreciated the freedom of being astral during the act itself, but now that I was once again prisoner in my chains of flesh, I recalled my OBE with more than a little longing.

I'd meant to wake Jacob and tell him what just happened, but I was exhausted—jetlagged and backachy and plain old wiped out, and before I knew it I was deeply, profoundly asleep.

After a few hours in the black pit of sleep, I stretched my legs to test the limits of my freedom, and when I found I could go all the way to the footboard, I enjoyed a moment of pure, unfettered relief. But then I realized that if I could stretch out to my full length, Jacob wasn't in bed with me.

I opened my eyes. Thankfully, I was still in the physical plane. Jacob was in the narrow center aisle with his arms outstretched, doing some kind of dramatic pose. Yoga. Tai Chi. Playgirl. Something like that.

"Hey," I said. My voice sounded gravelly, and I felt like I'd spent the night flailing around in a ball pit.

Jacob stopped posing and did a couple of neck rolls. "Hey. It's only five o'clock here. We're two hours off."

I sat up, experienced a twinge behind my glutes, and said, "I think I pulled something yesterday." Given my newfound neurosis about whether or not I was *athletic* enough for Buff Flexington over there, I was surprised I even admitted it. I was probably just distracted—because the thing that was really on my mind was my unscheduled flight in Astral Land.

Jacob perched on the edge of the too-small bed and rolled me onto my stomach. "Where does it hurt?"

"My back, my ass, all the way down my leg."

"Sciatic nerve. Which side?"

"Right."

He ran his thumbs over my lower back, firmly, but not hard, not yet.

It was easier to start talking when I wasn't looking at him. "So…about the TV."

"I've been thinking about that," he said. "Maybe we should start with every dial at a baseline of five and go from there. Maybe there's some sort of tension that's created when one dial is high and another is low, a tension that's not there when everything's the same."

"Ow…no, don't stop. It hurts good." Jacob dragged his thumbs over the meat of my ass and dug them in. I saw stars, semi-good stars. "There," I managed, through the pain.

"Uh huh."

"Did we leave it on?"

The sickening yet sublime thumb pressure let up. "The TV? No." He realized he'd stopped rubbing and sank his thumbs into the muscle again. "Why?"

"You didn't have…dreams or anything?"

"Nothing special. Something about being late for a lecture I thought I'd dropped…but I was the age I am now, not nineteen. And Carolyn was there. She was kind of my sister, though." He trailed off. The massage grew rhythmic, as if his attention had gone back to his dream in search of another detail or two he might recall. Once the massage had become truly excruciating, it stopped, hurt more for a moment, then felt blissful. "Why? What did you dream?"

"I'm not totally sure."

He rolled me onto my back and pushed my knees to my chest, and I gasped at the pain of the stretch—which gave me a second to figure out how to tell him. Why didn't I just come right out and say it, anyhow? The GhosTV must have done something to me that made me project. Either it did something permanent to me while we were twisting the knobs, or it worked simply from being plugged in, whether or not we thought it was actually on.

But I knew why I didn't start getting into any of that. Jacob had been in the room, too. He'd been wrapped right around me, protecting me, while I was the one cavorting in the astral with my old nemesis Faun Windsong, while I was the one playing in the ball pit. Frankly, Jacob was lucky he'd gone as long as he had without meeting Camp Hell's most arrogant medium—and the ball pit left a lot to be desired. Even so, he'd feel gypped. Personally, I wouldn't—but I've always been content to sit out the rides that made me puke.

Jacob took hold of my calf and crossed my right leg over my left. He pushed both legs toward my chest. The leg-crossing aspect of the stretch found the muscle group Jacob had been thumbing like a pain-seeking missile.

It shouldn't have come as any big surprise to me that Jacob always knew how to massage my hurts away. He was accustomed to putting his body through its paces, and then dealing with the results of it. How often did his rigorous training—which verged on self-abuse at times, if you asked me—result in soreness, stiffness, knots, or worse? Probably more often than I realized.

He didn't show it, though. Never. Jacob, limping around, favoring something that he'd pulled? Not only had I never seen it, I couldn't even picture it. And yet it didn't take an empath to know that my man of steel had plenty of soft spots just waiting to be jabbed. In the same way he'd picked up the ability to analyze the micro-expressions of a liar, I'd figured out how to gauge the level of his hurt disappointment by the depth and breadth of the vertical line between his eyebrows. Knowing that I'd been gallivanting through the astral while he'd been benched on the sidelines? It didn't take a genius to figure out it would sting to hear it.

But knowing that I'd lied to him? That wouldn't pain him any less. Damn it all.

I tried to figure out how to tell him, but it was like being ordered to chop off someone's body parts and trying to gauge the least horrible appendage to start with. Maybe it would help to blame the electronics, or at least it wouldn't make me look like as much of a jerk. "See, the TV…while we were asleep—"

Footfalls thundered down the hall, and then urgent voices sounded through the door. Jacob was on his feet and climbing over the spare bed in under a second. I scrambled to get my pants on.

Jacob unlocked the door and pulled it open, not as dramatically as he would have if his own body wasn't blocking its swing, but still fast. "Is there a problem?"

"Sir? Oh, I…I'm sorry to wake you so early. I just had the strongest impression that there was something really important in this room."

Faun Windsong. Oh joy.

Chapter 16

I stepped over the corner of the spare bed, still buttoning the waistband of my pants, and said, "Hey, Faun."

"How do you know that name?" Faun Windsong looked pretty much like she had in the astral—maybe ten pounds heavier and a few generations more Caucasian, but I could have picked her out of a lineup, no problem. What about me, though? Did I look that different?

It had been my physical body she'd recognized from the astral, though. So Miss I'm-The-Trainer must not have remembered.

"It's me. Victor Bayne."

"Victor…Bayne?" She slipped past Jacob, drawn to me like I was a ghost she'd spotted on a Psych aptitude test. "Wow…it is you. My name is Katrina Wojtowicz now."

"You don't remember…?" I glanced sideways at Jacob to see if he'd intuited "astral projection" from whatever I wasn't saying. He cocked an eyebrow. Damn it all. I'd really wanted to tell him alone.

She clasped both of my hands with both of hers and jerked them up and down, and I wondered if that's the way hippies were greeting one another these days. "Victor Bayne. Wow. It's been such a long time. When did you get here?"

"Yesterday. We're, ah…we're looking for Lisa. She's my friend."

"She's my friend, too." She sounded exactly like she had in the astral. Exactly. Only it wasn't as if the conversation was a continuation of the one we'd had outside our bodies. It was totally new to her.

"But how are you in the room that those…wait a minute. Are you still in the PsyCop program?"

"That's what the license says."

She looked me up and down, and I felt profoundly shirtless. "It hasn't changed you much. You don't look much older than you did when we were at Heliotrope Station."

Yeah, well, I wore my damage on the inside. "Thanks. You look great, too." She'd changed as much as Richie and Stefan, which was to say, if I didn't know any better, I wouldn't have recognized her.

"So you walk through murder scenes and look for cold spots?"

"Not exactly."

"And you thought you might find something here—what, some kind of clue?"

She said the word *clue* as if she was humoring me. What the fuck did she know? While she was busy traipsing around PsyTrain in her organic cotton yoga pants, I'd been putting three dozen wristlocks on a jerk named Sando so a criminal couldn't sue me for hurting him with my handcuffs. So she had no business taking that tone with me. "If you don't mind," I said, "I need to get dressed."

Jacob nudged her back across the threshold, shut the door and turned toward me. I reached across the corner of the mattress that separated us, and ran my hand along his forearm. "Last night, I went out of my body: you know, astral projection, like. I think it was the GhosTV's fault. I ran into her—Faun Windsong, I guess she's Katrina Somebody now, however they bribed her into changing her name—but remember, I told you when I knew her back at Camp Hell. She's a medium. And she came up here through the floor with me and said the GhosTV was glowing."

It wasn't exactly the "you lied to me" look that Jacob gave me…but it was still pained. "Don't you think you could have told me this fifteen minutes ago?"

"I was going to."

"You've been awake for how long? We could have put together a game plan. What were you waiting for?"

For the right words to miraculously occur to me—but I couldn't tell him that, so instead I said, "I was in the middle of starting to tell you about it."

He cut his eyes to the doorway. Through the gap at the bottom I could see two points of shadow, like she was standing there with her face pressed against the door just waiting for us to finish our conversation so she could rejoin it and have the final say on everything. I pulled a fresh shirt out of the garment bag and put it on. "I have a feeling," I said. Quiet. So someone with their nose against the door would have trouble hearing it.

Jacob gave me a tiny "go on" nod.

"They're not telling us something."

Jacob smiled—and he's not one for rolling his eyes, but he almost did. He was no stranger to questioning subjects who were hiding something from him.

I indicated the GhosTV with my eyes. "If that thing makes me project, and if I can figure out how to use it, I can poke through this place all I want and no one'll be any the wiser."

Jacob eased forward so that when he spoke, his voice was out of range of the door. "Won't someone astral see you?"

"If they do, they won't remember. I saw Faun Windsong last night and she has no idea—and she's the teacher."

Jacob eyed me. "Okay."

"The hard part of getting astral is staying that way without snapping back into your body—and thanks to the GhosTV, I can stay astral for a long stretch of time, no problem. Faun's so full of herself she underestimates everyone. I could probably do some research on OBE basics, get up to speed on projecting, and sneak under the wire—and if she does catch me, I'll play dumb."

"Is that…safe? What about that scumbag Barnhardt at Rosewood—what if you run into someone like him, someone who's up to no good?"

I doubted someone like him would have their very own psychic bodyguard curled around them like I did, though I couldn't quite figure out how to tell Jacob about that red ribbon of power snaking through my silver cord without sounding like some kind of parasite. "I'll be astral, too. And I've been sucking white light, huge amounts of it, since the Clinton administration. I think I could handle anything any astral sonofabitch could throw at me."

He wanted to say no. Not because he didn't think I was psychically strong. We both knew that while I might not be able to pick up the barbell he bench-pressed without the aid of a forklift—in the non-physical realms, if anyone could hold their own, it was me. He was scared because if I did it, I'd have to do it alone.

I leaned over the mattress, took his face in both of my hands, and pressed a kiss to his mouth. Believe me, I'm under no illusion that I can sway someone as determined as Jacob with something as fleeting as a kiss. I just wanted to feel his solidity, his presence, and let him know that I damn well appreciated him—besides, it was the only way I could figure out to tell him, in that half a second we had to ourselves, that I wasn't alone. He was with me.

His mustache and beard brushed over my lips, and beneath the whiskers, his mouth. Full. Warm. Gentle, since I'd caught him by surprise.

"We'll work out the details later," I said with our mouths still touching. "Right now, I want to keep my edge. That means keeping her away from the GhosTV."

Jacob caught my arms by the wrists and pulled my hands from his face. He placed a kiss on the backs of my fingers—firmly on my good hand, and gentle as a butterfly's wing on the hand that had been scraped to hamburger. He nodded, once, then turned and opened our door.

When Faun Windsong tried to elbow in again, he blocked her like a defensive lineman. "Ms. Wojtowicz?" He offered his hand in lieu of entrance to our room. "Jacob Marks, Chicago P.D. You'll have to excuse me, my badge is on the nightstand—and the nightstand is behind an impassable wall of furniture."

"I don't need to see your badge. Bert told me who you are." Her eyes darted from Jacob to the negative space in the doorway—but unless she could spew her astral body out as she was speaking to him, there'd be no way for her to get past him. "If we could just—"

"We have a lot to discuss. Over coffee? Somewhere we can all sit down?"

"But I was hoping Mister Bayne could tell me—"

"Detective Bayne," Jacob corrected.

I did my best not to smirk. It blows my "Don't mind me, I never notice anything," smokescreen when I give in to smirkiness.

"Give us ten minutes to get dressed," Jacob said, and then, to drive home the fact that he was *telling* and not asking, closed the door before Faun acquiesced.

◊ ◊ ◊

I resisted an urge to draw an anarchy symbol in the margin of my shiny new green notebook. Barely.

See, when I'd suggested during our crack-of-dawn coffee meeting that in my line of work I might benefit from a few sessions of Astral Projection 101, I hadn't anticipated that PsyTrain actually *offered* that specific class. Nor that they would take me seriously and invite us to join in.

"It's the curse of having such a deadpan delivery," Jacob murmured to me. He, by the way, was not beyond smirking.

The classroom wasn't like any kind of classroom I'd ever seen before. No chalkboards, no desks. But talk about chairs—any kind of ergonomic chair you might want to sit in, they had one. And even still, most of the students were sitting on the floor, on mats and cushions, in their bare feet.

I didn't want to sit on the floor. You couldn't stand up fast from the floor. Not with a bitchy sciatic nerve. Plus it'd be the surest way to make my holster dig into my ribs.

"Don't you just have a regular chair?" I said.

Faun Blowhard Katrina Windsong Wojtowicz looked around the room and pointed out something that didn't seem terribly comfortable, but at least didn't look like some updated Medieval torture device. "You might be more relaxed if you took off your shoes." I made no move to take off my shoes, and she added, "Euro-Americans carry so much tension at the backs of their knees."

What?

"Take a deep breath, and relax."

I breathed pointedly in and out in hopes of getting her to pick on someone other than me, but she was as persistent as Sando.

"Your problem is, you're breathing in your chest."

Someone needed an anatomy lesson.

Jacob and I sat, then—in chairs—and Faun Windsong said, "Let's all start with some breathing. In twice through the nose, hold two counts, out twice through the nose and mouth." She and the class did a sniff-sniff-pause-huff-huff thing, and since Jacob was playing along, so did I. Once we were done breathing, Faun said to me, "When you exhale, it's not a *ha* sound. It's more of a *huh* sound."

Huh was pretty much summing up my experience.

Sitting down seemed to divert Faun Windsong's attention from me, and she started her lecture. Finally, something I could use, something other than stupid chairs and *huh*-breathing through my knees. Faun Windsong turned to a small whiteboard on a tripod and wrote the words *physical - astral - ethereal*, and Jacob and me—we cracked open our notebooks. Jacob's not a doodler. He's a pen-fiddler. He twirled it, he tapped it against his chin, and he even mouthed the end a few times—like it wasn't hard enough for me to focus. Jacob got into what she was droning on about—something to do with the body/mind connection, and the silver cord. I got it. But I was busy thinking that now Lisa was four days gone, and it failed to hold my attention.

The rest of the class, eight other purported psychics, many of whom I'd spied on while they were asleep in their beds, listened with rapt attention. Really? I mean, what was there to say about the silver cord? It might or might not be visible. It might connect to your solar plexus, or your third eye—or maybe even your big toe, depending on your own particular psychic makeup. It did exist. I knew that much. I'd seen it in action, back when Jacob fed the rapist Barnhardt an antipsyactive and it reeled him back to his own stroke-riddled physical body like a gigantic fishing line.

Interesting stuff? I guess. But Faun had been talking about it for over half an hour, no lie, and she hadn't yet said a single thing I didn't already know. In fact, I'd experienced it all myself, and I understood it on a gut level, minus all the blah-blah-blah.

My pen tip clacked against the spiral notebook spine and I looked down, unaware that I'd even been doodling. Loopy-looking squiggles, repetitive, random. No anarchy symbols. I drew one, very small, to see how it felt. It didn't resonate with me. I wasn't a twenty-something tough guy with a mohawk anymore.

I missed it more on principle than in practice, this old me. It felt good to be able to fade into the background now, if I needed to. My badge and my gun were also pretty good consolation prizes. And I suppose we all need to grow up, sooner or later.

"Any questions?" Faun/Katrina asked. She looked around the room, hands on hips, and settled her gaze right on me.

I pressed into the chair and tried to seem not quite so tall.

One of the other psychics, an Asian guy around thirty, said, "In Friedmann's primer, it states that astral matter is bound to its physical counterpart by fine-particle vibrations. If the silver cord is a manifestation of those particles, does that mean if you damage the cord, you'll die?"

"It hasn't been proven. Marie Saint Savon mentions a *cordon* in one of her later interviews that she sees dissolve at the moment of death, but since that could also translate into 'ties,' she might be speaking metaphorically."

Her overly-French pronunciation of *cordon* made me want to slap her.

"A researcher in Glasgow seeking to disprove the cut-cord theory attempted to sever his own cord, but he only achieved lucid projection four times over the year-long experiment—and in those four successful projections, he tried pulling it, biting it, and even cutting it with an astral knife."

Astral knife. Cool band name.

"Each time, the substance of the cord flowed around the obstacle and reassembled itself. Something like mercury." Faun turned toward her whiteboard and wrote with her stinky blue marker: *mercury - quicksilver - silver cord.*

"Quicksilver," she said in a voice so patronizing it made me wince, "was the alchemical name for the element mercury, so theoreticians now believe this was how the silver cord got its name."

I was dying to close my eyes and think of anything other than Faun Windsong, but the group was too small, and if I was too obvious about zoning out, everyone would know.

"Most practitioners agree that the silver cord itself can't be cut. It is, as you say, a manifestation of the connection—but it isn't the connection itself."

I glanced at Jacob. Completely and utterly absorbed. Laser focus. Cripes, what I wouldn't give to be able to force myself to pay attention on command. At least if he was drinking it all in, I wouldn't have to. And it wasn't as if I wasn't attempting to listen—I was. Really.

"The first stage of an OBE is often the point at which a projection fails. Subjects in this transitional stage often report hearing clanging bells or feeling strong vibrations."

She went on to describe a dozen other things an unsuccessful astral traveler might experience fighting to free themselves, and more importantly their consciousness, from the prison of their flesh. "Many practitioners, when they do finally achieve projection, find they can't see—ironic, isn't it, since the astral body is known as the body of light. Either they experience their vision as if they're looking through a semi-opaque blindfold, or their eyes won't open at all."

Her gaze swept the room and landed on me again. I wondered if some part of her remembered that I'd had trouble opening my astral eyes my first time out.

"Why were you quoting Marie Saint Savon?" I blurted out instead, before it even occurred to me I had a question, let alone that I was verbalizing it.

Faun scowled. "Why wouldn't I?"

"She was a medium. Since when does that make her an authority on astral projection?" I sounded pissy, and I knew it, but I just couldn't hold back. The other students shifted uncomfortably. A few of them might've even held their breath.

"*Detective* Bayne," she announced to the class, "is understandably busy doing his police work, so he's not quite up to speed on the details of academia like we are here at PsyTrain." She turned and wrote something on the board, and then turned back around, blocking it with her body, to gloat.

"In January, the Center for Psychic Studies recommended the medium ability be reclassified to include not only psychics who could sense spirit activity, but shamans, remote viewers, and soul travelers, as well. Our ability has a new title." She stepped aside and revealed the words *light workers.*

"You're shitting me."

Her eyes went flinty at my failure to bow to her authority on All Things Psychic. "No doubt even the Midwest will get up to speed…one of these days."

The class began to snigger in response, but the amusement died fast when they looked at Jacob and me, cop-faced in our suits, and couldn't figure out which authorities they should be trying to toady up to: the teacher or the law.

"That wraps up the morning session. We'll meet back at one thirty in the floatation tank room for two shifts of focused breathing exercises. Bring your journals and your colored pen sets for your out-of-the-tank time."

Floatation tank? As in, sensory deprivation? My throat closed, and sweat prickled my low back where it curved away from the back of the chair.

Faun looked at me, smiling, as if she could hear my adrenal glands pouring fight-or-flight juice into my veins. "You're welcome to join us for a float, detectives."

Jacob looked at me and raised his eyebrows as if he was perfectly game to try it. Maybe he really was fearless. "No thanks," I muttered, barely restraining myself from telling her to shove her sensory deprivation tanks up her ass sideways. "We've got work to do."

Chapter 17

"I ain't no fucking light worker," I muttered in Jacob's ear as we headed back to our room to regroup. I'm not sure what I was so pissed off about. The suggestion that I was stupid because I didn't know about the crazy reclassification? Or the implication that I was a coward for not wanting to be locked in a coffin full of tepid water? Or both. "And 'soul traveler' is a ridiculous name for someone who projects."

"So as not to confuse them with the guys who run the films at the theater," Jacob said. I think he was smiling. Just judging by the back of his head.

"Y'know, maybe I have better things to do than to read all the journals and crap. All the junk mail, and the spam…who can keep up with it?"

"I hadn't read about it, either. I would have mentioned something."

"Right." Of course. Why follow anything myself when I could count on Jacob to follow it for me? "I know."

He opened the door, and a piece of furniture or two threatened to topple out of the room. We closed the door behind us and climbed over the spare bed. Jacob put his notebook on the nightstand and loosened his tie. I almost slammed my notebook onto the GhosTV, but caught myself at the last second and ended up pitching it underhand toward the bed. Its pages flew open like a dove flapping its way free from a magician's top hat.

"Don't get discouraged," he said.

"I'm not discouraged."

"You let her tone of voice get under your skin. Relax. Separate the information from the delivery; there's a lot you could learn from her."

"About what? The existence of a silver cord? Duh." I squeezed into the bathroom and unwrapped my hand. It had scabbed over valiantly. Now all I had to do was stop myself from opening the wound by making a fist. And punching Faun Windsong with it. Or Constantine Dreyfuss—either one would do.

"You get distracted pretty easily. You seem to have trouble focusing."

"Tell me something I don't know."

"I wonder if you have ADD."

Cripes. I needed more acronyms associated with my mental condition like I needed to lose another ten pounds and then book a vacation at a nude beach. "I do not have attention deficit disorder. That's just something the pharmaceutical companies made up to sell more Ritalin."

"And 'in your day' hyperactive kids were smacked into submission with the back of teachers' hands."

"Well...yeah. They were." I ran cool water over my scabbed knuckles. The cold stung for a moment, and then it felt good. Itchy, but good. "You too, right?" He was only six years older than me, but I couldn't resist. "Or did they make them stay after school to clean the clay tablets and sharpen the styluses?"

I turned off the water and blotted my hand on the towel. No new bleeding. That was good. No zinger forthcoming from Jacob, either. That was... unusual. He always gave back as good as he got, and then some.

I peeked around the doorjamb. Jacob was seated on our bed with my notebook in his hands, flipping pages, scowling.

"That anarchy symbol...it's a long story. It's nothing."

"Vic...."

"It's stupid. Just ignore it." Great. Had I written a single note? A sentence or two at the beginning of the lecture, but after that, nothing. More proof that I was mentally deficient. My stomach sank. Just when I thought I couldn't possibly disappoint myself any more, I found a new low to sink toward. Maybe the Ritalin would be tasty, I told myself. But even that failed to cheer me up.

"You wrote this?"

"They offered me a pre-doodled notebook, but I turned it down since I'm a hands-on kinda guy."

He jerked his head toward the bed. "C'mere a minute. Sit down."

I dropped down beside him, probably harder than I needed to. The bedframe creaked.

Jacob spread the notebook half on his thigh and half on mine, with the spiral spine between us. Two solid pages full of loop-de-loops. "You wrote this today?"

"I thought we already established that she didn't exactly inspire my rapt attention."

"Don't you see it?"

I looked down at my doodles again. Was there some sort of course on doodle analysis he'd taken at the Twelfth Precinct? I wouldn't have put it past him—he always goes for the extra credit. No doubt it had also taught him that guys who fill up pages of their new notebooks with loops have adult ADD.

"What?" I snapped.

He pressed his fingertip against the page, and whispered, "Words."

I lifted the page closer and began to formulate a jab about *someone* needing a prescription for reading glasses...and then I saw it, too.

nononononononono....

Two fucking pages of nothing but *no.*

My skin crawled as if it wanted to peel itself off my body and slink under the spare bed. I flipped back to the first few pages. My doodles had started as a bunch of nothing—other than the tiny Anarchy symbol up in the corner which, I remembered, had *felt* entirely wrong. And that symbol, with the pen pressure and the slant, actually looked like it had been drawn by a different person than the one who'd looped the loops. Except it was me. I remembered doing it. All of it.

The first several lines were filled with loops, which after a while grew shorter and rounder, and then flipped upside down. Once they firmly looked like letter-o's, they scrawled and spread, line by line, until they turned into scallops. Next page. More scallops. Then scallop-scallop-dip, which eventually tightened up into letter-n's. *Nnnn.* Finally, after a few wobbly attempts, the word *no* appeared, plain as day.

And kept on appearing for three more pages.

"I don't suppose it might say *on,*" Jacob suggested.

"Probably not." I squinted at the GhosTV. "Unless it was trying to tell me to turn that thing on." I checked the pages. "But every single line starts with a letter-n. So I'm going with *no.*"

"Karen Frugali," he ventured. "Lisa's roommate. Bert said she was a light worker."

I sensed his line of reasoning was headed somewhere so nasty I couldn't even bring myself to mock the title. "You're thinking she was astral, and she was moving my arm?"

"Not astral. If she was able to get her astral arm into somebody and send a message, wouldn't she have done it by now? I think it has to do with you. You're a…medium. What if she's dead?"

My stomach bottomed out and I swallowed back the urge to heave—because if Frugali was dead, then Lisa…well, I just couldn't think it. I'm not superstitious or anything—I don't think my thoughts manifest into reality just because I've thought them. But even so. I was not prepared to go there.

"Vic." Jacob put his hand over mine. He clasped it more toward the wrist instead of the backs of my fingers, but even so, the gentle pressure of his hand tightened my skin, and pain radiated from the layers of scabs across the backs of my knuckles. "Keep it together. We need to work fast."

"Okay. Yeah. I know it." What I didn't know was what, exactly, working fast would entail. My typical method was to find ghosts and talk to them—or let them talk at me. It usually worked. Except when it failed spectacularly. "But how?"

Jacob's gaze slid to the GhosTV. "We figure out how to work it."

"I'm sure Dr. Chance would be thrilled to help me."

After considering that for a moment, Jacob said, "She's in Dreyfuss' office. You have Dreyfuss here. And a plane."

"What? It'll take half a day to get there and back. If she's even willing to talk to me. If she's even still there."

"Do you think Richie would be able to make her cross over if she wasn't ready?"

Hell, I didn't know if even *I* could make her go toward the light. I restricted my exorcism efforts to repeaters. I knuckled my eye in frustration and ended up splitting one of the new scabs, and blood seeped out. Great.

If I refused, Jacob would think I was putting my loathing of Dreyfuss and the idea of spending eight more hours in a Learjet with him ahead of my desire to see Lisa safe and sound—and while that *was* how I felt, my hesitation went a lot deeper. Some simmering gut instinct that told me chasing after Dr. Chance was a big waste of time—one that we couldn't afford.

Jacob put his arm around me and said, "I wish someone could give Dr. Chance a spirit cell phone so you could call her and see how the TV works."

That sent my mind spinning. If I sent a fax, she could read it…but then how could she communicate anything back to me? Through Richie? Don't get me wrong, I'm crazy about Richie, but figuring out how to work through him would probably take longer than flying to Chicago and back.

Maybe someone at PsyTrain had a trick up their sleeve. It would have to be a hell of a trick. But supposedly everyone here was psychic. Right?

"Too bad," Jacob mused, "The only two people who knew how to work the GhosTV are dead."

Wait a minute. I seized his hand so suddenly I left a smear of blood on it. "You're a fucking genius." I leapt up from the bed, charged through the bathroom and pounded on the door to Dreyfuss' room.

"Okay, okay, keep your pants on." Dreyfuss opened the door at arm's length so I didn't have an excuse to knock on his skull. Typical Dreyfuss—track suit, ponytail, and a platinum Rolex just this side of gangsta-bling. "You got something?"

"I dunno—maybe *you've* got something. There was a third guy on the GhosTV team, the guy with the crewcut who played the world's most surly B&B owner. What happened to him?"

"Jeffrey Alan Scott." The info was right at the tip of his tongue. He hadn't even blinked. "Mr. Scott is the Feds' guest at the Metropolitan Correctional Center for 25 to 40, but he could always parole sooner for good behavior."

"Did anyone ask him how the GhosTV works?"

"Lots of people asked him lots of things. Lots and lots."

Pain shot through my knuckles. I hadn't realized I'd been so keen to pop him one I was making a fist. My blood dripped to the floor, dark red splatters against the octagonal vintage tile. I heard the clatter of Jacob pulling a hank of toilet paper off the roll to wipe it up.

I breathed and did my best to stay calm, and in my most reasonable voice, said to Dreyfuss, "We need to be able to work this thing."

He nodded. "I honestly wasn't trying to be a prick when I said that I figured you already had it down pat. Who would know better how it worked than the only guy strong enough to actually see the results? You say it's important? Okay. I'll see what I can do."

Just like that? Wow.

As he turned to retreat, someone started hammering on the room's front door. "Vic?" Faun Windsong. Or whatever her name was. Katrina. "Are you in there?"

"Yeah?"

"Did you want to come down for lunch in the staff dining room? You and Jacob?"

Jacob looked to Dreyfuss and said quietly, "What about you? You want in?"

"Nah, I've got a fetish for white bread and pudding cups. Plus I've got a phone call or thirty to make. Enjoy your carob and sprouts."

Katrina/Faun was a wall of chatter I tuned out from the moment we left our room to the instant we walked through the dining room door and found everyone staring at us. The staff lounge was quite a bit smaller than the cafeteria where we'd cooled our heels waiting for the rooms to be shuffled when we'd first arrived. Not small and cozy, though. Small and opulent.

We made the rounds of introductions. A telepath, an empath, a bookkeeper, two precogs (one specializing in dreamwork), and holy crap—a bona fide telekinetic. Everyone was an instructor, except the bookkeeper. Although I suppose it wouldn't hurt for a Psych to learn how to balance his checkbook.

A member of the kitchen staff took our order. It was kind of like being at a fancy wedding; we had a choice of vegetarian souvlaki or salmon. Here I'd thought Dreyfuss was being a smartass when he'd made his carob and sprouts comment. I went for the salmon. And I wondered exactly how familiar Con Dreyfuss was with PsyTrain.

"We weren't clear," Jacob said, smoothing the napkin over his lap, "what Karen Frugali was studying."

"Mediumship," said the dream coach, but Katrina/Faun corrected her with, "Light worker skills," before she'd even finished the last syllable of the word.

I took a drink of water and tried to size up the dream coach without being too obvious. She was younger than the rest of the staff, maybe thirty, with dyed red hair in a rockabilly ponytail and Marilyn Monroe eyeliner. There were a few extra pounds on her that she carried mostly in her midsection, though her plunging neckline and a heavy-duty pushup bra would draw the eyes of any straight man well away from her muffin top.

Everyone else at PsyTrain was in the forty-and-up granola demographic. Maybe dream girl wouldn't mind talking to a couple of PsyCops from Chicago.

If we could ever figure out how to see her without Faun butting in. "I'll bet you were surprised to find your old friend from Heliotrope Station here," Faun said to me.

Jacob caught my eye and quirked his eyebrow ever so slightly. I might not have said it out loud, and he might not be a telepath, but he seemed to hear *Which friend would that be?* loud and clear.

"I would never have pictured you as a cop," she said, "but, you know, I think it suits you pretty well. You look good. You look happy."

"Thanks."

The kitchen guy wheeled out the tray of lunches. The salmon looked too fancy for institutional food, more at par with something Jacob would have cooked up at home as a way of saying, *I'm sorry I stood you up at that party where all my friends were flexing so hard you could barely fit in the room with their delts.*

"I wonder sometimes," she droned on, "how my life would have been different if I would have accepted that PsyCop job."

If…what? Wait a minute.

"At the time it seemed like so much money, you know? Enough to tempt even you. We were all surprised you'd left Ste—" she cut her eyes to Jacob, then started the sentence over. "I mean, you just didn't strike any of us as a cop. You know?"

I stuffed some salmon into my mouth. It was okay. A bit on the dry side.

"But obviously it agrees with you. Really, you look terrific." She slid her gaze to Jacob again as if she thought he was a pretty good catch, too. Or maybe just to imply that the decoy bed wasn't fooling anyone.

"Thanks."

"It makes sense to put someone who's not quite so sensitive out there in the field where they're vulnerable to all the negative energy that comes with the job. Accidents, killings and whatnot…."

Whatnot? What the fuck was *whatnot*? "Just homicide," I said. "I'm a homicide detective. Not a beat cop." I was starting to get testy, and it carried in my voice. The bookkeeper and the empath were murmuring to each other, and Jacob was trying to catch my eye and give me a "calm down" look.

The dream coach leaned across the gap between her table and mine and said, "You don't think anyone's been murdered. Do you?"

I chewed a hunk of flesh with a small, flexible bone inside, clipped the bone in half with my incisors, and swallowed it.

"We have no evidence of that," Jacob said smoothly. *Yet.* That was unspoken.

"Of course not," Katrina/Faun said. "Think about the combined talent of everyone in this room. Sensitive empaths and telepaths and precogs. If someone, one of us, met a violent end…we'd know. I'm sure of it."

Bert Chekotah stepped into the room and Katrina's gaze swung to him.

Her eyes went wide and glittery with awe, and she smiled as if the mere sight of him transported her to a blissful plane.

Chekotah, on the other hand, just looked frazzled. Sure, his bone structure was still model-perfect, but his eyes were bloodshot, his hair was parted funny as if he'd washed it and let it dry without combing it, and his linen suit was more rumpled than the last time I'd seen it. "What would we know?" he asked.

Katrina hopped up and got him a glass of water with a lemon slice in it from the beverage cart. "Don't worry about it now. Drink—you've been staying up 'til all hours. You're fatigued and dehydrated. Have some food. Let it go for a few minutes and let your subconscious work through your problems."

He dropped into the last empty chair—next to me—shook out a cloth napkin and let it fall across his lap. "I heard you sat in on one of our classes," he said as he dug into the basket of stone-ground whole grain rolls. "You're welcome to, of course. But how does that bring you any closer to finding Lisa?"

"We can't discuss an ongoing investigation," I said. It sounded funny coming from me, since it was usually Zig who was the mouthpiece.

"Sorry," Jacob said. He managed to make himself sound sincere. I suspected that as strange as it was for me to be sans-Zigler, it must be a refreshing change of pace for Jacob to be partnered with someone who didn't flinch every time he lied.

Jacob made small talk while we finished our salmon, and I tried to get a feel for the personalities—but I can't say I was cut out for the task. When she wasn't raiding the bread basket, Katrina talked over everyone else. They let her, though I couldn't tell if that was because telling her to shut up was useless, or if they were treading lightly around her because she was Chekotah's personal cheering section.

I did notice the dream coach leaned away from the other teachers when they spoke—if they could get a word in edgewise around Katrina—and that she even crossed her arms a time or two. Not a member of the love-in, that one.

Once Chekotah finished his veggie-topped mound of meat substitute, the kitchen guy rolled out a cart of desserts, which was exciting for a few seconds, until I realized it was mostly fruit. When he rolled up to me, I spied some cookies that had been well-hidden between the mango cups and the slightly green bananas. Chocolate chip. Nice.

I grabbed one and took a big bite. It had the wheaty dog biscuit taste of something that was way too healthy. Even the chocolate seemed gritty… and then I remembered Dreyfuss' parting words. "Is this carob?" I managed around a mouthful of abrasive roughage.

The kitchen guy nodded. "You want another one for later?"

"No thanks." Would anyone believe I was on a diet? Doubtful. "I'm watching my gluten."

He wrapped one in a napkin and handed it to me, beaming. "It's made with brown rice and spelt. Today's your lucky day."

Right.

Chapter 18

I washed down my mouthful of minimally-processed twigs with all of my water, and as I drained half of Jacob's glass too, my phone rang. I pulled it from my pocket and checked the caller. Crash. The Psych staff was regarding me with varying levels of annoyance for being gauche enough to let my phone ring at mealtime, except for the dream coach, who thought it was funny, and Chekotah, who looked too wrung-out to care. I let Crash leave me a message and set the phone to vibrate.

The teachers began pulling napkins off laps, draining herbal teas, and pushing away from the table. Quarter after one, almost time for afternoon classes to begin. My phone vibrated against the outside of my thigh. I ignored it, and stood to intercept the dream coach before she got away. "Listen, uh…."

"Debbie."

"Debbie. Do you have a few minutes?"

"We'll have to talk on my way to class."

I glanced at Jacob, who gave me a small nod as if to say we'd cover more ground if we split up, so I tagged along to Debbie's classroom. She walked fast for a girl, especially a girl in retro tango heels, and when we got to the elevator, I saw she was breathing fast. She jabbed the "close door" button for all she was worth, and then we were alone.

"What's going on?" I asked her.

"I just wanted to talk to you without the Stepford Hippies listening in. Lisa talked about you a lot. I want to help you, any way I can. She was one of my favorite students: smart, focused, and totally genuine. It is *not* like her to just up and leave without saying anything."

"What makes you think the administration shouldn't be in the loop?"

"The Katrina-and-Bert thing was gag-worthy enough before he stepped into the Director position…but now?" She curled her lip. "Now she's acting like she's the Assistant Director, just 'cos she's doing him."

I hadn't even realized that Faun and Chekotah were an official "thing," though in retrospect, the signs were pretty obvious. Not only had I glossed over it because it didn't have anything to do with finding Lisa, but more likely, I hadn't wanted to envision Faun Windsong "doing" anybody.

"Lisa was studying, uh…what do you call your technique?"

"Sleep Paths." She rolled her eyes. "I wanted to call it 'Dream Analysis,' but I guess it didn't test well in the over-45-with-too-much-money crowd."

"So what happens when you dream? Do you uh…go somewhere?"

She narrowed her eyes. "You are a Psych, aren't you? Lisa was pretty slim on the specifics, but she let it slip once that you were really good at what you do."

"I guess I'm not up on all the vocabulary." Either because I didn't want to pay attention, or because I couldn't. The thought of not being able to learn anything even if I should choose to apply myself made the spelt I'd consumed do a nauseous flip in my stomach.

The elevator stopped on the second floor, and Debbie jammed the "close door" button in with her thumb and held it. "Dreaming happens in your brain. It's a bunch of neurons firing—electricity."

"What's the difference between dreaming and astral projection?"

"I've never gone astral myself, but the current theory is a part of you does actually travel when you're projecting. Probably some kind of wave or particle we don't have the equipment to measure. Think about radios—they emit electromagnetic waves, and a hundred miles away, someone turns a dial and gets to hear that asshat Don Imus on the way to work. Projecting's kind of like that, but your body is like a radio station, the world is your airwaves, and the rest of the astral plane is your car stereo."

I dry-swallowed, and not just because jagged bits of spelt were stuck in my throat. Debbie's explanation made total sense, not just to my head, but to my gut. "You're a great teacher."

She tried to quell a smile. "That's what Lisa said, too."

"What do you know about—"

An alarm cut me off before I could ask her what the hell she might think my page full of *no no no* was all about.

"Damn it." She released the close door button and the elevator doors creaked open. A couple of forty-something women in muted earth-tone clothing stared into the elevator car.

They eyed me—the tall guy in the suit—with no little amount of skepticism. "Are you okay, Professor March?"

"Why wouldn't I be?" she said, in a tone a lot sassier than the one she used with me. We filed out of the elevator and the newbie Psychs trooped in. Debbie gave them an ironic salute as the elevator doors slid shut to cut off their concerned looks. We walked down a hall filled with students on their way to classes.

"Can we go somewhere to talk?" I asked her. "Maybe that Mexican restaurant across the street. I'll buy you a margarita."

"Can I take a rain check? I need to get to class."

"Okay."

"You want to sit in?"

"No, I uh…I would." I actually wanted to. Weird. I'd been in class all morning, but I'd be interested to hear what was on Debbie's lesson plan. Unfortunately, I didn't think deciphering that dream where my teeth crumbled would help my investigation any. "Can't you skip out? Give 'em a reading assignment and have someone write their names on the blackboard if they talk while you're gone?"

"Are you kidding me? One of them would go running to Katrina bitching about how I'd deprived them of the full value of their tuition." She checked her watch. "They've determined my time is worth something like ten dollars a minute—and I'm almost late as it is." She strode into the thick of the crowd. I spotted one or two goth-wannabes and a smattering of Earth mothers, but most of the crowd was a typical mix of people like you'd see waiting in line at the DMV.

It was possible that Debbie's being in a hurry could work to my advantage. A lot of times when you interview a subject, they give you all kinds of ridiculous details, thinking they'll add up to something like they do in a Sherlock Holmes book. Usually it turns out the first thing someone thinks is closer to the truth. Unless you count the zombie employment agency. I doubt that was first on anyone's list.

"Listen…real quick…what do you think is going on?"

She paused in the hallway, as students streamed around her and filtered into classrooms. Weighing her answer. Which meant she knew something—she just wasn't sure how she wanted to say it.

"It's complicated."

"You're gonna leave me hanging? Just like that?"

She began to turn, but paused again in the doorway to her classroom. It was a lot like Faun Windsong's classroom, in that there were no desks, no world maps, no bulletin boards with construction paper turkeys made from handprints on it. Just a bunch of weird chairs, a watercooler and a whiteboard. And a dozen annoyed students all glancing at their watches then looking back at Debbie.

I put my hands on my hips so my jacket slid open enough that my sidearm showed, and the students immediately found something else to stare at. "You can't just dangle something like that in front of me and then take it back. C'mon—what if it's important? Anything you can tell me is more to go on than what I've got now."

"All right. But not here."

She turned toward her classroom and I caught her sleeve. "I'm serious about that margarita." I sounded a little desperate. "I need to know more about automatic writing, too."

"Okay. Class runs 'til five. Let me look up a few things and I'll come find you."

She closed the door, and just like that, I was alone. I leaned against the wall and stared at the empty hallway that had been full of fresh-faced, optimistic Psychs just a minute before, and wondered how my life would have been different if I'd learned about my abilities in a place like this—maybe even from a teacher like Debbie—rather than Camp Hell.

What use was it, though? PsyTrain didn't exist then, Debbie was in high school—and the idea that psychic abilities were real was so new that even the "experts" didn't know what was what. And if I were really being honest with myself by adding a twenty-three-year-old me to the equation, even with a better facility, better teachers and better subject matter, it didn't add up to me graduating in the top tenth of my class.

Still, I could have done without the sleep deprivation and drug testing.

My phone buzzed against my thigh. I checked the readout. Crash. Again. How persistent of him. I might as well answer. "Hello?"

"What are you doing?"

"Uh…nothing."

"Are you at work?"

"Not exactly."

"Uh huh. Did you check your email today?"

"Uh…no."

"Okay. I didn't think so. D'you know if Mr. Perfect did?"

"I doubt it."

"Really? Doesn't he get all his ducks in a row before he suits up for his crimefighting gig?"

"We're not in Chicago."

"Oh-kaaaay. You win the vague-contest. I give up. What's the skinny?"

Honestly, did he have to use that particular expression? I lowered my voice and turned toward the wall, even though there was no one else in the hall anymore but me. "We're at PsyTrain, looking for Lisa."

"What do you mean, looking for her? She's not there?"

"No. And whatever's going on, it's a whole big…thing."

He gave a long, drawn-out sigh. "If there's anything I can do…."

"Automatic writing. You know anything about that?"

"It's a tool. Like tarot cards and candles and incantations."

Like the invocation of Thor and the big iron spike? That explanation didn't ring true at all. Not that I'd ever dare to challenge Crash's encyclopedic knowledge of all things psychic, but how could I possibly be using a tool I didn't know existed? "A tool for what?"

"It's old-school divination. Victorian Psychs used it to find pen pals among the spirits and demons and whatever other unseen forces they were looking to chat with."

"Demons? Come on. Isn't there anything else it's good for? Something more modern?"

"Like I told you: old-school. Kind of like Ouija boards."

The hair at the back of my neck prickled. Even I knew about Ouija boards. They sold them in same aisle as the Etch-a-Sketch when I was a kid. Not that we were ever privileged enough to have anything fancier than a beat-up garage sale copy of Sorry with half the pieces missing.

"It's all about focusing your energy—"

The thing with Crash is that he can't stand the idea that someone other than him might be right, which made it hard to bounce ideas off him. Plus, the tone he was taking with me had started to sound annoyingly like Faun Windsong. "I gotta go…we're kind of in the middle of things."

"Wait a sec—before you hang up. Tell Jacob his email is bouncing."

The remains of the carob-spelt cookie tickled at my uvula, and I swallowed down the urge to hurl. "Which email—work or home?"

"His Q-mail."

My mind scrambled to put together a perfectly logical and benign explanation as to why Jacob's personal email account would be full. Maybe his mother's camera got switched back to its default settings. Maybe Q-mail reduced size of its inbox in an effort to cut costs. Or maybe his spam filter was on the fritz.

Except I didn't buy it. Lisa's Q-mail filled up, and now she was gone. Cause, effect, or some weird step in between—it didn't matter. "I gotta go," I repeated, and I snapped my phone shut and took off at a run to go find Jacob.

I skidded to a stop in front of the elevator, but the car must have been headed down. The cables creaked, and the pointer on top went from the number 1 to the letter B—very, very slowly. I waited for a couple of seconds while the pointer sat there on "B", and then I decided the stairs would be quicker. I thundered down the back stairwell, through the main floor, across the public areas, down the side hall that led to the dorm area, and up some more stairs to the second floor rooms above the empty ones Lisa and her suite-mate had shared.

By the time the door to our room was in sight—ten minutes, tops—I'd already convinced myself that an Internet demon was traveling through Psychs' emails, squatting in their inboxes, and devouring them when they checked their messages. I'd love to say I've never seen anything that messed up, but once you've seen the things I've seen, almost none of your theories land in the "too weird" category anymore.

Once upon a time, I would have assumed Jacob was immune to weird shit that preyed on Psychs. Lucky Jacob. He was a Psych now, too.

I staggered to a stop in front of our door, and hammered hard on it like I was practicing to take the point position on a drug raid. "Jacob?"

"Vic? It's open."

Relief flooded me so fast I swayed on my feet—and only then did I realize how well and truly scared I'd been to think that the minute I'd taken my eyes off Jacob, something had happened to him. Something bad.

I pushed the door in and it opened a couple of feet and bumped the crate. Jacob and Dreyfuss stood in the narrow aisle between the beds, both of them facing the GhosTV. Both of them stared at me expectantly—and damn it, did it really have to be Dreyfuss there with us? Couldn't it have been anyone else? I wanted to send him back to his own room so I could talk to Jacob in private, but he wasn't just employed by the FPMP…he was the goddamn director of the entire Midwest division. If anyone could help us connect the dots, it was him. But if he was even interested in helping us, or if he was just using us to further his own obscure motives—that's the part I didn't know.

My gaze dropped to a sheet of paper in his hands. Hasty handwriting. Directions for working the GhosTV? It looked that way to me. He'd done it. He'd pried those directions out of an inmate in the Metropolitan Correctional Center in the time it took me to have lunch. Just like that.

It pained me to let Dreyfuss in on my secrets, honestly it did, but between the full inbox, the *no no no,* and the way my best friend was fucking *missing*, it didn't seem like I could afford not to trust him. "Jacob," I said, "your email is full. Just like Lisa's."

Chapter 19

Jacob and Dreyfuss both pulled out their cell phones at the same time. It took Jacob a few seconds to navigate to the web. Dreyfuss had his secretary on the phone before I could even blink. "Hey, Laura. See if you can find any kind of pattern about email filling up." He listened for a moment, then locked eyes with me and said, "Any particular type?"

"Q-mail."

"Those accounts are huge. They never get full." He turned away from me and went back to chatting with his disturbing secretary. "Q-mail. Uh huh. I know, right? See what you can find. Bye."

Dreyfuss disconnected, but Jacob was still thumbing the buttons on his phone. The vertical line between his brows was as sharp as I'd ever seen it. "I can't get in."

"Let's see your error message," Dreyfuss suggested. Jacob handed his phone over.

Dreyfuss frowned at the little screen. "That's a new one. I'll send a screenshot to Laura to see if she can make anything of it." His fingers flew over the little buttons in a weird thumb-forefinger-thumb combo, and he worked Jacob's phone as confidently as if he himself owned the very same model. "I'll get your storage space upped so we can get in there and unlock it, too."

He could do that? Q-mail wasn't government. It was some little open-source thingie up in Seattle—or so everyone thought. Jacob and I met eyes, but neither of us said it out loud.

There was a thoughtful pause in Dreyfuss' thumbing, and then he said, "I'll score you kids some laptops, while I'm at it. Make it a little easier to keep an eye on the web. What's your flavor, Windows or Mac?"

I was fairly sure that even in my mohawk stage, I'd never been arrogant enough to own a Mac. "Windows?"

"Right. You can always spot a lifelong municipal employee." He thumbed in a few dozen more characters. "Cool beans. Hopefully the GhosTV's electromagnetic field won't do a number on the motherboard."

For real? Maybe he was just being a wiseass, but I turned so the pocket that held my cell phone was facing away from the console, anyway.

Dreyfuss' phone rang, a subtle beep of a ringtone that I would have taken for a piece of electronics resetting itself in a nearby room if I didn't see him answer it. "Uh huh? Yeah." He juggled phones, handed Jacob's phone back to him, climbed over the corner of our bed, and headed toward his room via the bathroom without even a typical Dreyfuss parting smartass remark.

I grabbed a Valium out of my suitcase and dry-swallowed it. "I want us to stick together from now on," I said.

"Why? You don't want me talking to Dreyfuss behind your back? Damn it, Vic, if you don't trust me by now—"

"That's not it—not at all." I planted my hands on my hips and looked around the room without even making sense of the jumble of colors and textures of crap stacked upon crap. "If Dreyfuss can dig up GhosTVs and hack into your full email account and whatever else he's gonna pull out of his sleeve next…fine. Maybe I'm selling my soul by getting into bed with him, but so what? What the fuck does it matter?"

He made an exasperated face. "Vic…."

"The only thing I care about? I want to make sure you don't disappear next. That's all that matters to me. If I owe him, so be it. He's got access to resources it would be impossible for me to scare up, and he's my best shot."

"I can take care of myself."

"You can't just go around thinking that—not without knowing whatever it is we're up against. Promise me we stick together, and you won't hear one more word out of me about Dreyfuss. For as long as we're here, he's part of the team…and I'll deal with the fallout later."

Jacob narrowed his eyes as if he thought I'd add a few more conditions on to my little lecture, but that was all I'd had to say. He nodded, and said, "All right. I can live with that."

Something clicked into place, as if I'd been trying to do one of those peg-and-hole psychiatric ward puzzles, and just realized that if I gave something a quarter-turn, it fit right in. Being able to stop struggling…that was a relief.

"The redhead?" he asked.

"Debbie."

"Did she have anything to say?"

A whole lot of nothing—I'd have to drill her later. With Jacob present. It wouldn't be as effective as talking to her alone, but at least he could be pretty damn charming when he wanted to be. "She's looking into the automatic writing."

He handed me the paper Dreyfuss had been looking at, a fax. "Dreyfuss sent in a telepath to pick the instruction manual out of the mind of your buddy at the MCC."

I looked at the fax. Handwritten words: amplitude, frequency, phase—numbered, so we knew which was which. A bunch of meaningful-looking arrows, like some kind of fancy football play. Cripes. I hoped Jacob would be able to make sense of it, because I sure couldn't. I handed it back to him. "You seriously think Dreyfuss telepathed the guy? Just now? How do we know he didn't have this piece of paper in reserve already so he could look like a big hero when we asked for it? Why have a lab team trying to figure out what makes the GhosTV tick if it was so easy to scrape the answers out of Scott's mind?"

"I guess it's possible." Jacob considered the diagram. "I don't get the impression that it *was* easy. I think it cost him."

Good. I didn't say it…then again, I probably didn't need to.

"But I thought you were done harping on Dreyfuss," he said.

Old habits die hard. "What does this mean, amplitude—ability—maximum 3?"

Jacob turned on the set and spun the innermost knob to three. "Let's find out."

Great. I could look forward to a full afternoon of *Can you see anything now?* and then a dinner of organic, free-range compost. I sighed, sat on the bed and leaned back against the headboard. "Okay," I said, hoping to move things along. "If amplitude has something to do with ability, what are frequency and phase? On the other GhosTV, one of the knobs made an old ghost fainter and a new ghost clearer." If only we had a handy old ghost and new ghost standing conveniently side by side, it would be a snap to figure out which was which.

"And what does it have to do with astral projection?" Jacob said. He looked at me expectantly, but luckily spared me from the *Can you see anything?*

I shook my head.

"You can see astral things."

"Yeah, if I've been drinking." And a stiff shot sounded really good just then. "But only because the booze lowers my shields. Last night when I projected, though, your shields didn't stop me."

Jacob stopped fiddling with the set and pivoted in his crouch to look at me. I was picking at a bit of toilet paper fluff stuck in the dried blood on my knuckle, so it took me a second to realize he wasn't going to pick up his side of the conversation again.

"What?" I said.

"What does that mean—my shields didn't stop you?"

I actually had no idea what it meant, just that my mouth seemed to be drawing conclusions on its own. Plus, I hadn't mentioned I'd seen his red energy all wound around me like the toilet paper around my mashed-up hand. And now that I'd stupidly let it slip…fat chance I'd be able to stuff that genie back in the bottle. "You know. Your shields."

He blinked slowly. I think he was counting to ten. "No, I don't know. What shields?"

"I mean, I think that's what I was seeing." I kept it as casual as I could so I didn't look like I was totally backpedaling. "This kind of, uh, energy. From you."

"Tell me."

I shifted under his laser beam focus. "It looked like my silver cord was a candy cane, and your energy was the red stripe swirling through it." Since the cat was out of the bag about his visible psychic energy, he might as well know it all. "It was totally different from mine, but the energies were interconnected. I might've even been, I dunno…feeding off your power—whatever it is that makes you a Stiff, a real Stiff and not just an NP. It was so bright and strong it almost looked physical."

He thought about it. Hard. His eyes searched mine as if he was trying to see if there was anything else I'd "forgotten" to tell him.

"And speaking of physical," I said, "your physical body had mine covered like you were trying to shield me from a grenade."

He stood from his crouch, slowly, without letting me drop my gaze.

"I guess that's why I figured it was some kind of shield. From the way it looked like you were trying to protect me, even though we were asleep."

When he sat on the bed, I thought he was going to grab me and shake me. But instead he pulled me against him, pressed our foreheads together, and said, "That's amazing." His voice was so full of awe it brought a lump to my throat.

"I thought you'd be ticked off."

"Why?"

"Because…well, because you couldn't see it yourself. You were asleep—regular-asleep, dreaming regular dreams."

"Of course I'd rather be conscious. But *you* saw it, so I know it's real. If you say I'm there with you, that's good enough for me." He kissed me then, slow and easy—and he'd probably meant to keep it brief, but somehow he managed to coax my tongue into his mouth, and both of us gave a small groan of pleasure. I slipped my arm around his neck and reveled in his closeness. Everything around us felt wrong, smelled wrong, tasted wrong. Every sensory detail I experienced reminded me I was no longer home, and I'd been ripped out of my comfort zone. Jacob, though…Jacob felt right.

Turning my head to break the kiss was brutal. "Not now. We don't have time."

"I know." He pressed his forehead into my temple, breathing faster than normal, like he could barely keep it in his pants. "I know." He pushed away from me, sat up, and adjusted his tie. I reached down and adjusted something else.

He ran a hand through his hair, stood up, and paced the aisle between the beds as much as the overstuffed room would allow. Two steps forward, turn, two steps back. He crouched in front of the console again. "So. A plan. We get the GhosTV working while Dreyfuss accesses the email."

I got to my knees so I could shift my shoulder holster where it had crept over to dig into my collarbone, then resettled my suit coat where it had pulled out of place during our impromptu make-out session.

Jacob was right, I decided. There'd be an advantage to going astral. I'd just stretch out on the gaudy sheets and try to pop out of my body to take a look around. Not only would I be able to see what the dynamics at PsyTrain were really like, but maybe I'd notice a sixth-sense detail or two that I wouldn't have spotted with my physical eyes.

Like the big glowing hotspot on our floor.

I walked forward on my knees to the foot of the bed.

"So with the amplitude at three, if I turn up the frequency…."

"Jacob. Stop." I looked up to make sure there wasn't some kind of bright light shining down from the ceiling. There wasn't—not that I'd really expected it. Some part of me knew that the glowing I'd just seen wasn't physical. "Can you back it down half a notch?"

"The frequency?"

"Whatever it was you just turned."

As I watched the floor, the beams appeared again. It looked as if holes had opened up in the carpet to reveal a searingly bright light below.

"Um…."

"What is it? Do you see something?"

"Light." I knew I sounded like a moron, but I was still trying to figure out what, exactly, that light meant.

"How's this? Better?"

The light brightened, then softened again. "Back a smidge. There. That's it. That's as bright as it gets."

"Okay. I'm going to turn up the phase. How is it now?"

The light didn't exactly fade; more like it went translucent. "Not good." I glanced over at Jacob. "I don't think it does anyth—" The bed behind him was moving. Or something in the big pile of suitcases and crap. Or something beyond it. "Wait."

Jacob stopped turning the knob, got a look at my expression, and pivoted to face the spare bed.

An arm shot out from the pile of stuff—a skinny, wasted arm—hand swinging as if it was grasping for something just out of reach. "What did you say this place used to be?"

"A hospital."

Actually, I believe he'd said "TB hospital." Which meant before the days of antibiotics, its patients never had any chance of going home. I climbed over the corner of the bed to approach the ghostly arm so I could determine what I was dealing with, a sentient spirit or a repeater. Repeaters didn't really scare me much more than, say, earwigs; they might be ugly, but they were fairly harmless. They were more like psychic film loops that kept re-playing their moment of death than actual ghosts. But sentient spirits usually had some kind of unfinished business, and when they saw me coming, all wound up in freaky psychic energy, they weren't above trying to carjack me out of my physical shell to go for a spin.

Ghosts never snuck under Jacob's skin, though. They couldn't. His talent was the equivalent of a permanent white balloon. "You wanna move those suitcases," I said, "so I can get a better look?"

He hauled both heavy suitcases off, one in each hand. The ghost in the bed didn't seem to notice.

I crept up beside Jacob and looked at the bed. The patient lying in it was a wasted, skinny guy, and what I saw of his haircut was worse than the hack job I'd been given at the twelve-dollar place. He grasped at a long-gone cord and pulled, pulled, pulled—trying to summon the help that wouldn't come soon enough, or if it did, it wasn't enough to stave off the inevitable. His body was sunk a good couple of inches into the mattress, and the plump, modern-day pillow surrounded a majority of his head—all but his forehead, temples, nose and chin, which peeked up above the cotton pillowcase like a backstroke swimmer breaking the surface of a swimming pool.

"Sir? Can you hear me?"

He kept on groping, grasping at that long-gone bell pull.

"What's he doing?" Jacob whispered. I gave him a quick imitation of the bell pull gesture without taking my eyes off the ghost.

"You can stop," I said. It had become the stock line I gave every repeater I stumbled across…not that it did them any good. It was mostly for my own comfort. "You can rest now."

My hand went to my pocket, where I normally kept a few fast food packets of salt—but my pocket was empty. I'd made sure of it before I headed off to O'Hare, fat lot of good it'd done me. It wouldn't have taken much with this repeater…old and faint, so weak it had been invisible even to my hypersensitive talent without the GhosTV bending its electromagnetic waves.

"You think they have any salt in the kitchen," I asked Jacob, "or do they season the rations with something like kelp, instead?" As I turned toward him and pulled my hand out of my pocket, a cascade of faint sparkles fell from my fingertips and bounced to the floor, shimmered, and disappeared.

Jacob saw the look I was giving my own hand. "What is it?"

"There must've been some kind of residue in my pocket." Perfect setup for a bad joke about where last week's tuna salad went, but neither of us followed up with a punch line. I stuck my hand back in and felt the seam of the pocket to see if a few grains of salt had been lodged in there. My fingertips closed around a surprising amount of gritty powder. Salt, or something else? Because maybe the drug dog at the airport would've pegged me even without help from the animal communicator.

I pulled out a pinch of grit to get a better look at it, but it was shining so bright in whatever wavelength I was viewing it that I couldn't tell what it actually was. It felt like salt, kind of, but it wasn't sticking to my fingertips the way salt would have. I parted my fingers and it cascaded from my grasp, leaving dozens of white tracers trailing through the air like itty-bitty comets.

The jacket was maybe three months old. I'd put it in the front of my rotation because the sleeves fit surprisingly well. Twenty guesses what I might have stuck in my pocket over the last three months. Auracel? Likely. Valium—definitely. Aspirin too. While I wouldn't have put it past myself to have crushed a pill in my pocket, I couldn't fathom why any of the pills that were likely to have been there would light up so brightly I couldn't even tell what they'd once been.

"What is it?"

"It's…I…" I pinched out another sample and it sifted out from between my fingers in a bunch of silvery-white sparkles. "Whatever it is, it's glowing so hard I can't actually see it. It's like staring at the top of a lit bulb and trying to read the wattage printed on the glass."

"So let me look."

Oh. Good plan. I reached in for more glowing grit, pulled out another pinch, held my fingers up right in front of Jacob's eyes, and gently released. A tiny shower of sparkles cascaded down. A couple bounced off my suitcoat sleeve, but I kept my eyes trained on my fingertips to try to see what was glowing.

"See anything?" I asked.

"There's some lint on your thumb."

I looked. Yep. Lint. "But nothing granular? Salty? Sandy? Chalky? Anything like that?"

I reached in for another pinch, and I'll be damned. It felt like there was even more there now then there had been before. I gathered as much as I could and pulled it out. It looked like I was holding the lit tip of a Fourth of July sparkler.

"There's nothing there," Jacob said. "Nothing physical."

A twinge of unease played over my molars—nothing too pronounced, like the heebie-jeebies I got when I saw dead things, really gross dead things. Just my body's acknowledgement that it would never really be numb to all the weird.

"What were you thinking about when you put your hand in your pocket?"

"Just looking for some salt."

"Because…?"

I nodded toward the bed. "To help this poor guy move along."

"Well…what's it going to hurt to try it? Use it like it's salt."

I reached in again. There was definitely more grit inside. "You think I'm summoning this stuff?"

"I hadn't thought about it yet." Jacob shot me a wry smile. "But apparently that's what *you* think."

I stifled the urge to flick some fairy dust at him, not only because he couldn't see it so it wouldn't really look very impressive—but also because I didn't know what it actually was. Proving how annoyed I felt wasn't worth the risk of smiting him with spirit crud.

The moves of an exorcism came to me quickly now, like the lyrics to the theme song of a syndicated TV show. Suck some white light through my third eye, strengthen my protective bubble—aha…my vision got a bit milkier when I did that with the GhosTV playing in the same room. Interesting. "It's time to move along," I said, not in a cop-voice, but not like a pushover, either. "Your business here is done."

I pinched some fairy dust out of my pocket and treated it exactly like I would have treated salt—which is to say, I imagined cleansing white light pouring into it just before I scattered it.

The resultant shower of sparks was so bright, my field of vision went white. But afterward, when I should have seen dancing afterimages of red and green, all I saw was an empty bed. My retinas hadn't been involved. I'd been watching it all with my inner sight.

So when tears sprang to my eyes, I couldn't really blame the light show. I knuckled them away before they had a chance to spill. Why the waterworks? I'm not sure. I'd had proof, time and time again, that the boogie man and the monsters under the bed were really real. Maybe what I'd never seen with my own eyes was the evidence that my own mojo was real, too.

Chapter 20

I stared at the empty bed for a few seconds while I composed myself, and finally, when Jacob couldn't take the not-knowing anymore, he asked, "You okay?"

I nodded. "Yeah. I'm good."

"So...it worked."

Another nod. My throat felt funny, and if I spoke, it would come out thick and emotional. If I were to guess, I'd say Jacob wanted to scoop me up and crush me against his chest, but he was holding back. The tension of him keeping himself in check reverberated through the room. But he gave me the space I needed to pull myself together.

When I was finally ready, I eased back on the white balloon I'd been holding, and the colors in the room grew vivid again. My skin prickled, then relaxed, like gooseflesh does when it fades as the furnace kicks in. Lightheadedness washed over me. Psychic fatigue? Nah, probably physical. No doubt my psychic shenanigans did things to my heart rate, blood pressure, and who-knows-what-else.

My eyes were dry when I finally blinked. I had no idea how long they'd been open. A neck roll released a loud, satisfying crack deep in my spine, and I pictured energy rushing up through the floor this time, rather than down from the ceiling. Grounding energy. Up through the soles of my feet, flowing through my chakras, setting all those rainbow-colored pinwheels to spinning.

I actually felt pretty darn good, considering I hadn't slept in my own bed, I'd just exorcised a repeater without any salt, and I'd swallowed something called spelt.

With my newfound energy and centeredness, I took another look around the room to see what there was to see with my GhosTV-augmented senses—and I spied the thing that had initially caught my eye, the light shining up from the carpet by the bathroom door. "Something over here." I crouched and wondered if I'd be able to see through the floor—and if I did, would it be considered telepathy, or remote viewing? And hadn't Faun/ Katrina said something about mediums being lumped in with remote viewers nowadays? Before, it had sounded pretty stupid. Not just because she was the one who'd said it, but because I didn't see how talking to dead people had anything to do with going astral or spying from the privacy of your own home.

But if a one-trick pony like me could do it…maybe it really was somehow connected.

A wooden door smacked into the side of my head and interrupted my epiphany.

"What," I snapped, "you don't knock anymore?"

"It was ajar." Dreyfuss looked slightly sheepish. Maybe. "And I thought Jacob might want to login to his Q-mail account and find out who the world's most memory-intensive LOLcats e-mail joke is from." He glanced down at the spot where I still saw light shining up through the carpet, despite the distraction of sniping with him, and his voice went marginally more serious. "What's with the blood?"

Blood? My heart hammered in my throat. Even though I knew Lisa had been one floor down when she'd disappeared, what if, somehow, her blood had risen up through the carpet?

"It's Vic's." Even as Jacob said it I realized he was right, and the calm in his voice ratcheted my adrenaline back down. "He cut his hand."

I looked harder at the glowing spots on the carpet, even tried closing one eye to see if it made any difference. Nope. It didn't look like blood to me. It looked like light.

"I can see that." Dreyfuss' track shoes were less than a yard from the shining blood residue. He hadn't made any move to go around me and wedge into the room. "So if you know whose blood it is, what's so interesting about it?"

With the idea of telling him to butt out for two seconds so I could gather my thoughts, I looked up and told him….

Nothing.

Because Con Dreyfuss had light leaking out from the perimeter of his eyeballs.

"Is there something you want to say, Detective?"

When he moved his head, his eyeballs multiplied, like maybe he had two pair. Or three.

I looked away, and although the impression that he had half a dozen eyeballs and a lit candle in his head like some kind of human Jack o' Lantern stuck with me, I tried to act like I hadn't seen a thing. He knew I'd seen *something*, though. Whether he was operating on visual, nonverbal cues like Jacob usually did, or he had some sort of empathic gift himself, I couldn't say. Obviously, he was on to me. I figured a partial truth would tide him over until I could decide exactly how much I wanted him to know. "We tuned the GhosTV to the repeater station and found a hundred-year-dead TB patient."

"Did you, now?" Dreyfuss swept the room with his flashlight eyes. "And here I'd heard this place was so clean you could eat off the floor." He stepped around me and crouched to look at the GhosTV's settings. Had Jacob and I just cracked the code that still stumped Dreyfuss' lab? And if so, what ramifications would it have? If those same settings worked for Richie and another GhosTV was in the FPMP's clutches, Dreyfuss would be able to boost Richie up a few classes, maybe to the point where he'd actually see the ghosts. Maybe to the point where he'd be able to exorcise Dr. Chance.

I was about to add some bullshit about the signal going in and out to buy us some wiggle room, but when he walked past me, the light leaking out from behind his jumbled-up eyeball caught his iris and lit it up like the taillight of a car.

I turned away. The spelt would be like sandpaper in my esophagus if I allowed it to come back up. Jacob waved at me behind Dreyfuss' back and caught my eye, scowling at me like he'd noticed my shiftiness, too—and he wanted to know what gave. There wasn't really any way to signal, "His eyes are all fucked up," to Jacob, so I shrugged instead….

And then I saw the veins.

The effect was subtle at first, like light bending above hot pavement. Jacob's veins were bulging. Not like he'd just hit the gym, either. They were bulging like someone was inflating them with a bicycle pump…and they were red. And now that I'd noticed it, I couldn't see anything *other* than the webwork of bulging, throbbing, ruby-red veins that seemed to hold him together like a mesh shopping bag.

Not only was he veiny, but his forehead…damn, his forehead was huge, and it throbbed in time with his veins. I stood up fast, and ran my fingertips over Jacob's cheek. It felt the same as it always did. Maybe a little more stubble than usual. I touched his temple. My fingers told me that was the same, too. But it didn't look the same. My psychic eyes were telling me another story.

"What?" he mouthed.

"Turn the TV off," I said. My voice sounded surprisingly calm.

Jacob reached around the crate and did it without me having to ask him twice.

The veins and the spooky eyes didn't disappear immediately. I looked all over the room so Dreyfuss couldn't see where I was actually looking, but I kept my eye on them in my peripheral vision. The weird special effects dwindled, the way the screen went from a gray field of static to a softly glowing point that grew smaller, smaller, and smaller, until finally, it disappeared. I looked at Jacob head-on again. He looked like I remembered him—my big, handsome lug of a guy with a vertical crease in his regular-sized brow. Thank God.

His focus, and Dreyfuss' focus, were on me, so I needed a plausible explanation for why I was acting so weird, and quickly. (I know, I know—just pick one, right?) Since both psyactive and antipsyactive meds had pesky physical side-effects, I figured it wouldn't be too far out to claim the GhosTV was making me woozy. "I was starting to feel light-headed from the TV," I said. If I needed to retract that physical symptom later, I could always blame the hippy food. "Maybe a little headache. But it could be jetlag."

Dreyfuss said, "You don't get jetlag from crossing two time zones."

Crap. I should've known better than to tell aviation-fibs to a pilot. I touched my temple, hoping it wasn't too melodramatic of a move, but knowing I didn't want to analyze my "symptoms" any further, since that would just give Dreyfuss more rope to hang me with. My hand was soaking wet. I jerked it away from my face. Maybe I wasn't bullshitting. Maybe I really did feel sick. I turned it palm up—both my hands—and the injured hand was wet.

Sticky-wet.

With clear goo.

Jacob and Dreyfuss both noticed, both swooped in to gawk at the freakshow. "My God," Jacob said under his breath.

What I wanted to do was wipe my spoogey hand off—but I didn't want that slime on my pants. I only had two pair with me, after all. Instead, I stuck my hands behind my back and glared at both of them, hoping they'd give me some space. Not that they really could, given that we were standing in the three-foot aisle in the middle of the room.

Jacob cut his eyes to Dreyfuss. "Is that…?"

"Ectoplasm. Nothing else it could be."

"Like Ghostbusters?" I scoffed.

"Like Victorian séances." Dreyfuss kept his smirking as low-key as possible, though I couldn't help but notice how amused he was by my distress. "Ectoplasm was supposed to be the outward manifestation of the medium's connection to the spirit world. I'd always figured it was a fraud—though I gotta say, I'm really getting a kick out of being proved wrong."

"Vic." Jacob gave me his biggest, saddest, most soulful, dark-eyed look. "Let me see."

What I wanted to do was tell Dreyfuss to turn around; it seemed too private to let him ogle. I was just as curious as Jacob was, though, so I brought the sticky hand forward. It looked like I'd been playing with the hair gel. Jacob caught me by the wrist—and did he really need to hold onto me all that tightly?

He gave the slime a sniff, and I nearly tossed my spelt-cookies. "It smells like ozone."

I had no idea what ozone was supposed to smell like, so I took a whiff, too. I guess it sort of smelled the way electronics smell after they've been sitting in the attic too many years and you plug them in to see if they still work.

Dreyfuss pulled a small plastic bag out of his pocket, and said, "May I take a sample?"

"Are you kidding me?" I turned my arm away, and did my best not to imagine myself strapped down to a gurney with a medical team standing by to amputate my right hand.

"You hate the government. I get it. But this is a big deal. And what if it turns out to be our key to finding Lisa?"

"Nope, you don't get to play the Lisa-card every time you want me to jump through the FPMP's hoops. This has nothing to do with Lisa. You just want to suck some stem-cells out of it and do something messed-up with my DNA. And it's not gonna happen. No way."

"All right. If that's how you're going to be." He looked me up and down. "How about this? Just let me see it. Unless this happens to you all the time—and judging by your reaction, it doesn't—it's ridiculous to lose the opportunity to at least look, all for the sake of being petty."

Frankly, my urge to keep my personal stuff personal was so strong that I was perfectly willing to sacrifice knowing what I could or couldn't do if it meant that Dreyfuss wouldn't know, either.

"Vic," Jacob said quietly. "Don't worry about him. Let me see."

I show Dreyfuss, then Dreyfuss has one up on me. I keep it to myself, then Jacob gets pissed. Talk about a no-win situation. Dreyfuss had already seen it, though. And when I clenched my hand and gave it a little squish, it didn't seem to me that it might actually do anything more than what he'd already glimpsed, which was to sit there and be slimy. And so I opted to make Jacob happy, and I pulled my hand out from behind my back and unclenched my fist.

There it was. Still goopy.

Jacob took a few snapshots of it with his cameraphone, which I let him do. If we were alone, I would have asked him if he planned to jerk off to them later. Sarcastically. Sort of. Obviously, though, I was in no mood to let Dreyfuss see the tender pink insides I keep hidden beneath my shell.

Within a couple of minutes, the glop of goo started to shrink. It felt even colder, which I didn't mention. I could tell Jacob later.

Toward the end, it dissipated so quickly it looked like time-lapse photography, shrinking smaller and smaller, following the lines of my palm, until finally it was gone, and the only difference between my two hands was that the ectoplasm hand still felt cold. And it was covered with scabs, though that was, of course, old news. Ectoplasm topped friction wounds any day, and long after my scabs healed, I'd still think of my right hand as my ectoplasm hand.

Someone knocked on the door, startling the hell out of me, and I actually shielded my hand from view—not that there was anything left to see. Jacob climbed over the corner of the spare bed and spoke in a low voice to whoever was on the other side. And then he started passing stuff over the top of the GhosTV console to Con Dreyfuss. Two more boxes, these made out of corrugated cardboard, roughly the size of suitcases.

"Your laptops made good time," Dreyfuss said.

And then, a pizza.

The smell of oregano and salty grease filled the overstuffed room. Suddenly, I was ravenous.

"Don't mind that," Dreyfuss said. "It's just my lunch."

Oh. The pizza was for him. Right. Because I'd already eaten lunch. If you could call it that.

I didn't want to eat an FPMP pizza anyway.

"I got you different models so you could tell 'em apart." He handed a laptop box back to Jacob. "Yours is ultra-portable. Detective Bayne's is built to withstand more punishment, though I don't recommend you use it to drive nails."

Jacob balanced his box on top of the garment bag that was resting on the crate lid on the spare bed. "These'll need to charge."

"Nope. I had them install fully charged batteries, and set up everything but the passwords."

I waited to see if Jacob asked for any clarification on the mysterious "them." He didn't. He didn't need to.

Chapter 21

I hated the computer.

It was lightning fast. The keyboard felt great. It looked pretty damn cool. No doubt it was recording every keystroke I made and dumping the info to a file on Dreyfuss' desktop.

After I opened up my e-mail and checked it, it occurred to me that the FPMP now knew my password. Damn it all. The last e-mail I'd read before I left Chicago was the one that had bounced from Lisa's full inbox. Since then, I'd received a dry cleaning coupon, an invitation to join the League of Hispanic Voters, a work-at-home offer, and interspersed with those, three emails from Crash. I hesitated to open them, but then I figured the FPMP was gonna see them whether I did or not. So I might as well read them too.

E-mail one: `just thought of a way u can get some xtra protein in ur diet`

Cute.

E-mail two: `so did Mr. Perfect dig ur hair or what? feel free to shower me with appreciation & french fries & a chocolate milkshake this time`

It seemed like forever ago that I'd been eating french fries at Sticks and Stones. It'd only been the day before yesterday, though.

E-mail three, from right around the time Crash called me after lunch: `jacobs Q-mail just bounced - wtf? i thought u were wrong when u told me about lisas - my bad`

If he referred to Jacob by his real name, I knew he was concerned. As I considered whether I should write him back and give him some sneaky reason to quit e-mailing me so the FPMP couldn't intercept it, at least until I had the chance to change my password from the safety of my old computer, Jacob started talking to his screen. Which he does at home a lot, although he denies it.

"What the...what is this?"

Dreyfuss put down the piece of pizza he'd been eating, dusted some cornmeal off his fingers, and came over to see for himself. "In the beginning God created the heaven and the earth. And that goes on for...how long?"

Jacob scrolled, and scrolled, and scrolled. "The whole thing."

"The whole...bible?" I said.

"King James 1769 version," Dreyfuss said, "if you wanna be specific."

Right. I was lucky I'd even guessed the "bible" part. It seemed icky that Dreyfuss could name the actual version.

"Do you recognize the sender?" Dreyfuss asked.

"No."

"Okay. How about the next email? Familiar?"

"No. I don't know any of these froms."

"Open this one here, by the bottom."

I was dying to get a gander at what they were digging up from Jacob's account, but I was too stubborn to give Dreyfuss the satisfaction. And I also didn't want him to see me drooling over the smell of the pizza.

"It's the same," Jacob said. "The entire bible. Again."

"Don't erase any," Dreyfuss said. "If you do that, they'll just keep filling it up."

"They?" Jacob didn't sound nearly as dubious as I would, but at least this time, he asked. "Who are they?"

"Whichever group set up a campaign to fill your inbox with the Holy Word."

Five Faith? I thought it, but didn't say it out loud.

"But where would they get my e-mail address?"

"Do you pay your bills online?"

Jacob looked disturbed. "Some. But isn't that...secure?"

I refrained from yelling out, *Come on, like anything's secure!*

"All it takes is a mole at the cable company. You're not exactly a low-profile guy, Detective Marks. Been a PsyCop for almost ten years now. And you're on the news practically every time I turn around. Using your real name."

Suddenly, the pizza was nowhere near as appealing, because my stomach just dropped like a broken elevator. If some extremist nut-job had Jacob in his sights, they could've done a hell of a lot worse than to stuff his inbox with thees and thous and begets and smites. They could've hired someone to put a bullet in his head.

"If it *was* some underpaid file clerk at the cable company," Dreyfuss went on, "then they now know where you live, too." He cut his eyes to me. "Just a matter of time before they get a gander at good ol' Victor Bayne shuffling out of the cannery bright and early, juggling his travel mug and the packs of convenience store donuts he thinks you don't know about, groping around for the keys to his underwhelming Ford Taurus."

"You need to leave," I said. "Now."

Jacob sighed, then ran his hand over his forehead like he'd suddenly come down with a splitting headache.

Dreyfuss closed the top of his pizza box, hefted it, and angled his way through the furniture toward the bathroom door. "Nothing threatens a bible-thumper more than someone who can confirm or deny the very existence of heaven." He put his hand on the doorknob, and paused in the doorway with one more thought. "Don't shoot the messenger, Detective. The world's a scary place. Maybe you'd rather bury your head in the sand, but I dunno how much longer you can afford to do it."

Bury my…that fucker'd been listening to Jacob and me talking the night before when we were discussing the crate…and when I was hammering home the point that I didn't trust Dreyfuss any farther than I could throw him.

He looked toward Jacob. "I'll have my lab run through and see if anyone was sloppy enough to leave something we can trace in the headers."

He left before my head blew up. But just barely. With Dreyfuss gone, it felt like there was space for more breathable air in the room. I took a good lungful and sat down hard on the bed next to my new, evil laptop. "Maybe all those e-mails are from the same person," I said. "Someone who signed up for a bunch of different free accounts just so he could mess you up."

Jacob shook his head. His eyebrows were all bunched together and he was staring at nothing, thinking. "Or maybe Five Faith managed to dig up my private information while they were house-hunting in Skokie."

"We could call Keith and Manny, have 'em set up surveillance at the cannery."

Maybe I'd thought he would jump at the chance to bring his brawny gym-buddies into the mix, but he didn't even seem to notice I was attempting to play by rules I thought he'd understand. He planted his hands on his hips, paced up and back, and finally wedged himself onto the bed on the other side of the laptop. "I've got to call Carolyn, make sure she's okay. You should probably let Zig and Maurice know what's going on, too."

Jacob and I don't have tons of friends; it comes with the territory of working a million hours a week. Among those friends we do have, the only Psychs are Lisa, Carolyn and Crash. Given our jobs, you'd think that number would be higher, but it seemed to jibe with the statistics for Psych distribution in the general population. I would have liked to think that, as Stiffs, Zig and Maurice weren't in any danger. But for all anyone knew, Jacob was also a Stiff. And I didn't suppose religious kooks thought any more rationally than mad scientists when it came to targeting people for their fucked-up agendas.

I waffled over calling Warwick, but I figured the FPMP wouldn't learn anything by spying on him that they didn't already know from Dreyfuss. Once I'd told him what was going on, the Sarge said one word to me. "Understood." That sent a chill through me worse than Zig's nervous questions, or Maurice's heavy sigh. Even if I'd been in the room with Warwick, I probably wouldn't have been able to read him. He'd been walking the FPMP tightrope a heck of a lot longer than I had. Or at least he'd realized he was on one, while I'd been staggering through life blissfully unaware.

As brief and pointed as we kept all the conversations, I still felt like I was running on fumes when we finally finished up our phone calls. I looked at Jacob, who'd been holding his cell phone in his lap, and staring at it ever since he'd hung up with Crash. He looked wrecked.

There's helpless, and there's helpless. Experimental Psych facilities and thuggish orderlies are one thing. Seeing the man you love looking like that… I almost preferred the wrist restraints.

"Hey," I said. I reached out to stroke his face—but hesitated when I saw the scabby knuckles and realized I was just about to touch him with my ectoplasm hand. Then again, nothing paranormal had befallen anything else I'd touched since the incident. Besides, that was probably Jacob's new favorite hand. I touched his temple—he had a few more grays shining through the black there than the last time I'd taken a good look—and did my best to put the image of his veiny, swollen-foreheaded GhosTV appearance from my mind.

"What about my family?" he whispered. "Jesus."

I swallowed down a sick twist in my gut and forced myself to look on the bright side. "If anyone can figure this out, it's us. We've brought down scarier sons of bitches. Now that we've got the GhosTV, I can project through the building and nose around." And see light leaking out around people's eyes… but that was a whole new can of shit. "Dreyfuss and all his money and connections are in our corner. And you're the smartest guy I know; there's no doubt in my mind you'll put everything together and figure out what the hell's really going on."

He slung his arm around me and rested his cheek against mine. His goatee tickled my chin. I could feel him breathing, slow and deliberate, getting himself calm and centered. I set my creepy hand on his thigh and felt his shoulders relax. Yep. His new favorite hand.

When he spoke again, he was the same old Jacob. Strong. Confident. Completely in control, and willing to do whatever it took to get the job done. It was probably just a veneer. But at least he didn't look so damn vulnerable. "Plus there's the automatic writing," he said. "Maybe we can use that to our advantage."

My ick-factor kicked in—because the thought of someone else moving my arm was too close to possession for my taste—but even I couldn't deny automatic writing might turn out to be a valuable tool. Besides, maybe it wasn't as scary as I was making it out to be. Maybe it was less like someone using my arm as a sausage casing for their ghost arm. Maybe it was more like radio signals, or Morse code, where an electrical impulse tells a stylus when to move. I suspected whatever it was, Professor March could probably explain it to me in a way I would actually understand. "Debbie was supposed to come help us at…" I checked the clock.

Almost six thirty.

Shit.

"At when?"

"She was supposed to be here over an hour ago." She had said she was coming over after her class ended at five, right? I might be scatterbrained, but I usually had a good sense of time. Although she'd said she needed to look it up. Maybe the research was taking longer than she'd anticipated. There had to be a way to talk to her without running all over the building. Was there a phone in each room, like a motel? I scanned the mountain of stuff. If the phone did exist, it was buried. It probably wouldn't have mattered anyway, given that Lyle had pulled the plug on the phone system.

Lyle. We had his cell number. And it wasn't buried under a suitcase, either.

I picked up his card and handed it to Jacob. "Here, call your boyfriend. See if he can help us find her."

"*My* boyfriend?" He handed it back.

"C'mon," I said. "He wore perfume for you and everything."

"Grey Flannel. And who says it was me that he was trying to impress?"

I tried to give Jacob a "just call the guy" look, but he'd turned back to his new ultra-portable laptop already. "Besides," he said without bothering to look up. "He gave the number to you. Not me."

While it cut the tension to spar with him on something as dumb as who was getting cruised and who wasn't, I couldn't afford to get into the whole debate. I needed to see if Debbie was just fashionably late or if she'd actually stood me up, so I gave Jacob a parting sigh, checked the business card, and dialed the cell number of a Mr. Lyle J. Peters, Office Manager, PsyTrain LLC.

He answered, and I said, "Mr. Peters, this is Detective Bayne. Is there a way I can get in touch with Professor March?"

"Well, sure, I can buzz her room…wait a minute, no I can't. Um…."

"I need to speak with her."

"I'm not allowed to give out personal numbers, sorry, but I'll call her myself and have her call you right back."

We hung up. He still sounded edgy, to me. But that was the way people who didn't normally chat with cops tended to sound. Pacing seemed like a good idea, but there was nowhere to pace. I tossed my phone from hand to hand as if that might make it ring faster, but then I remembered the slimy feel of ectoplasm in my right hand and wondered if it was even safe to hold the phone with that hand anymore, or if I was emitting some kind of electromagnetic jelly that would fuck up the circuitry.

There was still enough gauze in the first aid kit to go around my fist a few times—but instead of protecting my carpet burn from dirt and germs, this time I was shielding the outside world from my weird right hand. My phone rang again, and I recognized the number as the one I'd just dialed. "Any luck?"

"She's not picking up her phone. I knocked on her door and nobody answered, so she's not in her room."

She'd seemed really keen on talking to me before, in the elevator, so the no-show didn't make any sense at all. "Is there anyplace she might go to do some research?"

"I'll check the library." He huffed and puffed as he went from room to room, but who am I to judge? "No. She must have gone out. I'm sorry. If I see her, I'll be sure to tell her—"

"Lyle, do me a favor." He shut up fast, in the way people do when you bark their name at them like I just did. "Stand outside Debbie's room and call her again, and see if you hear her phone ringing. Can you do that?"

I hung up with him and found Jacob watching me. "What are you thinking?" he said.

"Nothing. Yet. I just want to see—" my phone rang. Lyle again. "Yeah?"

"You're right. Her phone is in there. Maybe she went to the cafeteria for a snack."

Maybe. Except the sick, cold feeling settling in the pit of my gut was telling me otherwise. I hung up with Lyle and told Jacob, "Let's go check with the security guards in the lobby. Maybe I'm wrong…but I think something happened to Debbie."

Chapter 22

Fact: Deborah March was not in the building.
Fact: the security guards in the front lobby hadn't seen her leave.
Fact: the security camera on the back door hadn't, either.

I made my way around the building's entryway for the umpteenth time, sucking white light through my forehead like a giant SUV guzzles gas, *looking* with all my might for something that could tell me where Debbie was.

As I pictured a white balloon surrounding myself, I realized I'd been chugging white light since Jacob and I left our room. The sudden stoppage of the flow actually left me lightheaded, and I had to plant my feet for a second, close my eyes, and re-orient myself to keep from tipping over.

While I know that psychic stuff is really real—unlike portions of the general public who still aren't convinced—I still don't give a concept like "white light" as much credence as I give "a rock hard spelt cookie," for instance. So in a place like PsyTrain where everything was set up to facilitate psychic experience, a guy like me, in all my profound sensitivity, could get his skinny white ass into some serious trouble. Sure, whatever Feng Shui might have once existed in my room was history the minute they crammed in a second bed. We still had a dozen instructor Psychs and over a hundred bright, eager newbies continually conscious of raising the energy. As much as I scoffed at the idea that positioning your furniture at weird angles made any difference in those elusive "energies," I'd need to keep reminding myself that those energies did actually exist. And that I was drinking them up like a binge-drinker at a kegger.

Plus I had a big hunk of scary electronics in my room that was making said energy do all kinds of unheard-of things. Like causing me to sweat fairy dust and ectoplasm.

Like ejecting me from my body.

I patted down my chest as if I was looking for something in my jacket, but really, I needed to ensure that my subtle bodies were still anchored in my physical one, where they belonged. As far as I could tell, nothing was sticking out where it shouldn't have been. Then I focused on the room.

Nothing. The lobby was clean, of ghosts, of psychic residue…of everything but the dust that had gathered where the receptionist used to sit—back before they needed to worry that a nutjob with his head screwed on too tight would lob a grenade through the front window in the name of Leviticus.

Jacob was talking to Chekotah…actually, he was practically propping the guy up. Chekotah was so stressed out he looked about ready to collapse. While I was noticing the way Jacob steered Chekotah toward a chair, like he really was worried he might need to call a paramedic, Lyle hovered near the doorway, took a couple of steps, then blanched when he saw me notice him. Maybe he'd know something. The security guards sure didn't.

He had fair skin that blushed easily, and blushed blotchily. He was looking pretty blotchy at that very moment. His eyes darted all over like he couldn't figure out where to look when I approached, and he gave me a tight, weird smile. I know it's bad when I'm the one wishing I had Carolyn at my side to figure out what's what. "How long have you been with PsyTrain?" I asked him.

"A year? No, wait, it's almost two years now."

"And you live here—in the building?" I said. He nodded. "You ever been tested yourself?"

He stared at me for the duration of an awkward pause, then said, "For what?"

For gonorrhea. Jesus H. Christ, what did he think? "Psychic ability."

"Oh." Nervous laugh. "Yeah, of course, I…well, my first test showed an empathic tendency." He sighed. "But after that I tested random-normal. The first one was a fluke. Sometimes you can do that. Score high. Score low."

I knew all about that. Two whole years of my life I'd been put through more tests than the dials of the GhosTV. "All right, maybe you don't have an extrasensory edge. But living here's gotta count for something. What do *you* think is going on?"

Lyle's eyes flicked to one side. He was thinking about what he was going to say. People filter before they verbalize, which is why you need to knock them off-balance so they don't have a chance to clean up their story. I caught his eye and held it—and then propped an elbow on the wall and leaned in closer to him, slouching a little so I didn't look like I was towering over him quite so much. The potential for me coming off as ridiculous rather than cool was astronomical, but somehow the move worked. Lyle didn't back away when I got close. Careful, so as not to be totally over the top, I dropped my voice subtly and said, "You can tell me." His eyes widened a little. Pupils, too.

He *was* into me. Jacob had been right.

I'd never hear the end of it.

"It's really nothing concrete." Lyle sounded like he was just about ready to spill. What would Zigler do? Scratch that, Zigler never would have been angling at a witness like I currently was, and the mere thought of Zig even trying nearly destroyed my illusion of coolness.

I gave a small shrug, like I could care less about how concrete it was, and I kept on staring him in the eye.

His cheeks got blotchier. "Five Faith."

Another long pause. I leaned in closer, and when it became obvious he'd hit another roadblock, I said, "Uh huh."

He wet his lips. His eyes darted. And, damn, just as I figured my working-the-witness mojo had been all in my head and he wasn't going to give me a damn thing, he said, "If they were trying to target someone, what better way?"

"Target who?"

"Lyle," Chekotah called, and the spell was broken.

Lyle flinched, looked at me apologetically, and took off at a fast trot toward his boss. "Wait," I said, but evidently my powers of seduction only went so far.

"Take the detectives to Debbie's room," Chekotah said. "Just them, okay? Let them have a look around, see if they see anything useful." Lyle nodded, and Chekotah repeated, "Just them."

I glanced at Jacob to see if he had the same feeling I did—that something was churning around under the surface—but there was only so much our non-verbal eyelocks could communicate. Lyle led us to the classroom wing of the building, then up to the third floor to the area where the bigwigs lived. He pulled out a master key. Jacob snapped on a latex glove, took the key from Lyle and opened Debbie's door.

Clothes were strewn on the bed, the floor, the dresser. Jacob said to Lyle, "Stay in the hall. The room's been tossed. We'll need to call it in."

"It's always that way." Lyle held up his hands as if to tell us, *just sayin'*.

Jacob took a closer look, then said, "If that's the case…." He pulled out another pair of gloves, handed them to me, and said, "Be careful. Lisa's room was already contaminated when we got here. But if there's any evidence the locals can pull from this room…."

"Right." Contaminated? Hell, the dipshits at PsyTrain had been in Lisa's room moving furniture, burning incense, and who knows what else. Not only was evidence contaminated, it was probably destroyed. I might not have graduated at the top of my class, but I knew better than to shuffle evidence around. I pulled on the gloves. My scabby, spooky right hand felt taut and prickly as the latex dragged over the scabs. It also felt vaguely weird, though maybe that was just me worrying that I'd fill the glove up with ectoplasm and end up carrying it around like a baggie full of goldfish I'd won at a midway game. Still, it seemed to me that if my hand had the potential to spooge on the evidence, it was probably best for everyone that I kept it sheathed in latex.

"We'll treat it as a crime scene," Jacob said. "What do you want to do? Sketches or photos?"

Like I was any good at either of those things. I'd never needed to be. That's what techs were for. I took a covert peek at my phone to see if it might telepathically relay the instructions for the camera to my brain, but it didn't. With my best impression of confidence, I said, "Sketch."

I think Jacob bought it. He was already sweeping around the room with his cell phone clicking away while I still lingered at the threshold, struggling to pick the starting point. It was harder than you'd think. No body, no obvious sign of a struggle, and—judging from a quick glance—no ghost.

Not so great for me, I supposed, but good for Debbie.

Unless the Internet demon had sucked her in. But I'd see something obvious, like a computer with a curl of brimstone wafting up from the keyboard, if that were the case. Right? I told myself Internet demons were only a figment of my overexposed imagination. They didn't exist. And if they did, they wouldn't stuff inboxes full of bibles unless those bibles were penned by Anton LeVay.

Back to the sketch, which wasn't drawing itself. Begin at the beginning, I decided…the front door. I pulled out my pad and pen and considered the room. As far as messes go, it was mostly clothes, like maybe she'd tried on a couple of outfit combos that day. She'd hung plenty of retro crap on the walls to mark her territory; B-movie posters, a neon light in the shape of a lipstick tube, and a full-sized vintage jukebox all warred for my attention. Despite the kitsch-and-clothing explosion, it was a pretty spacious layout. Probably doctors' quarters originally, rather than patient rooms. I craned my neck to peer around Jacob. Private bathroom, too. Not too shabby.

A pair of scrunched-up fishnets lay on the floor, and a red bra was draped across the leopard bedspread. Given how most women feel about strangers who aren't potential bedmates looking at their lingerie, I was guessing she hadn't been expecting company.

I might not have a tape measure on me, but supposed I wasn't too bad at judging distance. I paced the length of the bedroom, drew a rectangle on my pad, and marked the dimensions. Ten feet, same as ours. It was wider, though, a whole window-width wider.

I placed the windows, doors and furniture, then did a slow circuit with my shields down and my feelers up, in case anything happened to be sending out any helpful psychic signals. Jacob emerged from the bathroom, sweeping his gaze back and forth to cover anything mundane that I was likely to miss, and the sleeves of our jackets brushed as we passed each other in the center of the room. I paused for a heartbeat, but decided not to remark on the fact that I was surprised it felt so natural to work with him, even here, totally out of my element. I suspected he knew.

The bathroom was more cluttered, since Debbie had a thing for makeup that bordered on fetish. The outfit she'd been wearing earlier lay in a pile in the middle of the bathroom floor, as if she'd come back to change after class. Did she feel the need to slip into something a little more comfortable while she looked up automatic writing for me?

I scanned the sink area. There, on the wall—blood? I crouched to take a better look at it, and my days of helping my ex, Stefan, go from a sassy bleached blond to a magenta siren came flooding back like they were yesterday. The spatter shape on Debbie's bathroom wall looked like it'd been made by something thicker than blood, and its position relative to the sink led me to think it was hair dye. It was old and long-dried. Plus, it wasn't glowing.

"Someone's coming," Jacob called from the bedroom.

I guesstimated the width of the room and added the measurement to my sketch, put an X on the wall and marked it *red spatter 10 in. off floor.* Then I filled in the rest of the details. Tub. Toilet. Window. Door.

"A few someones. And your friend Katrina."

Wait, what? I looked at the opposite wall from where I stood in the doorway to Debbie's bedroom. Door? There was no door on the opposite wall, not like our shared bathroom, where we were stuck flossing our teeth with Dreyfuss just a keyhole away.

I looked down at my sketch. I'd definitely drawn a door there. Huh.

"Give us a few minutes," I heard Jacob say, his voice projecting out toward the hall. I glanced over my shoulder and saw he was blocking with his body. All right, I thought. I'd worked under a hell of a lot more pressure with a lot smaller of a barrier between myself and the people who didn't want me around. I could figure this thing out.

I squinted at the wall where I'd drawn the door. Nothing. White light, faucet wide open, energy pouring in through my forehead. Breathe in. Breathe out. Indigo chakra spinning—wow, that was a new one. I didn't think I'd ever known which way those things were supposed to turn, but there it was, whirling so fast behind my forehead I felt dizzy again.

I looked at the wall where I'd drawn the door. Nothing.

The sound of people pushing into the room was marginally distracting, but Faun Windsong's voice—my own personal form of water torture—insisting that her precog and her clairvoyant needed to have a look…that voice was the thing that finally broke my concentration. When I clicked the pen cap so I could stick it back in my pocket, I felt something cold creep over the inside of my wrist.

Holy hell. That glove full of ectoplasm I'd imagined earlier? Yep. I had it.

Chapter 23

Voices amped up as Faun Windsong forced her way in with a couple of Psych students, and while Debbie's room was spacious enough, jamming a bunch of people into it, especially relatively untrained people, was the surest way to botch evidence I could think of. And I don't mean contaminating it so it was inadmissible in court, either. I mean obliterating it so we couldn't use it to find Debbie, and ultimately, Lisa.

It was tempting to wad the spent ectoplasm-rubber into my pocket and rinse off my hand in the sink, but on the freakish off-chance that the fine folks at PsyTrain wouldn't totally destroy any evidence that might be in the room, I just couldn't. Hell, I couldn't even bring myself to steal some toilet paper to wrap around my wrist; I'd had "don't touch anything, leave it for the techs" branded into my brain for too many years.

While I figured if I was loudmouthed enough I could distract Faun Windsong from noticing I was keeping my right hand in my pocket, I didn't want anyone to think I might draw on them. Sure, I didn't keep a gun in my *pocket* like some junkie out to rob the Stop 'n' Go, but I knew better than to assume a civilian would follow that logic.

Instead, I held my elbow at an angle and kept my hand at my side, pretending it was glued to my ribcage. Hopefully no one would notice I was standing funny. And hopefully my exuberant astral jam wouldn't spill.

Surprise, surprise: Faun was shooting her mouth off at Jacob when I slipped out of the bathroom. "...and you think we can't see anything just because we don't have state licenses?"

"What I think," he replied just as loudly, and while he remained outwardly polite, I could tell he wanted to strangle her. She was lucky he's practically made of patience. "...is that there could be physical evidence here along with the psychic evidence. They could both be critical."

The way NPs tend to get jumpy when Psychs come in to do a sweep? I saw the same thing unfolding here, only in reverse. I said, "Listen, Faun." Katrina, whatever. "This makes three women, up and gone. Not just students—teachers now, too. What if you're next?"

She opened her mouth to argue, then closed it again and gave me a good, hard stare, and when she spoke again, she'd taken it down a few decibels. "You think this has to do with gender?"

Actually, it hadn't yet occurred to me. When it had just been Lisa and Karen missing, I'd assumed it was something to do with them being roommates. But now Debbie was gone, too—from the opposite side of the building. Jacob's stuffed inbox didn't fit the theory—but Faun didn't need to know about that. I gave her the patented non-answer, "We're looking at all the angles."

Her shoulders fell and she took a half-step back. "If you think this is some kind of thing where women are being targeted…I can't take that risk. I'll need to postpone the semester and send everyone home."

Bad idea. We needed to interview people. And mostly, we needed to see if anyone was acting hinky—because no matter how hard it was to land a spot at PsyTrain, if there was a group of religious weirdos targeting Psychs, I wouldn't put it past one of them to weasel their way in somehow. "For now, the best thing you can do is sit tight," and stay out of our way… "and let us do our jobs."

"I couldn't agree more." Dreyfuss. My favorite person. Right on schedule. He slipped around Lyle, who didn't move to stop him, since as far as PsyTrain was concerned, he was with us.

He managed to intimidate all the Psychs out of his way—him, with his stupid ponytail and his track suit—took a deep breath, rubbed his hands together, and said to us, confident as you please, "Okay, kids. Brief me."

I let Jacob handle it. Like I said, he's *made* out of patience.

Since just looking at Dreyfuss made me want to punch something, I ducked into the bathroom to see if the not-door was there. It was not. There. Maybe I'd just imagined it, since I was busy comparing and contrasting Debbie's room to ours. I couldn't just discount it, though. What if my hand had drawn that door of its own accord, kind of like the notebook pages full of *no no no?* Or what if I was tweaking so hard on white light—hard enough to start seeping ectoplasm—that I was catching glimpses of ghost doors?

Could buildings have subtle bodies? If they did, it would explain why spirits didn't sink through floors and keep on falling through everything solid until they reached the molten core of the earth.

Weariness washed over me at the thought of how much I didn't know, and I almost sagged against the wall—but I thought better of it, seeing as how it was the wall with the not-door on it. I glanced at the bathtub and considered perching on the edge of it, just for a second, while I knuckled grit out my eyes and wished that Calgon really could take me away…and then, on impulse, I pushed the shower curtain open with my pen.

Debbie had at least ten kinds of shampoo and shower gel—why was I not surprised—and one of those nylon puff things dangling from the showerhead. And on top of that…jewelry. Someone had thrown a necklace over the sprayer.

It wasn't the fact that a necklace was hanging in the shower that was unusual. Who hasn't stumbled into the shower with a watch on and tossed it onto the nearest convenient surface? Debbie's rooms were brimming with makeup and accessories, so it wasn't the presence of the necklace that was puzzling. It was the necklace itself.

The style…totally not her.

I took a quick peek in the direction of the medicine cabinet, where some earrings and necklaces littered the ledge above the sink. Debbie had a specific "look" going on. She wore funky chains and polka-dotted, studded things in black and chrome and bubblegum-pink plastic. The necklace in the shower was beaded, but not the big, round, retro-fifties fake pearls I'd expect to see on Debbie. This necklace was turquoise, onyx and sard seed beads. I almost touched it—almost—as if my hand might be able to tell whether the semi-precious stones were real. But of course they were. I could practically feel them singing to my sixth chakra.

Hippy dippy stuff. Not Debbie's bag at all.

I held my gloved hand about an inch away from the dangling necklace, sucked some white light through my third eye, and tried to see if any impressions came to me. They didn't, not like the glowing blood spatter on my carpet. What did I expect? I knew beyond the shadow of a doubt that I wasn't a precog.

"Vic? We gotta get going." Jacob was in the bathroom doorway. I glanced at him. "Did you find something?"

I cut my eyes back to the necklace. "I dunno. Take a picture of this."

He raised his phone and snapped, though he didn't seem nearly as curious about it as I was. Between him and me, Jacob might be better at picking out a tie, but I'd been the one with the mohawk and the bad attitude, albeit many years before. I knew when something didn't belong in an alternative chick's wardrobe.

We waded our way out of there through the sea of wannabe-Psychs. They were getting a stern lecture from Faun Windsong to not touch anything, even as one of them was groping through Debbie's desk drawer and another one put his fingerprints all over the windowsill. "Let's get back to our room," I told Jacob. "I think the day is catching up to me." We passed by the soda machines on our way there, and I managed to slip out of my latex gloves and pitch them into the trash, with the apple cores and granola bar wrappers, without anyone being any the wiser to my most recent ectoplasmic spurt.

Chapter 24

"I'm just gonna rest my eyes for a second," I told Jacob.

A tap sounded on our door as I was taking off my shoes. I ignored it, so Jacob did another cardio-healthy bout of climbing the furniture to answer it. Dreyfuss. "Good thing you processed that scene before the Odd Squad got there," he said. "You know how it is when the sixth sense is the only sense someone's using. Common sense goes right out the window. And you weren't the only ones who totally scored."

He reached behind his back, and for a split second I thought he was reaching for a small-of-the-back concealed holster—but the thing he pulled out, with a very self-satisfied smile, wasn't even remotely gun-shaped. It was a netbook.

Not just any netbook: a silver netbook covered in stick-on sequins like a twelve-year-old girl's cell phone. Three guesses as to whose computer it was. And two of those guesses, I didn't need. "What about you two?" he said. "Find anything juicy?"

A door that wasn't there. Which I didn't want to volunteer...because it meant nothing? It might mean nothing. Or it might have something to do with my player-piano hand. My brain insisted Dreyfuss was working with us, and while I didn't need to be his buddy, I did need to share evidence. But I wasn't sure what the door was evidence of—something to do with PsyTrain, or something to do with me. And I wanted to keep the me-evidence to myself.

But Debbie March was missing now, too. So I couldn't. I tore the sketch out of my pad and gave it to him. He glanced at it and said, "Red splatter?"

"Hair dye."

Thanks to the Miss Clairol, he didn't notice the extra door.

"I photographed the scene." Jacob said. "I'll send you the pictures."

Dreyfuss turned to go and clocked his hip on the GhosTV. "And what about this?"

"I saw the one repeater," I told him. "That's it." Liar, liar, I know. But I told myself that Jacob's veiny forehead and Dreyfuss' weird eyeball trick had nothing to do with the case, so it didn't matter if I told him or not. Same with the astral projection.

"Maybe no news is good news," Dreyfuss said. "I'd prefer to keep telling myself no one's gonna turn up dead." He patted the top of the console, and went back to his room.

Jacob stared at the door for a few seconds after Dreyfuss closed it, then said, "He almost sounded like a human being for a minute there."

"Tell that to the wire tap."

"I wish I could run him past Carolyn. She'd know how to separate the truth from the bullshit." Thankfully, that was the extent of what Jacob had to say about Dreyfuss. He started to get undressed and ended up knocking the crate lid on the floor with his elbow. "I'm gonna try to organize some of this stuff," he told me. "Maybe move one of the dressers into the hall."

I grunted, and he knew me well enough to take it as, "Knock yourself out." I was so drained, both from working a case I had a personal stake in, and from the time change that supposedly shouldn't have affected me at all, that "resting my eyes" went the route it usually does when I'm at home in that recliner of Jacob's I've taken over. The light, the strange bed, the sound of Jacob moving furniture…none of that could prevent me from conking out so hard and fast it felt like one of those rides where the bottom falls out.

Later—maybe much later, given the time warp that happens when sleep hits hard—Jacob pressed into bed behind me. We've always fit together well. My last boyfriend was always bitching about my elbows and knees, especially when he was crabby because his pot dealers had run dry, but Jacob probably couldn't even feel my pesky bones through his solid wall of muscle. I sighed back into him. Falling into bed after a long day is great. Settling in with Jacob wrapped around me, though…that's amazing.

He snuggled up harder, and the snuggling wasn't the only thing that was hard. It felt like someone had nestled a salami between the cheeks of my ass for safekeeping. I smiled to myself and enjoyed the warm, stiff length of his heavy cock against me. That was about all we would enjoy, given the fact that if I had even one iota of spare energy, I intended to use it in finding Lisa, and not getting my rocks off. Plus, there was no lube.

Jacob's mouth pressed into the back of my neck, and an electric thrill shot down my spine. "What do you think you're you doing?" I said.

He mostly mumbled, but I made out, "I love the way you feel."

The sensation of the words against my skin played along some poorly mapped erogenous zone, and that combined with his sneaky flattery—in an arena where I so sorely needed it—made my body start to respond to his subtle grinding. My nuts hitched, and that telltale tingle started at the base of my cock.

Still, it felt like I should be getting some rest, not some jollies. "Here?" I said. "Seriously?"

"Please…don't say no."

He sounded awfully forlorn. I figured the investigation must've been wearing on him. Hell, if it meant that much to him, I'd give him a quick beej so we could both get some rest. He'd probably sleep better without that huge boner weighing him down, anyway. I started to roll over, but Jacob had fit himself against my back curve for curve so close I couldn't muster the leverage to move. "Okay," I said, and pushed back to get him to give me some room. He didn't. "I'm trying to go down on you, but I can't do it if I'm facing the other way."

"Don't just get me off…that's not what I want."

He flicked his hips and slid that stiff piece of meat up and down my ass crack again. It felt like skin on skin.

"It's no big deal," I said. "C'mon. I want to."

He trailed his fingertips down my arm, and my skin danced like we were rubbing socks on a carpet to create static. "Don't you want me?"

Talk about a conversation I was tempted to deflect with a well-placed sarcastic comment. I couldn't do it, though. Not the way he sounded. Raw. Really raw. "Sex just isn't on the top of my list right now. When this is all over, once we get home—"

"When you were talking to that guy…."

I knew exactly which guy he meant. The little doughy guy with the Grey Flannel cologne. "Right, I'm sure I looked like a big idiot playing sexy-cop for Halloween. Are you giving me shit about that? 'Cos he was just about to tell me something important."

"I dream about you looking at me like that."

I shoved against him to try and turn around to get a look at him now, but it was like shoving against the side of a building. "I don't look at anybody like that in real life, mister, because I look like a huge fake doing it."

"Really? You weren't into him?"

"What? No, I wasn't into him." If I were single, and itching for some company? I supposed I wouldn't turn him down. But he wasn't anyone I'd do a double-take at and think, wow, that guy's tasty. Not like Jacob.

"I thought…when you were inside me…I didn't think I could satisfy you."

Cripes, is that what this whole thing was about? "Jacob, that was like…I dunno, days ago. You're reading too much into it. It was just different from our usual. That's all."

"You might find someone with a sweeter ass…."

"Are you high?" It was just an expression, but once I'd blurted it out, I realized he did actually sound kind of strange. In an attempt to get a look at his eyes and see if maybe he'd been sampling my Valium, I pushed with my shoulder, hard, and he still didn't budge. "Scoping out a sweeter ass couldn't be farther from my mind. You have a great ass. Beyond hot."

He ran his fingers up and down my forearm again, and his touch sent such thrills down my spine he might as well have been stroking my cock. He forced his fingertips between my fingers to clench his palm against the back of my hand, and the way my hips bucked from the feel of his fingers parting mine, I could swear I was getting my legs spread instead. Something was going on. Some byproduct of me sucking white light all day, most likely, some fluke that left me as hypersensitive as a drilled-down tooth.

"Besides," I added, "who said I wasn't perfectly happy with the way things were?" Not that I've ever thought of myself as a "bottom," but him pounding me really was my idea of a good time.

"Are you happy?"

"Yeah." The need to kiss him flooded over me, because he shouldn't have needed to ask me that. He should have known, and if he couldn't tell that he was everything to me, it was my fault, not his.

I craned my neck, but couldn't reach him. "Kiss me," I said, and the mammoth hard-on that was cozied up to my ass felt gargantuan as I strained to find Jacob's lips. He kissed me at the hairline with that fine, generous mouth of his, then began working his way forward, kissing around the back of my neck, below my ear, along the corner of my jaw. By the time he fit his lips to mine—not perfectly, but against the corner of my mouth—I was as hard as he was.

His tongue swept over my lower lip, and the taste of his mouth washed over me. I was disappointed when he let go of my hand, with that strangely appealing tingle-touch he had going on…but not for long. He reached between us to line himself up and fit us together even closer. Him inside me.

"You don't need to change things up to keep me interested," I said. "The way you smell, the way you taste, the way you breathe when you're turned on…the feel of your cock plowing me 'til I'm sore—that's all I need. Not role-playing. Not games."

"You'll get bored."

"Come on, you know me better than that. Yeah, my attention span isn't stellar, but I have the same cereal for breakfast every day and watch the same scene of the same porno every time I jerk off. You know that's the truth."

He pushed into me, so big I would have sworn he'd decided to add fisting to our repertoire to incorporate the variety I'd just said I didn't want—except that there wasn't any pain. Pressure, yeah. Delicious pressure, stretching pressure, everywhere I liked it. Plus he'd wrapped his arm around me so he could tug on my ballsack while he fucked me. Since I'm not double-jointed I couldn't really touch him anywhere but his arm, so that left me with nothing to do but writhe around on the end of his huge dick while I hurtled toward my peak.

"If anything…" damn, he was nailing me perfectly, each and every thrust, "I would think you'd get sick of doing all the work."

"I get off on making you come." He raked his teeth along my spine, then clamped his mouth onto the meaty part between my neck and shoulder and started sucking on me. I felt like I might implode from the sheer goodness of it.

"How can you just say things like that?" I was breathing hard by then, and he stopped diddling my balls and started jacking my cock, instead. "Sometimes I can't believe the things you say out lou—yeah, right there. Oh God."

Before I knew it I was shooting, and the orgasm was as hard and sudden as a lightning bolt. I soared, or maybe I floated, and even though it was just for a brief, shining moment, time stretched in that way time does when some small miracle has occurred.

For that one moment, I was light. I would have thought it would be scary, the lack of me-ness. But instead of being scared, I felt elated.

By the time I regained some sense of myself, Jacob had stilled, clasped against my back. This time, when I moved to turn toward him, he actually yielded enough to let me do it. "How could I ever be bored when—"

Jacob was in the decoy bed. Asleep.

But he was in bed with me—kind of hard to miss it seeing as how he'd just fucked my brains out.

It was like one of those trick drawings that can either look like two faces or a wine glass, depending on how you shift your own perspective. Yes, Jacob was in that other bed. And, yes, Jacob was in bed with me. Which Jacob felt more real depended on how I focused on him.

Once I wrapped my head around that idea, I started picking up his silver cord in my field of vision…only it wasn't silver. It was red. And it was a huge, badass, ropy-looking thing right out of a sci-fi movie.

What about me? Most people, seeing their man in two places at once with a magic umbilical cord between them, could safely assume they themselves were on a big head-trip, too. But me? I could very well be awake. I touched the bed. My fingers made a depression in the bedspread. Still, that didn't mean anything. It could be an astral representation of the bedspread I was moving. When I tried to shove my hand through it, though, and didn't get that familiar passing-through-the-ball-pit sensation, I began to entertain the possibility that I was actually awake.

Maybe that was why I was able to turn over. Jacob's astral body could block my astral body, but not my physical body, and after I'd had my spiritgasm, I woke up and snapped fully into the physical. I looked behind me, figuring he'd snap back into himself. Nope. Still there. And down by the foot of my bed, the GhosTV was on, flickering, tuned in to a non-channel.

So that amazing pounding I'd just had…did it even happen? I was still dressed. And no squishy surprise packages in my underwear, either. The memory was still there, though, bright and clear.

It seemed to me someone at Camp Hell had not only thought we could do each other in the astral, but that the astral plane itself was one big orgy. Maybe Dead Darla…and maybe our teacher, being an ex-nun, changed the subject whenever Darla brought it up. Or maybe I was reconstructing Camp Hell to fit my current experiences since my memory of those years was so iffy.

That creepy Barnhardt guy at the old folks' home had seemed to enjoy sowing his astral oats. So, yeah, I could probably conclude whatever had just happened was…real. It just wasn't physical.

Shit. Figuring out one level of reality was hard enough. Now I had to deal with two. Although, to be honest, I'd been dealing with two realities ever since I hit puberty. Not dealing particularly well, either.

I inched toward the wall, and naked astral-Jacob rolled onto his stomach. Leave it to him to figure out a way to take up all the space on *both* beds. Since I figured he'd be game to do some experimenting with me—and since he deserved it for turning on the GhosTV before he went to bed—I poked him in the astral shoulder to see if he'd feel it.

My hand passed through him. Neither Jacob stirred.

"If your astral body is here," I murmured, "then where's mine?" Since I was conscious, it would have to be inside of me, wouldn't it? Inside, and aligned with my physical. But if that were the case, then when I poked Jacob's astral body, it should have felt solid like it had when we were doing the astral nasty.

When I thought that, my perspective shifted. I poked him in the shoulder again, and this time, it felt…not quite solid. But substantial. Jacob's astral body grumbled in its sleep.

"Why're you wasting your astral time sleeping?" I asked him. "You should be so jazzed about this you'd practically wet yourself." Unless he didn't know. That was probable. And unless he wasn't going to remember… now, that was just sad. But if Faun Windsong (who'd always thought she was the world's most sparkly light worker) had trouble remembering her astral projections, did Jacob even stand a chance?

I shifted so I was face to face with Jacob's astral body and I sucked some white light. What I really concentrated on was maintaining that mental shift of mine—the faces instead of the wine glass—and I ran my fingers down his bare arm. "Hey, you really need to remember this."

Jacob made an exhausted, "leave me alone, I just shot my wad" noise.

"You're gonna be really pissed off if you don't." I got my face right up to his. The hair on his astral head was shorter, like it had been when I first met him. I think he looked a few years younger, too…though I'd never be brutally honest enough to tell him so. I sucked a little more white light, until the hairs on my forearms felt tingly with static, and tried to visualize my astral body inside my physical body touching Jacob while I pressed my mouth to his.

It felt like a ghost-kiss. Only not scary. Not at all.

Jacob's astral eyes opened, and he looked at me all lovey-dovey.

"Hey," I told him. "You're having an OBE." And then, duh, I realized the acronym probably wouldn't translate well. "You're astral. You need to remember it, okay?"

"You *are* looking at me that way. It's not fake. Not at all."

Jacob Marks—psychic putty in my hands. Did our astral bodies have different personalities…or maybe, more accurately, did they showcase different facets of our existing personalities? It definitely wasn't the Jacob I usually lived with who needed this level of reassurance. Physical Jacob would've been all about the Psych, not the mushy stuff. "Seriously. You've got to remember."

He slung an arm around me and tried to pull me toward him. I didn't budge, so he rammed himself up against me. It was freaky, the way I could half-feel him pressing me against the wall. "I know you think I'm only attracted to your talent, but that's not…" he tried to find my mouth and lose himself in more kisses, but I had a hard time keeping that duality of astral and physical aligned. "You being a PsyCop, like me. You get it. You get me."

And here I'd thought Jacob was uninhibited about discussing his feelings in the physical. I should have realized something was up sooner, given the extent of our conversational skills while he was reaming my ass. That, and the way we magically hadn't needed any lube.

"I get that you'll be totally pissed off if you forget your projection. Tell me you understand. You're astral. And when you wake up, you're gonna remember."

He ran his hand down my back, but jerked it away when my concentration slipped from arguing with him and he found himself inside me—and not in a good way. "What's happening?" he demanded.

"I told you. You are astral. Get it? Astral. You're astral and you need to remember."

He waved his hand as if he was trying to shake something gross off of it. "I think my hand just went through you. It's got something to do with the GhosTV, doesn't it?"

How frustrating, that he was so close to understanding what was going on…and yet, so far. "That's about the size of it. You fell asleep watching the astral channel and here you are. Astral projecting."

On the other side of the wall, I heard a door open and shut. It made me realize how spoiled I'd become living in my very own building—a building with industrially-thick walls that blocked out the outside world so effectively it was just Jacob, and just me. I lowered my voice. "Hey. Can you say it? Tell me you're astral and I'll stop harping on it."

There was a knock on our bathroom door, and Jacob's astral body snapped back into his physical so quick it looked like the subway speeding by. He sat up, squinting, mostly awake in no time flat. I climbed out of bed, impressed that he'd cleared enough space in the room that I could actually call what I was doing *walking*. I turned off the GhosTV, and went to get rid of Dreyfuss before Jacob completely forgot his bodiless jaunt.

When I opened the door, I only did it far enough to see one of Dreyfuss' eyes, and I said, "Now is not a good—"

"We cracked Professor March's email."

Chapter 25

Visions of gospels and testaments danced in my head. I steeled myself to hear that Debbie March's email was full of the bible, just like Lisa's, just like Jacob's. And I started spinning out a theory that maybe Jacob hadn't been nabbed yet because he was a Stiff, which wasn't a very good name for his red, ropy power, but it was all I had. Or maybe the holy roller who was supposed to grab him got a load of his scowl, and his Glock, and his six-foot-three of hard-pumped muscle.

And maybe they went back for reinforcements.

My mouth had gone dry and my throat felt fluttery when Dreyfuss interrupted my impending panic attack by saying, "No weird emails. Well… plenty of weird emails. She's got friends into some kinky cosplay stuff. But no weird bible emails."

"What are you saying? There's nothing suspicious going on?" I checked my watch. "It's the middle of the night and she's nowhere."

"I didn't say there was nothing suspicious—I just said her email's clean… er, clean-ish, anyway."

"But she's still missing."

He turned his hands palm-up and gave a shrug that was way too flippant for the situation.

"You think this is funny?"

He actually considered his answer before he gave it. "I can't even recall the last time I found something funny, Detective." He turned back toward the bathroom door to retreat to his room, but before he closed it, he added, "A detail that might or might not matter—it wasn't a Q-mail account. She had her own domain, and her email went through that—so someone could've tried to bible her and got caught in a filter. We won't know 'til we subpoena her webhost."

Some filter.

Once Dreyfuss was gone, I turned around to face Jacob. He gestured toward the decoy bed and said, "I slept over here because you looked so beat, I wanted to make sure you got some rest."

I laughed. So help me. His so-called "consideration" had just sideswiped a reaction out of me.

"That's funny?"

"I don't know. Maybe. Maybe it's just ironic. Maybe Dreyfuss is right, and nothing's actually funny, and laughter's just a way to keep our heads from blowing up." I maneuvered around the console, sat down hard on the bed where the dirty astral deed was done, and said, "You left the GhosTV on all night and you projected, but you snapped back to your body when he knocked on the door."

Jacob planted his hands on his hips like he wanted to challenge me. "When? Just now?"

"Just now."

"And you saw it."

"Saw it, felt it, took the tour and bought the postcard." I decided to drop the smartass act, since he looked so profoundly bewildered, and instead I patted the bed and invited him to sit down beside me. He sat. The bed dipped. I took his hand between mine and said, "I was trying to make sure you'd remember. I guess I didn't hammer home my point forcefully enough."

"Was I doing anything, or was I just…I dunno…floating around?"

"Oh, you were doing something, all right," I said. He looked at me sideways as if to see if I meant what it sounded like I meant, and I added, "Horndog."

His eyebrows shot up. "Really?" He sat with his amazement for a few seconds, and then said, "Was I any good?"

I could have kept teasing him, but I decided that, thanks to all his secrets that came to light during the astral honesty session, I'd feel like a grade-A jerk if I smart-alecked my way out of this one. I slipped my ectoplasm hand around the back of his neck, drew his face toward me so our foreheads clonked together, and said, "The aftershocks rocked the astral plane." He looked pleased. "I just wish you could remember."

"I'm trying. I don't know. It feels like it does when you know you just had a dream, but you can't grasp it, not at all, even a single detail."

I kissed the corner of his mouth. "There. Does that bring anything back?"

He licked his lips and considered. "I think I need another reminder."

I kissed him again, fit my lips against his more squarely, and lingered over his lush mouth for a few seconds so I could really appreciate the contours, and the texture, and the taste. When I opened my eyes, he was watching me. I looked back…and I wondered what it would take for me to look at him "that way," like he wanted me to so badly. I wasn't sure. I spent most of my time trying to be totally devoid of expression, to not let anyone, living or dead, sneak past my own personal brand of shield. Quite possibly, I wouldn't know how to really look at anybody "that way" even if I tried.

If I couldn't figure out how to make my face convey my feelings, I suppose I'd need to settle for words. "You know how much I love you, right? I don't say it enough, I know. It's…I…" I sighed. "I do. And I've never felt like this before. About anyone. Only you."

While my face was the white noise of the facial expression continuum, Jacob's was more like a symphony. His eyes softened and went all smitten, and he grabbed me by the shoulders, pulled me against him and stopped just short of kissing me hard, and instead, brought our lips together soft as a whisper while his whole body trembled with tension.

I could take a lesson from him. Really. Literally. Get him to feel an emotion and watch what it did to his face—then turn to a mirror and try to see what it might feel like to look the same way. If I really wanted to try it, he'd do it for me. He'd probably do just about anything for me. Somehow, though, I couldn't see myself actually asking him.

Because that would be weird.

◊ ◊ ◊

"I think it'd be okay if you let me out of your sight," Jacob said. "So some religious freak spammed my inbox. I can defend myself. I'm armed—Lisa wasn't."

No disrespect to Lisa, but if she wasn't flashing a badge and a gun, I'd have to agree, she was nowhere near as imposing as Jacob. Even so. "Maybe, if I knew I was leaving you where a bunch of people could see you. Dreyfuss to watch your back. And then maybe Chekotah to keep an eye on Dreyfuss. Maybe then. But we're only working this one angle before breakfast, so it's not like you need to be somewhere else. There's no reason for us to split up now."

I stopped in front of the door number Lyle had given me, and raised a hand to knock.

"Vic," Jacob said quietly. I looked back over my shoulder. "You'll get more out of him without me there."

Talk about a conversation I had no desire to revisit—though Jacob didn't remember having it the first time. "I'm not any good at batting my eyelashes to try to build rapport with my witnesses. It doesn't work, seeing as how they're usually dead. Besides, you take better notes than I do."

I knocked. Lyle let us in, and then got flustered because he only had one chair to offer, the computer chair from his desk. "Just pretend I'm not here," Jacob said, and he strolled over by the window so I could sit down and look Lyle in the eye while I interviewed him.

Lyle perched on the edge of his bed. His lamps and accessories were all Ikea. The bed was made, the surfaces of the dresser, desk and nightstand were all clear, and the scent of Gray Flannel hung in the air. Nothing bad, as far as smells go. Just something that would undoubtedly live in my brain forever after as "that smell from PsyTrain."

I leaned forward, planted my elbows on my knees, did my best to arrange my face like a warm and caring person might, and said, "Something you told me last night—I was hoping you could expand on it."

He swallowed, and went a bit blotchy. "I really have no idea…."

"You said Five Faith was responsible, and that they were targeting someone by going after Lisa, Karen and Debbie."

"Not Debbie. Oh, hell, no. Debbie would never…this was before Debbie disappeared too."

Debbie would never what? I was itching to ask, seeing as how whatever this thing Debbie would never do was, Lisa had apparently done it. I pitched my voice to sound as casual as I could, even though I felt like a big fake. "Then just satisfy my curiosity." I smiled. I was so out of practice it almost hurt. "What was this first theory of yours, the one that doesn't fit because Debbie would never…."

"She'd never let Bert get in her pants, is what." He gave a nervous laugh. "Maybe students get starry-eyed about the power and the prestige, they're naïve, and they're so blown away by his Indian shaman thing—but Debbie was too grounded to get sucked in by all of that. Just goes to show you, I've seen way too many episodes of Law & Order. Dreaming up this whole convoluted thing where Five Faith gets back at Bert for being a heretic by offing the women he's slept with one by one."

We had no proof that anyone had been "offed."

And also...what was that Indian necklace doing in Debbie's shower? *It's complicated*—that's what she'd told me. Maybe she didn't buy into the Chekotah Fan Club. That didn't mean she wouldn't take him for a spin out of boredom, or isolation, or a sense of camaraderie. Or the desire to get back at Faun Windsong.

Faun Windsong. Who was head over heels for Bert Chekotah.

"How long have Chekotah and, uh, Katrina been an item?"

"Ever since I got here."

"Then when did he have time to be dating these other women?"

"Who said anything about dating? I just said they were sleeping together."

"And then Katrina, what? Turns a blind eye?"

"Denial ain't just a river in Egypt." I think he just barely stopped himself from calling me "girlfriend."

"So if Five Faith wanted to get at Chekotah by going after someone he was seeing, why wouldn't Katrina have been at the top of their list?"

Lyle looked baffled. "I don't know. Maybe they're saving her for last." His laptop gave a little chime. "That's breakfast. We need to go; the vegan sausage tastes pretty nasty when it gets cold. Sorry I couldn't think of anything more useful."

We stood, and Jacob, who was already standing, got to the door first. As he opened it, Lyle put his hand on my forearm and said, "Could I talk to you alone for a sec?"

Jacob gave me a raised eyebrow as if to say, *See? I told you one-on-one would've been better.* "I'll be right in the hall."

I didn't think I could handle knowing any more of PsyTrain's dirty little secrets, but I supposed I didn't have any choice but to hear them. After Jacob closed the door behind him, I turned toward Lyle with my arms crossed and said, "Okay. What else?"

"Well, I...was wondering if you wanted to get together for a drink after my shift. Five thirty? Happy hour at El Dorado across the street?"

Whoa. "That wouldn't be a good idea."

"Oh. My. God. You're not gay." Lyle's blotches turned fuchsia. "I'm so sorry, I totally misread—"

I cleared my throat. "Uh, I am, but...I'm seeing somebody."

More nervous laughter. "Thank God. That would've been beyond awkward! So you're seeing someone in Chicago, so what? It's just a drink."

"And I'm on duty. I don't punch a time clock at five and call it a day."

He let out a huffy sigh, crossed his arms to mirror my stance, and gave me a "you're such a partypooper" look.

"Sorry," I said lamely, and turned toward the door.

"Well, if you change your mind and decide you're up for a quickie, you know where to find me."

Once I got out of the room, I'm not sure why I was more relieved—that Jacob was still in the hallway, unabducted, just as he promised he would be, or that I was no longer alone with Lyle "quickie" Peters. No one said a word on the way to the fancy staff dining room, but I couldn't tell if it was everyone who felt awkward, or just me.

We paused outside the dining room, and Lyle turned to look at us as if he couldn't fathom why we weren't charging into the room to load up on sprouted wheat bagels and fair trade coffee. "You go on ahead," I said. "We're right behind you."

Lyle headed into the dining room and started pouring coffee.

"So?" Jacob asked. "What did he have to tell you in private?"

"He invited me for drinks. It wasn't my place to out you, so I just kept it vague and told him I was seeing somebody."

"Oh." Jacob smirked. He didn't look nearly as threatened by my potential date as astral Jacob would have been. "I was hoping he'd dish some more dirt."

I wasn't sure I could handle any more dirt—especially when it was Lisa getting dirty. Lisa. And Chekotah. I know, I know, Lisa's a grownup and, if it was even true, I was sure she had her reasons. But the thought of Chekotah putting the moves on her for a little side action made me want to clock him in the face.

Which would make breakfast pretty interesting.

"So we look at Chekotah?" Jacob said.

The boyfriend is always the logical place to start, and yeah, we did need to take a better look at Chekotah. Maybe we'd see something in light of our new perspective—but did I think it'd point to him sleeping his way through PsyTrain and driving off his conquests before they could tattle to Faun Windsong? No. In fact, I didn't think he had any idea what was going on. He'd seemed upset when we arrived, and genuinely distressed when he heard Debbie was gone too.

"And keep an eye on Katrina," I said. "She might be a lot of things, but she's not stupid. Maybe she's not as oblivious as Lyle thinks."

Chapter 26

Jacob and I were the last ones in the dining room. Three seats were open: one by Lyle, one by the bookkeeper, and one by Faun Windsong. Katrina. Whatever. Although I was seized by a profound urge to get to know the bookkeeper better, it was easy enough to identify my avoidance for what it was, and I sat beside Katrina. Jacob took the seat next to Lyle. The bookkeeper was on his own.

Breakfast was served family style, with a big cauldron of oatmeal being passed around each table. One look at the glistening, slimy surface brought back the memory of ectoplasm so sharply that I nearly regurgitated yesterday's spelt. I took a banana instead. The sticker on the peel proclaimed that it was organic in extra-smug letters. I put it back and decided that maybe I'd try the oatmeal after all. After I scooped it into my bowl, I topped it with a big squirt of honey, then drowned it in enough cinnamon to exorcise an evil spirit. Not bad.

I dragged my spoon through the bowl and watched as the beige oatmeal-colored layer eased shut behind the spoon, and then, a moment later, the cinnamon-colored layer. And I wondered if maybe they had huevos rancheros across the street. Lyle would know. I did my very best not to look at him, in case he'd interpret that as an invitation for a "quickie."

I ended up looking at the final empty seat, and I said to Faun, "So, where's your guy?"

"My guy?" She laughed. "You're so funny." Real laughter, or head-exploding laughter? Sounded like actual amusement, not nerves or awkward release. "*My guy* is spirit walking."

Was that like astral projecting? It seemed like it would be—but if it were, wouldn't she have just said "astral projecting," since she's the big expert? My head hurt. "Does he...spirit walk...often?"

"On the solstices and equinoxes, of course."

Oh yes, of course.

"And whenever he needs guidance from our ancestors." Most of her ancestors were haunting castles back in Europe, but I'd pointed that out enough times at Camp Hell that it was apparent she was determined to let it roll off her back. I did glance at Lyle then, over at the next table. He was spooning raw sugar onto his oatmeal, smiling to himself. Maybe he really was on to something in regards to Katrina's obliviousness.

"Is there a ritual, or…?"

"Absolutely. Shamanic tradition is rich in symbolism and ritual."

The narcissism was killing me, but I forced myself to sound normal and prompt her with, "Such as?"

"Fasting. Drumming. Chanting."

"Peyote?"

"No." She looked down her nose at me as if I couldn't possibly have said something more juvenile. "He's Seminole."

Gee, I wasn't as up on my Native American traditions as the chick who used to call herself Faun fucking Windsong even though she was fifteen sixteenths as lily-white as me. Imagine that. I slashed into the oatmeal with my spoon. Not eating it. Just funneling my aggression. "Summer solstice isn't 'til next week," I pointed out.

"He's trying to figure out what happened to Professor March."

"By burning sage in her room?"

"Not in her room—I don't see how that could affect evidence, but you said not to touch anything, so we didn't touch anything. He's in our room."

"Our" room? They lived together on campus? Quite the happy couple. Or were they? Did Faun say the words *Professor March* with a hint of cattiness, or was I imagining it because I'd seen that necklace hanging in Debbie's shower? Maybe the three missing women had nothing to do with a bunch of bible-thumpers, and everything to do with the fact that they'd known Chekotah in the biblical sense…and then Faun Windsong found out, and one by one, arranged for them to take a permanent hike.

I must have been looking at her funny, even with that expressionless face I've cultivated over the years, because she said, "Our room is a very sacred space."

I almost laughed. But the knowledge that Bert Chekotah had been stepping out of their "sacred space" to stick it to Lisa left me entirely unamused, which killed the laughter dead in my throat. I stabbed my oatmeal a few more times before the other Psychs at my table started looking at *me* funny, and then I decided that eating would probably be my best bet. It might not be pleasant, but I was pretty damn hungry—and at least it would keep my mouth busy so I didn't say something I'd regret.

When I looked down into the bowl, four oatmeal-and-cinnamon colored slashes looked back at me—oozing shut, but definitely there. Not only that, but they spelled out two letters.

TV

I stirred the word out of the oatmeal and pushed the bowl away.

◊ ◊ ◊

While I had no definitive proof that "spirit walking" and astral projection were the same thing, I suspected there were only so many types of psychic phenomena in the world—not necessarily six, like the government's got printed on all their pamphlets and brochures. But few enough that it didn't surprise me when the same mojo went by a different name. And what interested me about astral projection was this: if I could catch Chekotah while he was astral, I might be able to get him to really spill his guts in that same sort of radical honesty Jacob displayed while he floated the ridiculous theory that there was a better ass than his somewhere out in the world. Judging by my prior two trips, if I did manage to drag Chekotah into an astral conversation, I'd probably remember it just fine—and if I was really lucky, he wouldn't.

Jacob thought it was a good plan. When I told him I wanted him to watch over me while I was doing it, he thought it was an even better plan. But even though slipping out of my flesh suit would be the best way for me to take advantage of Chekotah's spirit walk, the knowledge that my right arm had suggested turning on the GhosTV wasn't sitting very well. "I was thinking about trying it without the help of the TV set," I told Jacob.

"Any reason in particular?"

Because I wanted to rebel against my oatmeal. "I just thought I might have a little more control over snapping back into my body if I needed to."

"But that's why I'll be here. I can always wake you up. And besides, since when can you just decide you're going to astral project and fly right out of your body? I thought it was the type of skill that takes people whole lifetimes to perfect."

"I won't know until I try." I took off my shoes and jacket, removed my holster, loosened my tie and sat down on the bed.

"Do you want a drink? Something weak, like a hard lemonade."

The itchy hunger-like feel at the back of my tongue told me half a tab of Valium would not be unwelcome...but supposedly most drugs made it harder to project, not easier. "It's fine. All I need to do is say the magic words—just resting my eyes."

I closed my eyes and folded my hands on my stomach, sighed, and tried to remember what it had felt like to project. Floaty. Foggy. Stuck in a ball pit. I lay still and thought about the sensations, tried to feel those feelings somatically. I remembered...but I didn't feel them. I tried harder, and harder still. Nothing. "How long has it been?" I said, finally.

"Twenty minutes. No luck?"

"Zilch."

"Here, I have an idea." A computer made its "ta-da" startup noise, and then there was the quiet sound of a new keyboard clicking. I kept my eyes shut so as not to undo my twenty minutes of effort. "I'll read a guided meditation for you. Maybe that'll help."

"We can give it a shot."

"Okay, here's one," he said. I settled back on the pillow, and he began reading. "Take a deep breath, and hold it. Imagine your diaphragm stretching, and breathe deeper still...."

Breathe in two counts, stretch the diaphragm, out one count. We'd done all kinds of breathing at Camp Hell. Old news. Jacob reading it—that was new. I could tell he was reading rather than talking, not that he stumbled over the words or anything. But he wasn't smooth, like Stefan was smooth when he induced hypnosis. Fucking Stefan. He was probably the last person I wanted to think about.

In. Out. Focus on your toes. In. Out. Focus on your ankles. Your calves. Your knees. My ass felt like it was asleep—my sciatic nerve again, or did that count as a tingle? Maybe it was a tingle. Maybe I was astral, and I just hadn't opened my astral eyes yet. I opened them. Nope. Still awake. Closed them. And Jacob kept on reading. Breathe. Breathe. Focus on my fingers, my hands, my wrists.

"Hey," I said finally, when I was supposed to be focusing on my chin.

"Yeah?"

"It's not working."

"No big deal. Just go to plan B and turn on the GhosTV."

"Yeah, but…" I rolled onto my side, opened my eyes, and pissed away the last forty-five minutes of focusing and breathing by coming fully awake. I couldn't tell him I was hell-bent on disobeying the oatmeal. That sounded pathetic, even to me.

"We'll turn the amplitude dial down to 1," he said. "How about that?"

"I really don't feel like—"

"Vic, how long do you think Bert's going to be on this spirit walk? Grab him now, while you can." Do it for Lisa. He didn't say it in words, but his eyes said it plenty.

I didn't want to. Really didn't want to. But….

"Fine." I figured if I was successful and I actually did find Chekotah out of his body, I could have the satisfaction of giving him an astral kick in the astral ass, and he'd be none the wiser in waking life. I settled back down and watched Jacob turn on the set and adjust the dials. "But how will you know to wake me up if I need to come back?"

"I'll watch your face."

Yeah, knowing he was staring at me as I was attempting to drift off wouldn't be distracting at all. "That won't help. I don't think the physical body knows what the astral is doing."

"But yours does. Doesn't it? Isn't that why you remember?"

He had me there.

"And as a backup plan, I'll have Lyle call me when Chekotah emerges from his 'sacred space.' If you're still asleep at that point, I'll wake you up. Deal?"

Jacob Marks. Always making so much goddamn sense. I sighed. "Oh, all right. Deal." I closed my eyes, tried to relax myself yet again, and pretended Jacob didn't sound like he was smirking when he called Lyle and talked him into being our sentry.

"Do you want me to read the guided meditation again?" he asked me.

"I guess it couldn't hurt."

"Take a deep breath, and hold it. Imagine your diaphragm stretching…."

The totally unwelcome thought occurred to me that Stefan, with his velvet voice, would've probably had me floating already, and it got me so agitated that I sat straight up and snapped, "Fuck this, I hate it. There's gotta be some other way."

"Breathe in two counts…one, two…and out one count."

Talk about persistent. That was my first notion, until I whipped around and saw my own head back there on the pillow. Jacob wasn't ignoring me. He couldn't hear me. I looked at Jacob, and then back at myself again. My hair really did look pretty spiffy—but I thought my face looked a little rough around the edges, in the smattering of sparkly gray stubble amid the black, and the creases at the corners of my eyes and across my forehead that announced to the world that forty wasn't all that far off.

"Focus on your toes...."

I glanced down at my solar plexus in search of a silver cord, but there wasn't one. I felt my forehead, and again, no luck. Not with anything cord-shaped. But it did feel taut, kind of like my sunburned scalp. I looked back at my body again. As much as I didn't care for the fact that it was aging, I preferred that to the alternative. When all was said and done, that body was still mine. I'd prefer some guarantee that if I roamed, I'd eventually find my way back to it.

But some things in life don't come with guarantees.

I swung out of the bed and stood, and the floor felt firm beneath my astral feet. Was Jacob's red energy shielding me, or was I shit outta luck because he was awake? I took a good look at him and searched for the red energy. For the veins. "Notice your thighs." He smirked. "Your buttocks. Your lower back."

No veins. And he couldn't even say the word *buttocks* with a straight face. Still, I had faith that he would keep my shell of a body safe while I was out. "Okay, mister," I told him. "I'm trusting you not to let anything nasty happen to me while I go put the thumbscrews to Chekotah."

And with that, I pictured the instructors' wing of the building, steeled my astral body, and hurtled through the wall.

Chapter 27

Either the other two times I'd already projected had been good practice for me, or we now had the GhosTV at just the right setting…or maybe a little bit of both. Morning classes were in session. The only other person in the hallway was a fifty-something lady in a flowered smock with a housekeeping cart, an iPod and a vacuum cleaner. I considered calling to her, waving, trying to see if I could make her see me. She looked physical, but I wasn't really experienced enough to attest to her physical state with a hundred percent certainty. Besides, if she was astral, she probably had her astral iPod turned up good and loud, so she wouldn't hear me either way.

I thrust my head through the first door. Empty room. Moved on to the next door. The same. It occurred to me that I should have told Jacob to ask Lyle which room was Chekotah's "sacred space." I might not be able to read the number on the front of it, but I'd at least know which floor I should start on. Some rooms had plants and pretty curtains and natural light. Some were sleek and Asian-inspired. None of them had personality like Debbie March's room had—and that thought just made me all the more determined to wring an answer out of Chekotah.

Frilly room. Plain room. Room with pentagrams on the walls and candle wax on the dressers. Room stuffed with books. I challenged myself to a little game of guess-what's-next as I moved on to the next room, decided it was time for another frilly room, stuck my head through the doorway to have a look—and found myself sprawled in the hallway with my feet sticking through the opposite wall and my head half-sunk through the floor. Damn. I half expected to find little astral birdies tweeting in circles above my ringing head.

I definitely needed to start being more careful about where I stuck my body parts.

More cautiously, now, I reached out with my astral fingertips and touched the door. It felt as solid as a physical door. No reason I needed to use the door to get into that room, right? I touched the wall to the side of the door. It felt equally as solid. I worked my way down the wall until I felt the flex-and-give I was accustomed to, and I carefully put my hand through. When the wall didn't complain about it, I followed with my head to take a look.

The room was frilly. The bedspread was lacy and the walls were covered in pressed flowers with fancy frames. While I wasn't entirely sure I'd find a whole bison hide on the wall of the room Bert Chekotah shared with Faun Windsong, I suspected there'd at least be a dream catcher or two. I'd overshot.

No problem. I'd approach Chekotah's room from the side. I felt my way around the flower room. Every wall was permeable, except for the one it shared with Chekotah's room. Damn. All right. How about the ceiling? I rose up easy as you please, patting myself on the back all the while for my fine control of my subtle bodies, pushed my head through the ceiling, and found myself face to face with a dried up raccoon carcass. I jittered back a yard or two and told myself to stop being a smug jackass and start paying attention.

I scanned the attic. No ghosts. Nothing glowing. Nothing hinky, other than the long-gone critter.

Good.

And, hey, at least the body marked the spot where I'd come up through the rafters so I could get my bearings.

I felt my way along the ball pit of the floor, pushing my fingers through every few feet as I worked my way toward Chekotah's room. I knew when I'd found it, all right. My fingers bonked against the ceiling like it was made of cement. I could trace the whole perimeter of the room, it turned out, all by poking around and seeing where my hand didn't break through.

I routed myself back through the frilly room and then down another floor in an attempt to come at Chekotah from below. There was an empty classroom down there, unused, judging by the way the furniture was stacked inside as if it had only been put there for storage and not for actual use, and the sheen of dust covering everything. There were rows of books lining the wall, the types of texts you'd find at Sticks and Stones. Someone had drawn a sun with a smiley face in it on the whiteboard. How fucking optimistic.

The ceiling was rock solid. Great. Now what?

I floated there with my astral hands on my astral hips and glared down at the classroom as if it could help me figure out what to do. I couldn't read the books, since sticking my head between the closed pages would no doubt be confusing. I couldn't pick up the whiteboard stand and drive it through the ceiling...could I? I floated down and tried to grab it, but my hand passed right through. Besides, I'd hardly sneak up on Chekotah if I came crashing up through the floor.

The physical floor.

I looked up at the ceiling again and tried to help the thought that was attempting to form in my head. I didn't need to get through a physical barrier. I needed to get through a psychic barrier. And if I needed to get through a psychic barrier, I'd need a psychic tool, like...what was that band name? Astral knife.

I grabbed toward my pocket, the one that had filled itself with fairy dust when I'd been trying to summon salt, even though I had no pocket there since I was wearing an astral T-shirt and jeans rather than a suit. Even so, my hand brushed against something, though whatever it was, once I overthought it, it slipped out of my grasp.

Remember the fairy dust, I told myself, and I imagined a big, heavy blade, something substantial enough to cut through the protection keeping me out of Chekotah's room. I made a grab for it, then, doing my very best to ignore the niggling of doubt that insisted this was all some kind of stupid dream and I was making it all up. No. It wasn't just a dream. It was real, all real. And damn it, I was good at it.

My hand closed around something hard. Big, and hard, and weighty. I gathered my courage and looked down. I'd summoned an astral axe.

You'd think I would be pleased, but mostly I was disconcerted. I hadn't been picturing an axe. In fact, if I were to be honest, I think I'd been picturing the cleaver from the last Ginsu Knife infomercial I saw. But I'd summoned an axe.

Did that mean my subconscious was forming it when I'd been busy focusing conscious thoughts on something else, or that the axe had an astral existence totally separate from my imagination? I didn't know. I wasn't sure *anyone* even knew. If projecting was anything like dreaming, Debbie might have a theory. But Debbie couldn't exactly explain it to me in nice, simple words if she'd been kidnapped by Five Faith, driven out of town by Faun Windsong, or spirited away by an Internet demon.

Or killed and dumped in the ocean.

No. I gripped my astral axe tighter and gave it a swing. Because Debbie wasn't dead. She couldn't be dead, because if she'd been murdered, she would have stuck around long enough to tell me.

Because if Debbie was dead, chances were, so was Lisa.

The axe bit into the ceiling, shuddered, stuck there for a moment, then came free when I gave it a yank. I swung again, grunting with the effort, and felt something split. I pulled the axe free and stared up at the ceiling, panting. My breathlessness was more from panic than exertion, I think, given that I wasn't currently physical and didn't actually need to breathe. Also, I realized I'd probably just given myself away big-time with all my chopping and grunting. So much for sneaking up on Bert Chekotah.

The ceiling looked exactly the same, but I knew what I'd felt. I reached my hand up into the split I'd made with my astral axe.

It pushed through.

I snatched it back, just in case Chekotah was waiting up there for me with an astral axe of his own, and I sucked some white light to gather my courage. He'd be on to me by now. But I needed to face him, to see what the hell was going on. What had happened to all those women. I sucked harder, and my vision went sparkly. Now or never. I tensed all over, and I shot myself up through the rift.

I erupted from the ball pit and into Chekotah's room in a cascade of astral sparks. I had the axe raised over my head and I was ready to swing it around to show I meant business. I took in the room with one sweep. Only one thing was moving, barely—a figure in the corner, sitting cross-legged on the floor with its back to me. It trembled.

Nothing glowed. Nothing shimmered. Nothing sparkled, once the backlash of my appearance died down and fizzled out.

Nothing else was astral. Nothing besides me.

Focusing on the figure in the corner made me shoot up closer to it before I could second-guess myself. I craned my neck to get a look at its profile and ended up flickering into existence perpendicular to it—Chekotah. No problem, though. He didn't seem to see me.

A shrine area was set up in the corner, with wall hangings and feathers and carvings defining the perimeter of the space. No dream-catchers. The walls were painted in earth tones and the floor was tiled in pale orange terra cotta.

I must've been expecting to find Chekotah wearing a Village People getup, so I was surprised to see him in a red hat that was a cross between a pillbox and a turban, and a blouse of patchwork squares that looked like it was sponsored by the local quilt shop. He sat on a woven mat with a drum cradled in the crook of his crossed legs and a smudge stick billowing smoke at his elbow. An MP3 player docked in a speaker system on his other side played the sounds of Native American drumming and chant. Chekotah's hand fluttered as if maybe he'd begin to drum along, but then it collapsed, defeated, and left him there to sit and squint against the smoke.

Maybe Faun Windsong had been wrong about that whole peyote thing—'cos I could tell he wasn't astral. He'd be glowing blue, or at least sort of transparent, if he was. He could have been high, staring into the smoke like that. Unless "spirit walking" wasn't a form of astral projection at all, and it was more of a trance, an inner journey, and Chekotah was actually more of a clairvoyant than a medium.

Although, if that were the case, if he wasn't a medium, how had he managed to exorcise the Criss Cross Killer? Maybe "spirit walking" was just his name for meditation. After all, I was a high-level medium, and before I'd started watching the projection channel, I'd never experienced a lucid astral journey of my own.

I tossed the axe aside in disgust, and it made a couple of wobbly loops in the air before it disappeared into the wall beside Chekotah's bed. "You were supposed to be astral," I snapped at him. He stared straight ahead, while the Indians on the tape continued their atonal chanting and drumming.

"You know something more than you're telling us," I said. "I know you do. Damn it. There you are, with your stupid sage stick, and your stupid drum—and what the fuck is happening to these women? Women who trusted you. You ought to be ashamed."

The chant droned on.

I glared at him for a few minutes, which he didn't notice, and I considered whether or not it might be possible for me to make Chekotah's astral body come out and play. His astral body existed—it was just lined up with his physical body at the moment. He was already in some kind of trance. Maybe if I focused, I could pull it out of there and make it give me a straight answer.

Where I should grab him, though? That was the question. I don't really like touching other people. Not people I don't intend to sleep with, anyway—and he might be some new age, ethnic prettyboy, but given what I'd learned about his reputation, I'd sooner head over to Lyle's room for a "quickie" than do the nasty with him.

His arm seemed impersonal enough. I made a grab for it, and my hand passed right through. Damn. I squatted next to him, and I glared some more. "I went through all this trouble to talk to you," I said, "you'd damn well better come out here and say something." I sucked white light again and grabbed for his arm.

I might as well have tried to grab the sage smoke. In fact, that would've probably been more effective. At least in the physical, when you pass your hand through smoke, it moves. Grabbing Chekotah's arm? Nothing.

So he couldn't hear me, wasn't going to talk to me, didn't feel it when I grabbed him, and didn't look like he was going to do anything but sit there and look miserable. Talk about a bust.

The floor where I stood felt too solid to sink through, as if Chekotah's protections still held. I turned around to head back the way I came, and froze to the spot.

There was a door next to Chekotah's bed that hadn't been there before, and framed in that doorway, a blood-covered woman stood, holding the astral axe.

Chapter 28

"Are you okay? Ma'am? Ma'am?" Thank God for cop-mode or I swear I'd just shut down like an unplugged blender. I'd never injured a civilian in the line of duty, and frankly, given that I almost never need to draw my weapon, I thought I'd retire free from that particular privilege. Leave it to me to nail someone with a careless toss of an astral axe.

If she even was astral.

She had the bluish, whitish, transparent and glowy look that Faun Windsong had when I'd first discovered Faun in the astral. The blood…well, that was different. It looked like the axe had cracked her sternum right in half. The blood looked black. It spread over the front of her flowing white dress in a rapidly-spreading stain, with sparks playing over the edges of it as she moved. It was hard to take my eyes off that bleeding, sparking wreck of a wound, but for just a second, I did. Long enough to determine she had no silver cord.

She flickered like a ghost from a B-movie and appeared beside Chekotah. The axe stayed there beside the ghost door, dropping first on the top of the blade, like it had actual weight and heft, and then dissolving into the floor as it tipped over sideways, gone by the time the handle would have hit the floor. Flicker—her, staring down at him with a grief-stricken look on her face. Flicker—her hand reaching toward his hair to stroke it.

"Ma'am?"

No reaction. If she was a ghost and I was astral, she probably couldn't hear me. Different planes, right? Er…maybe. Then she wound her hand in Chekotah's hair and tugged—and his hair moved.

She could touch him.

Her face contorted, and at first I thought it was just the facial acrobatics people do when they're gonna start bawling, but then I realized that she wasn't exactly sad. It was more like she was…triumphant. She pulled harder, and Chekotah's hair starting glowing where it was wrapped around her hand.

"Step away," I barked, because her body language told me she'd be happy to tear the astral hair right out of his head.

She ignored me and yanked.

Chekotah's head blurred. Or maybe it stretched. His physical body was just sitting there, like it didn't feel anything at all—but the top of his head was stretching like a piece of Silly Putty.

"Police, step back." Useless, I know, since it carried zero weight in the astral—and besides, she couldn't even hear me. But that's the thing about training. You repeat it enough times, and when push comes to shove, your body goes through the motions for you while your mind is busy looping on the words *holy shit.*

Since I now knew how to do a wristlock from every conceivable angle, I grabbed for her wrist. I must not have thought I'd actually make contact, because it shocked the hell out of me when I grabbed, pulled and twisted, and ended up with a bloody ghost in restraint. Chekotah's head snapped back to normal. Maybe he felt it—I think he sagged forward a little. Or maybe he was just getting tired of sitting there staring into his smoke.

The ghost cried out, or maybe she roared. It wasn't a human sound from a human throat. It was like feedback and static channeled through a disembodied voicebox. Vinyl tie. I reached in my pocket to grab it, but right as my hand closed around the spot where it would be, I realized that I was in civilian clothes, so of course I wouldn't have the vinyl tie with me.

At that moment, the moment I doubted myself, I lost my grip on the bloody ghost. She flickered and disappeared.

I'd touched her? Maybe she'd been able to hear me after all, and she'd just been ignoring me—at least until I subjected her to the ol' snap-and-pop. A chill ran through my astral body. I hadn't realized it was possible to be astrally cold. I scanned the room. The door? Gone. The axe? Gone. Chekotah? Useless excuse for a man. Some big-time shaman he was, if he didn't realize blood ghost and me were having a wrestling match right behind his head.

Unless she'd done something to him. Messed him up, emotionally, mentally. As the thought occurred to me that I needed to get a better look at Chekotah and make sure he was all right, the room changed, and I was right up against him. "Can you hear me?" I hollered in his ear. Either he was paralyzed, or he couldn't. I took a look at his hair. It seemed to still be there. Not even messed up. Whatever had just happened, it must have left his physical intact and instead affected his subtle bodies. It had sure as hell looked like his physical body was stretching, but physical molecules and cells and atoms couldn't actually do that.

At least I hoped not.

I circled around him to try to get a good look at his eyes. Thanks to my time in the nuthouse, I knew crazy eyes when I saw 'em, and it looked to me like there was someone home upstairs in Bert Chekotah's head...someone who wasn't doing anything particularly useful at the moment, but at least the attic apartment was occupied.

I was itching to get back, but I figured I should do a final check for injuries—astral injuries—if there even was such a thing. I checked him out the best I could. Face, hands, body, all normal. As I was getting ready to fly back to the relatively safe confines of my own skin, I noticed the light catching on something that had been camouflaged by the checkerboard pattern on the yoke of Chekotah's traditional native smock.

I squared myself up to it and looked harder. It was glistening.

He'd been slimed.

By the blood ghost? Or by me? The goo glistened just below the spot where I'd grabbed her in a wristlock. Since Chekotah was in the same position, I attempted a reenactment to see if I could tell where the ectoplasm had originated. It had all happened so fast it was hard to tell, even if I hovered my hand around the back of Chekotah's head and tried to imagine that eerie stretching effect. Which I had totally seen...hadn't I?

I checked out my hand. It was dry. So it couldn't be my hand-juice on Chekotah's shirt—evaporating, growing smaller even as I tried to figure out where it had come from. In fact, I didn't even think I was capable of producing ectoplasm while I was astral, because it was a physical manifestation of my power. That's what Dreyfuss had said. And he wasn't being a smartass at the time, either.

Could I, though? If I tried? Both times I'd slimed myself, I'd been wound up tight with anxiety and siphoning white light for all I was worth. I currently had anxiety in spades—so I opened up the floodgates, and I pulled.

My astral body glowed, and a wave of disorientation washed over me. But my hand stayed dry.

While I was busy sucking light, someone managed to approach the room in the physical just as I was too dazzled by white light to notice. I flinched at the sound of a door opening, and Faun Windsong slipped into the room. "Bert?" she loud-whispered, in a voice that conveyed *I know I'm interrupting you so I'll do a funny voice to make up for it.* "Did you want me to chant with you? Maybe it'd help you focus."

Seriously—they talked like that in the privacy of their own room? *Do you want me to chant with you?* Although I guess I shouldn't throw stones, given the fact that Jacob was probably telling me to focus on my forehead or my collarbone or my elbow at that very moment.

Chekotah's shoulders sagged. "It's not going to help. The problem is me. The ancestors won't talk to me because…my heart is closed to them."

Maybe so…but the top of his head seemed pretty accessible.

Faun approached and knelt beside him just beyond the fringe of his mat. "How can you say that, after everything you do for us—all of us—here?" She took his hand and wove their fingers together. "Taking over for Dr. Park when he was too much of a coward to deal with Five Faith. That took courage. Your heart isn't closed. It's stress that's bothering you, pure and simple. That's all it is." She moved behind him and began to rub his shoulders, and I backpedaled until I was flat against the wall from my sheer horror at the thought that I might be about to witness Faun Windsong's seduction technique.

"Did you ever think that maybe the missing women brought it on themselves?" she said. "They never fit in here. None of them. The students were always complaining about Debbie…."

Brought it on themselves? I'd had myself convinced that Faun Windsong was an innocent bystander in this whole mess…but hearing her talk when she thought no one was listening but Chekotah made me wonder. I was straining forward to make sure I caught every bit of their "private" conversation when a sudden lurch knocked me on my astral ass. Blood ghost, back for more? I tried to rally, to whip around and face her, but before I knew it I was flying through the ball pit so fast I thought I'd end up with skidmarks on my forehead.

My flight ended with a bodyslam into the physical that left me gasping for air. Blood ghost hadn't dragged me down; my own silver cord had.

"Vic?" Jacob shook me by the shoulder. "Are you with me?"

My head spun. Not like Auracel-spins, and not even like sucking-too-much-white-light spins. It was the feeling, I suppose, of having my astral and my physical lined up so suddenly, and so violently, that my subtle bodies were reverberating like a big Tibetan gong.

"Lyle called. He said Katrina was heading for their room."

"No kidding—and she was saying some pretty fucking incriminating shit." I pushed myself up into a sitting position and my hand landed in something wet. Actually, no. My hand *was* wet. Ectoplasm. "Sonofa—why'd you pull me back now, right when they were getting to the good stuff?"

"What was I supposed to do? Leave you standing there so Katrina could see you questioning Bert in the astral?"

"See me? She couldn't see me in the astral if I poked her in the eye."

"I figured you'd rather play it cautious."

Right…like I always do. "Chekotah wasn't astral. And Faun couldn't see me."

Jacob took my hand by the wrist—gently, for all that we were currently none too thrilled with each other—and turned it palm up so he could see the psychic jelly cupped in my hand. I sighed hard and gestured for him to go ahead and touch it. He dragged his finger over my palm, and I shivered.

"Why did this happen again?" he asked. "Is this how I'll know that you're really astral and not just asleep?"

I almost said, "How should I know?" in a fit of snippiness, but I had to admit, it was a legitimate question—and if I didn't know, who else would? "I don't think there's any way for you to tell if I'm projecting or not. I didn't slime myself on either of my other trips…so this must've happened here in the physical while I was trying to see if I could summon ectoplasm there in the astral." I explained the whole thing to him—the astral axe, the blood ghost, the slime on the back of Chekotah's blouse, and even the stretched head. I felt a little crazy talking about that last part. But you never know which piece is going to make the whole puzzle come together.

Jacob didn't say anything when I finished. He just sat there cradling my hand, which was long-dry but still a little bit cold, and he stared at me.

"What?" I said finally.

"Do you realize how big this is?"

"I dunno. What, specifically?"

"The ability to travel anywhere, to see a location without being physically present, to hear a private conversation?"

He made it sound awfully empowering. What it had felt like to me was that I was flailing around, making up the rules as I went along. Like usual.

In Jacob's assessment, I was some kind of superspy. And that was exciting for maybe two seconds, until a few more realizations sank in. The CIA had been trying to crack remote viewing since 1972, and I had no desire for the government to be any more interested in me than it already was. Even the remote viewer the FPMP supposedly had was only spoken of in whispers. "We gotta be careful who we tell," I said.

Jacob squeezed my fingers. It hurt the tight scabs, but even so, the feel of his hand surrounding mine was a comfort. He sat that way for a moment, and then when he spoke, it was quiet, and very measured. "You know how, when we figured out that I actually had something other than a big psychic void inside me, right away we told Carolyn and Crash so we could get their take on it?"

"Yeah."

"Let's just keep this to ourselves."

Being on the same page with Jacob, especially right after we'd been snarling at each other over him pulling me out of the projection, should have been a relief. Instead, the fact that he'd agreed with me sent an icy finger of dread sneaking down my spine. Not only would federal recruitment efforts step up if I made this new facet of my talent known. If the wrong people found out I could sneak around at will and return to my body with a full understanding of what I'd just heard and seen, I might as well paint a big ol' target on my forehead and kiss my ass goodbye.

Chapter 29

Thanks to my enviable new method of gathering evidence, Jacob and I could agree that we had more direction in figuring out what was going on with all the disappearing girls. Agreeing on which direction that might be was another story.

"Faun Windsong actually said they deserved it," I repeated for the umpteenth time. "If that's not a big red flag, I don't know what is."

"True, but you can't ignore the bloody ghost. She was gruesome, right? And she was trying to touch Bert."

I wasn't sure exactly what she'd been trying to do to him—slime him, possess him or lobotomize him—but whatever it was, it didn't look too savory.

"I think we need to find out who she is." He pulled out his notebook and poised his pen over it. "Give me a description."

"Other than the gaping black wound in her chest that was throwing off sparks?" I sighed. "Caucasian. Twenty-five to thirty. Five foot five, average weight, dark hair, pale skin." I thought back to her features in search of anything that might help me pick her out, though unfortunately she hadn't had any astral tattoos or name tags. "Maybe a little long in the chin."

"And if you saw her here, she died here. Right?"

"Either that, or she blames Chekotah for her death and she's following him around. Not that I see him as a murderer—he doesn't strike me as the type—but maybe someone who convinced her to do a hippy-dippy herbal cure that stopped her heart and landed her in the hospital with her sternum cracked open." Figuring out who'd died on the property in the last ten, twenty years shouldn't be hard if the local PD was willing to pull some records. Figuring out who Chekotah knew that had died a sudden or violent death, one in which he was somehow culpable, without letting him know we were sniffing around him? Nearly fucking impossible. "Look, never mind the ghost. I need to get back there and see what Faun was saying."

"Never mind the ghost? Listen to yourself. You're carrying such a grudge against Katrina that you're writing off the most important witness."

"There's no grudge."

"Are you sure? Because she seemed to come through Camp Hell pretty much unscathed—in fact, she doesn't even call it that. It's Heliotrope Station when she's referring to it."

I yanked my hand out of his lap and balled my fist a few times to bring the feeling back into my frigid fingers. "You keep on talking to me like this, I'll be too ramped up to fly back over there anytime today."

He kept gnawing at that same old bone as if I'd consented to be part of the conversation. "She might not be as strong as you, but she's still a decent medium, isn't she? It's more than just cold spots for her, right?"

"So?"

"So…it would stand to reason that she would have been in demand just as much as you. Or at least nearly as much."

"If you try to tell me I brought whatever happened at Camp Hell on myself…you'd better get used to sleeping in the decoy bed."

He grabbed me and pulled me against his chest before I had a chance to flinch away. "You're putting words in my mouth. What I am saying is that you might be pissed off at her for not deflecting some of the attention off you. That's all."

Seeing as how Jacob typically makes so much sense, even though my brain was trying to spin into a heated panic, I had to admit that being pissed off about something like that did sound an awful lot like me. Why hadn't she taken some of the heat? Maybe she had…and she'd just processed it differently than me. Taken those sleep-deprived exercises in futility and reframed them as exciting, multi-day cram sessions in search of a brave new world of Psych.

Or maybe the powers-that-be had played catch and release, and allowed her to swim back to her non-traumatic Heliotrope Station experience since she was just a minnow, while they had a great, big catch they could be feasting on instead. Maybe it was only the big fish who'd been trawled in the nightmare net. Movie Mike. Stefan. Me.

"I'm not saying we don't look at Katrina." Jacob's voice was gentle and low, and he spoke into my hair. "I'm just saying that a bloody spirit in a building that's supposedly clean—that's important, too."

"Even if the locals were on board, which I'm thinking they're not, it'll take us forever. Back home, we've got people we know who can dig through records for us, people willing to cut us a little slack. Here, I don't even know how to figure out who we're supposed to call."

"Then let Dreyfuss do it." Although I gave pulling away a pretty good try, Jacob had me in a bear hug, and he just crushed me to his chest harder. "He's got the contacts. He's got the resources. Let him dig up the records, and in the meanwhile, you see if you can get back to Chekotah's room."

I suppose it could've been worse. At least Jacob was on board for the astral eavesdropping portion of the program. He could have told me to physically go and question Chekotah and Faun, after all. He was too accustomed to getting a psychic edge on his statements, I guess, to go back to needing to dissect a witness' actual statement to pick out the truth.

It was a good enough plan, one we could both live with. And while I was tempted to tell myself that giving Dreyfuss some paperwork to pull would keep him out of our hair, I did have to admit—we really hadn't seen much of him. Only those couple of times he was in our room giving us electronics.

I went through the bathroom and gave the door to Dreyfuss' room an ungentle bang. Shuffling, footsteps. He opened the door. "Any news?"

Although my goal had been to get him working on the photo lineup and get back to what I'd been doing, my curiosity spiked. What, exactly, did he do all day? He didn't interview anyone. And, other than his walk through Debbie's bedroom, he hadn't been combing for physical evidence. I glanced over his shoulder. He had a laptop on his desk, but it was off. That didn't mean anything, though. Maybe he had it set up to power down the second he shut the cover. "Another ghost," I said as I tried to get a better idea of what he'd been up to. "In the hall outside Chekotah's room."

"Sloppy cleanup work. They should ask for their money back."

"She wasn't talking. I thought you could dig up some info and help me figure out who she was."

I wasn't entirely truthful about my location and astral state, but when it came down to the blood ghost herself, I gave him the same description I'd given Jacob—minus the touching Chekotah and the ectoplasm parts. He didn't write anything down. "And how does she fit in?"

"I won't know until I figure out who she is."

"A theory. A guess. Is she victim number one? A witness? A fluke you're trying to rule out? A little something would help me know which rocks to start turning over first."

"Maybe she lived here? Maybe she was someone Chekotah knew, since she was near his room?" I shrugged, and did another visual sweep of Dreyfuss' desk, what I could see of it beyond his head and his half-closed door, via the space he was mostly blocking. No clue what he'd been up to all this time. I had myself convinced he'd been busy spying—it takes time to monitor all those bugs and little cameras, after all—when he turned his head and I noticed a ridge on his cheek. The GhosTV had me seeing things again, veins and bulges that didn't exist. Or so I thought. Until it didn't shift or move or do anything supernatural at all, and I realized it was a pillow mark.

That asshole'd been sleeping.

"I do think you're on to something," he said. "But your vagueness needs work."

"What're you trying to say?"

"You were just standing there in the hall outside Chekotah's room when this ghost appeared, didn't say anything to you, and didn't do anything in particular?"

"That's not what I—"

"Stories have beginnings, middles and ends. Why were you hovering around Chekotah's doorway? What did you say to the ghost that she didn't answer? Why did she disappear, when it was all said and done? If she even did. Maybe she's still standing there in the hallway, waiting for you to bring a photo lineup and see if you can put a name to the face."

"I wasn't being vague—I was trying to get to the point. I went to Chekotah's room to ask him a question, I saw the blood ghost in the hall, I asked her if she was okay and she didn't answer me, and when I touched her wrist to get her attention she disappeared."

"There you go. Was that so difficult?" He winked at me. *Winked*. "We'll make a proficient liar out of you yet."

When I went back to our room, I closed the door very carefully behind me, because if I slammed it as hard as I wanted to, it'd fall off its hinges and Dreyfuss would be able to peek in at us any time he wanted. "Don't let him get to you," Jacob told me. "I can tell you're ticked off. Ignore him. Just think about relaxing and getting astral again."

Which had taken me an hour the first time I'd done it. Chances were, Faun Windsong would be long gone by the time I got my astral ass back up there. But the problem did seem to center around the Native American couple of the year. And since there was a chance, albeit slim, that I might learn something important they weren't willing to say to my face, and because I wouldn't put it past her to annoy Chekotah all morning while he was busy moping, I settled myself back down on the bed and tried to get astral.

Tried being the operative word.

I closed my eyes and imagined I was looking down at myself, and Jacob read through the relax-this-and-that script, and the GhosTV was tuned the same as it had been before. And nothing. No drifting, no floating, no astral at all…because my stomach kept moaning and groaning like I hadn't fed it in days. "I don't think spelt agrees with me."

"Are you sick?"

"No…just hungry." Hungry enough to eat the packing crate.

"It's not even eleven, although we are two hours off. It says here that any kind of physical distraction—stuffy nose, cold room, noises, hunger—will make it really hard to project. That's probably why they do the sensory deprivation tanks in Katrina's class."

"I'm not shutting myself up in any—"

"I was just thinking we should order you a burrito. That's all."

"I'd blow you for a burrito."

"You'd blow me anyway." True. But the burrito would make it especially satisfying. Jacob dialed information, connected to the Mexican restaurant across the street, listened for a long moment, and then hung up. "They don't open 'til four."

"Four? But they're a restaurant. Why aren't they open for lunch? Everyone opens at eleven for lunch. Eleven thirty, tops."

"We don't have time to waste on this. Give me Lyle's card."

"Aw crap, not more cardboard and lawn clippings. Can't you just look in the phone book?"

"Don't worry, I'm not sending him to the kitchen. I'll just ask him the name of a nearby restaurant that delivers."

Not a bad idea. It was probably faster than calling around and trying to give directions to where we were when we didn't exactly know, ourselves. Plus, he'd lived here nearly two years. He should have a shortlist of decent restaurants. It seemed like a good plan, until Jacob explained to Lyle what we wanted, stopped to listen, and the vertical line made a reappearance between his eyebrows. What, was it a national restaurant holiday, now? First no direct flights from Chicago, and now this. Fine. There had to be an open grocery store. Or even a gas station. The green chile microwave burritos at the gas station minimart went down okay with an antacid chaser.

I was about to signal to Jacob to just forget the whole thing when he started giving Lyle the order. Two chicken burritos, rice and beans, extra guac. He thanked Lyle and hung up.

"He's playing concierge now?" I said. "When we first got here, he didn't even want to deal with answering the phone."

"It might just be an excuse for him to try and get in your good graces… but I'd rather play it safe. He's going to go pick it up himself. He said people stopped having food delivered to PsyTrain once Five Faith showed up on their radar."

"They're worried an anti-Psych delivery guy's gonna spit in their food?"

"Or worse. Radiator fluid. Rat poison."

My stomach should have clenched up at the mere thought of it…but it didn't. I was way too famished for a little anti-freeze to kill my appetite.

Jacob pulled his laptop onto his lap and scrolled down the astral projection site to pick up a few more pointers while we waited for our food, only he wasn't really reading it. Just looking. "We're sitting ducks," he said finally, disgusted.

"You and me, or…?"

"Psychs. In general. I would have expected this to happen fifteen years ago. Not now."

I made a noise that didn't mean much of anything, since it sounded more like he was venting than trying to elicit a response from me.

"And you know what the worst part is?" he said. "It's not the criminals trying to take us out. It's regular people."

I couldn't say I was particularly shocked. Maybe I'd never thought society would thank us for all the monsters we helped put away. At the very least, it would be nice to be allowed to live in peace…but deep down inside, maybe I never expected even that much. Not in the long run. "Someone who's going to feel threatened by another poor schmuck's ESP probably felt the same way fifteen years ago. It's likely a charismatic instigator met up with the right hotheads at the right time, and convinced them to start a movement, and now they've got somewhere to channel the hate."

My assessment didn't make Jacob feel better. Poor guy. He just wasn't accustomed to being hated.

Chapter 30

While it was only eleven o'clock in the morning, and while I usually am a morning person, I'd managed to drift off by the time Lyle showed up with lunch. I lurched awake with some difficulty, feeling bone-tired, disoriented, and of course sore from wrestling the GhosTV out of its crate two days ago. Even so, the delightful smell of chicken simmered in salsa verde urged my laggy body to shake off the dregs of sleep. I sat up and ran my fingers through my hair while Jacob retrieved a twenty out of his wallet to pay Lyle for our food.

"Not there," he said, as Lyle moved to put the bag on the GhosTV.

"This isn't…what is…" Lyle did a triple-take at the worn console. "Where did this old thing come from? I can have the security guards move it to the dumpster."

"It's ours," Jacob said calmly.

Lyle looked as if he thought he was getting punked. "This? The TV? That's what the big delivery was?"

"It's a long story."

I stood up, grabbed the bag out of Lyle's hand and started rifling through it. I was so enthusiastic the paper tore. There were chips in there. Warm, crunchy corn tortilla chips that stained the bag dark where the oil wicked out of them…and there was probably extra salsa in there too, but I'd shoved a whole handful in my mouth without even checking for those little plastic tubs. Salt. Grease. Corn. Really good, even with a pointy triangular corner digging into my soft palate.

Jacob looked at me sideways. "I'm starving," I said. A few flecks of corn chip blew out of my mouth as I spoke.

"You don't say."

Lyle flushed a bit—no doubt vicariously embarrassed for me—but I couldn't stop eating. I jammed in another few chips. Also pointy. He started to back toward the door, unsure where to look: at me, eating like I'd developed a sudden and profound tapeworm, or at the seventies-style TV in the middle of the room. No doubt I came off so weird he was relieved I hadn't taken him up on that "quickie." And that was some trick, coming off as weird in a building full of Psychs where the fact that I spoke to the dearly departed was par for the course.

He was just about to make a run for it when Jacob slid between him and the only exit, and said, "Got a minute? I have a few more questions for you."

"Well, I..." he looked as if he might try to give Jacob the slip and run for his life, but then he glanced at the decoy bed, which had obviously been slept in, and said, "sure. I'm happy to help."

I sat back down on my bed, tore the bag the rest of the way open, and pulled out one of the burritos. It felt like it weighed a pound. I unwrapped an end and briefly considered swallowing it whole, boa constrictor-style, but supposed it would be less of a choking hazard if I chewed it first.

Jacob gestured for Lyle to have a seat at the desk, which was piled high with packing crates, while he settled himself on the decoy bed. "I was wondering about Katrina's relationship with the missing women."

Lyle crossed his legs and bobbed the top leg up and down anxiously. "Well...it's no secret she and Debbie didn't exactly see eye to eye. Lisa? Everyone liked Lisa, although she was fairly shy and kept to herself." He gave an awkward laugh. "Other than the rendezvous with Bert."

Ha ha. My stomach throbbed, and I realized my burrito was half gone—and I hadn't even dripped any sour cream or guac onto my shirt. Gravity probably hadn't had a chance to affect it, I'd inhaled it so quickly. Even as I thought as much, I swallowed another huge bite half-chewed.

"And Karen?" Jacob prompted.

"Oh, Karen got under everyone's skin." More nervous laughter, and I hoped to God there wasn't gonna be a comment about Chekotah's foreskin in there anywhere, or I'd probably go Linda Blair on him and cover him in guac. Thankfully, he refrained from making any such remark. "It was always Karen, Karen, Karen. Her room wasn't big enough. The classes weren't advanced enough. Her instructors didn't give her enough attention. And none of us realized how talented she was. Level six, at least."

"I fought oo idn' do 'evels?" I said.

Somehow, Lyle understood. "We don't. But everyone knows about them.

You'd need to be dead to not know about them. And some of the students were tested before they got here, so of course they throw their ranks around. It's human nature to try to figure out where you stack up against everyone else. Especially if you see them as your competition."

"And Karen was competitive?" Jacob suggested.

"Competitive! You'd think the girl was training for the Psych Olympics."

"In 'ight 'orker?" I swallowed a wad of rice, chicken, and flour tortilla, and repeated, "In the 'light worker' games? How could anyone here know whether they were a medium or not, let alone how strong they are, if there aren't any ghosts here to talk to?" Aside from the blood ghost, anyway.

"She was no medium—she was an astral traveler. Said she could run astral loops around Katrina and remember every last bit of her projection."

Jacob and I both turned to look at the GhosTV. Lyle followed our gazes, then stood up, reached behind it, and pulled the plug from the wall.

Jacob narrowed his eyes. "What are you doing?"

Lyle stared at the power cord in his hand for a beat, blinked, and then said, "It's safer this way. Old building, old electronics. Total fire hazard." He flushed harder.

"So was Karen just trying to get a rise out of Katrina," I said, "or was she really that good?"

Lyle shrugged. "I dunno. She certainly seemed to think she was God's gift."

I looked down and my burrito was gone. I finished the chips. Then I pulled the lid off the salsa fresca and drank it.

Jacob stood and offered a hand to Lyle, who shook it, albeit a bit hesitantly. "Thanks—for the information, and the food. Vic was…really hungry."

Lyle paused in the doorway, gave that nervous laugh of his again, and said, "It's so weird you should get me talking about Karen just now. That's exactly how she used to eat."

◊ ◊ ◊

Jacob didn't say a word when I finished his burrito, too. He did watch me, but he held his tongue. And when I was done, I felt like I could have eaten more, but the sheer pain of my stomach being stuffed to capacity would've prevented it.

"I suppose you could look online and see if I'm supposed to carbo-load before I go for a spin," I said. I was so full that even talking hurt.

Jacob weighed his reply carefully. "I think…we might want to go more slowly with your projections. We've been acting like there aren't any physical consequences, when obviously, there are."

"Yeah, but…I really feel like we're on the verge of something. Don't you?"

He didn't deny it.

"It's probably shitty of me to admit this," I added, "but if it were a bunch of strangers involved? Yeah. I'd pace myself. But not for Lisa." I settled back down and did my best to ignore the fact that my stomach was straining against my waistband like the distended belly of an African kid in one of those dollar-a-day charity commercials. "Whaddaya say? Let's see what's playing on the projection channel."

Jacob picked up the GhosTV's power cord and looked at the prongs. "So what was the deal with Lyle?" he said. "Did he know what this thing was? Maybe angling to get it for himself, see if he could uncover a latent Psych ability?"

"That wouldn't make any sense—how could he know what it did? Who would have told him? And if he did actually know, he would never have assumed we'd be willing to toss it in the trash, so he wouldn't have even suggested it."

"He did seem sincere," Jacob mused, and even without Carolyn there to verify it, I suspected he knew what he was talking about.

He plugged in the set and turned it on. Static.

I relaxed, and I listened as Jacob went through the script, and I let my mind wander. What *was* Lyle's deal with the GhosTV? Maybe it offended his Ikea-honed sensibilities, something mundane like that. It wouldn't be useful for anyone other than a medium—a light worker—because its wavelengths were tuned to subtle bodies and not whatever psychic stuff made a dreamer dream, a TK bend spoons, or a Carolyn spot lies. Right?

I sighed. Even with Dreyfuss' explanation, I couldn't claim to have any real idea what the GhosTV actually did.

Jacob finished the projection script. I could've sworn I felt him staring at me expectantly, maybe even holding his breath. I cracked one eyelid open. "It's a no-go. My stomach hurts."

"Maybe you shouldn't have had that second burrito."

I sat up and pressed my palm against my stomach. It felt rock-hard, and not with a six-pack, either. "No kidding."

"The full stomach is probably anchoring you to the physical. Chalk it up to the learning curve. What about seeing spirits—can you still do that?"

Without a handy-dandy ghost to glance at, I couldn't say for sure. But speaking from experience, I didn't think my eating binge would matter. When a ghost got in my face, the only things I knew of that would keep them at bay were a tab of Auracel…or a carefully sanctified space.

"Vic?"

I'd been staring at the snowy screen, hard. "What if Chekotah knew about the blood ghost?"

"Okay," Jacob said. "I'll buy that. He's a medium, isn't he? Calls himself a shaman, but when you come right down to it…."

"When you come right down to it and cram it into the parameters we're used to working with, him talking to 'the ancestors,' chances are he's basically a medium." I shuddered at my memory of my stunted attempts to project into one of Chekotah's sacred spaces. "So what if he knows she's around—feels her, hears her, catches some kind of vibe, even if it's not quite as visual as the one I get—and…."

And that was about it. Maybe his room was ghost-shielded because at some point he'd pissed off a spirit and he wanted to keep her out. But I didn't see what that would have to do with Lisa.

Jacob waited for me to put the pieces together, but when it became obvious there really was no second piece, he said, "You told me the blood ghost wouldn't talk to you. Maybe she couldn't hear you. Maybe we should turn the GhosTV to the setting that allowed you to see that really old repeater so you can try to interview her."

Again with the blood ghost—though I shouldn't have been surprised that Jacob would manage to steer me back to the ghost angle. Plus I only had myself to blame for eating that second burrito. Who knows, I thought. Maybe I'd get lucky. Maybe, if the blood ghost had a bone to pick with Chekotah, once I was able to communicate with her, she'd be able to tell me something about him I could actually use.

Jacob consulted his notes and turned the knobs to the ghost channel. "Okay." He turned to look at me. A webwork of thick red veins shot from his jaw up to his cheekbones, and his forehead bulged. "Anything?"

Crap. Where to begin? "Uh, yeah…I think it's on."

We had no idea of what kind of range we could expect out of the GhosTV, but since our options were either leaving it in our room or dragging it downstairs, across the lobby and over to the instructors' wing, we opted to take the subtle approach and hope the signal was strong enough to carry. Lunch was just letting out, and the PsyTrain students were filtering out of the big cafeteria in twos and threes. I almost strode right by, until I realized one of them was glowing.

"Hold on," I told Jacob. I backed against the wall and pulled my phone out of my pocket, and toggled the vibrate on and off a few times so it would appear that I was actually doing something with it. "Look busy. I need to see something."

Jacob pulled out his notepad and pretended to consult it. "Anything I can help you with?"

I was about to tell him no, but then I decided a few notes might not be a bad idea. "Here's what I've got. Caucasian female, fifty, glowing." I looked harder. "Asian man, thirty…" I looked harder at him to try and figure out what I was seeing. "Uh…transparent skin. Black male, forties…oh, hell, he has a third eye, literally." The two burritos and the bag of chips might have made a move to come back up, but they were packed in too tightly to budge.

"Want to tell me what this is all about?" Jacob said.

"The GhosTV. Apparently, what's playing now is *PsyTrain's Got Talent.*"

Some people just looked like people, but most of them, it turned out, had an extra eye or see-through skin—and the special effects varied in strength, with some of them so visible I couldn't tell the difference between the talent and physical reality, but some of them flickering in and out of visual range. Only a handful of the students were glowing, unless I missed it because it was a soft glow that settled around them like a trick of the light. But once it was all said and done, what had initially looked like a big free-for-all turned out to be a surprisingly limited range of talents.

If the different window-dressing indicated different talents, chances were that the glowers, third eyes and thin-skins represented precogs, clairvoyants, telepaths and empaths. I wasn't sure what corresponded to what, just that those were the most common flavors of Psych.

After the cafeteria had emptied and I'd detailed the last thin-skinned student, I said, "And guess who's got a mystery talent? Dreyfuss. He's got extra eyeballs, and they glow like a pair of headlights."

Jacob cleared his throat, shifted, and didn't write anything down.

"What?" I said.

He chewed on whatever was bothering him for a minute, like maybe he didn't want to ask, but in the end he couldn't resist. "What about me?" he said quietly.

Oh.

"You're...especially pumped." He looked a bit Cro-Magnon, actually. "And you've got this red, uh, I guess I'd call it energy. It's marbled all through you."

His eyes went wide. "You can actually see it?"

"Kinda hard to miss."

"And nobody else has...?"

"Nope. No one."

Jacob considered his weird talent for a moment, then said, "And you?"

And me. I didn't know what my talent looked like—and seeing as how I hadn't been even the least bit curious, evidently I didn't want to know. As Lyle had so recently reminded us, denial ain't just a river in Egypt. "So far the TV's signal's holding up pretty good. Let's get up to Chekotah's room and find us a ghost."

Chapter 31

We trailed the students to the classroom wing of the building where the instructors lived upstairs in the more spacious single rooms. Since they had their backs to us, and since none of the talents manifested as the proverbial "eyes in the back of the head," I didn't notice the GhosTV's signal decaying until I glanced at Jacob and saw his veins weren't as disturbingly red and bulgy as they'd been back by the cafeteria. "We're getting out of range," I said.

Jacob paused. "Completely? Or does it fade?"

I squinted at the students as they filed into their classrooms. I caught a hint of a glow and a glimpse of muscle showing under a semi-transparent cheek. "It fades. And Chekotah's room is just upstairs. If the blood ghost is still there, I'll probably be able to see her just fine." Despite the cilantro-flavored cement that was setting up in my gut.

As the creaky elevator carried us to the second floor, I watched Jacob's reflection in the mirrored brass surface of the walls. Veins? Yep. I could still see 'em. I supposed there was no avoiding it—I looked at myself. Nothing special, other than hair that still looked pretty damn good considering I hadn't washed or styled it recently. But I wasn't glowing, I wasn't see-through, and, thank God, I didn't have a spare eyeball in the middle of my forehead. 'Cos that would've really sucked.

The hallway outside Chekotah's room was clear. We approached the room. The smell of burnt sage lingered in the hall, but there was no movement, and no telltale glowing. We stopped directly in front of the door and looked at each other. Jacob shrugged, and knocked. No answer. "Bert?" Jacob called through the door. "Can we talk to you?"

Had they gone somewhere, or were they still hunkered down in there, hoping we'd go away? Jacob tried the doorknob. He must have been fully expecting it to be locked. I know I was. But it turned, and the door swung open.

The part of my mind that dreaded finding them in some kind of ceremonial mating ritual recoiled from the sight of Faun Windsong on her hands and knees, but only for a split second, because the other parts of my brain were quick enough to engage and really take stock of what was going on. Her back was to us. She was alone. And clothed. And she was scrubbing something off the pale terra cotta floor, something black that hadn't been there on my astral fact-finding mission.

At least, I thought she was scrubbing, judging by the big, sweeping motions of her arm. I slipped past Jacob to get a look at it, whatever it was, in case she hadn't quite managed to obliterate the evidence before I could see it. I approached from the side. Something crunched under my shoe. Her glasses had fallen to the floor, one lens missing…now broken. The floor they lay on was covered in huge, black scrawls, and her fingers were black. It wasn't a sponge or a scrub brush in her hand—it was a hunk of charcoal. And she wasn't scrubbing the marks away. She was making them.

I crouched, and I looked. Not just marks. Letters. All jumbled up on top of each other, at least that's what it looked like at first, until I stared at it long enough and words emerged.

Oh God.

I followed the thick, charcoal scrawls.

OTVNOTVNOTVNOTVNO….

No TV.

"Faun," I said, and I touched her on the shoulder. She turned to look at me. Her mouth hung slack and her eyeballs were white, and her big, ugly necklace of rocks and hemp was glowing like a string of Christmas tree lights.

I stood and spun away so fast I ended up crashing into Jacob, who'd snuck up behind me quiet as ever. He made a grab for my arm but I dodged him and staggered out into the hall to suck air, and if those burritos and chips had been sitting bad before, now I was strongly considering having my stomach pumped.

Jacob's voice drifted out of the awful room, low, but urgent. "Katrina, can you hear me? Katrina?" A pause. "Vic—help me out, here. Do we call an ambulance, or…?"

"How the fuck should I know?"

"Vic," he snapped, and my brain stopped the panic loop that had been swirling around inside it like something nasty on its way down the toilet. "I need you."

Run. My gut—what I could feel of it around the burritos—was telling me to run. Ghosts and repeaters are inconvenient and annoying and sometimes bloody, but they don't actually frighten me because, as long as I'm not on any kind of psyactive, they can't actually hurt me. Not that I thought Faun Windsong could. But what about the thing that was inside her?

"Shield her," I said—from the doorway. Faun's arm was flapping like it was still trying to write, even though the charcoal was no longer touching the floor. A string of drool dangled from her lower lip.

"What?"

"Imagine red energy, a web, a net, that fits around you like a second skin—and then use it to shove out whatever's in her." Even as I said it, I realized what a flawed plan it was. Jacob's psychic veins blew up big and red as he focused and ramped up his energy, so I knew that although he couldn't see or feel his own power, he'd totally understood me. It wasn't the plan's failure I needed to worry about. It was its success—'cos if he drove some homeless ghostie out of Faun, which medium did that leave standing there like a big, inviting flesh suit?

Run. My overstuffed gut was still telling me to make tracks, more urgently now than ever. But ghosts move a hell of a lot faster than I could ever hope to run, so instead I sucked white light, hard, and threw a super-thick white balloon around myself. If you can't outrun 'em, bounce 'em.

"Is it working?" Jacob said. He glowed red, I could see as much even through the hazy white membrane of my protective barrier, but Faun's arm was still writing letters in the air.

"No. You're shielded, but not her."

He looked at her, hard, and I imagine he was struggling to wield this tool he had no way of controlling. I had some idea what he needed to do, but I was fighting with myself over whether or not I should let him in on the secret. This whole dread thing, weirdly enough, was foreign to me. It was different from the panic I'd felt at the threat of being locked in a room and strip-searched. I'd been locked up before, and come out of it more or less intact. I'd even let my late doctor play puppetmaster with me to get us both out of a bind. But the thought of a hostile spirit hijacking not only my body, but my mind—leaving me a white-eyed, drooling wreck?

I'd rather stick my gun in my mouth and swallow a bullet.

Unfortunately, as much as Faun Windsong drove me completely and utterly nuts, I couldn't leave her that way, either.

I backed up another step, sucked even more white light, and told Jacob, "You must need physical contact to work your shield. Put your arms around her." He did it—awkwardly, but he did it—and I winced back and poured every last bit of my white light into maintaining my own barrier. My vision went mostly white. White eyeball syndrome? No, thank God, no. Just my own barrier so pumped-up it was as opaque as milk glass. Faun went rigid—I saw her move in silhouette—then she gasped and fell limp. I steeled myself for the rush of the displaced spirit looking for someone else to ride, but it never came. Cautiously, bit by bit, I thinned down my white balloon until I could see clearly again.

No ghost.

Faun had dropped in Jacob's arms like a yo-yo, then snapped back up nearly as fast—and when she did, it was as if she'd suddenly gone psychedelic, leaving a tracer of light behind her in the shape of her body. "What… how…?" She looked around at her room, at Jacob, and then at her own hands, which were black to the knuckles with charcoal—and two of her fingers were blistered as if she'd grabbed it, still smoldering, right out of the incense burner. "What happened?"

"Are you okay?" Jacob asked.

"Yes, fine." She sounded impatient, as if the state of her physical body was hardly worth noticing. She knelt on all fours again, just as she'd done when she was scrawling the letters, and she took a closer look at what she'd written. I saw a double-image trailing a split second behind her as she knee-walked.

"I wrote this?"

"Yes." Jacob's voice was careful.

"I don't get it. What's 'Not V'?"

I can't imagine there was any way Jacob had missed what the letters really said, but he didn't correct her. "Any ideas? Maybe impressions you had while you were writing?"

"That's just it, I don't remember any of it. I wasn't even *trying* to go into trance." She straightened up, cocked her head and did a sweep of the lettering, as if maybe looking at it from a different angle would illuminate the meaning, and she started retracing her steps without any prompting from

Jacob. "I came in to check on Bert, and…where's Bert?"

I stepped over a stretch of charcoal lettering and tapped on the bathroom door. No answer. I opened it. Empty. A cell phone began to ring, and I turned. The ringing was coming from the shrine corner of their room—no, not from the shrine. From a pile of clothes in front of the shrine.

Something was wrong about those clothes. I knew it, fully and completely, before I'd even analyzed why. People didn't take off clothes like that. They throw 'em around, or they fold them. But they don't leave them in a pile—in the exact order in which they'd been wearing them. Chekotah's ceremonial garb was all there: turban on top of tunic, on top of pants, with a couple of sandals poking out the bottom, and a ringtone threading up from the midst of it all.

I looked back at Jacob and Faun. She had her cell phone to her ear, and she was staring at the pile of clothes like she didn't quite know what to make of it.

Stepping around the lettering on the floor as best I could, I approached the shrine, crouched beside it, and lifted the red turban with my pen light. A mucous-like strand of slime stretched from the edge of the hat to the hollow well in the neck of the tunic, which held a mass of quivering goo like a bowl of clear gelatin. I prodded the clear gel with my penlight and then smelled the tip. Ozone.

"You might want to get a picture," I told Jacob. "Now, before it's gone."

"A picture of what?" Faun said.

Jacob joined me and snapped a few shots—which probably rocked his world, seeing all that ectoplasm. And seeing that creepy pile of clothes, lined up as if Bert Chekotah had just melted right out of them and turned into ectoplasm himself. I'd been thinking that sarcastically…but actually, that was exactly what it looked like.

"What are you looking at?" Faun's voice turned edgy, and started growing shrill as the realization that something was very wrong sank in. "Is there blood on Bert's clothes? Oh, no. No."

She dropped her phone and barreled across the room with no concern at all about smudging the lettering on the floor, and fell to her knees in front of the slimy clothes pile.

"Faun, wait a minute," I said, as Jacob said, "Katrina, stop," but she wasn't hearing either of us, or either of her names.

"What happened?" she cried, as she tore the tunic from the pile, and strands of ectoplasm stretched and snapped. "Was it Five Faith? Did they…?"

As shocked as she was, that line of logic was too bizarre for her to follow. Five Faith—abducting Chekotah, stripping off his Indian gear, filling it with slime and leaving it just so? Unlikely.

"Think back," Jacob said. "Anything you can remember. Sounds, smells, anything. You came in to check on Bert, and what?"

"Well, I…he…he was upset about Debbie, and I was telling him it wasn't his fault, and…" she stopped, froze, and for a second I thought maybe "trance" was catching up to her again, and she'd grab some more lit charcoal and set herself on fire. But it wasn't trance that was washing over her. It was memory.

I waited to see if Jacob was going to prompt her again—because he was the people-person, not me—and then, all of a sudden, Faun Windsong's face twisted up, and the waterworks began. Faun Windsong, not exactly my nemesis, but a smug and superior annoyance ever since I could remember, was crying. And I felt bad for her. I patted her on the arm, and said, "You're okay," which was the only thing I could think of that sounded even remotely true, and comforting at the same time—and she flung herself at me, grabbed me around the waist, buried her face in the front of my jacket, and sobbed.

When I put my arms around her, I tried not to be as obviously awkward about it as I felt…but I doubt I succeeded. I patted her back gingerly, and said, "We're here," which, again, was not particularly comforting, but at least it was true.

Her spiky gray hair tickled the bottom of my chin, and whatever hippy fragrance she had on smelled like herbal cough drops. She squeezed me so tightly I had a hard time taking a good, deep breath, but at least from the new overhead angle I was watching her from, I was so close I didn't have to see those freaky light-tracers trailing from her movements anymore. She squeezed, and she cried. I patted. Her sobs turned into wails. I looked at Jacob over the top of her head, and he gave me a "sorry, can't help you" shrug. I patted some more, and eventually, her wails began turning into words.

"Heeeee…he…he…."

It was so not funny.

"He…." She snuffed, a few long and wet-sounding times. I imagined she was leaving her own brand of slime on the front of my jacket. "I was talking to him, and the room went cold, and…he…he…he…. He dissolved."

Not funny at all.

Chapter 32

So much for my idea that Faun Windsong and her shaman boyfriend knew what was going on, since Faun was such a wreck I'd needed to spot her my last two Valiums, and Chekotah appeared to have gone the way of all his flings. So if they weren't responsible, who was? I wanted to blame the Internet demon, but it hadn't bibled Debbie's email, plus Faun and Chekotah didn't even keep a computer in their room. What about Five Faith? That'd be a pretty neat trick, to make people dissolve—if that was what had actually happened—using totally mundane, non-psychic means.

Jacob and I stood in the doorway marked Quiet Room, while inside, Faun drifted in a Valium cloud on a big, cushy couch with an afghan pulled up to her neck. She didn't want to be in her own bedroom, not after what she'd allegedly seen there. I didn't blame her.

"We need to check out the blood ghost," Jacob said. "What if it wasn't a ghost? What if it was…something else? Something more powerful that can turn people into ectoplasm?"

"Maybe it's not a ghost," I agreed. "I see spirits when I'm physical. I saw the blood ghost when I was astral." I glanced at Faun. "So we should keep an eye on her. I'll bet she's the next target, given the relationship of everyone who's disappeared so far…and the fact that she probably didn't disappear them herself." In fact, I was surprised she'd been left unslimed back in the bedroom, since now that made her an eyewitness.

Maybe only so much ectoplasm was available for sliming at any given time. Or maybe Faun was immune because she was a medium, and her subtle bodies fit together differently than other people's. Or maybe…hell. I really had no idea. "So how're we gonna manage that? If blood ghost was really an astral demon or something, she was never human. It's not as if we can pull her birth certificate and driver's license." I lowered my voice and said in his ear, "Plus I think I'm too full to go astral again. It might even be a day or two before I'm back to…normal."

Jacob glanced down at my stomach. It felt as if a protrusion the size of the take-out bag should have been visible, but my jacket hid the evidence of my gorging well enough. The lapel was shiny where it had served as an impromptu handkerchief, though. "What if we turned up the GhosTV signal?" he suggested. "Between that and your natural talent, maybe it would be enough to help you launch."

Gotta love how blasé Jacob is about the whole thing—but my overstuffed gut was telling me different. "Cranking the knobs on the GhosTV *did* something to me. I'm not sure it's totally safe to cross my fingers, spike the amplitude, and hope for the best."

He frowned. "It did something psychic to you."

"Something that turned me into a competitive eater. I don't think we can say, 'It's just psychic so it must be harmless.' Intangible? Yeah. But that doesn't mean it can't mess me up."

His red veins got bulgier as he pondered the GhosTV's effect on me. "But the…entity…keeps ordering you to turn off the TV. First in your notebook, now on the floor of Bert and Katrina's room."

And the oatmeal, though I hadn't mentioned that to anyone.

"And then there's Lyle." Jacob said.

"Lyle?"

"Right. The way he unplugged it."

"He just wanted to toss it out because it clashed with the décor."

"You know the secretary's usually the most important witness, don't you? Everyone underestimates them, so they're like a fly on the wall."

He watched me, like he was waiting for me to see what he was getting at. I had no idea.

"You have an in with him," he said finally.

"I hope I'm hearing you wrong. There's no way you seriously think I'd be able to play Mata Hari."

"I'm just saying, put a few drinks in him, maybe he'll slip up."

"And tell me what? He already dished the dirt on Chekotah and all his fooling around."

"He knows more. I'm positive he does." Jacob warmed up to whatever idea he was brewing. "Plus, he was the one who brought the burritos. And he knew that light workers had big appetites, because he made that remark about Karen Frugali right before he left—so maybe he also knew it was hard to project on a full stomach. What if he did it on purpose, brought you all that food so you couldn't project, because he had something to hide?"

"Like what? An embarrassingly big ABBA CD collection? You ordered that food, Jacob. He just brought what you ordered."

"The guy lives on his cell phone. What if you were out for a drink, you remembered something you needed to tell me, and you notice your phone is dead?"

"I'm not leaving you alone."

"You said it yourself, I have red energy all around me—I'll bet you're looking at it right now." I tried hard to focus on anything but the veins webbing his cheeks, but my gaze must have infinitesimally strayed, and, of course, he saw. "I'll be fine. So you borrow his phone."

"Seriously," I said, "this plan of yours is getting worse and worse."

"You pretend you're having trouble hearing me, you go outside with it, or maybe into the bathroom. And you get a look at the list of the last people he called."

"There's no way I'd ever sound natural enough to fool anyone."

"I know you're scared, since this is so far beyond police procedure—"

"I'm not scared."

"—but we're not on duty, so we're not limited by any of that now, which means we don't have the same kinds of resources we'd have if we were on official business, so we need to do what it takes to figure out what's going on."

"I'm not scared of Lyle, okay? I just think it's a shitty plan."

◊ ◊ ◊

El Dorado, the Mexican restaurant across the street, might have been closed for lunch. But just my luck, it was open for happy hour when I called Lyle and told him I wanted to take him up on that drink. The sight of the chips and salsa on the bar made me want to hurl, but the mariachi music was loud enough that Jacob's phone-borrowing plan might actually work. I got there before Lyle did and ordered a virgin margarita to make it look like I was drinking an actual drink, planted myself at the bar, and tried to imagine how I was going to make Jacob pay me back. 'Cos he totally owed me one for talking me into this ridiculous stunt.

On top of the bar, a plastic holder showcased laminated cards printed with glossy pictures of nachos, taquitos and jalapeno poppers. I flipped through the cards, and was seriously considering the fried ice cream when someone hopped onto the barstool beside me and the smell of Gray Flannel told me my date had arrived. "Sorry to keep you waiting. The phone company put me on hold for twenty minutes."

"No problem."

He waved to the bartender and ordered a vodka cranberry, while I pondered the fact that I'd actually been considering dessert.

"Seriously, how can these Christian Soldiers keep finding our unlisted numbers? There should be some kind of law against it." He looked at me expectantly, as if I'd have something to say about "the law," given my career, when my vision flickered. I assumed it was just my metaphorical vision, anyway, though I imagine I still did that staring-thing with my physical eyes I've built a reputation for, just to make sure.

"There should be," I answered blandly, because most of my processing power was trying to figure out what had just moved.

"But anyway, enough about work. What are you into?"

Another flicker. It was his face, but it was subtle, a trick of the light, almost. "Uh." I couldn't think of a single hobby, so I borrowed one of Jacob's. "Running."

He took a gulp of his drink, leaned toward me, and said, "In bed."

There it was—that flicker again, as he moved closer to me. It was his skin, doing that holographic thing. Now you see it, now you don't. If I looked at Lyle from the proper angle, he was see-through. I glanced at the bartender. Solid. I looked at a table full of middle-aged women. Solid. I looked at Lyle, and his skin flickered briefly and gave me a glimpse of his musculature beneath, which looked like the primo London broil at Moo & Oink.

"Don't be shy," he said. "I'm really hard to shock."

"Just your typical…stuff." So the GhosTV's range reached all the way across the street.

"Typical, how? Oral? Anal?"

The flayed look that flickered in and out of my range of perception distracted me enough that I didn't blurt out, "Who actually talks that way to someone they've just met?" Instead I said, "Regular stuff."

"Because one guy's kink is another guy's vanilla." He batted his eyelashes at me.

Oh shit, was that supposed to be alluring? "Uh huh."

"How about role-playing? Do you get into that?"

"I dunno," I said.

"Because sometimes authority figures like to hand over control, even if it's just for a few hours."

Is that what was going on with Jacob when he wanted me to be bossy, or was he just switching it up for the sake of a little variety? And what about when I let him order me around and totally own my ass? That wasn't exactly play-acting. He really could overpower me and force me to do anything he was inspired to demand of me. It should have triggered the aversion response that had roots in my interactions with Camp Hell orderlies, but instead it made me feel safe....I guess because of the mechanics of the rest of our relationship. I felt my cheeks get hot, and reminded myself I wasn't actually talking about my own sex life with some guy who I was gonna get it on with once he was tipsy enough and we'd grown tired of the verbal buildup. I was just trying to grab a look at his phone.

"You like playing Good Cop/Bad Cop?" Lyle suggested.

"Not really. I like the balance of power to be on an even keel."

"So you're a switch."

"Uh huh." Great, all these painfully awkward questions to determine if I wanted to top, bottom or blow him. I couldn't picture acting out any of 'em. And I desperately wanted the conversation to be about anything but me. "What about you?"

"My favorite thing...in the whole world...is felching."

I didn't even know what that was. And so I stared.

He held my gaze with his eyes sparkling and a big smile on his face while his skin glinted transparent for a long couple of seconds, and then he burst out laughing. "I totally had you going...I'm kidding! No one really *likes* felching. No one actually *does* it. Even John Waters says he's never met anyone nasty enough to try it."

I gave a totally unconvincing laugh.

"Unless you're talking about porn—I've got a couple of really gritty, eastern-European twink vids where everything's bareback and they'll eat come out of anything."

The words *eat come*, combined with the horrible pressure in my stomach and the photo of the Mexican fried ice cream, made my throat start to flutter.

"You like porn?" he said. "I've got a huge porn collection."

And here I'd assumed it would be ABBA. "Who *doesn't* like porn?"

"I know, right?" He sipped his pink drink. "Ohmigod. I have this awesome set of comeshots you just have to see. There's these three guys on a pickup truck with a big black dildo—"

Enough. "Can I use your phone?" I blurted out. He stopped, mid-comeshot. "My battery's dead," I said, "and I need to check a case." Over the *ais* and oompahs of the mariachi piping through the speakers, the phrase "check a case" didn't even sound made-up. Or maybe my delivery was better than I'd hoped, given how desperately I wanted to stop talking about dildoes and comeshots and felching, whether I was a top, bottom or switch, and how many times I shook off my dick after I took a piss.

I probably shouldn't have actually called anyone, because that would only serve to bump someone else off the end of the "recent calls" list, but I thumbed in Jacob's number anyway.

"Marks."

"It's me. So. How's that…case?"

"You got the phone, great. Do you have anything to write on? Maybe you should go outside."

"What?" I said. I could hear him perfectly fine.

"Do you have anything to write on?"

I sat there for a minute while the mariachi music bounced along in the background. And then I said, "What?"

"Vic? Go outside."

I covered the phone, leaned over to Lyle, and said, "The music's a little loud. I'm gonna go outside."

He nodded and started digging into the basket of chips. I strode off and considered demanding that Jacob tell me what felching was, specifically… although if the director who'd talked Divine into eating a dog turd on film thought it was gross, I undoubtedly didn't want to hear about it on a stomach full of semi-digested Mexican food. As I burst out onto the street, I said, "This…sucks."

"You're almost there. The phone menu, is it pretty similar to yours?"

I hadn't even checked. "Close enough."

"Good. Don't forget to catch the times and dates of the calls. They might be important." And with that directive, he hung up.

Bossy. And not in a suck-that-cock-mister way, either. The thing with Jacob is this: he might look like a big, musclebound gym rat. But I don't think that's what his fitness regimes are really about. All his eating right and exercising has more to do with his mental focus—and his preternatural ability to get other people to do what he wants. In this case, me.

I pulled up the menu on Lyle's phone, and nope, it was nothing like mine. Damn it. I scrolled down, fat-fingered something, and ended up in his settings. And it wouldn't be suspicious *at all* if I accidentally changed his ringtone. I backed out carefully. Text messages…none. Either he wasn't into texting, or he kept them erased. Back up. Scroll. Where the heck were the call lists and the voicemails?

I snapped a photo of my shoes. Great. I fumbled for the delete button, and a stored photo appeared on the little screen.

A photo of me. Not my shoes. My whole upper body and head.

I was standing there in the lobby at PsyTrain in my cop-suit, hands on hips, scowling at something. My hair looked pretty good.

I scrolled back. Another one of me. Same expression, this one closer up and angled to one side. Back again. Another one. In all, eight snapshots of me, seven of them scowling, one of me talking to Jacob. A sick wave of dread washed over me. What if Lyle was some kind of Five Faith mole? What if he was nowhere near as harmless as he seemed—and he wasn't interested in sleeping with me at all—he was just a really great actor? What if he'd sent those photos to his base camp, and now every violent religious zealot in the country would be able to identify me…since apparently I always looked the same, because I'd scowled too much when I was a teenager and my face froze that way.

I backed up one more click and found the first not-me photo, a picture of Lyle and a buddy of his in a coffee shop bending their heads together and smiling, obviously taken by Lyle himself with an outstretched arm, given the unflattering angle. He didn't look like a religious zealot at all. He looked like a gay white guy having a cappuccino with another gay white guy. And before that, he'd taken a bunch of pictures of one of the security guards at PsyTrain—a tall, lanky guy like me, though one who didn't scowl nearly so much.

Not Five Faith, then. Just pervy. And here I'd thought all I needed to worry about was Jacob and the picture of my ectoplasm hand. If it weren't for Five Faith, I would've been spooked by the idea of someone actually taking pictures of me to whack off to later, but now I was practically giddy with relief. It really goes to show how everything's relative.

I backed up even farther and found more PsyTrain stuff. A graduation party, it looked like, since there was a cake and a *Congratulations, Sophie* banner and a bunch of smiling Psychs. Mostly smiling, anyway. One of 'em looked a little more like me, cursed with a permanent scowl. Where had I seen her before? The cafeteria? Faun Windsong's class? Or maybe in the hallway?

In the hallway.

My brain seized up with the notion that the hallway was really important, though it hadn't quite connected the dots yet. I backed through a few more photos—Sophie cutting her cake, Faun Windsong gesticulating as she said something self-important—and then that was it. No more pictures.

"There you are."

I flinched and turned. I'd been hovering near the restaurant doorway so long Lyle had come looking for me. Maybe I should've ducked into the bathroom instead—at least I would've been behind a locked door.

"Sometimes the signal cuts out if you hold it with your thumb over the… ohmigod." He was staring at the phone in my hand. I'd been caught rifling through his photos—he knew it, and I knew it. And I'd caught him taking jerk-off pictures of me—and all of this was conveyed by the look of complete and utter dismay on his face. He didn't flush this time. He went white.

Then he made a grab for the phone.

I raised it up above my head. He'd either have to jump, or climb me to reach it. He started to jump, as if batting it out of my hand would make any difference now that I'd seen the snapshots. "Stop it." Jump, swipe. "Cut it ou—so help me God, I will pistol-whip you if you don't quit it."

He stopped jumping at me and crossed his arms defensively. Now he was flushed from all the aerobic activity. His hair was messed up, but the Grey Flannel still smelled pretty good. Once I was fairly sure he wasn't going to try anything that made it obvious I wouldn't know how to pistol-whip someone if my life depended on it, I lowered the phone and thumbed back to the first shot of the party. I held the phone under his nose, jabbed my finger at the scowling woman, and said, "Who's that?"

He cocked his head and squinted at the photo. His skin flickered transparent. "That's Karen Frugali."

Really? Karen Frugali took off long before I'd come to California. So why was I convinced I'd seen her before? I squinted at the tiny photo myself. If I'd known her back at Camp Hell, I would've remembered—after all, there were only a handful of us mediums there, and lately all of us but Dead Darla were present and accounted for. Even if Dead Darla had grown out her cherry-red hair and managed to lose half her body weight, she'd still be around forty years old. Too old to re-emerge with a new name and a new identity as this thirtyish Karen Frugali. Plus, Faun Windsong wouldn't have been able to resist telling me about her, in a know-it-all kind of way.

"Look," Lyle stammered, "I can explain. I was just—"

"Shut up." Karen Frugali. Where had I seen her? I tried to picture her outside, then in the lobby, then in the hallway. Why was my brain stuck on the hallway? Maybe there was a photo of her, hanging on the wall inside the PsyTrain building. I didn't particularly remember seeing any photos, but maybe my subconscious did. The hallway. Photos hung in hallways, right? Except I remembered stucco walls when I thought of PsyTrain hallways, not collections of framed photos.

Okay, so what else was important about the hallway? The main thing that came to mind, not that it meant jack squat, was that when I'd lied to Dreyfuss about seeing….

I stared at the tiny scowling face harder, and my pulse started to pound in my temples.

The blood ghost. That was her.

Karen Frugali was the blood ghost.

Chapter 33

Karen Frugali's story, once we put it all together, was rough for me to contemplate—because it seemed that while she and I'd had different timing and different circumstances, some parts of our history ran uncomfortably parallel to one another. She'd been a waitress in Kentucky who married her high school sweetheart and tried for nearly nine years to have a kid. When she finally did, one day she found the baby boy in its crib, motionless and blue.

The students and teachers who'd known her all described her personality in general as being extreme—and apparently she'd been as extreme in her grief over her son's sudden death as she was about every other aspect of her life. So extreme that not only did her husband file for divorce once he'd checked her into the psychiatric ward of the local hospital for observation, but extreme enough to trigger her latent psychic talent: astral projection. She spent her days shuffling from counselor to counselor, and her nights wandering in search of the spirit of her baby boy.

In this day and age, I would've thought the medical profession wouldn't be so quick to lock someone up in the nuthouse—then again, I've seen what passes for a modern Psych testing kit, so maybe I shouldn't be so shocked. Karen was diagnosed with paranoid schizophrenia, evidenced by elaborate fantasies of grandeur and exacerbated by the tragic loss of a child. And since she came from a "good" family where people didn't talk about things like mental illness, she was mortified.

Although her only resource consisted of half an hour of recreational computer time per day, Karen used that time to research astral projection, lucid dreaming and remote viewing online, until she was able to not only think clearly enough during her OBEs to stop aimlessly searching for her son, but also to remember the projections clearly when she woke back up.

Once she'd mastered projecting, a graphic description she provided of the chief psychiatrist listening to Mozart and conducting an imaginary orchestra with an emery board—all while he took a lengthy and explosive crap—was enough to merit a new volley of Psych screening, and then, a reversal of the schizophrenia diagnosis.

Which wasn't to say Karen Frugali was emotionally healthy. Just that she really could travel without her body holding her back, and then remember what she'd seen.

She'd been the first one to disappear. Everyone else who vanished after she did was part of the Bert Chekotah Fan Club—including the star of the show, Chekotah himself. Circumstances pointed to Faun Windsong flying into a jealous rage, eliminating her competition, then finishing off her straying man as the icing on the cake. Except...that didn't jibe with her genuine distress, and the whole "No TV" writing marathon I'd caught the tail end of.

"Our best bet," Jacob said, "is to try and see if Karen might be able to help us out. Find her spirit. Talk to it. Figure out where her body is, and maybe...." he looked away without finishing that thought. Maybe we'd find the others. Debbie. Lisa.

Although, that didn't seem quite right, either. Maybe Karen had been butchered, but Chekotah had simply disappeared...or dissolved. There were piles of clothes in Debbie's and Lisa's rooms, too. Hard to say if they'd been full of ectoplasm at any point or not. But they might have been.

I walked the halls and grounds for hours searching for a glimpse of Karen Frugali's ghost, but no dice. Dreyfuss pulled everything he could find on Karen, from her high school transcripts to her MySpace page to her dental records. Jacob interviewed students, instructors, janitors, guards. The sun set, and PsyTrain residents ate their dinner—which I skipped, as I was still packed with burritos—although, disturbingly enough, it was tempting to try to cram a little more in.

It neared midnight—I no longer bothered converting things to "my time" since I'd been so sore, exhausted and sleep-deprived since I'd arrived that my subjective time seemed irrelevant—and I took a quick shower and fell into bed. Jacob was busy jabbing keys on his laptop and scowling at it. "Come to bed," I told him. "Maybe sleeping on it will help."

"In a minute."

He sounded snippy. Since there was no arguing with him even on the best of days, I rolled over and faced the wall, and ignored that little itch in my throat that told me a Valium would be really, really nice, or maybe an

Auracel. Deadening my Psych sensitivity for the sake of the floaty feeling the Auracel would give me was no kind of option, plus I'd sacrificed my Valium to Faun. Enough Mexican food had moved along that my stomach didn't hurt quite as much, that was a bonus. I focused on that, and on my breathing, and how good it felt to finally lie down and rest my eyes.

That seemed to do the trick, relaxing and breathing, because my aches and pains fell away, and eventually I realized I felt pretty damn good. I gave a stretch and prodded something with my hand, something that resisted, and then gave.

I opened my eyes. My hand was inside the wall.

I sat up. Jacob was down on one knee in front of the GhosTV, frowning at his notes. He tweaked one of the dials, and my head started to buzz a little bit. He checked his watch and jotted down a few more notes, while I rolled my astral eyes. I had nothing against testing the damn GhosTV, but it would have been nice of him to consult me first.

I'd be hungry as hell come morning, but I supposed I should be grateful for the opportunity to carry on with the investigation even in my sleep—plus, there was always the chance I'd get someone to really open up and tell me all the things their internal censors wouldn't let them say while they were physical, the way Jacob had admitted he was worried I wasn't attracted to him while he was pounding my astral ass. I attempted to float out into the hall, and found that I didn't need to. I was just there. I took a good look around. Yep. It looked like the hall. Pretty spiffy. I dropped through the floor toward Karen's and Lisa's rooms. The ball-pit sensation was fleeting. I found myself downstairs in a split second. The hall looked the same—but the people in it…those were new.

I recognized both of them from Faun Windsong's astral projection class. A middle-aged woman who'd had a bad perm in real life was standing by the elevators with her eyes closed, groping along the wall. She had astral hair like Lady Godiva, long and blonde, hanging down to her thighs in heavy, luxurious waves. Thankfully, unlike Lady Godiva, she wasn't naked. And the Asian guy who'd asked the insufferable question about the silver cord—he was floating by the ceiling like a big, guy-shaped helium balloon, and he was dressed like the Matrix. "Hey, Leather Boy," I called. "You're astral."

"Am I out?" he said. He floundered and bobbed against the ceiling. "I feel like I'm out."

"You're astral. C'mere a minute. I want to ask you a few questions."

He floundered some more, elbowed the ceiling, then floated in a slow rotation until his back was to me and his nose was against the textured stucco. His long, black duster didn't look particularly cool dangling like that as he struggled to control his astral body. "Am I out? My head is buzzing. What do I do?"

I sighed, left him to find his footing, and went to chat with perm-lady instead. "Hey…you're astral," I told her.

"Maybe I'm dreaming. It feels the same."

Did it? Not to me. Dreaming had weird time-lurches and jumps of logic in it, and people who were really composites of two other people, and usually I was naked but I only realized it at the most embarrassing time. At the moment, I was still in my jeans, my black high-tops and my favorite T-shirt. "Nope, you're not dreaming. Definitely astral."

"It's so hard to see."

"Your eyes are closed."

"But if I open them, I'll wake up. I've been trying to do this all year and I can't screw it up now—I don't want to wake up."

Given the range of the GhosTV and the frequency it was playing at, I was guessing she'd be pretty safe opening her eyes. "You won't know 'til you try. Give it a shot."

"I can't. I'll wake up."

"I promise," I said—which was a lie, since for all I knew she really would snap awake if she opened her eyes, "you're totally astral and you won't wake up."

She groped the wall some more, then ran her hands down the front of her body, through the silver cord that snaked out of her solar plexus, then back up where she touched her own face. I waited expectantly for her to open her eyes, but instead she found the wall again and started working her way away from me. "Where're you going?"

"I don't want to wake up."

Behind me, the Asian guy said, "Am I out?"

I sighed. Astral witnesses were nowhere near as helpful as I thought they would be.

Jacob had been so rational while he was astral. Weirdly vulnerable, and he didn't remember a lick of it after he woke up, but still rational. And Faun Windsong—she'd made plenty of sense, too. Faun had experience, while Jacob had proximity to the GhosTV, and, it would seem, a pretty highly developed talent. Not light worker talent…but maybe the type of talent didn't matter. Just the strength. He'd be pretty stoked to hear that theory, though I'd probably need to think of a better name than "the red veiny talent."

I thought about Jacob, and found myself back in our room. My physical body was in bed with its face to the wall. Jacob was sitting at the piled-high desk, stroking his beard and staring at the GhosTV. He looked tired—but he also looked stubborn enough to stay up all night, if that was what it took.

So I couldn't expect him to go astral anytime soon, but Jacob wasn't the one I needed to talk to, anyway. He didn't know any more about the case than I knew. Faun Windsong, though…maybe she hadn't been entirely truthful with me after Chekotah dissolved. Or maybe she remembered something that was so horrible her conscious mind blocked it out, but her astral body would be able to fill me in on the details. Either way, I figured she'd be my best bet.

I thought about the Quiet Room where I'd last seen her swaddled in an afghan, felt a sense of rapid motion, and then, there I was. The lights were low, but it was the Quiet Room all right, all recliners and bland artwork and philodendrons. Faun was still bundled up on the couch, zonked out with her burnt hand wrapped in gauze sticking out from a fold in the afghan, but there was someone else with her now—a guy sitting in one of the recliners with his upper body leaning forward and his hands clasped between his knees, watching her anxiously.

An astral guy. He was angled mostly away from me, but the silver cord was a dead giveaway.

He was a skatepunk in sloppy, cutoff camouflage shorts and a ratty flannel shirt, with a wispy beard, stoner tattoos showing above his slouchy gray tube socks, and white-guy dreadlocks tied back from his head in a grungy bandanna. I didn't recognize him from PsyTrain—but Faun Windsong had told me distance didn't matter. Maybe he was some long-distance relative who had an emotional connection with Faun. Maybe she had a brother, or a son.

One of us high-level mediums procreating—how's that for a creepy thought?

Faun was asleep, although she wasn't astral. In fact, she probably wouldn't be astral anytime soon, thanks to the Valium. I regretted giving her both tablets, but I'd had no idea I could get out of my body again so soon after the burritos, and there was nothing to be done for it now. I cleared my astral throat so I wouldn't spook the skatepunk by sneaking up on him.

"What?" he said dismally. He didn't bother to look up.

"How's she doing?"

He shrugged. "She's a wreck. Not very surprising, considering what she saw."

Not only did he seem to know something about the case, but he was also phenomenally lucid. Jacob-level-lucid. Faun-level-lucid. I collected myself and tried to formulate a strategy for approaching him that wouldn't send him flying away. "So…you know what happened?"

He sighed heavily and knuckled his astral eyes without deigning to answer, like he was sick of me already, before our conversation had even gotten started.

"You know you're astral?" I ventured.

"Unbelievable." He leapt to his feet and swung around, and I got that weird feeling again of knowing the face but being unable to place it—a lot like when I'd spotted Karen Frugali on Lyle's phone. "Of course I know I'm astral. You think I can't tell when I'm astral? Newsflash—I'm in charge of the whole fucking Midwest. Including you." Oh. My. God. "So I think I'm quick enough to figure out I'm having a projection."

Hello, Constantine Dreyfuss.

Chapter 34

I tried not to look too surprised to see him, and especially, not to let on that he looked a whole hell of a lot different in the astral than he did in the physical. Why? Well, it seemed to me that it probably meant something. Jacob was younger in the astral. Faun Windsong was thinner in the astral. And my astral body didn't float around in a cheap suit.

Judging by his apparent astral age and the whole getup, right down to a well-worn Beastie Boys T-Shirt, I'd say I was looking at a Dreyfuss from the early 90's. The FPMP didn't exist, not yet, since back then psychic powers were thought to be made up of stage magic and hoaxes, and ghosts were still the stuff of Hollywood B-movies.

And yet, although astral Dreyfuss was a throwback from the first Bush administration, he was well aware of who he was in the present, what he did for a living—and who his friends were. Or weren't.

He seemed a lot edgier in the astral than he did in waking life, where he was so unflappable that everything just rolled off his back like it'd been greased with Vaseline. Jacob had been vulnerable in the astral, too. No censors. But if I played my cards right, maybe I could exploit this opportunity to talk to the real Dreyfuss, the one hiding behind the nonchalance and the big pretzels.

"I'm not surprised you take me for an idiot," Dreyfuss said. "You think I'm stupid enough to buy all that shit you shovel."

"I never thought you were stupid. Ever." Where had that come from? I'd need to be more careful—because evidently my censors weren't in the on-position, either.

"Really? Because you do the polar opposite of everything I want you to do, you lie like a rug, and you put less faith in me than you do in the Cubs winning the World Series."

"Faith?" My lack of sensors was seriously impeding my ability to steer the conversation the way I wanted it to go. "You're tapping my phone."

"And it's your loss that I've never been able to hack into Jacob's Q-mail—because now someone's stalking your boyfriend and I've got no idea who it is."

"Oh, so all this invasion of privacy is for my own good." I waved him off in disgust. "I'm never gonna fall for the line that you're just looking out for my best interests. Give *me* some credit for having a brain in my head. I'm not Richie."

"Speaking of whom—for a borderline moron, he seems pretty damn fulfilled, don't you think?"

"He's got nothing to worry about," I said.

"Because he's slow?"

"Because he's weak." Let it go, I told myself. Find out what Dreyfuss knows about Chekotah, about PsyTrain, and then drop it. But I just couldn't. "The Psychs who've gotta watch out for themselves are the high-level talents."

"Like you?"

"Like Warwick's nephew."

My God, when was I going to shut up? Meeting a dead medium in the basement of Camp Hell was my secret—mine—and Dreyfuss was the last guy I wanted to share it with. And he was watching me now with those shrewd eyes of his, the same eyes I'd come to know and hate, set in the face of a guy who was twenty years younger in the astral. "You, knowing about him?" he said. "That explains a lot. A heck of a lot."

"Forget it." As if saying that ever worked. I could only hope that with us being in the astral, it might. "It doesn't matter."

"Not so surprising, given that you both trained at Heliotrope Station—but you couldn't have known each other. You would've been there long after he slit his wrists. What happened, you wandered into a records room one day when you were bored and you did a little reading? Or maybe the rumor mill was still grinding out gossip when you showed up, and they couldn't wait to tell you about the medium who took the bloody way out." He watched my face for a reaction, and I felt my patented blank look failing me. "Or maybe you had a little chat with him yourself."

Every fiber of my astral being was straining to say he didn't kill himself, but I sucked some white light, and I managed to grit out, "Fuck you—I don't know what you're talking about."

"That's what you'd like everyone to think, isn't it?" He held up his hands as if to show me he wasn't concealing a weapon...or maybe a one-hitter. "I'd tell you that your secret's safe with me—but I don't suppose you'd believe me. Alex, Warwick's nephew, what happened to him...that was before my time. Not only was I not a federal agent yet, but if you'd told me that was what I was gonna be when I grew up, I would've figured you were high."

"So what did you do?"

"I flew my buddy's Cessna for weekend skydivers...and I played bass in a band. Maybe you've heard of 'em?"

Evidently I hadn't, because he said something slippery that was lost to the astral. I shook my head, no, and said, "Sorry."

"I wasn't looking to be any big, psychic so-and-so when I hooked up with the FPMP. I just wanted the cash. Do you know how much it cost back then to cut a record? And I'm not talking about a digital download or even a CD. Back then, you had to press vinyl. And we were dragging our gear from gig to gig in a hatchback. We needed a van." He gazed down at Faun Windsong sadly, and said, "My kingdom for a horse."

While I was trying to tell myself I didn't give a damn about his story, I couldn't help but wonder how joining the FPMP seemed like a promising way to make a quick buck to a kid with dreadlocks and pot leaf tattoos—especially one with a pilot's license. "So, what? You regret that you cut off your dreads to grab an entry-level position as a private pilot? Looks like it worked out in the end; you don't seem to be hurting for money anymore."

"And that just goes to show how far out of whack you are. I've never flown anyone anywhere unless I wanted to fly 'em. And aside from my initial contact, it's never been about the money—not once I got myself tested."

Tested? Dreyfuss? Shit, shit, shit, Dreyfuss and his glowing eyes. He wasn't just the president of Hair Club for Men, he was also a client. And whatever mojo he was working, it was something rare, something different, like Jacob's. Something that didn't blend in to the crowd at PsyTrain.

"It's not safe out there," he said. "It's never been safe, not since Psych went public. And the better you are at what you do, the riskier it is."

What did Dreyfuss "do"? That's what I wanted to know. But my head started to buzz when I thought about it too hard, when I got too damn excited, and I started getting scared I'd lose control and float up against the ceiling like the dumb Matrix guy in the hallway. "So you felt safe at the FPMP," I said, hoping to draw him out—to ask him what his deal was without coming right out and saying it.

"Once we took care of …." He said a name I didn't recognize. "Once he was gone, yeah. Once we'd cleaned house, at least I didn't have to worry about getting plugged by my own team."

"And so now it's perfectly safe—one big, happy family. Who just happens to be spying on me."

"Look—we can watch you, or we can watch the whole entire rest of the world while we keep our eyes discreetly averted from your oh-so-private life and hope to keep you covered in our peripheral vision. You might think you're fascinating, but lemme break it to you: you're not all that special. Everyone else eats and shits and fucks and sleeps, too. The things about you that're even marginally interesting, no one else can see. So get over yourself."

I was only too happy to oblige. If I was astral and prone to venture into TMI-territory, the last person I wanted to talk about was me. "So, what's next? You point your snipers at the bible-thumpers and shut them up for good?"

"You're confusing me with James Bond. I don't carry out hits. I just crunch the numbers that pick out the targets."

"Oh." Not just a river in Egypt. "That's completely different."

"It is, actually, because I follow parameters. I check with all my top-level Psychs, and if their collective data confirms that some thug's living results in my Psychs dying…." He shrugged. "I gather the info and I pass it along to the military."

"You have people eliminated based on psychic evidence."

"You didn't have much of a problem with Detective Marks' evidence treating the Criss Cross Killer to a lethal injection."

"There's no comparison. He had due process. A jury convicted that guy, and a judge sentenced him."

"I guess Hardcore Vic has officially retired." Dreyfuss stood up from the physical chair, and an astral skateboard appeared in his hand. He let it drop to the floor with an astral clatter easily as loud as any physical skateboard would produce, then popped the nose up with his heel and caught it. "And he's been replaced by Detective 'Law and Order' Bayne—who'd rather put his life in the hands of twelve potentially bribeable, ignorant, prejudiced pinheads than trust a team of certified Psychs like him."

Hardcore Vic had left the building some years ago—though I wouldn't exactly classify the guy who'd filled his Chuck Taylors as a proponent of the straight and narrow. Did I trust a Psych any more than I trusted an NP juror? Maybe, maybe not. But executing someone based *solely* on psychic evidence made me question whether or not I believed in free will, and that, in turn, made me want to swallow a couple Valiums, curl up in bed, and pretend the whole thing was just a crappy TV show I was better off forgetting.

Dreyfuss dropped the board, then popped it up again. "It's something you saw in my office that's got you spooked, isn't it?"

"Duh." What I'd meant to say was *no.* God damn it.

"There's a good chance that anyone noncorporeal you see is just some poor schmoe I inherited from the old guard—"

"Jennifer Chance. Did you inherit her?" Shut up. Shut up. Shut up.

"I knew it!" He flickered, and then he was right in front of me, young and thrashy and way too fucking smart. "I knew you could see Dr. Crazy-cakes."

"You had her killed."

"What I did—and believe me, I ran all kinds of scenarios—was determine that any jury that could possibly be assembled would take one look at her, with her blonde hair, easy smile and an M.D. after her name, then take one look at your surly self, with your history of drug use and mental illness, and let her go scot-free. And if she didn't come back and find you, which was the predominant possibility, thanks to the trial you'd pop up on some other wacko's radar and end up full of holes."

What I'd always assumed was that Roger Burke and Jennifer Chance had been erased because they were hypothetical threats, loose cannons with potentially FPMP-damaging ammo. Not because they were threats to me, specifically. And normally I would have assumed that Dreyfuss was just making it all up—because he was good at cooking up enough specific-sounding detail to make the things he said seem totally plausible—except that we were astral. And even for the most dishonest of us, every conversation in the astral was so painfully truthful it sounded like the inside of Carolyn's head.

"If you're so smart," I said, "then tell me what you really think happened here."

He dropped his skateboard again. I steeled myself for the clatter, but this time, it hit the floor with a gentle whumpf like he'd dropped a couch cushion instead, and it broke apart into hundreds of tiny, sparkling astral motes that flickered, then winked out. "Bert Chekotah."

"But he got slimed, too."

"I'm not saying he did it. I'm saying his insatiable pit of neediness was what set the vortex spinning."

"You know this for a fact?"

He flickered, and reappeared right beside the couch where Faun Windsong was zonked out. "I know it in my heart. All those women…and he didn't deserve any of 'em. Not even close. Chekotah had a dichotomy working for him that sucked in strong women like a gravitational pull. Here he was, a physical leader, a spiritual leader, strong and proud—and, of course, dreamier than Lou Diamond Phillips. And yet, at the same time, he was a wounded little boy who just wanted a great, big hug." His voice was dripping with disgust. "That's got more pull than an electromagnet for a powerful Psych chick. Especially a woman like her." He gazed down at Faun sadly. "She wanted to gather him up in her arms, snuggle his darkness away and make it aaaall better."

Ew. Maybe once I was physical again I'd forget the mental picture I concocted of Faun cradling Chekotah's head to her bosom. But I doubted I'd be so lucky. "So what're you saying—Chekotah stirred up too much psychic energy by hopping from Psych to Psych?"

"Not at all. I'm saying hell hath no fury like a woman scorned."

I looked at him, looked at the incapacitated afghan-mummy on the couch, and looked back at him again. "So you're saying Faun Windsong did it."

He knelt beside the couch and tried to take Faun's wounded hand in his, only his fingers passed right through her. "You said yourself she seemed genuinely distraught when Chief Feelumup disappeared. I say we look at the other women."

"It wasn't Lisa," I said. Intellectually, I knew that the amount of stress she'd been under was probably enough to make anyone snap. Although she'd probably built up a pretty big emotional callus to make it through the police academy, plus whatever other horrors she'd seen over the years walking the beat, it wasn't as if police officers never cracked. But I knew Lisa. And I just couldn't see her going all Fatal Attraction over a man.

"How about Professor March?" he suggested.

I shook my head. I could see Debbie having the potential to be a Grade-A bitch if you crossed her. But she'd told me herself that she liked Lisa. Plus, Debbie had a life outside PsyTrain. She had interests—and although those interests were primarily clothes and makeup, I had a feeling they connected her with a social circle that had nothing to do with "spelt" unless they thought it was Rockabilly slang for something dirty. Plus, she really didn't seem smitten enough with Chekotah to go all psycho over his other women.

Psycho, like Karen Frugali. "But it can't be Karen," I said out loud.

And while Dreyfuss hadn't been privy to my entire line of reasoning, he followed along well enough. "You sure 'bout that?"

The buzzing in my head, the one that made me worry I'd float up to the ceiling, intensified to the point that I felt like I needed to shout for Dreyfuss to hear me. "She's dead. Maybe Chekotah had another affair going on with someone even more desperate who we don't know about yet."

"Yet another woman?" Dreyfuss batted his ear with the heel of his palm like he was trying to force some pesky water out of his ear canal. "Unlikely. His dick hardly had enough time to dry off between his current mistresses. You should take a better look at Karen. After all, we never found a body."

"I don't need to see her physical body," I said. "I saw her astral." Mother fucker. That was *my* secret.

Dreyfuss stopped trying to tamp water out of his ear and gave me a big-eyed *caught you red-handed* look. "Astral?"

Wait a minute, I'd meant her *ghost*. Hadn't I? My head buzzed so hard it sounded like he was talking through a really shitty cell phone connection. "Never mind."

"But don't you get it?" He seemed so pleased with himself for catching me in a lie—the one where I said I'd just been hanging out in the hall, minding my own business when I saw Karen's ghost—that he was actually hopping up and down. He said something else, but it was lost to the astral static.

"What?"

He cupped his ear and shook his head like he couldn't hear me, either.

The buzzing swelled, and I started feeling shaky. As I fought down the astral equivalent of vertigo, it occurred to me that Dreyfuss was gesticulating like crazy, trying to tell me something. He grabbed one of his dreads and pointed to it, and then he pointed at my sneakers, and he nodded at me, wide-eyed and grinning, as if to say, *Isn't it obvious?*

With the sensation of the cord tethered to my third eye suddenly burning against my astral forehead, I couldn't make heads or tails of whatever he was so worked up about. And while most of me was hoping beyond hope he'd forget all the secrets I'd let slip during the conversation, a tiny sliver of me realized that if he forgot his astral outing, whatever big idea he was trying to tell me would die with his current projection.

He must have figured as much too, 'cos he seemed keen on getting me to understand. Since he could tell I was clueless, he made a fist and cradled it over the left side of his chest, making it go *pa-pump, pa-pump* like a human heart. Then he pretended to rip it out. He looked at me harder and spread his hands. *See?*

See, yes. Understand, no. Was he trying to be Karen? I squinted at him and he went sparkly around the edges, kind of like his astral skateboard had when it hit the floor for the final time. He pantomimed ripping out his heart one more time, then he held up two fingers behind his head and did the woo-woo-woo thing in front of his mouth with the flat of his fingers, like a little kid playing cowboys and Indians in the years before political correctness existed.

Chekotah ripped out Karen's heart? No doubt she saw it that way…and just as my astral vision went hazy, and I suspected that I probably looked like I was turning into sparkles too, I realized that astral bodies don't have much to do with how you actually look in your physical life. Sparkles turned into streaks as I rushed across the building and through the ball pit of the floor to hurtle toward my own body. I careened into my physical shell with a sickening, buzzing lurch that filled my mouth with bile, and even so, I clung to one single, crystalline thought. The way astral travelers see *themselves* is the way they look to other astral folks. So if Karen Frugali *felt* like she'd been eviscerated, maybe she wasn't the ghost of a murdered woman. Maybe she was the astral form of a jilted lover.

Which would mean Karen wasn't dead, after all.

◊ ◊ ◊

"Karen Frugali," I blurted out. I sat up and my head hurt, bad. Thanks to Auracel, I'm no stranger to headaches, but this was a scarier headache, like maybe something was really wrong. Jacob was crouched in front of the GhosTV, and he looked at me over his shoulder. I told him, "You gotta crank down the astral channel, now."

"You feel it?"

"Yeah, I feel it."

He consulted his notes and twirled the dials. My headache stayed right where it was, so maybe what I was feeling were the consequences of being forced out of my body with a bag of Mexican takeout in my system.

I slung my legs over the side of the bed. Holy hell, everything on me hurt. Everything. "Get Dreyfuss." It even hurt to talk. "He knows."

"He knows what?"

I pointed toward the door that joined our room to the bathroom we shared with him, as if to say, *Just go get him already, before he forgets. And can't you see I feel like crap?*

Jacob ducked into the bathroom. I heard the knock, not quite pounding, but still urgent. Low voices, and then he came back into our room with Con Dreyfuss trailing him.

Dreyfuss' hair was flat on one side and huge on the other, as if the pillow had displaced it. His eyes were squinty and red. "Did you find something?"

"Karen Frugali," I said.

Both Jacob and Dreyfuss eyed me expectantly and waited for the money shot. I searched Dreyfuss' bloodshot eyes. Didn't he remember? He'd been so phenomenally lucid back there in the Quiet Room. How could he not remember?

Once they both started to look as if they were getting exasperated with me, and once I realized no corroboration would be forthcoming from my new astral buddy, I said, "What if she'd thrown herself into her relationship with Chekotah as hard as she did with everything else? And what if she realized she wasn't the only side action he was getting—that Chekotah had the gall to put the moves on her roommate, too? Her heart getting ripped out—what if that was a metaphor? And what if what I saw wasn't her ghost, but her astral form?" I took a careful breath. Breathing hurt, too. "What if she's not dead?"

"I'd totally buy it," Dreyfuss said, "except for one thing. If she's astral, where's her body?"

Chapter 35

It wasn't so much that we thought we'd find Karen Frugali's physical body in her room. It was just the only logical place to start looking. Since my headache didn't let up no matter which way Jacob spun the GhosTV dials, I had him set it to the channel that made his cheeks streak red like the skin of a cuttlefish and also caused Con Dreyfuss' eyes to multiply and leak light. With the psychic channel playing, hopefully a really good piece of evidence would take pity on me and sparkle, or glow, or jump up and down and point to itself.

While I'd stopped converting California time to "my time," it seemed pretty clear to me that anyone who had the authority to open the door to Karen Frugali's room was asleep. Either that, or jerking off to a picture of me on their cell phone. The clock was ticking down on our missing Psychs, though, and we weren't particularly concerned about anyone else's beauty rest. Jacob pulled out his cell and said, "I'll have Lyle send a security guard."

Dreyfuss said, "Don't bother." He pulled out a keyring and stuck a key in the lock, and right as I wondered when he'd managed to get a copy made for himself, he wiggled it, gave it a sharp smack with his pocket flashlight, and pushed the door open. Bump key, the type of thing a locksmith would use… or a burglar. Very illegal, in Illinois, anyway. Very useful, though.

Karen Frugali's room was the same way I'd remembered it. Bed at an awkward angle, red screen protecting the rest of the room from her stack of books. I swept it with my GhosTV-sensitized gaze, but nothing lit up. Jacob and Dreyfuss flitted in ghost-quiet, each of them combing over Karen's possessions with a flashlight and a scowl. "Anything?" Dreyfuss asked me, and yeah, I realized I'd never actually told him I was seeing Psych, but we seemed to be so close to finding something I didn't really care.

"Nothing."

"Go through her books," Dreyfuss told Jacob. "See if she kept a journal—although, if she was paranoid, she probably didn't."

"She wasn't paranoid." Yeah, that was me, defending the main suspect.

"She wasn't schizophrenic," Dreyfuss said, "but let's face it, the girl had problems." He turned back to Jacob and said, "When you don't find a journal, see if she underlined or highlighted anything in the books. If not, see if anything's bookmarked or dogeared, or if they fall open to a particular page."

I made my way around the diagonal bed and looked down at the picture of the baby. Karen's baby, I presumed. The picture frame was a cutesy ceramic thing painted with wooden alphabet blocks, jacks, and a teddy bear. The kid itself was not attractive—and I wasn't just thinking that as someone who didn't particularly go for children, either. His head was kind of peanut-shaped and his creepy milk teeth had big gaps between them. Still, he'd never grow up to get braces, or a more flattering haircut. And for that, I felt bad.

I pulled on a latex glove and picked up the photo, looked at the back, and looked at the front again. Nothing buzzed, nothing glowed. I put it back down, and I wondered what the hell I'd expected to see with the GhosTV tuned to its current channel. Outward manifestations of psychic ability? Check. Old repeaters? There probably weren't any to see. Faun's necklace, would that still be glowing? Probably. I glanced down at my ectoplasm hand, the hand covered in carpetburn, then slipped off my glove and picked off one of my scabs. Then I realized it would probably not be a good idea to leave a scab at a scene that might eventually be combed by a forensics team, and I flicked it into my pocket. Hopefully I wouldn't follow it up after I'd forgotten about it with a cookie I wanted to save for later…but given the ingredients of PsyTrain cookies, I doubted I would.

A bead of blood welled from the hole in my knuckle, and I wiped it on the cuff of my black jacket, then squinted. Yep. Glowing.

Though all that experiment seemed to prove was that nobody had bled recently in Karen Frugali's room.

"Anything?" Dreyfuss asked me.

I shook my head no.

"It's totally possible there's nothing here for you to see. Don't forget, Chief Feelumup ran in here and started burning sage and messing with the energies the second he realized something hinky was going on."

That was the same exact thing he'd called Chekotah back in the Quiet Room. Was that a hint? A challenge? Or what? I stared at him, baffled…and he shrugged and gave me a thumbs-up, then turned and went to search the bathroom. What the hell was that supposed to mean? Did he remember our whole astral conversation, or not? Everything about him was so ambiguous, I'd never know without coming right out and asking him…which would leave me totally exposed, if it turned out he had no memory of his astral trip.

Damn it.

I went past Jacob, who was dutifully picking through each and every one of those textbooks to see if Karen decided to scrawl her evil master plan in the margin, and I followed Dreyfuss into the bath. "So." How could I ask him if he remembered tripping without coming right out and saying it? "You been sleeping okay?"

He'd been scrutinizing the contents of the medicine cabinet. He shot me a dubious look over his shoulder with his lighthouse eyes, then turned back to take stock of the contents. His eyes left tracers when he turned his head, kind of like Faun Windsong's body had. He peeked inside a bottle of vitamins as if he'd hoped to find something illicit hidden there, and was disappointed to find only One-a-Days. "I haven't had a good night's sleep in fifteen years. Why should it be any different here?"

And just like that, he knocked me off-balance again. Constantine Dreyfuss, vulnerable? Or maybe just misdirecting me. Because I'd damn well caught him with pillow marks on his cheek in the middle of the day, though who's to say he knew I'd noticed them? My chewed-up hand started to itch—not with ectoplasm, I saw. And hopefully not with a newly-developed latex allergy. I chalked it up to the healing process, and pressed my fingernails into the bumpy texture of my skin to seek a little relief without actually dislodging any of the scabs. "You're always bragging about being able to score me Valium, or something even better," I said in an attempt to keep him on the tightrope between truth and defensiveness. "Maybe you should skim a few for yourself."

I leaned against the white-tiled wall and watched his profile to see if he'd try to tell me his sleeplessness had something to do with guilt—which, I gathered from our astral chat, he didn't actually feel, not over having Dr. Chance executed sniper-style. Or if he'd try to feed me some line about having to stay clean, especially after I'd seen he liked his ganja well enough to have it inked into his own hide. But instead he just shuffled a container of skin cream aside with the end of his pen, and said, "Women. How many kinds of moisturizer do they ne…?"

He turned and caught my eye—heck, maybe he was even gonna *wink* at me again—but his face went still. Hard to totally read his expression, what with the way his eyeballs were lit up like the Terminator. But something was definitely wrong. "What?" I said.

He pitched his voice low. "What are you doing?"

"Nothing," I said automatically. But even with his glowy eyes, I could tell he wasn't looking at me. He was looking past me at the wall beside the sink.

I turned and took a look for myself.

NOT
VIML
ISA

There it was, scrawled on the white tile wall in ten-inch red letters, just above the towel rack. If there was any doubt in my mind that I'd just written it in my own blood, the knuckle of my forefinger throbbed where I'd torn it open, and the damn letters started to give off a gentle glow. I blinked a few times, and then I saw the message plain as you please.

No TV. I'm Lisa.

◊ ◊ ◊

Of course, it occurred to me that if Karen Frugali wanted me to pull the plug on the GhosTV so I couldn't find her, the smartest thing she could do was tell me that Lisa wanted me to shut it off. But what if I was wrong to second-guess myself, and what I really needed to do was take that writing at face value, because it really was Lisa, and she'd been telling me all along to turn the damn thing off?

"Tell me this," I said to Dreyfuss, as he and Jacob and I all stood around the snowy-screened GhosTV and tried to determine if we should put an end to prime time. "If that was really Lisa, why would she be able to move my arm? She's not a telekinetic. She's not an astral traveler." And she wasn't a ghost—at least that was a huge consolation—because if she'd been a spirit, I would have seen the rest of her.

Jacob planted his hands on his hips like he was eager to hear the answer to that one, too.

Dreyfuss considered the question, then said, "Because with the power of *si-no* and nothing but time on her hands, if Lisa needed to make something happen, she'd figure out a way to do it."

"Maybe we're looking at the wrong angle," Jacob said. He turned to me. "You can sense astral activity if you've had a couple of drinks, right?"

He knew damn well I could *see* travelers after I'd knocked a few back, but I gave him credit for not airing every last detail of my secrets in front of Dreyfuss.

"Maybe we turn off the set and try alcohol instead." Jacob looked sideways at the TV, as if he didn't want it to know he'd been talking about it. "We can always turn it back on later."

Whatever the GhosTV actually did—and given the crazy spectrum of effects it was broadcasting, I couldn't have pinpointed what, exactly, that thing was—it wasn't only doing it to me. Those waves were hitting the whole building and sinking into all the Psychs in range. Maybe it did make sense to draw on a resource that affected just me. "I guess a couple of drinks wouldn't hurt."

"You do know that booze actually decreases psychic ability," Dreyfuss said. "Don't you?"

I'd heard as much, yeah. But I wasn't in the habit of letting the facts get in my way.

Dreyfuss dug in his pocket and came out with a pillbox like you'd find at the corner drug store, a cheap plastic affair with Monday through Friday compartments. It rattled as he opened it. "Let's see." The lid popped, and my eyes went right to the long red pills smack-dab in the middle. Seconal—my one true love…aside from Jacob. And phenomenally difficult to find. Right beside it was that Valium I'd suspected he was carrying too, but Valium's everywhere. In contrast, Reds had been shuffled from manufacturer to manufacturer and gone in and out of vogue. Or maybe they'd gone out of vogue at the end of disco and pretty much stayed that way. There had to be almost a dozen pills in there; the compartments were deep. Simply seeing that telltale flash of red set my whole body on high alert, and actually had me swallowing back a surge of anticipatory saliva.

Talk about a big pretzel. With frosting, coconut flakes, sprinkles and all.

He didn't wave it under my nose. In fact, he didn't even linger with the lid open very long. He picked out a bullet-shaped capsule that was half green and half white, closed the pillbox and stuck it back in his pocket. "This is the latest and greatest in psyactives. Nothing like those old vasopressin uptake inhibitors from back in the day—those things'll fuck you up for good."

That tingle on the back of my tongue, the one that made me long to swallow a pill, drained away at the memory of Movie Mike twitching in his wheelchair.

"What does it do?" Jacob demanded.

"It pumps up the ligands that bind with your sigma receptors."

"In English."

"If you're not a Psych, it does nothing worthwhile. But if you are…it makes you better."

Jacob narrowed his eyes, which he couldn't tear away from the green and white pill. For someone willing to pay twice as much for a carton of hormone-free coffee creamer, he seemed strangely keen on attaining better living via pharmaceuticals. And if he liked me as a level-five (or probably six) medium, chances were he'd *really* like me as a seven.

I was so ready to hear him encouraging me to take one that it took me a second to process what he really said, which was, "If Vic takes it, then so do I."

Chapter 36

"So much better than partying alone," Dreyfuss said. He pulled his pillbox back out, retrieved not just one more green and white pill, but two—and he swallowed one himself, then handed one to Jacob and one to me. "This works a lot faster than an uptake inhibitor, but it's not immediate. We're talking maybe half an hour instead of a few weeks."

Since I was none too proud of my gullible tendency to take candy from strangers, what with the whole Roger Burke "muscle relaxant" fiasco, it did set my mind at ease to see Dreyfuss go first. Yes, it was entirely possible that he'd planted a placebo for himself to take while he dosed Jacob and me with something we'd both regret, but somehow, I didn't think so. He'd held all three pills in his hand at the same time, and he hadn't even looked to see which one he was popping.

Even more interesting: since Jacob's mysterious talent wasn't common knowledge, and Dreyfuss' mysterious talent wasn't either, joining me in a psyactive cocktail struck me as a major act of trust. On the parts of both of them.

I dry-swallowed my magic bullet. Jacob went into the bathroom and washed his down with some water. Amateur.

Dreyfuss eyed the GhosTV. "If you leave that on…well, I dunno what'll happen, but it'll probably be pretty intense."

He didn't specify if that was intense-good or intense-bad, I noted. But since I'd made up my mind that the writing on the wall really was a message from Lisa, I switched off the set and pulled the plug out of the wall. The eerie psychic light in Dreyfuss' eyes dimmed, then died.

California time, my time, whichever time I framed it by—it was really late. Or really early. People inside the PsyTrain building were beginning to wake up as we headed once again toward Lisa's suite. Mundane TV sets played the morning news, and the sounds of generic co-anchor banter carried through closed doors and into the hallway. I kept my eyes peeled for ghosts—there were none—and for glowing clues. None of those, either. I could cut myself and bleed on something and see if that lit up, but I'd already left more blood smeared around PsyTrain than I was comfortable with. We piled into the elevator and I checked the mirrors. No one veiny, no one glowing. Con Dreyfuss caught me looking at him and *winked*.

At least that was out of the way.

The kitchen staff was reporting for duty as we emerged on the first floor. They weren't glowing, either. And none of them were ghosts. As I pondered that, I wondered what good a psyactive would actually do for me if there were no ghosts around, and began to worry that the answer to that question might be nothing at all.

What good was talent if I couldn't tell whether it was working or not? And if it was actually working, how could it be of any use if I couldn't figure out what to do with it?

"Faun's necklace," I said, just before we turned to head toward Lisa's suite. Jacob and Dreyfuss both hung on whatever I was going to say next, and which, of course, I hadn't particularly thought through. What could I say—that it had red energy when the psychic channel was playing? That it sparkled in the astral? "I want to take a look at it. D'you think she's still wearing it?"

Dreyfuss said, "I've never seen her without it," and he turned down the hall that led to the Quiet Room.

Faun Windsong had the afghan bunched around her middle, with her head and feet sticking out either end. She must have woken up at some point between my last astral projection and now. There was a tissue box on the floor beside her, with a handful of used tissues scattered beside it. Since she wasn't in motion, I couldn't tell if she was leaving tracers behind her when she moved, like when I'd viewed her with the ghost channel playing. Her necklace just looked like a weird tangle of rocks and twine, so I was guessing the psyactive hadn't kicked in yet, was all.

I got down on one knee beside her and patted her arm awkwardly. "Hey."

"Lyle? You found more Xanax?"

No wonder she was still too doped up to project. "It's me, Faun. Vic."

Her eyes opened and she squinted a bit with her glasses missing—and I wondered if her astral glasses were broken too. "It's funny," she said, "how everyone calls me Katrina but you."

"Habit. Sorry."

"It's okay. I don't mind." She gave me a smile that was wistful, and mostly sad, but not entirely. "I feel young again when I hear it. I remember what it was like when life seemed so full of possibility."

I suppressed a shudder. If I thought about what "feeling young" meant to me, I came up with cold sweats and a bunch of memories I'd just as soon forget. "So, this necklace of yours…."

She covered it with her gauzed hand as if she'd meant to stroke it and had forgotten about her second-degree burns. "Isn't it wonderful? Bert made it for me."

Gee, what *couldn't* that guy do? It made sense that he'd craft a functional amulet—he was the guy who'd sent the Criss Cross Killer's spirit packing. The guy whose room I'd needed an astral axe to break into…the room I'd then left with a big ol' hole in its protection to let Karen Frugali come rushing in.

Faun struggled to half-sit and remove whatever was holding her necklace on so I could take a better look at it. I drew a breath to tell her to stop, but then the charley horse that had originated in Chicago several days ago came roaring back—and it brought its friend, the sciatic nerve pain, with it. I didn't know whether to stand, sit, or just keel over, howling. I brought my second knee down to the floor and curled in on myself in a sort of kneeling fetal position—which helped the pain in my ass but not the cramp in my calf, which hurt so suddenly, and so bad, it left me gasping.

"Vic?" Faun sounded dreamily concerned. All that Valium. I really should have kept one for myself—because now I had no choice but to score some from Dreyfuss. Who knew what strings would be attached? Though I was in so much pain, I couldn't really say I cared.

What was worse, I realized I hadn't summoned that astral axe. I hadn't even been thinking of an axe. Karen Frugali had put it in my hand to break through Chekotah's astral barriers. Jesus.

I drew breath to say something, and that hurt, too. Bad. Like I'd just done way too many whippits and there'd be hell to pay, just as soon as I could breathe again. I hoped Jacob knew a Vulcan nerve-pinch that would allow me to breathe again, but when I turned to ask him, I saw he was gripping the back of his own neck with a grimace of pain on his face.

Dreyfuss was doing a triceps stretch with one elbow in the air. He looked none too comfortable himself. "Muscle rigidity...temporary."

Now he tells us.

"Vic?" Faun was too doped up to notice her three visitors were moaning and groaning like they'd just completed a triathlon. She shoved the necklace at me. "See the turquoise? That's an heirloom. It was blessed by three generations of tribal elders. And the wool came from a damaged prayer mat of an 18th-century shaman that was unraveled and spun back into—"

"Wait," I said, but she was on a roll—and since when had the locomotive of her conversation ever stopped for me once she'd started talking about herself? Maybe Faun Windsong had worn that necklace every day because her prettyboy shaman had told her he'd made it especially for her—but even if she didn't see it was more than just an ugly piece of folk art, Chekotah knew. He knew he'd tomcatted one woman too many, and he knew that woman was mind-blowingly talented. He'd protected his room, his "sacred space"—he'd even tried laying down some hocus-pocus in the rooms of his other mistresses—but he'd put the Real Deal Necklace around Faun Windsong's neck. Did he perceive her to be in more danger from astral Karen than he was? Or did he think the necklace made up for the way he betrayed Faun's trust by slipping it to every other woman who would let him? I might never know. All I knew was that he had a good idea of what kind of power was in that necklace, and he'd given it to her.

And now she was giving it to me. Just to show me. Or rather, to show it off—once a showoff, always a showoff. "...and only four skeins of the yarn exist..."

"Wait." I spread my hands wide to make it obvious I did not want her to give it to me—but she'd convinced herself that my life would be incomplete if I didn't see this marvel of Native American craft. When I didn't take it from her, she just shoved harder, slotted it into the gap between my chest and thighs, and let go. "Faun, no."

Despite the fact that I now had cramps in both legs, really brutal cramps, and my arms too, for that matter, I uncurled myself and tried to give the necklace back. Only when I moved my arm, a jarring sensation swept through me—the feeling that I was somehow not in synch. It was as if I felt one thing and experienced another. My arm should have been straight out, touching her, in fact. Only it wasn't. At least, I didn't think it was. When I looked at it, I saw three arms...no, wait, multiple arms...each of them occupying a different place in the trajectory of the movement I thought I'd made.

And then, I felt a snap, and all of my arms lined up.

That tracer-thing I'd seen happening to Faun Windsong, back when I'd viewed her with the psychic channel playing? I was doing it. Big time. And I felt every last incongruity of it.

"Fuck." That was about the most succinct way I could express my frustration. I dropped the necklace, because I couldn't tell where my hand really was as opposed to where it felt like it was—and on top of that, where it looked like it was to me, and whether or not I'd moved my fingers, or just thought I had.

"Are you okay?" Jacob was down beside me so quick I heard his knees crack against the tile floor.

"I…." I wasn't. But I couldn't just say that, not to him. He must've had his own psyactive trip to deal with. And besides, what could he do about it? A crash behind me. I turned, felt the queasiness of multiple, unsynchronized turns snapping into alignment at the end of the motion, and saw Con Dreyfuss with his hands out, eyes unfocused, and an uncomfortable-looking butterfly chair on its side in front of him.

"Just a little disoriented. I'm cool."

He then tripped over the chair and went sprawling. And I probably shouldn't have felt glad about it, but at least, I reasoned, I could be fairly sure he'd swallowed the same green and white pill that was currently coursing through my veins. "I'm okay," he insisted.

Jacob pressed his mouth to my ear and said, "What's with him?"

"His eyes are messed up. What about you—are you okay? Do you feel anything?"

"Muscle cramps."

"Hold onto my arm," I told him. "It doesn't feel…right."

He grabbed hold of my arm, no questions asked.

"What're you doing?" Faun sounded bemused.

I ignored her and told Jacob, "Okay, now move it around."

He pumped my arm up and down a couple of times. No tracers. Not on that arm, anyway. The opposite side of my body felt like it was fanning out from the anchor point of his grasp. I couldn't see his red shield, not like I could under the influence of the GhosTV, but it seemed to be there anyway. Would he understand what I meant if I asked him to hold my subtle bodies in, if I told him I felt like they had all come loose? I wouldn't know unless I tried. "Hey, I need you to—"

I saw movement on the wall behind Faun Windsong's couch. Light. A finger of light snaking upwards, as if the wall was splitting open and a bare 1000-watt lightbulb was shining behind it. The crack was slow at first, and small, but then it shot up toward the ceiling, took a right turn and shot across, parallel to the corner where the wall met the ceiling.

"Do you see that?" I whispered.

"What?"

Damn it. It was right behind Faun Windsong's head. I pulled my hand out of Jacob's grasp and went for the necklace. Getting it back around Faun's neck where it was supposed to be was the only quick course of action I could think of. Only my hand wasn't closing around the necklace. Did I feel something? Was that it? I made another grab. Used tissue, moist. No necklace. Damn, damn, damn!

Another crash behind me, and Dreyfuss said, "I'm gonna stay on the floor for now."

"The necklace," I said.

I'd expected Jacob to hand it to me, but instead it was Dreyfuss who said, "To your right."

I moved my hand right, and sure enough, there it was. Only Dreyfuss couldn't have seen it, not from behind me where he was flailing around on the floor. So his sixth sense really was in overdrive just as much as mine. And his funky eyeballs didn't need to be lined up with something to see it. I grabbed the necklace and tried to slam it down on Faun, but the swing went wild. I punched her in the arm and dropped it again. Meanwhile, the crack of light took another right turn and crawled down the wall until it disappeared behind the couch. "Jacob..." once it formed a rectangle, the glowing cranked up even harder, and the section of wall in the center began to...dissolve. "Put the necklace back on her. Now."

Chapter 37

Jacob grasped Faun by her uninjured hand and gave her an alley-oop. He was moving fast and efficient, but Faun was like a floppy rag doll. Who's to say if Jacob would've moved faster if he could see the big, honking, scary-assed door to another dimension opening directly behind her head. But I knew in my gut that the only one who had a visual on it was me.

"Now," I said, and somehow, despite the feeling that my muscles were brittle enough to shatter if I forced them into motion, I rose into a crouch, and then stood.

The cold light shining from the magic door was scary, but once my psychic eyes adjusted to the brightness, the figures lurking beyond it were ten times worse. The figure in the forefront resolved itself as it moved closer, and closer still, and the haze of overbright light receded, and revealed the stain down the front of her dress where her heart had been torn from her chest, and that long, wet stain was pulsing blackish red. I wasn't sure what scared me more, all that blood, or the look in her eyes. Because sane people's eyes didn't look that way—I know that for a fact.

Most of the cops I've worked with over the years have a particular fear of crazy people. Not just because crazies are so unpredictable, but for some deeper, subconscious reason, like the fear that their mental imbalance might be somehow contagious. Luckily, I shed that phobia probably a week after they locked me in the loony bin. Nutjobs are people too, after all, and unless they've got a history of violence or maybe a weapon, I don't find them any more intimidating than your average joe. So here's the part that was spooking me: most nutjobs think they're sane, at least on some level, and so Karen Frugali's astral form shouldn't have been staring out through those glittery, crazy-girl eyes.

But Karen saw herself as crazy.

And crazy Karen looked pretty damn happy to see Faun Windsong without her lucky necklace on.

She didn't just reach for Faun Windsong's head. She reached *into* it, like a horror-flick zombie looking to grab a quick snack. Faun gasped—a small inhalation, as if maybe she'd just remembered something. She'd felt it, though. She'd definitely felt it.

"And here comes our buddy, Lyle," Dreyfuss said, "just in time. Detective Marks, keep him in the hall, would you?"

Jacob started to turn toward the door, and I snapped, "Stay with Faun." He listened to me and not the federal agent on the floor behind me—I give him that much credit. But even though he finally got that ugly-assed necklace fastened around Faun Windsong's neck, he was too late. Karen had already broken through.

She felt around inside Faun's head as if she was searching for the last piece of chocolate in a plastic jack o' lantern full of cheap lollipops, and the moment she seized on whatever it was she'd been looking for, I saw it. Karen's face lit up in a wide, brutal smile that showed way too many teeth. Faun Windsong's face changed, too. Her look of mere surprise shifted, intensified, and became fear.

Karen clutched hard, and she pulled.

I thought I was the only one who saw the top of Faun's head stretch—but then Jacob dropped her and jumped back with a very un-Jacob-like, "What the fuck?" and I realized that Karen had somehow managed to bridge the gap between astral and physical.

I tried to shove Jacob back toward Faun, but my arm wasn't where I thought it was and I only managed a girly slap across his shoulder. "Hold onto her," I barked. "Protect her." Faun's head stretched like taffy, and glistening globs of ectoplasm burst from the point at which her physical body stretched into the astral. That, I gather, Jacob saw—the slimy stretched head—and he didn't budge. She howled, and it didn't sound like a human howl. It didn't even sound like an animal howl, or anything else from the physical world. I tried to give Jacob another shove toward her, and might as well have been beating him up with a wet noodle. "Go on, protect her. Isn't that what your talent is for?"

"What's happening?" Dreyfuss demanded, but if he couldn't see anything while he was hopped up on psyactives—not in the sense people normally see things—I didn't have the luxury of calling "time out" to explain things to him.

I said, "Karen Frugali." Hopefully that'd convey enough.

Her head snapped up at the sound of her name—yeah, she could hear me all right. Her crazy astral eyes met mine, confirming that she knew I could see her—while I was physical and she was astral. How's that for a parlor trick?

Jacob forced himself to take Faun Windsong by the shoulders, even though her head was stretched two feet into the astral, and she was covered in slime and making that horrible, hollow, bone-chilling wail. "Karen's pulling on her," I said. "Pull back."

And then another voice joined the fracas. "Oh. My. God." I recognized it from the Mexican restaurant, so I didn't need to risk a disorienting glance over my shoulder to know Lyle had just graced us with his presence. Some photo op.

Dreyfuss tried to round him up. "Don't move. Stay calm—" but stretched heads had never been among the psychic phenomena on PsyTrain's lesson plan. Lyle started shrieking, louder even than Faun Windsong.

Karen set her jaw and started hauling at Faun's head even harder. Faun's face was at least four feet long now and her features looked like a melted multicolor candle. Her screaming sounded echoey, and more astral than physical. "Grab her fucking head," I told Jacob. Because he was the one who'd always wanted to dig in, and get his psychic hands dirty, right? Well, here was his chance.

He didn't want to—I could tell he was straining to do what I'd ordered. Hell, if he'd actually wanted to touch it, I'd probably have good reason to be freaked out by the extent of his Psych fetish. But he summoned up his courage, and he forced himself to wrap his hands around that long, slimy, rubbery, wailing thing that had been a human head mere seconds ago, and he pulled.

"Red energy," I told him. "You're stronger than a damn necklace. Suck white light and send your red energy up to zap her free."

Even though I couldn't see what Jacob was doing, it must have had some effect. When Karen saw what was going on, she blazed sparkly-astral and pulled even harder, gaining a few more inches on Jacob. The weird wailing sound Faun made was so far away now, when Lyle drew breath to keep panicking, I realized there were more voices—small and distant, but definitely voices—coming from behind Karen.

"Police. Drop it. Drop it now. I will shoot."

An astral cop? A female astral cop, at that...and then the slight Spanish accent clicked in, and everything else fell away—Jacob and Faun, Dreyfuss and Lyle, and the world's loudest Quiet Room. Because that was Lisa's voice. Lisa.

I surged forward and found myself face to face with crazy-eyed Karen... which didn't make sense, because how could I be in the doorway when the astral door was way up by the ceiling, and I was half-crippled with drug-induced muscle cramps. Only I didn't feel crampy at all. I looked down and saw the top of Jacob's head. Then I glanced over my shoulder and saw myself.

I'd projected...standing up.

It was useless to look at my physical body, stooped and glassy-eyed—it only gave me vertigo. What was the worst thing that could happen, anyway? I'd fall over? I've survived worse. Or maybe someone else could carjack me while I wasn't behind the wheel...but no time to think of that. Not now. I poured all my focus into Karen Frugali, coordinating with Lisa to get her to let go of Faun. "Drop it," I shouted, directly in her face—and I felt the familiarity of my holster on my left side, and the gel insoles of my work shoes. I wasn't ex-Hardcore Vic, a guy with no hobbies besides pretend-jogging and porn. I was an astral cop too, and now I was on-duty. "Police. Drop it. Now."

I'm not sure whether she would have been scared of my astral gun or not—heck, I didn't even know if my astral gun was even loaded—but that dumb training session with Sando I'd endured came back to me clear as ectoplasm, and instead of worrying about guns and bullets and how they would or wouldn't function in the astral, I grabbed her by the wrist, leaned in, and snap-pull-pop, I'd jarred her funny bone.

While I hadn't expected it to work on her a second time...I hadn't exactly thought it would fail, either. I think my sliver of confidence was the catalyst that converted the physical maneuver into its astral equivalent. Karen let go of Faun's head and screamed—if you could call it screaming. It sounded more like the squeal of brakes right before a car crash.

"Watch it, Vic. She's dangerous." Lisa. My God, it was so good to hear her voi...wow. There she was. I'd expected her in a J-Lo type velour tracksuit, or maybe a poorly-fitted woman's blazer, but astral Lisa was wearing the navy uniform of a beat cop, complete with a masculine black tie and a big, gold badge over her heart. She held her gun like she meant business, and I wouldn't have been surprised if she was a better shot than me. The weird thing was, in the astral…Lisa didn't quite look like Lisa, not the way I thought of her. Astral Lisa was plainer. Harder. Like if you saw her from the wrong angle and you didn't notice the tight single braid down her back, you might mistake her for a short Mexican guy with thin eyebrows and biggish hips.

"Don't let her pull you in." Debbie—holy hell, astral Debbie looked like a pinup girl. She could give Betty Page a run for her money. She didn't glow as brightly as Karen, though. Neither did Lisa. Or that weaselly little dark-haired kid beside her…Chekotah. Cripes, Chekotah really was as pathetic as Dreyfuss said.

I didn't think I needed to worry about Karen trying to pull me in. Just the opposite. "Get out," she bellowed, and her voice was like thunder. It knocked me back a couple of feet, and the magic door began to dim. I could make out the texture of the stucco wall behind it, or through it…or however it was situated in relation to the physical.

I started to feel panicky around the edges, because Lisa and Debbie—and that weirdo Chekotah—were within reach, and since I had no intention of taking one of those evil psyactives again, I needed to figure out how to bring them back to the physical *now.* I sucked white light and rushed back toward the door. The closer I came to it, the more defined it became. But Karen was right on the threshold this time…and now she had the astral axe in her hands.

"Get out." Karen hefted her axe like she damn well meant to use it.

Given that she was so adamant about guarding that doorway, I figured it must be important. Behind her, Lisa motioned for me to get going—right, as if I'd turn tail and just leave her trapped there beyond the looking glass. I was in cop-mode just as much as she was, and on top of that, Karen's craziness didn't scare me—though it probably wouldn't be a bad idea to watch out for that axe. I glanced down—Jacob was cradling Faun Windsong, who was gasping out huge sobs and covered in slime, but her head looked round enough. If I could pull Lisa and Debbie back through that door, maybe they'd be okay, too.

Of all the various scenarios I'd trained for, hostage negotiation was not one of them. Maybe that was another of Sando's many skills, and we'd learn it during next fall's training inservice. Even so, I knew the value of staying calm. So while Karen was bugging out and Lisa was screaming at her, I decided to take it down a few notches. I showed her my empty hands so that she could see I wasn't going to draw on her—yet. Then I motioned for Lisa to stop the *Drop the weapon!* routine, and said, "Look, I just want to talk."

Karen clenched the axe, but her psycho-eyes went slightly puzzled.

"This isn't what you wanted," I said, "is it?" Karen didn't contradict me, so I went on. "You're a smart lady—think about it. Yeah, Chekotah's a creep, and yeah, he strung you along. But it doesn't look like revenge is gonna make anything better. Keep going with this, and there's no way it can end well."

"There never was," she snapped.

Behind her, Lisa motioned for Debbie to take Chekotah and start circling around so they were flanking Karen.

"Right," I said, "I get it. Sometimes everything's just another shade of crap. But listen, here's something else I know. You've got a ton of talent—and you could do more with it."

She must've been waiting for me to tell her to tone it down, because the look of confusion on her face was priceless.

"Forget the 'light worker' bullshit. You're a medium."

"No...." she didn't sound very sure.

"You are. Your subtle bodies come apart like a bunch of nesting dolls. But you've only been working on one muscle—the astral muscle—and leaving everything else to go flabby." As someone who'd never had any idea he could project, but who saw ghosts like they were right there in front of him, I should know. "If you can do this astral thing, then you can sense spirits." She was so strong, level-five at least, that with the right training, she'd probably be able to *see* them as well as I could. "It's just a matter of focusing on a different subtle body."

"Why should I care?"

"Because that's really what it's all about, isn't it? The afterlife?" I searched her face. "Your son?"

Chapter 38

At the mention of her dead kid, her expression froze, but her energy shifted palpably. She flickered. The door flickered. Lisa saw the change, and made the call to get out of there while the getting was good. "Go-go-go," she barked, and tried to herd the civilians through. There was a blur, and a whooshing sound filled my ears, and the three of them distorted and began to stretch—but Karen reached into the smear of light and astral matter, snagged something, and pulled.

Chekotah's astral body pulled free from the stream and snapped back into the astral. Lisa and Debbie, it seemed, had broken through. Commotion in the physical started up behind me, lots of shuffling and yelling, but I didn't dare take my focus off Karen. She flickered, hard. But there was no way for Chekotah to get past her. It would serve him right for me to leave him behind, but I supposed I should at least attempt to pull him out, too. "Listen," I said, "just listen a second. I know about spirits. Okay?"

The flickering stabilized. Karen stood before me, still blocking the doorway, but now the axe was dangling at her side and she was making major eye contact—not looking there occasionally and then looking away again, like normal people do—but unflinchingly staring deep into my eyes.

"When people die," I said, "and you'll be able to verify this for yourself—most of 'em move on. A few of 'em stick around. But the ones who stick around are usually messed-up. Murders and suicides, or people with unfinished business. As for accidents and illness—at the very worst, they leave a little residue. A repeater. A psychic impression of the final moments, like a moving snapshot. I think the spirits of those repeaters, they're fine. They go wherever it is people...go. When they die."

Karen was so still, I almost thought her astral pause-button had been triggered. But then she said, "Heaven?"

While I knew she probably wanted to hear that heaven was full of clouds and angels and Jesus and all-you-can-eat, calorie-free buffets, I couldn't bring myself to lie to her. Not Psych to Psych. I felt something pulling at me, voices in my ear. It was getting hard to think, but I managed to say, "Maybe it's heaven, or maybe it's some higher plane. Call it what you want. I know there's something more, though. I've seen spirits go there...and join up with their loved ones again."

She didn't cry. She was beyond crying. Her face twisted into an expression of such raw despair I had to look away.

"Don't you get it?" I said. "You'll see your kid again. When it's time. But until then, what good's it gonna do to rack up a bunch of casualties, all over this...guy?" I did my best to ignore the sensation of being shaken when it seemed to me I was standing still. I gestured at the sniveling little nerd she'd trapped beyond the door. "Forget about him. He doesn't deserve you."

While it blew my mind that I'd actually been in full agreement with Con Dreyfuss, especially to the point of repeating him verbatim, Karen seemed to experience a headful of epiphanies, too. Her expression registered a series of shocks. She released the astral axe, and it dissolved into a shower of sparks as it slid from her grasp. She was still blocking that door, though.

"Let him go," I said gently. "I have no idea if there's a big scorecard in the sky or not—but just in case there is, do you want to take the chance you'll screw up your afterlife—for *him*? And even if it turns out to be one big free-for-all once you go into the light, what about the rest of *this* life? You can be so much more without him."

I'd been trying to appeal to the childless mother in her, but inadvertently, I ended up speaking to the dog-eat-dog part of her that wanted to be the best, the brightest, at everything she did. She whirled around to get a look at astral Chekotah, and even though I had serious doubts about whether I'd have any aim when my physical body was being jostled around, I slipped my astral gun out of its holster in case the axe made a reappearance. But instead of splitting Chekotah like a cord of firewood—which I have no doubt she could have—Karen gave him a look of such pure contempt it made him shrink even smaller, and she pointed her finger in the direction of the Quiet Room, and she said, "Go."

I couldn't stick around long enough to see if he made it or not. My physical body was pulling at me hard, and the sickening psyactive in my system was the only thing that kept me from snapping back like a lightning bolt. It felt good to let go, to let it drag me into that shell, in the way that puking feels good after you've been hovering over the toilet half the night waiting to hurl.

My hearing came back first—pandemonium—while my vision took a moment to clear. And it seemed like there were hands all over me, though I was too stunned to recoil from all the unwelcome touching.

"Can you hear me?"

"Call an ambulance."

"I think he's okay, give him a second."

"Don't—what good's a paramedic going to do?"

"If this has anything to do with that pill you gave him…."

Jacob's face was the first thing I saw when gray sparklies dissipated, and I felt like I was back a hundred percent in the physical again. He'd hauled me onto his lap with my head cradled in one hand and the other one stroking my cheek. I put my hand over his—and saw tracers. Three or four hands that snapped into position one after the other. Okay, maybe ninety-five percent back.

"Vic?"

"No ambulance." I tipped my head back to try to make heads or tails of what was going on in the rest of the room. From my upside-down vantage point with my subtle bodies rattling around inside me, I saw Debbie March wrapped in the afghan. She was huddled against the far wall with a notebook on her lap, scribbling in it so hard I was worried she'd tear through the page. Her red hair hung in straggles, wet with goop, and her makeup was gone.

Bert Chekotah was as naked as the day he was born, and just as goopy—and the little creep had a much hotter body than he deserved, which, although it was pretty superficial, did explain some of his appeal. Maybe. Faun Windsong and Lyle were huddled around him, wailing. Con Dreyfuss stood with his back against the wall, gazing off into the distance. Or maybe he was listening. If I'd been looking at him with the GhosTV tuned to the psychic channel, I had no doubt his psyactive-enhanced flashlight eyes would be too bright to physically see through. Or maybe he had so many sets of eyeballs that they saw too much for him to navigate.

"Vic, are you okay?" Lisa's voice. I cast around until I found her kneeling right beside me in Jacob's blazer, crying, with ectoplasm and tears glistening on her cheeks. The realization that she was the only other one besides Jacob touching me was a big relief.

"If you don't write it down," Debbie called to her, "you're going to forget."

"I...don't...care," Lisa said, between great, wracking sobs.

Wait a minute. *I* cared. I needed to know who'd been using my arm as a telegraph machine. I reached for her—more tracers—and patted her hand. It was freezing. "Were you really the one telling me to turn off the TV?"

"Yes," she said, certain at first...but then she grew puzzled as the specifics of it slipped from her mind, just like a dream.

"How?"

"I think I...I asked the *si-no*, I remember that. And then...."

Come on, she'd been physical again for, what? All of two minutes? And she didn't know how she'd managed to move my arm? "Think, Lisa. How did you do it if Karen had you trapped behind the door?"

"I asked the *si-no*..." her crying abated as she strained to recall the sequence of events. "And the *si-no* told me to pray. And so I prayed to my guardian angel."

What? Come on—give me a break. That couldn't be it. She might as well have said she drove an iron spike into the ground and invoked the power of Thor.

Jacob didn't care about the specifics. All that mattered to him was that we'd found Lisa. He gathered her against him, and me too, and held us both, and maybe he shed a tear or two himself. And for a moment it seemed it was just him and me and Lisa, and the rest of the world dropped away while we were reunited, and safe, and whole. He kissed the top of her head, and mine...and then kissed my cheek, the side of my mouth....

"Well no wonder you weren't interested," Lyle huffed. "You could have mentioned your partner was doing you. Honestly."

He wasn't the only one not feeling the love. Faun Windsong hauled off and slapped naked Chekotah so hard he staggered, and the sound was so loud it echoed through the Quiet Room. He was lucky she was on a Xanax and Valium cocktail, otherwise he might've lost a tooth. She didn't say why she'd belted him; she was too enraged. But she didn't need to. Dreyfuss coughed—or maybe it was a snigger he'd covered with his hand, and although he was looking at a spot on the far wall, I could tell he'd just enjoyed that whack as much as Faun Windsong had.

As if it wasn't chaotic enough, a couple of the students shoehorned their way in, with one of the security guards from the front door in tow.

"Dr. Chekotah?"

"Professor March!"

As still more people packed into the room, Jacob rested his forehead against Lisa's temple, and gave me a world-weary smile. "You scared the hell out of me. I thought you'd had an embolism, or a stroke."

"Nope. I just don't have enough brainpower to be awake in the physical and astral at the same time." Although, if I did…that'd be a pretty neat trick up my sleeve.

"How do you feel?"

Relieved. Disoriented. Surreal. But mostly… "Hungry."

Chapter 39

I took a long, deep breath, and I held it. Savored it. And wished I could roll around and rub my face in the smell of it.

Bacon. Crispy. Just the way I like it.

I was so famished I probably would have eaten anything, even spelt. But once she'd taken a quick shower and swiped on some bright pink lipstick, Debbie hustled us over to a 1950's diner on the beach called Sambo's where the waitresses still wore polyester, the chrome napkin holders were shiny, and the coffee was strong enough to keep my mind off the tracers. And while we had plenty to celebrate with both her and Lisa back in the physical again, I think mostly we wanted to get away from the melodrama vortex at PsyTrain. Lyle'd had the good sense to know he was in over his head, and he alerted the board of directors, who swept in with their bifocals, briefcases and very disappointed frowns. Chekotah stepped down from his four-day directorship to try to spare the organization some of the scandal, and Faun Windsong…I mean, Katrina Wojtowicz…was being considered to take his place. I thought it made sense. She always acted like the boss of everyone. They might as well make it official.

It seemed to me like something was missing—that I should file a report, or head into Warwick's office to brief him, or feel vaguely guilty about Bob Zigler doing all the boring paperwork. Given how much of my time as a detective is spent wrangling red tape, the luxury of being able to catch my breath felt positively decadent. But I wasn't on duty. Not with the Chicago Police Department, anyway. I suspected I might have been acting as day-labor for the FPMP in this whole debacle…but I'd never signed anything formal. And so I decided to tell myself I'd been here as a favor, helping out a friend, and that was that.

We sat in a big, semicircular booth, me on the outside, and Lisa next to me, pinned between me and Jacob like we were worried she'd disappear if we didn't anchor her between us. Debbie was on Jacob's other side, and beside her, opposite me at the other end of the bench, was Dreyfuss. I still felt somewhat out of alignment, but given that I caught Dreyfuss searching my face a couple of times, I was guessing his eyesight was almost back to normal.

Debbie chugged a giant mimosa, then flagged down the waitress and asked for another. I wondered if I might come down faster if I had one myself—or at least a Valium—but I decided the green and white pill was too potent to risk mixing it with anything else.

"What's taking them so long with the food?" Debbie said. The waitress had taken our orders less than five minutes ago. "I think my stomach is digesting itself."

If projecting my astral form gave me an atomic tapeworm, I couldn't imagine how hungry I would end up if I'd been fully astral, like the girls were. Which I hadn't known was even possible—but we'd all seen it, so apparently it was. Psych tends to be like that. Full of big, hairy surprises you'd just as soon do without.

Lisa didn't complain about being hungry. In fact, she didn't say anything at all. She stared down at the edge of the formica tabletop like she was sorry she'd ever been born. Even though I've never been sentimental, I knew enough to see that I should probably offer her some kind of comfort—though the thought of anyone being comforted by *me* was a laugh and a half. I was glad to see her, of course I was. But now that the glow had worn off the giddy relief, I also wanted to grab her by the shoulders, shake her a few times, and ask her what the hell she'd been thinking, inviting a scumbag like Chekotah into her bed.

Jacob reached down, took her hand and squeezed it. He was good at things like that—acting like a normal person should.

"While we're waiting for the food," Dreyfuss suggested to Debbie, "maybe you could treat us to a reading from your dream journal and shed some light on what happened."

Debbie knocked back most of the second giant mimosa, pulled a few sheets of folded paper from her pocket, and began. "I'm in my bathroom fixing my hair, and I'm going to see Detective Bayne in a few minutes, and I'm thinking about this book on automatic writing with a yellow cover when suddenly I feel dizzy and really cold. And then I was in the biology lab at Chemeketa Community College, and Karen was there. And she said I couldn't go anywhere until I finished my lab notes. Only she wouldn't give me a pen. How could I finish my lab notes without a pen? Then I saw Lisa was there, over by the refrigerator full of shrink-wrapped frogs and fetal pigs. She was working hard on a computer, and she told me I needed to focus. And I said what good would focusing do if I didn't have a pen?"

"What are you talking about?" Lisa said, when Debbie paused to finish off her mimosa. "That never happened."

Debbie frowned down at her notes, and said, "I guess that depends on your definition of *happened*."

"What did *you* see?" Dreyfuss asked Lisa.

"I remember being cold and dizzy, but then I was somewhere else. It was misty, I guess. And Karen was there."

"What did she look like?" I asked.

"Pretty much the same as always." No blood? I gather she would have mentioned the blood, unless Karen *usually* looked like she'd just had open-heart surgery and left before they stitched her back up. Which I kind of doubted. "She was mad at me—she was always pissed off about something—but then I realized she knew about...Bert." Lisa stared down at the table as if that was all she had the energy to say.

"And you remember when Debbie showed up?" Dreyfuss prompted.

"Uh huh. It was better with Professor March there because we could pray together, and it was easier then for the angels to help us."

Debbie had been busy trying to get the waitress' attention and order another mimosa, but Lisa's description of events stopped her mid-wave. "I haven't prayed since I missed my period after I slept with Arthur Mirar on a dare from my cousin Junie. You told me you would type up my lab notes on your computer, so we started working together."

Subjective, much?

"So you didn't see the angels?" Lisa asked her.

The waitress finally emerged from the kitchen then, and she had the busboy in tow. It took two people to haul the groaning platters of pancakes and omelets to the table. Debbie asked for her third giant mimosa, but after that, we were all carefully silent as they laid out the food, refilled the coffee, and made sure we didn't want anything else...although, with the equivalent of breakfast for twelve, I didn't see what else we could possibly need.

I hacked off a big wedge of a pancake stack with the edge of my fork, crammed it into my mouth and swallowed it. Then I started to hiccup.

"Put more syrup on there," Debbie said, "or you'll choke."

Lisa was more practical. She started with the eggs. They went down faster. She ate them grimly, as if she would just as soon starve. Debbie washed down a mouthful of pancakes with a swig of coffee followed by more mimosa, and then she said, "What difference does it make if I saw angels or not? I don't go for organized religion. You know that."

Lisa shrugged. If she was feeling shitty about herself, and the angels were willing to help her anyway, I imagine it really would suck to be told they were just symbolism being spewed out by her own brain while it tried to make sense of what it was seeing.

The only two people who weren't inhaling their food were also the only two who were more interested in listening than talking. Instead of speculating on what had happened, thereby contaminating whatever the three of us actually did remember, Jacob and Dreyfuss started making arrangements to get us back to Chicago. Dreyfuss invited Lisa and Debbie to come with us. Debbie looked at him like he was nuts, and said something about being a "West Coast girl" around a mouthful of corned beef hash. Lisa said she'd think about it.

What I wanted was to talk to Lisa alone, but crowd logistics were keeping that from happening. Or maybe I managed to subconsciously avoid a one-on-one because I was scared I might lay into her about the piss-poor judgment she'd displayed in sleeping with Chekotah, and then she'd never want to come back home. Still, by the end of breakfast, despite the fact that her stomach must've been as painfully stuffed as mine was and the thought of getting on a plane was pretty damn daunting, she told Dreyfuss she would pack her bags. And when she did, I felt more optimistic than I had in a long, long time. I don't think it struck her as weird that I stole a play out of Jacob's playbook, covered her hand with mine, and squeezed.

◊ ◊ ◊

Once the GhosTV was crated up and transferred to FedEx's capable hands, we ended up taking a van to L.A.X. and flying commercial back to Chicago. My overtaxed adrenal glands grudgingly surged into fight-or-flight mode as we passed through the gate, but nobody stopped us, or seemed alarmed about our sidearms, or even made us take off our shoes. A quick glance at my boarding pass showed a four-figure number that I'd taken at first as a seating assignment, but then I realized was the cost of the last-minute, first class ticket. I supposed it was a veritable bargain compared to the cost of flying us there on a Learjet.

The interior of the 757 was, of course, nowhere near as snazzy as the white leather opulence of my first official flight—but I frankly felt a lot better having a hundred-some-odd people around, as opposed to being alone with Dreyfuss. Not that he spooked me anymore, at least not to the extent that he used to. It wasn't just a matter of familiarity, of knowing what he looked like with pillow marks on his face, or finding long, curly hairs in the sink when I went to shave. It was that whole astral conversation where I'd actually seen eye to eye with him, if only on one particular issue. And maybe the notion that I remembered it, while he likely didn't.

It also helped that I now knew who the FPMP's remote viewer was. 'Cos if I let that classified info leak to the right nutjob, Dreyfuss would end up with a higher bounty on his head than me.

Jacob climbed into his window seat, then I stuffed my garment bag into the overhead compartment and moved to plunk down beside him. A cheerful stewardess with blindingly white teeth checked my ticket and directed me instead to the window seat across the aisle. Jacob raised an eyebrow and caught my eye, but I shrugged. I was nearly forty. I should be able to survive having a few feet of space between us for the duration of the flight. And then Lisa deflated into the seat next to mine, and I decided that maybe things were looking up. Con Dreyfuss parked himself beside Jacob. Better Jacob than me. He's made of patience.

Lisa was inscrutable behind her big, dark Jackie-O sunglasses. I wondered if she'd been crying again—she cries an awful lot, for a cop—or if she was so wrung out that she was past tears. She looked over at me and gave me a tight, somewhat chagrined smile.

"Hey," I said.

"Hey." She took off her glasses. I don't think she'd been crying recently… but her eyes were a bit puffy. We both stared at each other. I don't think either of us knew where to begin. A few other first-class passengers herded up the aisle, leading awkwardly with carry-on bags that jostled Lisa in the shoulder. Some of them grabbed pillows and blankets from the overhead and settled into their seats like they were at a pajama party. I didn't look for a pillow. Neither did Lisa.

I dug Faun Windsong's necklace out of my pocket and put it in Lisa's lap. "I think you should take this…it's nothing to look at, but it'll keep you safe."

Lisa plunked it right back in my lap. "What do I want with that thing?"

"But, wait. It's really real."

We played "hot potato" with it a few times, and finally Lisa said, "I don't care what it can do. I don't want it—I can take care of myself. Give it to someone who needs the protection. Someone like…" her mouth worked as she consulted the *si-no*, "…Crash."

Crash? I supposed I could visualize it hanging from the epaulet of his leather jacket. And I supposed, as Psychs went, he did need more protection than Lisa, or me, or Jacob, since his talent wasn't strong enough to really give him much of an advantage, and since he didn't carry a sidearm.

Yes, it did make sense. Though I wasn't sure it was really the *si-no*'s idea. Maybe Lisa just didn't want a reminder of the whole Chekotah fiasco.

I couldn't think of anything to say. Trying not to be critical of her taking up with Chekotah was like trying *not* to think of an elephant—good luck with that—so I figured I might as well throw it out there so we could get past it. "It happens to the best of us," I said, meaning sleeping with someone we totally regret later. But at the same time, she blurted out, "You did your best."

We both stopped, then, and tried to figure out where the other one was headed with that. But considering that she made it sound as if I'd given something my best shot and then failed, I said, "I did my best with what?"

"Well, with…that TV set. Trying to help me."

Trying? It seemed to me I'd done more than just try.

"I mean," she went on, "you couldn't have known that every time you turned it on, Karen got stronger. I was saving up my energy, praying hard, getting strong enough to open the door myself…but then suddenly she was twice as powerful as before."

What? Whoa. The thought that I'd been feeding Karen's mojo the whole time knocked me off my high horse with a swift kick in the pants. "I guess that makes sense. I didn't actually know she was a medium until fairly late in the game." Even if I had, I'd felt such a sense of ownership in regards to the GhosTV that it probably wouldn't have occurred to me that I wasn't the only Psych in the path of its waves. And then there was the other area in which I hadn't been particularly helpful: Chekotah's sacred space. I waited to see if Lisa had witnessed me hacking through Chekotah's defenses with the astral axe and leaving him wide open to attack—but if she did, she didn't mention it.

"I didn't know you were the one writing those messages." I sounded somewhat defensive even though I was trying not to. "I didn't know you could send automatic writing from the astral. Hell, I didn't even know you *were* astral."

Lisa shook her head. "Not me, I didn't do it. The angels did. When I saw that no matter how strong I got, Karen would always be stronger, the *si-no* told me to pray to them. So I did, and they sent you the message."

While I pondered who the purported "angels" could be, and what they might look like through *my* jaded eyes, the captain sent a message of his own over the speaker system—one that I didn't understand any better than the automatic writing. A stewardess did a pantomime of what we should do if an airmask dropped down from a compartment over the ceiling. It was nearly impossible to focus on the instructions, but I figured if it came to the point where the airmasks unfurled and I needed to use my seat as a floatation device, I was screwed anyway.

"Did the *si-no* tell you falling for Chekotah was a good idea, too?"

Lisa glared at me, said, "Oh, you've never done something you wish you didn't do, even though you knew better," then turned and faced the underside of her tray table.

Smooth move on my part. I sighed. "Yeah," I allowed, "he was good-looking enough, but PsyTrain was full of guys. Wouldn't you have been better off going for one that was single?" And not cheating on his girlfriend with your roommate?

The loudspeakers mentioned something about emergency doors—whatever—while Lisa turned back to me and said, "You wouldn't get it." And I must have looked sufficiently sorry for the tone I'd taken with her, because her lips moved as if she decided to ask the *si-no* whether or not I'd understand...and was told that I would. In a small, small voice that I needed to strain to hear over the whoosh of the powered-up engines, she said, "He made me feel pretty."

She looked at the aisle while I found something absolutely fascinating out on the tarmac. I doubted it would help any if I told her she *was* pretty, at least she was to me—especially since I knew she saw herself as a hard, mannish beat cop. And especially since I really could relate, with my wimptastic physique. I patted her on the knee a couple of times, then sighed again and looked up at the modern-day hieroglyphics on the panel above my head.

While they explained what the no-smoking sign meant, I pondered whether or not I'd actually accomplished anything at PsyTrain. It sounded as if Lisa had been working on her equivalent of sucking white light, and that she'd nearly had enough to break free. But then, thanks to me, the GhosTV came along, and it got Karen so pumped up she was not only able to hold onto Lisa, but to make off with Debbie, too.

If I'd never come charging out to California, once Lisa was full to the brim with white light, she probably would've popped out of one of the PsyTrain walls, naked and slimy, but unharmed. Debbie, Chekotah and Faun Windsong would have been spared the sensation of being stretched into the astral. Karen Frugali would have managed to get away, any way you slice it—'cos who'd be able to go after her? Not me. I liked my subtle bodies right where they were, so no one else could hijack the cockpit while I was having some cheese fries in the Captain's Lounge.

Also, I wasn't necessarily sure I saw Karen as the villain in the whole debacle. Bert Chekotah—he was lucky I'd bargained to save his sorry ass from finishing out his life as an astral prisoner. Maybe that was the one thing I'd actually achieved. Go figure. The only ones who'd seen me do it were him, and Karen, and me.

Chapter 40

By the time we touched down at O'Hare, I'd convinced Lisa she needed to forget about grabbing a motel room and stay with Jacob and me—just for the time being, while she figured out what her next move was. Even though Five Faith hadn't been responsible for the disappearing Psychs at PsyTrain, we now had a better appreciation of how vulnerable Psychs actually were to the superstitious nutjobs who perceived us as serious threats.

It'd been a long flight, so Lisa and I both hit the airport restrooms while Jacob waited with our luggage. I must've been walking fast, and thanks to my good seat, I'd been one of the first ones off the plane. While I was in the stall wishing I'd gone easier on the pancakes, the ambient sound of the restroom changed as other people from my flight crowded in, dragging suitcases, flushing urinals and toilets, running the taps and working the hot air driers. When I stepped out of the stall, the previously empty room was now crowded with exhausted and stressed-out travelers jostling for space.

I waited for a sink to become available, then stepped up to wash my hands. A quick look in the mirror gave me pause. After all I'd been through, my hair still looked good.

Then a spot at the sink next to mine opened up and Con Dreyfuss slotted himself in, met my eyes in the mirror, and smiled. Thankfully, he didn't wink.

"You did some good work back there," he said.

I was pretty sure that wherever his compliment would eventually lead, I didn't want to hear it. I said, "Thanks," in a way that indicated I saw it as the end of the exchange, and I shook the water off my hands and headed toward the towel dispenser. It was empty. I went for the air drier instead. Once the air stopped running, I wiped my still-damp hands on my pant legs and turned…and almost tripped over Dreyfuss.

"Ever wonder what it would be like to be able to work like that all the time—to really pull out all the stops and just let 'er rip? No endless paperwork and reports and procedures. No meathead patrol officers swaggering around your desk. No ridiculous liability training."

"Oh, that's right, you spy on me at work, too. Thanks for the reminder."

I moved to step around him, but he sidestepped and easily blocked me. "Okay, I rub you the wrong way. Point taken. Look, the fact is, I've been trying to keep you on your toes—on purpose."

I attempted to step around him but there were too many guys with rollerbags rushing toward the urinals for me to dodge him.

"Some people can afford to get complacent," he said, "but not you."

I saw a gap in the crowd and I went for it, but damn it all, Dreyfuss was just as fast. He trapped me between the empty towel dispenser and a trash can and stretched on his tiptoes to look me square in the eye. The only way I could get away from him then would be to physically knock him down—and with a wall at my back, I didn't think I even had the leverage for that. Although, maybe if I made a fulcrum out of my foot…nah. It would only create a scene.

"You're not replaceable," he told me. "Get it?"

I forced myself to stop trying to figure out how to slip away and tried instead to determine what his angle was. Probably some ulterior motive. I narrowed my eyes at him.

He leaned in and dropped his voice so that only I could hear it. "You know you're a seven."

Dreyfuss had never struck me as someone who was any more interested in levels than the folks at PsyTrain who wanted to ensure that everyone got sufficient ego-stroking for their tuition money. Hell, look how happy he always was with Richie—and Richie was a strong two.

"Using you to solve a domestic is like swatting a fly with an Uzi."

"Karen Frugali's more talented than I am," I said—which was a weird thing to say, because you'd think I might want to revel in getting credit for being good at something for a change. But Karen was scary-good. She could turn the physical into astral. And once she saw beyond her own hurt feelings, she'd figure out that she could practically teleport. And kidnap. And then hide out in the astral where no one could ever find her. Holy hell. "She's definitely better."

"Not better. Different. And way too unstable to withstand the pressure of being a government agent. The minute the going gets tough, she loses it. Not you, though. You bend instead of breaking."

Either his description was an incredibly poor choice of words, or an incredibly perceptive one, because it convinced my PTSD that I was about to be tortured. Sweat prickled at my low back and a wave of pronounced nausea washed over me. Dreyfuss must not have meant to yank my chain quite so hard, because he took half a step back and looked me up and down. Then he shrugged and pulled a Tic Tac dispenser out of his pocket. Only those weren't cinnamon Tic Tacs inside…those were Reds. Thirty pills. Forty. At least. He flipped the rattling plastic case in the air, and I caught it and stuffed it into my pocket.

"You want to waste your time working with a bunch of Neanderthals… why? What's in it for you?" He gave me a sidelong smirk and pretended he was weighing out an option in either hand. "Tedious paperwork…or chasing astral kidnappers." He looked at each hand as if he couldn't determine which side carried more weight, then spread his hands wide as if both pretend options had just turned to astral sparkles. "Do you seriously see yourself as being so mediocre that staying with the police department is even an option?"

While my knee-jerk reaction was to defend the Fifth Precinct, the memory of all those cops standing around and smirking at me like a bunch of assholes while Sando made me practice about ten thousand wristlocks on him was still fresh in my mind. Not every case was a painfully obvious domestic; I got my fair share of spirit action as a PsyCop…but other than Zigler, and to a lesser extent Warwick, I wouldn't say I gave a rat's ass about anyone there.

And so I opted to not answer Dreyfuss. I just stared.

Dreyfuss held my gaze for a long moment, and then turned away and headed toward the exit. "You decide you want to hook up," he said breezily over his shoulder, "gimme a call. Your man's got my number."

I'm not sure how long I stood there with travelers streaming around me, going in and out of the restroom. Probably not quite as long as it felt. Eventually, I pulled myself together, took a step toward the door—then thought better of it and took a little detour to the water fountain to make sure the red Tic Tac didn't stick in my throat.

◊ ◊ ◊

It had been almost four days since I'd last seen the cannery. It felt different. Not like someone had snuck in and moved the furniture around or anything. More like I was the one who was different, and the way I fit into the space had changed. It was nearly midnight when I turned the key in the lock and eased the door open with my hip. I didn't remember the ride home—I'd fallen asleep the minute I slid into Jacob's passenger seat, and now I felt wobbly and disoriented, though thanks to the Seconal, I wasn't terribly concerned about the notion of falling down. The small mountain of unread mail beneath the mail slot turned into an avalanche as the door tipped it over. I stepped on a slick piece of advertisement and skated halfway across the vestibule in it, then let my rollerbag tip over sideways, and sagged against the wall.

Luckily, everyone else thought I was just exhausted.

Lisa took my arm, draped it over her shoulder, led me into the living room and said, "C'mon, sit down."

"I got him," Jacob said. He transferred my arm to his shoulder and half-dragged me upstairs. Which was good, because if I sat down in the living room, chances were I'd never make it to bed. Jacob must have taken care of locking down the fortress for the night and helping Lisa get situated. My thoughts ran somewhere along the lines of, *There's my light fixture. Hello, lamp.*

When the mattress sagged beneath his weight, I was drifting on the hazy cusp of sleep. My battered body wanted to keep going, but some part of me realized that although we'd been together this whole time, we hadn't really had a chance to talk since the astral door opened in the Quiet Room and all hell broke loose. Not alone.

I rolled against him and threw an arm over his chest. Did he pause for a fraction of a second before he hugged my arm to him? He had. He'd paused. My exhaustion cried out for me to ignore it and just go to sleep. But I couldn't.

I steeled myself and forced my protesting body to wake up. "What's wrong?" I said. I'd pretty much guessed the answer—he knew I was high. But fuck it. After everything I'd seen back there, the goop and the blood and the stretched heads, I didn't give a shit.

He sighed. "It's fine. Go to sleep."

I sighed louder, propped myself up on one elbow, and turned on the reading light clamped to the headboard. "Obviously it's not fine. What?"

Jacob rolled onto his side, reached up and turned the light back off, but then he put his arm around me and pulled me against him. Our chests pressed together and my face settled into the crook of his neck. "I don't think I realized…seeing the…I don't know what to call it. What happened to Katrina."

Stretched head? His moodiness wasn't even *about* me. What a relief.

"We probably saw two different things." That would be an apt metaphor for my whole entire life, but I set the notion aside and added, "You only saw the special effects. I had a peek at the behind-the-scenes production footage." Not that seeing crazy-eyed Karen pulling the strings was any less scary…but knowing often felt preferable to not knowing. It provided the illusion of control.

"I saw enough," he said. "I almost bailed."

So…that was the real problem. The Man of Steel noticed a spot of tarnish. "But you didn't bail. Jacob, cripes, who else would've thrown themselves on Faun Windsong and kept her from getting slurped into Bizarro World? Yeah, you had second thoughts. Only an idiot wouldn't."

"I used to think I understood. Maybe I didn't see things like you saw them. But I could watch you and gauge your reaction. You could tell me there was a guy in a tux or a woman in chains on fire, and I could imagine what it would look like. And I could tell how bad it was, whatever you were seeing, by the look in your eyes. At most, I might see a candle snuff itself out. But to actually see the phenomenon, really see it myself…." He paused, and it seemed like he might just trail off there. But then he finished his thought. "I almost couldn't handle it."

"But you did. You handled it great."

It would've been nice to pile on some more reassurances, but they would've only been repeats of what I already said. Besides, Jacob must've been as bone-tired as me. Although he didn't have Seconal luring him into sleep's sweet embrace, he'd gotten even less shut-eye than me over the last few days. Still, as I slipped away, I heard him whisper, "I never really understood how brave you are."

I didn't have the energy to force myself into wakefulness enough to respond to him—but if I had, I would have brushed it off. Because bravery had nothing to do with it. It wasn't like I had any choice. I saw what I saw and that was that.

◊ ◊ ◊

A special delivery woke me up—woke all of us up—bright and early. I staggered to the door in bare feet, sweatpants, and a t-shirt I'd used for dusting off the bedroom electronics. A guy in a stiff-looking navy uniform stood on the front stoop with a clipboard in his hand. He didn't seem any more thrilled to find me at home than I was to find him on my doorstep. "Yeah," I said with zero enthusiasm.

"I have a shipment for a V. Bayne." He seemed hopeful that maybe a few numbers on the packing slip had been transposed, and he could leave the heavy lifting to someone else. But I nodded, so he said, "I'll need to verify your I.D."

I dragged out my unflattering driver's license. He checked it, then schlepped back to his delivery van and started strapping the big plastic crate to his heaviest hand truck while I gathered up all the junk mail to ensure he didn't fall and break his neck on it. He seemed reluctant to bring the massive crate any farther than my front hall, but I told him there was twenty bucks in it for him if he hauled it down to the basement for me, and he grudgingly acquiesced. The noise of it thumping down the stairs one tread at a time was enough to finally roust Jacob, who managed to get the guy to help him uncrate the damn thing on charm alone. It occurred to me as the console emerged that Jacob and I probably came off as a couple of nelly antique collectors…but I'd rather have a deliveryman think that about me than know the truth—that I was a prime target for Five Faith, or any other nutjob flavor of the day, if they ever figured out who I was and what I could do—so I could live with the queer stereotype just fine.

And there it was: the GhosTV. In my house. Or the basement of my house, to be more specific; I try to pretend the basement doesn't exist. I'd always thought owning a GhosTV of my very own would be awesome—that I'd be in control of what I saw, or didn't see, and with that kind of power, I wouldn't be anybody's bitch ever again. But instead it just reminded me of stretched heads and slime coatings. The basement where I never went was the best place I could think of for it…at least until I figured out if I could even handle cranking my talent up higher than seven, or not.

Lisa and I stared at it in silence for a good few minutes, and then finally she said, "Maybe you can use it for something positive. Like making sure there aren't any really old spirits here."

"There aren't," I said quickly. The ghost who'd sold me the cannery told me so. And if she'd been wrong about that, and I'd been living among repeaters all these months...well, I didn't want to burst my own bubble. Lisa glanced at me to see if I was okay, then dropped her gaze to the stack of junk mail I suddenly realized I'd been holding in front of my chest the whole time like a shield.

"What's that?"

"Nothing."

As Jacob jogged back down the basement stairs, she pulled an envelope out of the stack and said, "This doesn't look like nothing." She checked the address, then handed it to Jacob. Red lettering on the envelope caught my eye. It had been stamped, *Important: Do Not Discard.* "It's from your gym," she said. "Thick paper, too. Really official. Did you let your membership lapse?"

Heaven forbid. "How do you know what his gym's logo looks like?" I asked her.

"He brought me there on a guest pass last time I was in town. Cute trainers. Too bad they all like boys."

Jacob opened his letter and read. His eyes skimmed side to side at first, but then the telltale vertical furrow appeared between his eyebrows. Lisa and I both caught on that maybe it actually was important. We watched him intently, and finally, once the tension was thicker than the fancy envelope, he started to read aloud.

"We regret to inform you that our confidential customer email list has been breeched. The unfortunate incident occurred last weekend, when a new hire who passed all of our background checks copied the database and forwarded the information to a group that claims to promote the 'sanctity of marriage.' We at Halsted Fitness Club appreciate the business of all our clientele, and we would not be the top-rated fitness center on the north side four years in a row without the support of the LGBT community. Halsted Fitness Club intends to pursue damages to the fullest extent of the law. Also, please be assured, your credit card information was not accessible to this individual at any time."

So Jacob's email hadn't been bibled by Five Faith because he was psychic. His whole gym had been targeted—gay and straight alike—by a bunch of anti-gay creeps. Even Lisa, who'd only been there once. I supposed it was a relief. Maybe.

"They're giving me a free month," he said.

"I guess that's better than nothing."

Chapter 41

Jacob folded the letter and slipped it into his pocket, then planted his hands on his hips and scowled at the GhosTV. Did he want it upstairs...or did he want it gone? I couldn't tell. "Maybe we should put it on a pallet," he said. "What if the basement floods?"

Just as I was thinking we probably would have noticed in April or May if the basement took on water, Lisa said, "No."

We both looked at her.

"It won't," she said. "It's safe here."

Okay, then.

As we headed toward the stairs, I wondered if maybe I'd gotten off easy in regards to the *si-no* up until now, at first because Lisa was hiding it, and then later because she was unsure of the moral ramifications of using it. Her time in the astral had changed her. I might not know exactly how pronounced that change was until we were able to spend more time together, but I had the sneaking suspicion that her days of being able to fake normalcy were over.

The land line started ringing when we were halfway up, and by the time we got upstairs, the machine caught it. "It's me." A woman's voice. Barbara. "Listen, I know it's last-minute, but if you and Vic can make it, Clayton's team has a tournament in Beliot at one." Beloit was the approximate halfway mark between our place and theirs...or maybe it was just the point at which I always had to stop and take a leak when we were on our way to visit. Jacob paused with his hand hovering above the handset, and looked to me. I wasn't especially interested in soccer, particularly children's soccer, but I realized I wouldn't mind seeing Jacob's mom and dad, and his Uncle Leon. Especially now that the "Level-Five PsyCop Medium from Chicago" was just "Jacob's boyfriend," and Leon's ghost arm didn't make such a spectacle out of itself for me anymore. It would be a normal thing to do. Like normal people. It might even be…dare I say it? Fun.

"…he could have mentioned it sooner," Barbara yammered on, "he always pulls this…"

"We should go," I told Jacob.

"Really?"

I nodded. "Yeah. Let's go."

He picked up the phone. "Hey, Barb…."

If we wanted to make it, though, we'd need to get our asses in gear. The poor performance of the water heater actually got us all showered in record time, since with Lisa there we only had about three and a half minutes of water apiece instead of our usual five. I made sure I wasn't being stingy with the sunscreen. I even scrubbed it into my scalp along the part in my hair.

As I stood in my bedroom wondering which drawer I might have shoved my baseball cap in, a tangle of crap on the top of the dresser caught my eye instead. I hate clutter. It lurks there in your peripheral vision and hides the nasty supernatural stuff you'd rather be able to avoid. Jacob's usually the culprit behind clutter, however, this particular offense was mine.

Faun Windsong's necklace had twisted up with one of the nylon ties from the wrist restraint training in the pocket of my blazer. It sat there like a tangled jumble of trash you'd spot in the gutter grate after a big storm. We'd be going right by Sticks and Stones on the way to the expressway, since it was easier to hop on 90 from there than it was up by our place. If I shoved the necklace in a drawer, I'd probably forget it even existed—so I might as well drop it off.

It seemed like a plan. Until we actually got there, and realized every parking spot within five blocks of the store was taken. Jacob's mood had been subdued all morning long, and though the idea that I actually seemed interested in spending time with his family had raised it up a couple of notches, the luster wore off a little bit more with each time he circled the block.

On the third revolution, I'd finally untangled the nylon tie from the necklace—although I found myself somewhat carsick from looking down. I shoved one in each pocket of my flannel shirt to keep them from getting tangled up again, and then I called Crash to see if he could meet us out front before Jacob ground his molars down to a powder.

It rang five times, and then his voicemail picked up.

Weird, the store should be open. I waited a few seconds, and tried again.

Voicemail.

I checked the time. Five after eleven. Maybe he was with a customer… but now we were running the risk of being late for the game, especially if we hit any snags by the tollbooths.

A car in front of us slid into a parking spot, and Jacob made a sound of annoyance deep in his throat. I tried Crash's phone one more time—voicemail—and then I said, "Fuck it. Let's just go. We'll stop on the way back."

"No."

I glanced over my shoulder at Lisa in the back seat.

She gave me an exasperated look that conveyed, *Look, pal. How should I know why? It's not called si-no-WHY.*

I rolled my eyes. "Okay, then double park and I'll run it upstairs. I'll be in and out in two minutes."

Jacob flicked on the hazards. "Fine."

Hopefully, I really would be in and out in two minutes. Crash was probably dying to hear about the California trip. Dying to see Lisa. I wished he could have come along with us, but in a sense he was married to his store, and if he wanted to do anything social during the day, he'd have to close up shop and take a financial hit—and probably alienate his regulars who wouldn't take too kindly to walking up all those stairs for a Fast Luck Money Drawing candle only to find "closed" scrawled on the door in chalk.

I saw the door was ajar as I rounded the landing—which was good, because I'd been starting to think that maybe Crash wasn't answering his phone because he'd gotten lucky—so lucky that his good time had extended all night, all morning, and right though store hours—and that I'd be setting myself up for a really awkward moment of, "Hey, Vic, this is…what's your name, again?" And there was no doubt that whoever'd been rocking Crash's world would be very, very athletic.

But, no. No awkward moment with a nameless trick, not today, at any rate. Incense was burning, the radio was playing, and the fake dollar bills that hung from the ceiling on fishing line fluttered silently as I shouldered open the door. I was just about to call out, "What, you don't answer your phone anymore?" when I saw the top of a head through a gap in the shelving, and realized Crash actually had been with a customer the whole time.

They were talking, and as I drew closer I could pick out the customer's voice through an ebb in the music on the secondhand boombox. "…don't believe in evil, like Christians believe in evil. But there's still darkness in the world..."

Ugh. I'd had about as much New Age philosophy as I could handle at PsyTrain. I'd be glad to ditch the ugly necklace and...oh, fuck. The guy had a knife.

And I recognized him, even from the back—his hair was all tangled, and there was lint stuck in it. His knife hand shook. It was the same guy I'd seen there the other day. Same time, come to think of it. The regular who was always buying curse deflections—Crash had said that guy creeped him out. He should have listened to his gut. "You should thank me," the creep said, and his voice was getting louder, and edgier. Crash, I now saw, was filling a plastic bag with the money from his register.

Where was Miss Mattie? Then again, even if she was there, what could she have done? I reached for my sidearm and patted empty flannel. Great. The one time a gun would do me any good and I was unarmed. Call for backup, then. I went for my phone.

"Money is so, so dirty," the creepy guy said. His voice was a little sing-song, in a pretend-friendly sort of way. Gooseflesh sprang up on my arms from the mere sound of it. "They don't call it 'filthy lucre' for nothing. It's a stain on your karma. Don't you get it? I'm saving you from the darkness... wait a second—you're not holding out on me, are you?" Crash's arm trembled as he extended the bag to the guy, who didn't move to take it. It did seem like a really paltry amount of bills there in the bottom of the bag. Given the utterly dismayed look on Crash's face, I'd guess that was the whole register. Shit. "Don't you know that lying blackens your soul? When you speak an untruth, the one you hurt the most...is yourself."

I really didn't like the way his voice was pitched—and the way his knuckles went white as his grip tightened on the knife, either. It was a kitchen knife, not a fighting knife. Whacked-out schizos with kitchen knives are a hell of a lot more dangerous than hardened criminals who just want to get the money and get out.

As I chose the most covert path back to the stairwell so I could call him in, I heard him say, "Do you suck cock?" Conversationally, almost—the way he'd observed that Crash cut hair. "You look like you'd be good at it." And that was when I realized I couldn't wait. Not for a patrol car. Not even for Jacob, who was right outside. From where I stood in relation to the creep, he was ripe for a chokehold, but since I was one of Chicago's Finest, a chokehold would only end up getting me sued. Normally, my reaction to that would be, *fine—sue me.* But I'd recently done half a million wristlocks on my buddy Sando. From every conceivable position.

I'd always figured training maneuvers couldn't possibly carry over into real life. Perps move faster than trainers. Perps are actually trying to hit you, and to run. They're holding real weapons. But I'd never accounted for the fact that I'd be looking at my friend on the opposite end of that real weapon, and that my own adrenaline would be sky-high.

"You'd hold back on that too, wouldn't you?" the creep said. "You think you're better than me? What makes you so—" Right hand, wrist, left hand, chin. I didn't need to execute a chokehold when grabbing someone from behind by the chin and yanking their head back to throw them off-balance was totally whitelisted. Sando had even encouraged me to master the chin maneuver, since it works best when the perp is shorter. And so far they've all been shorter.

Snap, snap, pop and twist. Fulcrum—wow, I even got the fulcrum in place—and the smelly-looking guy was face-down on the floor before I'd even hollered, "Police—drop your weapon."

The tone of my voice was enough to make him think some thick-necked beat cop had caught him in the act. Sure, I was unarmed, and I was wearing my Converse All-Stars, a T-shirt under an old plaid flannel, and my favorite pair of jeans, but seeing as how his face was mashed into the floor, he didn't know that. I planted my knee between his shoulder blades and got him trussed up with my nylon tie, and then I turned my attention to Crash. "Are you okay? Did this asshole hurt you?"

Crash shook his head slowly from side to side. I think it was the first time I'd ever seen him speechless. I was glad he wasn't hurt. Otherwise I might need to "accidentally" punch the creep in the neck. Five or ten times. My sciatic nerve twinged hard as I straightened up, and my hand was bleeding again. All in all, though, I felt pretty damn pleased with myself.

I called in the robbery attempt, then immediately called Jacob to let him know what was going on. So much for the soccer game—but that was the way it was, being a cop. I'd caught on pretty fast that scumbag criminals had no respect whatsoever for my social life.

Jacob and Lisa both left Jacob's car where it was, and thundered up the stairs. "Are you okay?" Jacob asked Crash, and then me. We said we were. Then he looked down at the creep, considered him for a moment, and asked me, "How are those nylon cuffs, anyway?"

"Not bad."

I glanced back at Miss Mattie's closet door, but I didn't see the telltale flutter of the paper Saint Anthony fan. It didn't make logical sense to me that she'd just stood by while a paranoid schizophrenic who'd gone off his meds threatened her little Curtis with a knife. Then again…if the *si-no* was something that existed outside Lisa, something that was more than a simple channel to her inner knowing…when she asked about the necklace, someone out there had told her what to do with it. Guardian angels, she'd called her contacts, when she saw them in the astral. I didn't think Miss Mattie would mind the Judeo-Christian connotations of that term—though, like everything else in the world of Psych, I imagined it was also incredibly subjective.

Crash made his way around the counter, caught me by the upper arm, and turned me to face him. When he draped his forearms over my shoulders and pressed himself against me, he did it so deliberately that I was relieved Lisa and Jacob were both there—because if he'd mashed himself on me like that while we were alone, I might have gotten the wrong idea. He cocked his head to one side and stared me in the eye for a second or two, then put his mouth to my ear and whispered, "Can I take back every single time I've ever teased you about being a wimp? 'Cos I'm not ashamed to admit when I'm wrong."

"Yeah, well." I took a step back to put some distance between us, but it didn't work. His body flowed with mine, and somehow he managed to use the motion to fit us together even more tightly. "Good thing all your friends are cops," I said.

"Not all my friends." He pressed his cheek to mine, and tilted his head slightly, so his skin brushed against mine. The bristle of his stubble dragging over my jaw sent a fresh bolt of gooseflesh down my arms. "Just the hot ones."

Chapter 42

The cops who showed up to collect the creep were not particularly hot, but they were efficient—and they didn't realize I was a PsyCop, either. Just a detective. I let them think that. They'd probably hear about it later and kick themselves for not sneering at me, but for now, it made the afternoon a hell of a lot easier.

Lisa decided to stay with Crash, which I was glad for. But she told us that if we left right away, we'd make the second half of the game. And also that we should go.

So, we went.

Being exposed to the full force of the *si-no* was definitely going to take some getting used to.

We arrived in Beloit at the end of halftime, just as the players were straggling back out onto the field. Parents sat on the sidelines in folding chairs. A typical kid's cheering section must have been one person strong. His mom. And most of the moms weren't even looking up. They were talking to each other, or talking on their cellphones, or reading books, or even knitting.

Clayton, however, had an impressive audience of four—now rapidly swelling to six, as Jacob and I hauled our chairs along and got them set up. So many family members, we made up our own cluster. Barbara was the only one who seemed particularly into the game—not that the older generation didn't dote on Clayton just as much as she did. Just that Jacob was a lot more interesting, seeing as how they only got to visit with him a handful of times each year. I shook Jerry's right hand and Leon's left as I sidled past them, gave Barbara a stilted wave and tried to tell myself the annoyed look she was giving me was only due to the angle of the sun in her eyes, and then I parked myself next to Jacob's mom.

Shirley's purse was so big, it took up as much space as a human being—a large one. She shifted it so I could get my chair right beside hers, and she slung her arm around me and squeezed when I sat down. "So…uh, who's winning?" I said.

"I have no idea." She leaned back to size me up. "Well, don't you look handsome today. Did you do something different to your hair?"

"Just a haircut." The first couple of times I'd hung out with Shirley, I kept waiting for the other shoe to drop. *"…but too bad you're not a woman. Because I was hoping for some additional grandchildren, since Clayton's not exactly the most lovable boy."* Except, the "but" never came. Shirley actually liked me. Weird, but true.

She dug into her massive shoulder bag and found a can of Pepsi, somewhat cold with a bit of tissue stuck to it, and handed it to me. I took it from her, cracked it open, and swallowed a long pull. "No, not just your hair. There's something more."

Was the sense of self-satisfaction I'd acquired by successfully manhandling a creepy bad guy showing through? Maybe. "Stand up," she said. "Let me take a look at you." I felt myself blush, but I stood, and kind of shrugged. Shirley gave me a good once-over, then patted the seat of my lawn chair again. I sat, and pressed the cool can to my now-warm cheek. "You keep yourself in such good shape, too. Do you run?"

I might lie about running to a casual acquaintance, but not to Shirley, so I answered, "Not if I can help it."

She laughed. I really enjoyed her laugh. "Don't let Barbara hear you say that."

She looked back at the soccer field as if the thing she'd just said made perfect sense. I stared at her profile for a few seconds, and then finally said, "Why?"

"What's that, dear?"

"Why shouldn't I let Barbara hear?"

Shirley scanned the field, then took a covert glance over her shoulder in her daughter's general direction, and finally leaned toward me. "She's always been so sensitive about her weight. If the only reason you're so slim is a good metabolism, she'll be jealous, and…well, I suppose you don't know how she can be. Let's just say you don't want to get her started."

I slipped on a pair of plastic sunglasses and stole a look at Jacob's sister through the dark lenses. She'd stood up, hands cupped around her mouth, bellowing, "Run, Clayton!" Sure, she was big-boned. But so was everyone in the Marks family. The "athletic" remark being caused by jealousy? Craziness. The thought that anyone in their right mind would find anything in me to be jealous of was totally insane.

Barbara sat back down with an annoyed harrumph, which then put Jacob in my line of sight. Frankly, as far as I was concerned, I had only one thing anyone could possibly be jealous of—my man. Great hair, killer bod, mind like a steel trap, great in bed, and those phenomenal, expressive dark eyes. He gazed out onto the field with a look in those eyes I didn't really get to see much. It was soft around the edges, a faraway gaze. Very serious. It looked hot on him—but no big surprise there. Jacob wears so many looks well. But I supposed, having grown up with him, Barbara was immune to all of that. I guess it was always possible she resented me being in her brother's life, maybe subconsciously, because she thought there'd be less of him left over for her now that I was around.

Shirley pulled her digital camera out of her handbag and showed me a picture of Jerry and Leon on the small viewfinder. They were outside somewhere with lots of leafy stuff in the background, holding up a three-foot catfish between them.

Families. Never a dull moment.

Youth soccer matches don't last all that long, which I previously had no reason to know. Less than forty-five minutes after we got there, the game was over. Everyone had driven more than two hours for the privilege of watching Clayton run around and kick the ball a couple of times, so Jacob suggested we extend the get-together by heading out for pizza. Since Jacob and I had skipped lunch in an effort to catch at least some of the game, and since my appetite was still voracious from my astral adventures, I found the prospect of some pizza very welcome, indeed.

I had my hand resting beside me on the seat of the car as we drove to the pizzeria, and Jacob surprised me by dropping his big hand on top of it and meshing our fingers together. Jacob's just not a hold-hands-in-the-car kind of guy. Not that it bothered me or anything. Just that I noticed.

The intensity that he focused on the road with seemed unusual, too. Traffic in Wisconsin was a walk in the park compared to Chicago streets, but the way Jacob had his eyes glued to the car in front of him, you'd think we were navigating the Loop during rush hour in freezing rain. His jaw worked, like he had something to say, but wasn't quite sure how to say it. Had Barbara said something nasty about me to him? I didn't think so—she'd seemed so focused on the game. Maybe something about the game, then? Something about Clayton, something about kids…holy hell, Jacob didn't want kids now, did he? He must realize that neither of us was ever home. We'd already determined we weren't even home enough to consider a dog. And whether I was home or not, I'd be the world's most pathetic father. Shit, I so didn't sign up for kids….

"I'm really glad we came today," he said. And I held my breath for several tense seconds waiting to see what the "but" in that statement might be. It was a lot like talking to his mother, though. There was no "but."

The pizza parlor was empty at mid-afternoon except for us, and a few retirees sharing a newspaper. The waiters shoved together a couple of tables for us. I ended up sitting between Uncle Leon and Jacob. Leon's spirit arm, though visible, simply rested on the table beside his silverware. I could handle that.

Once the pizzas came, and I'd helped myself to a third piece, and a fourth, I did notice Barbara looking at me through narrowed eyes. I looked right back at her and asked if she'd like another slice. You'd think I was offering her a drowned kitten. Huh. Shirley'd been right. That whole "athletic" bullshit had more to do with Barbara's own issues than it did with me. And to think, I'd nearly started working out over it.

Somewhere around my fifth piece, my favorite jeans started to feel a bit tight. I set the crust down and I watched the vacant tables around us begin to fill as the early dinner crowd trickled in.

"I'm glad you're all here," Jacob said. I was looking out at the parking lot through the window, where someone had left their dog in the car, a little yippy dog with a bow in its hair that was showing its teeth to everyone with the audacity to walk past the vehicle. But then his tone struck me as particularly serious. And I realized he was holding my hand yet again. At the dinner table. With his entire family there.

"I've been giving it a lot of thought…a *lot* of thought…actually, lately I can't think of anything else. And given the way certain…things…have come to pass…." he squeezed my hand and looked at me.

I stared back at him. Jacob didn't get tongue-tied, not him. So whatever it was he was trying to spit out—I wasn't sure I even wanted to hear it.

"It hasn't been an easy decision, but I really think it's for the best…."

I squeezed his hand, hard. He caught my eye again and nodded. What I'd meant by that squeeze was, *what the heck?* But he took it as a show of support.

"I'm going to retire."

Stunned silence. Everyone's face froze somewhere along a spectrum that ranged from shock to confusion. My expression must have registered all of the above. Retire? Jacob? Sure, he had his twenty years in…but he'd never mentioned anything about retirement. The guy's whole life was about trapping dirtbags in their own webs of lies and making sure they couldn't bother decent people anymore.

His whole life was about being a PsyCop.

Once his family picked their jaws up off the floor, they congratulated him. But it didn't seem to me that their hearts were really in it.

Soon after that, Barbara and Clayton broke off from the group to head back home. Clayton was worn-out and cranky, and besides, they'd just seen us a week ago. Leon left after that. He played cards on Saturday. I tried to imagine playing cards one-handed, and came up blank. That left Shirley and Jerry. The four of us sat together in silence for a while. I glanced at Jacob. He had a very Claytonesque expression on his face. "Did something happen?" Shirley said.

Jacob's eyes tracked back and forth as he filtered through…what? PsyTrain? Was the stretched head what had made him come to the conclusion that it was time to throw in the towel? Because I guarantee, stretched heads were a once-in-a-lifetime type of phenomena, and Psychs with enough power to do something like that were few and far between.

"I just don't want to keep pushing it 'til I'm totally burned out. That's all."

Jerry and Shirley glanced at each other, then looked at Jacob again. "If there's anything I can do to help," Jerry said, "you just let me know. Anything."

Jacob looked at them, each of them, and then said, "You lock your doors at night. Right?"

They both gave a shrug that said maybe, maybe not. It was my turn to stare. Seriously? They didn't lock their doors? Where did they think they lived, Candyland? Jacob worked his jaw a few times and said, "I need you to start doing that. Promise me?"

The patented Marks family stubbornness flared up in Jerry, who said, "You're the one living in the country's murder capital, not us—"

Shirley cut him off. "Fine. I will make sure the doors are locked. Every night." She stood, and hoisted her massive handbag onto her shoulder, then kissed Jacob on the temple. "I promise." She lingered with her hand on his tense shoulder for a moment, and then she and Jerry said their uneasy goodbyes, and Jacob and I were alone.

While we sat there at the empty table staring each other down, a waitress came to see if we needed anything else. When neither of us responded to her, she backed away.

"Damn it, Jacob," I said, when I couldn't keep it inside me one second longer. "You could have maybe, I dunno, *discussed* this with me first."

"I couldn't. I didn't know for sure. Not until..." he planted his elbows on the red-checkered plastic tablecloth and buried his face in his hands, took a few breaths, then raked his fingers through his hair and met my eye. "I didn't know for sure until I saw them."

"Who?"

"My family."

Obviously, I was missing something. Something big. Because other than a few dirty looks from Barbara that hadn't particularly fazed me, I thought we'd all been having a pretty good time. Jacob caught my hands, both of them this time, including the scabby one that had leaked ectoplasm all week, and said, "Who's the next Five Faith going to be? We don't know, do we? But look at me—all these years I've been representing my precinct, I've been in the paper, on TV. And look how easy it would be to track down my sister, my parents, Clayton. They're less than four hours away."

"Yeah, but...why is Five Faith freaking you out now? They weren't even the ones screwing with your email. They weren't the ones stealing people at PsyTrain."

Jacob squeezed my fingers together so hard it hurt. "But what if it had been? I worry about them targeting you, me...but face it, we can protect ourselves. My mother? My grandmother?" He shook his head. "I can't let that happen."

"And so that's it? You're gonna take your pension and...what? Build a model train set in the basement and putter around the yard?" I was shocked at how sickened I was by the thought of Jacob declawed and defanged. I thought I'd loved him for who he was as a person. I had no idea I was so attached to who he was as a cop. Surprise, surprise.

He almost-smiled. "Could you actually see me turning into a househusband?"

Actually, I could...and I didn't like what I saw. I narrowed my eyes at him.

"No." He squeezed so hard I needed to pull my hand free for fear of bleeding on him. He released my hands like he hadn't realized his own strength. Which I'm sure he hadn't. "I might not be safe at the Twelfth Precinct anymore, but that doesn't mean I just roll over and surrender. I couldn't."

"Okay," I said, relieved. "Just as long as you don't—"

"So that's why I'm signing on with the FPMP."

I waited for the rimshot, the point at which he'd break into his big, contagious smile, cuff me on the shoulder, and say, *I really had you going there.*

Except that point never came.

Nope, Jacob looked completely earnest. Painfully so. And I realized, as I stared deep into his eyes, that I hadn't been seated next to Lisa on that flight back to Chicago so that I could catch up with her. I'd been put there so Dreyfuss could start working on Jacob. So he could drop a few carefully selected notions into their conversation—ideas that would make Jacob fear not for himself, or even for me—but for his family.

I could argue, remind Jacob that the FPMP was tapping our phone. That they assassinated people, for crying out loud. But Jacob had that mulish expression on him that told me I'd be better off biding my time, since any argument now would only make him dig his heels in deeper.

I stood, and picked up the check. "C'mon," I said. "Let's get going."

It was gonna be a long ride home.

About the Author

Jordan Castillo Price writes and produces the PsyCop novels from her home in rural Wisconsin. Since she shed her day job, she no longer needs to endure embarrassing staff inservices like the one in which Sando makes Vic do a million wristlocks. Though she imagines you never know when a wristlock might come in handy.

About this Story

I re-discovered an old friend of mine who'd had a career as a forensics tech since last we knew each other. I badgered her for a good long while to try to get an idea of how crime scenes are treated. Interestingly, some of the things she said around the specific questions really informed the Vic/Jacob relationship, like, "Not too many people, in fact none that I know, ever wanted to hear too many details of the scenes I went to. My husband has heard the most but at some point he would tell me to stop." After hearing this, I reasoned that Vic and Jacob get along well because they understand each other on a level that a civilian wouldn't. My friend's descriptions of sketching the scenes gave rise to the part in the story where Vic draws the astral door without knowing it.

And I recruited help with the more mundane aspects of the storytelling, too! Another friend has two pre-teens in Wisconsin soccer, so I totally picked her brain about what happened at soccer games, if it would be plausible for Clayton's team to play in Beloit in June, and how people acted at the games. There are these plastic red and yellow penalty cards the ref keeps in his pockets. They're shown to the kids when they've broken rules, and I really wanted to include a yellow card, but explaining what it was seemed to bog down the action too much, so I dropped that idea. That part where no one's actually paying attention to their kids playing soccer and they're all knitting? That doesn't really happen; I just took artistic license to show what a special little snowflake Clayton is. Plus it seems whenever I go somewhere, there's someone completely oblivious to their surroundings, knitting. I often add in details like that just to amuse myself.

Some aspects of the story I figured out via first-hand research. I took a day-long meditation retreat to get some ideas for PsyTrain—and believe me when I say everyone there was nice! But Vic needs to be disgruntled and roll his eyes at everything so you're seeing it all through his annoyed filter.

I actually even looked for some spelt cookies so I could enjoy the wholesomeness, but alas, I couldn't find any, only spelt crackers with lots of seeds. I ate something called Chunks of Energy Carob Spirulina, figuring Vic wouldn't put something called spirulina in his mouth without vociferous protest…but, it wasn't bad. Kind of like an herbal crispy rice treat. Then again, I don't mind hippy food. I'm not Vic. (I would've spewed over that bone in the salmon.)

Also by Jordan Castillo Price

Channeling Morpheus series

Petit Morts series, with Josh Lanyon and Sean Kennedy

Sleepwalker

Hemovore

Zero Hour

The Starving Years

CPSIA information can be obtained
at www.ICGtesting.com
Printed in the USA
BVHW060531021021
617948BV00001B/71

9 781935 54022